rules of
engagement

rules of engagement

a novel

Stephanie Fowers

Covenant Communications, Inc.

Printed in Canada
First Printing: May 2005

11 10 09 08 07 06 05   10 9 8 7 6 5 4 3 2 1

ISBN 1-59156-809-9

To the 73rd World,

my family,

and to all the wacky people I know

(yeah, redundant, but that's why I love you).

WARNING

This book will scare you—scare you silly—that anyone could be as irrational as I am. But the fact is, maybe you need an irrational perspective. Just about everyone is irrational when it comes to the dating game, the LDS dating game to be more specific. I'm warning you that I'm basing this book loosely (what am I talking about loosely—solely) on my life, and since I'm a little clueless, this book will hardly delve into the depths of human intellect. It won't win any Nobel Peace Prizes and no one will quote it, unless they're mocking me because I'm about to make a bigger-than-life fool of myself . . . even more than usual. It's amazing how surprisingly easy it is, but what do you expect? This is about dating. And yet, it's about so much more . . .

You see, I had a big problem—guys. And I always liked the wrong one. I just didn't know who was going to save me from myself—it wasn't going to be me. I'd already proven that. It's interesting, but I believe help came from the most unlikely source . . . the wrong guy.

CHAPTER 1

"I'm not sure we're such a good idea."
—Marcus Gray (Mon, Nov. 22nd)

Now, where do I begin? Ah, yes, Marcus—incredibly sweet Marcus, incredibly hot Marcus. It's funny how some guys get cuter the more you get to know them. But at that particular moment, Marcus's hotness was dwindling before my very eyes.

"What are you doing, Samantha?" Marcus snapped. "You're driving too fast. Slow down."

I just laughed, my short, blond curls blowing against my face. The heater in my car was broken. It blew out burning air and the only way to cool down was by opening the window, even though it was late November. "I've been speeding for years," I said. "I'm just making sure that I really deserve the speeding ticket when I get it."

Marcus didn't think that was funny. He was way too serious sometimes. It made me wonder why he liked me since I bordered on the mischievous side. Even when I tried really hard to tone it down, my smile gave me away every time.

"This actually isn't a race," Marcus said. "In fact I'd rather live than be on time, you know." He pulled his Cardinals cap over his eyes. That's what he did when he was nervous. Aside from his verbal protestations, he didn't even have to use the ghost brake on the passenger's side for me to know that he hated my driving. "I'm sure the cops have been waiting for someone like you all day," he said.

"All day?" The corner of my lips curled in amusement. "Well, we'd better hurry. We can't keep them waiting." I was trying to get Marcus to unwind, but I think I was driving him crazy.

He snorted. "Well, I guess I wouldn't care if I crashed this piece of junk either," he muttered.

Now it was my turn to be astonished. "What are you talking about? I love my car." It really was a piece of work. Sometimes it amazed me it even ran, but with the help of DI accessories, I'd souped it into a mean gangsta hoopty and accurately dubbed it the Loner.

The windshield was fogging up and I could barely see the snow-covered mountains in the distance, let alone the street. I leaned forward, my pink corduroy flairs rubbing noisily against the leopard-print seat covers. I peered through the bottom half of the windshield, but I couldn't see a thing. "Hey, quit breathing," I said.

"Watch for pedestrians," he said. He was getting testy, and I tried not to take it personally. I chalked it up to nerves. I was pretty high-strung before an exam too.

"Don't worry. They always get out of the way in time," I tried to reassure him, but it wasn't working. He never got my jokes. Instead he pulled his cap down even farther, hiding the few rogue freckles on his face. Several stray blond hairs curled beneath the rim of his cap. He was due for a haircut, which meant finals were coming and he was busy. Last time he practically buzzed his head, and though I was grateful that he hadn't done that again, he'd have a hard time getting in to take his test at the testing center with the scruffy look.

I lurched to a stop at the next stop sign and hung my head out the window, feeling strangely like a dog. "See, no pedestrians," I said to appease him. I pulled forward until I was hanging halfway across the intersection so I could look past the line of cars parked on the road.

My furry green dice and SpongeBob cube swung wildly from my rearview mirror, and Marcus pushed the cube roughly from my view. "Who got you this stupid thing?" he asked. "Your worst enemy?"

SpongeBob? I felt myself stiffen. He had gone way too far. "What's wrong with SpongeBob?" I asked softly. Interestingly enough, he didn't recognize the danger signs.

"He's annoying."

Like you're annoying? I clenched my teeth tightly over the retort. "Have you ever watched SpongeBob?" I managed finally.

"No."

"Green eggs and ham. Don't dis it until you've tried it, buddy. SpongeBob is more kind and loving than any guy that I've ever met."

He tilted his head to the side, and I waited tensely for his response. "What are we listening to?" he asked in a confused voice.

What was wrong with him? Marcus acted as if I didn't just bare my soul to him. He could at least have given me some sort of reaction to my passionate outburst, but instead he was talking music.

"Avril Lavigne," I told him angrily.

"You got any Foo Fighters or Radiohead in here?"

I did, but there was no way I was going let him listen to it after completely ignoring my SpongeBob soliloquy. To make things worse, he didn't even notice that he was being a jerk. Well, I'd show him. "No," I clipped. I slammed on the brakes with the chunky soles of my boots for good measure. "I didn't bring my CD player. You're stuck with my old-school radio."

I stomped on the brake after enunciating each word.

To my complete fury, he tried to change the channel. "Hey," I cried, diving for the radio. He caught my hand before I could smack him, and then he still had the nerve to change the station. "What do you think you're doing?" I demanded.

Marcus stopped on some Depeche Mode song. "That's better." He still had my hand, and he turned my long fingers over in his. My nail beds were my best feature. I had painted my nails a sparkly pink. I couldn't help it. I loved sparkles. "When did you do your nails?" he asked. He didn't look impressed.

"None of your business." I snatched my hand away from him, too furious to think straight. I was quite capable of reciprocating any move he made—I liked him a lot, but he was being way too bossy right now. My hands landed on the steering wheel, and I turned the corner hard.

"Park in front of Ben's apartment . . . there." His voice broke, and I swerved my car in front of his brother's apartment complex and lurched to a stop. He looked a little sick, and I didn't know why that gave me so much satisfaction. I felt like I was driving with my dad.

"Man, sometimes I think you actually *are* from Utah," he said.

"What's that supposed to mean?"

"You fit in with the other drivers here."

"Oh, really?" I pulled forward, then slammed the brakes and glanced back so I could parallel park.

"A little closer to the curb," Marcus said, "back a little, closer to the car in front of us."

For crying out loud, I was just *dropping* him off at his brother's. I put the car firmly in park and his lips twisted. The green, furry dice and SpongeBob swung overhead, and I smiled brightly at Marcus, making it obvious that I wasn't going to listen to him anymore.

"Have fun studying for your test," I said in an overly cheerful voice.

He took off his seat belt, but stayed right where he was. "Did you want to tell me something?" he asked.

"Uh yeah . . ."

"Well, what is it? I need to get Ben's notes before he goes to class . . ."

I glanced at him in disbelief. It wasn't what he was saying . . . it was how he was saying it. How did this happen? One moment I'm the hot commodity, the next he's bossing me around. But that didn't stop me from saying what my roommates had forced me to rehearse last night. Maybe he was just having a bad day.

"Did you want to get together tomorrow night?" I asked. "We're having a Christmas party—"

Marcus interrupted me. "Sorry, I made other plans."

"Oh," I said. "Well, have fun . . . with whatever you're doing." I faked a smile, wanting him out of my car and my life. He unwittingly obliged.

He slid out, and after throwing back the school papers that came out with him, he leaned against the crunched-in side of my car, watching me with expressive eyes. He had thick eyelashes for a guy, and I had to admit that I melted for a second. "I don't think that I can make it for dinner tonight," he said. "Thanks for inviting me though. I'm playing basketball with my roommates."

I turned from him to stare straight ahead—and he didn't invite me? "Don't worry about it . . ." I found myself saying, and I almost meant it.

"Is that okay?" The snow was falling heavily over him, but he didn't move from my car.

"Fine." I realized that I really wanted my punching bag right now. I pushed down the gas instead, barely giving him time to close the door behind him. Marcus watched me speed away with shocked eyes, and I hoped that was the last time I would see him—except he was still in my ward and he was my FHE "dad." Tough luck on my part.

"Dash diddly dog!" I said. That's what I say when I'm really angry. I gunned the engine. How did I read him so incredibly wrong? I thought that he liked me. But since the moment I started liking him back, he began walking all over me. Was I just being too nice to him? I thought that I had good self-esteem. I mean, I was well-adjusted, so why did I always end up with the wrong guys?

The problem with Marcus was that he had seemed so sweet in the beginning. It made me realize that I had no idea how to read a guy. Either that or he had changed his mind about me when he'd gotten to know the real me. You see, I'm not very coy about hiding my true self. In fact, I'm an idiot when it comes to men. I laugh too much, I talk too much, I'm too affectionate—which means I break every rule; I sit by him whenever possible, *attempt* to cook if he comes over looking like a pathetic dog, want to see him every night, and think he's the greatest thing that ever came to earth . . . until he pulls something like this.

I turned the corner, my wheels squealing. My cell phone went off and I picked it up, seeing Marcus's cell number on it. With a dropping heart, I answered it. "Yeah?"

"Samantha, listen . . . you're a great girl, but . . . I've been thinking about our relationship. I'm just not sure if we're such a good idea."

I couldn't help it—I smiled in relief. Even though we didn't have much of a relationship, it had been more wearing on me than I thought possible, and this was the perfect solution. The fact was that I liked to be the one rejected, not the one rejecting—that way I could avoid the guilt . . . and the lectures I'd been getting lately from my dad about being too picky and making myself inaccessible, and other formulaic advice I couldn't take seriously.

Things were getting hot for me at home. Normally I could count on getting lost in the shuffle, but I had just returned from my youngest sister's wedding, which left me the only unmarried girl in a family of seven. Now my parents had no one to concentrate on but me, and I had to cling to any excuse I could find.

"I completely agree," I said, staring through my windshield. It had finally cleared, giving me a good view of the mountains. They cut a jagged line across the horizon, the low clouds wrapped lovingly over them. I cleared my throat. "It isn't anything that you've done . . . it's me. You're a really nice guy, and any girl would be lucky to go out with you. We just didn't connect . . ."

He was silent on the other end, and I mentally tried to stop myself. He was the one trying to break up with me. I might as well let him do it instead of trying to take over everything. Breaking up with me would make him feel better about himself anyway, and since I had no pride really, I didn't mind that he was trying to rip it to shreds.

"But I still want to be friends," he said. "Maybe we can get together sometime."

My brow wrinkled. I sincerely hoped that wouldn't be the case. I didn't even spend time with my *real* friends. Why would I spend time with some guy that I didn't even like anymore? But of course, he was lying, and that gave me comfort.

"Uh, yeah sure, that would be great." I hung up the phone and flung it onto the seat next to me.

It was time to start looking again, but I didn't really want to. No. In fact, I started doing what I do every time I get frustrated with my life. I started making plans to go to Hollywood so I could waste my life away in an endless round of meaningless parties and fashion. And then I would look at the camera with sad eyes, and maybe all the guys that I once liked would say to themselves, *Oh dear, did we drive her to that?* Or I could join the Peace Corps and explore the deepest jungles of Africa, and maybe get attacked by a lion while protecting a whole village of orphans, because hey, if you're gonna go, you might as well go as a martyr. I had to dismiss that idea because my mom wouldn't like it very much. She never liked any of my plans, really . . . except the marriage ones.

I started aiming my goals a little lower. I could write a really good angry-girl song, form a punk band, and tour the country . . . or maybe I could just write a book. Yeah, that's what I usually do when I'm mad. Write and write, deep down thinking and hoping something will come of it all, even if it's just explaining myself to this world.

Basically, this was a girl's lot in my world: she had to plan like she was going to be single for the rest of her life, but she had to be ready for a major change if marriage happened to come along. Now lump that with my own personal flaws, and you had *me.* So, where was I because of it? I was firmly on the shelf; not just by Mormon standards, but by the world's too. I was twenty-five with nothing to show for it, and oh, I had so many plans in the meantime. I wanted to be a rock star, a surgeon, an actress, a cop, a wife, a mother . . . oops, no, that's a *no-no.* One must never admit they're a female with maternal instincts, because that makes one less desirable and more vulnerable to attack.

I parked the Loner outside my apartment complex and stared up at the three-story building. We lived on the top floor. Silver garland twisted through the rails of our balcony, lights blinked blandly over our porch, an unusually silent wreath hung on our door. What happened to Thanksgiving? We were now the pathetic poster children of what happened when you hurry the season. Our overdone Christmas décor made the apartment look like the set of an '80s slasher movie. Well, that's just how everybody else would describe it. I just called it home. I climbed up the three flights of stairs and entered the horrific confines of my apartment, knowing that I was about to do something rash.

I closed the door behind me and muffled a scream. Normally I had nerves of steel, but I had no idea that Christmas decorations could multiply. Nothing outside could even prepare me for the newest monstrosities in the living room. Candy canes and tinsel hung over lights strung unevenly around the walls. Our apartment rivaled the Christmas displays in the toy stores at the mall, except we had horrible, green paisley couches and orange shag carpet with matching overstuffed chairs to add to the holiday cheer.

My eyes were drawn unwillingly to the empty corner of the room. The punching bag was gone. Where had it disappeared to? Had my roommates gotten rid of it to leave space for a tree? We hadn't even picked one out yet! Dash diddly dog.

I felt my blood thicken as I began scanning the apartment for something else to hit or kick or throw, and that's when I felt the heater blow full force into my face. *Emma.* Dear, sweet, Relief Society president Emma—she liked it hot. That meant she was here. My fingers clenched into fists, and I stormed through the organized chaos.

"Emma! Emma!" I felt like I was calling for my mommy, and I stopped short when I saw my guitar leaning against Emma's bass. The bass was propped against the wall next to heavy amps and Ashley's drums. That wasn't such an unusual sight—we hadn't moved them back to our rooms since the last time we had practiced them, which had been way too long ago—except now they were a part of the Christmas display. Tinsel was woven carefully around their long necks. Red bows covered the off-white polish. Normally I would've thought this was a prank, except that Emma was involved.

"Emma!" I pushed the door open to the room that she shared with Ashley and exhaled slowly when I saw her sweet, upturned face. She had been caught in the act of tucking her blankets neatly into her old mattress. It made quite the contrast to Ashley's messy bed on the other side of the crowded room. "There you are," I said.

Emma gave me her motherly smile and my fists uncurled, even though my foot itched for me to do something with it. I crossed it around my ankle instead and leaned against the doorframe. Emma was too nice to kick. Besides that, I needed her.

"Samantha, you're back already?" Her soft voice held the utmost compassion. Emma had just returned from her mission in Guatemala and was trained in the arts of kindness and diplomacy. And since every apartment needs a conscience, poor Emma was forced to work overtime on us.

"Did you have a good day?" she asked, rearranging the *Ensigns* next to her reading light.

I leaned my weary head against the doorframe. "Sure, sure, everything's good if you look on the bright side."

"Oh dear." Emma sat down heavily on the yucky green chair next to her bed, her brown ponytail bobbing with her head. "What happened?" she asked.

I felt the tears come unbidden to my eyes. Emma always got to me; any sympathy would, especially hers. "Let's just say that it's good to find out early that the guy you *thought* you were kinda dating is a noncommittal, freaked-out fraidy-cat."

"What?" Emma flipped her bangs away from her eyes. "What happened?" I shrugged, realizing I couldn't say anything too poignant right now or I would just end up bawling. Sometimes I really hated having emotions.

"Oh," she said, seeing me fight my tears. Her voice grew too serious. "Marcus isn't coming to our little Christmas party, is he?"

"You could say that."

She stood up to hug me, her head barely reaching my shoulders. "I'm so sorry, Samantha."

"Why?" I quickly pulled away from her. "You didn't break up with me." I gave her a watery smile as I jumped onto Ashley's bed. The hard mattress creaked dully beneath me.

Emma sat on her neat little bed across from me. "Oh, I know, but . . ."

"But nothing, it's not anybody's fault but my own." I shrugged, trying to pretend I didn't care, which was hard with Emma's pitying gaze. I stared up at the scriptures that she had taped all over the wall just above our reach.

Proverbs: Who can find a virtuous woman? for her price is far above rubies . . . My gaze quickly shifted from it and I sighed. I could never be a ruby, especially with stupid guys in the way, knocking me off course. I tripped myself up enough on my own. I didn't need their help, so why couldn't I learn my lesson and stay away from them?

"*I'm* the one who keeps setting myself up for heartbreak," I said. "I get one sign that a guy I like is interested, and I pounce."

Emma smiled, hugging a pillow to her. She began tracing the flowers with her fingers while she patiently listened to me ramble on.

"My mind races all the way to the wedding altar, and I'm picking out names for our children! Did you know that Justin and Maggie go really well with Gray?"

"Oh dear."

"Yeah, way attached, way too soon, and then I go crazy. That's the only way to describe it. And I don't even know what I'm doing, or what signals to send, or anything . . . and then I smother the guy with sweet something somethings until he starts taking me for granted and acts like a jerk because he thinks I'm stupid or something, and that's when I know he doesn't feel the same way about me, and then I have to kill whatever we had going." I fell back, landing hard on the mattress. "I try too hard and ruin everything."

"We all do that," Emma said.

"Well, we shouldn't," I said. We both stared up at the sparkles on the ceiling. "You don't . . ." I finally ventured.

"Well, maybe if you didn't have everything weighing on what guys think . . ."

My jaw dropped. I couldn't believe Emma just said that. "What are you talking about?" I said, lifting my head. "I *don't* care what they think." In fact I had been trying to do a reversal. I had been a jerk to the right guys for years, and yes, I probably deserved what I was getting now. Maybe that's why Emma was so confused. I was actually giving guys a chance now—even ones that I wasn't particularly attracted to . . . as long as they weren't mass murderers, right? I'd even given potential stalkers a first date. Of course, it didn't mean that I was going to marry them, though maybe I'd have a change of heart. Who knows? I was just tired of feeling like a failure.

I wanted to do what was right. I wanted to be good and get married in the temple, but the weird thing was that I was almost afraid of it. Everything else that I had ever wanted that badly, every-thing that I thought I was good at, had fallen through—my music "career" was nonexistent, I had bounced from one major to another, and I *still* had no idea what I was going to do with myself when I was done. Nothing I wanted was very practical, so why would I want to complicate things further? Marcus had actually done me a favor by breaking it off.

I smiled mockingly in remembrance, turning on my stomach. "He said he still wants to be friends." My words were smothered in the mattress.

"Well, that's nice of him."

I snorted and felt like kicking something again. *Nice?* Nice that he used some overdone line of how I was a great girl instead of telling me why he just wasn't interested? Nice that he gave me the runaround until he was forced to admit that we just didn't connect? Were all guys like that—liars?

"Guys aren't nice, Emma. That's the first thing you've got to learn, or they'll walk all over you."

Emma looked shocked and I knew that I had done it. I had been way too dramatic, and now she was going to let me have it. I squinted and waited for the onslaught.

"Samantha, you don't mean that," she said. "Don't you dare get bitter. That's the worst thing and you know it. Things will get better. You just can't give up on guys. Promise me you won't."

I gulped, having a hard time meeting her impassioned eyes, and I almost felt guilty. Of course I wasn't going to give up on guys, even though I really wanted to right now. Most likely I'd do the exact opposite. Where was my pride anyway?

"Promise me," she said.

"Emma," I pleaded. She wouldn't actually make me promise, would she? It was too demeaning to give in.

"Promise," she said, "that you won't become some social recluse and shut yourself away from the world with your army of cats."

I wrinkled my nose, but then had to wipe it. I laughed through my sudden tears. "Of course, Emma. I wasn't going to anyway." Marcus hadn't broken me. I'd become the flirtiest flirt who ever flirted and I'd forget all about him. I was sure of it. And then he'd be sorry.

Now I just needed to find something to kick.

CHAPTER 2

"It is common knowledge that a hook that hangs
from the ceiling must be kicked."
—Logan Smith (Mon., Nov. 29th)

"Kick the hook! Kick the hook! Kick the hook!"

My roommate Ashley guarded her drums, keeping them safe while the guy in front of me took a running start and jumped through the air, kicking the hook attached to our ceiling. A shout of applause marked his progress.

"Stay right where you are, Logan," I said. "Work on your pose or something. I'll be right back." I ran to get my digital camera to take his picture for the Kick the Hook wall of fame. It was huge now. The collage of wallet-sized pictures covered almost half of our living room wall, and it was growing bigger.

It was time for WWFHE again. Well, that's what they called us downstairs. I guess we were pretty loud, but at least we weren't playing mafia again or Rambo like we usually do . . . or pigs on a couch. No, we were kicking the hook.

Okay, this probably calls for an explanation. We originally hung the hook on the ceiling so we could fly our pig, which calls for another explanation. A flying pig is a plastic pig with wings. When you attach it to the ceiling on a hook, it flies in a circle around the room. My roommate Ashley got it in Vegas. Well, after my conversation with Emma, I saw the hook just hanging there (minus the pig) and wanted to kick it, so I did. I told you I was going to do something rash. It's because I'm a flibbertigibbet. Do you know what that means? A daydreamer, a visionary sorta. I can't keep my feet on the ground . . . especially when it came to kicking the hook.

The night I broke it off with Marcus, I demonstrated my new trick after we had roommate prayers. Every one of my roommates wanted to try it out, even little Emma. Even though she is only five foot two, she was one of the first. She had to bend completely in half to do it, but she got her foot up there.

Immediately afterward, Ashley smiled with her perfect, cupid-bow lips and kicked it effortlessly, demanding we take pictures to document it, which is how the Kick the Hook wall of fame came about. Brooke dragged her feet the longest, but she finally got them up there. How could she not, with us egging her on to kick it every night for nearly a week after roommate prayers?

It just got out of control after that. Everyone wanted to kick it. You see, Mormons don't have to get drunk to do crazy things; we just do them and accept the fact that we're crazy.

"Alright, give me a pose." I held up my camera, and Logan made a karate-kid stance. I stepped back, making sure I got the writing on his blue T-shirt, *Mr. Bo-Jangles and me.* Below it was a drawing of a bald cat. What did that even mean? I guess it was supposed to be funny.

I snapped the picture, the crammed front room the perfect back-drop.

Overstuffed couches lined the walls, and our pathetic *Charlie Brown Christmas* tree stood desolately in the corner, decorated with only a bit of red construction paper. Apparently it wasn't enough that our everyday junk took on a life of its own and crawled out from the hall to infest the living room; we had to assault the public eye further by becoming the Great Christmas Spectacular for the holidays.

"Did you get my picture?" Logan asked.

I nodded, lowering my camera amidst the talking and laughter that filled the room, the typical FHE scene. Lots of fun, right? Being single? Nothing beats it? Give me a break. Let's take a closer look at this scene, shall we?

I'm the blond punk with the dark eyes taking pictures of kickers and egging everyone on. Then there's Marcus, sitting next to a girl on the overstuffed, green paisley couch—and flirting wildly with her, might I add. He's my FHE "dad," the one wearing the baggy jeans and the pink T-shirt, well, the "new" pink anyway—orange. He just got a haircut too. Why did he always have to cut it so short? But yeah, now you get the picture—the heartbreaker. Except I wasn't really heartbroken, just embarrassed about looking so stupid for falling for a seasoned flirt. I'm sure I'll get over it. The jerk. Anyway, enough with the setting.

"How are you doing, Samantha?" he asked kindly.

"Uh, fine." I turned from him, the thick soles of my black Docs catching on the shaggy, orange carpet.

Okay, so maybe I'm overreacting. Marcus isn't a jerk. He's a really nice guy when it comes down to it. All these guys are . . . they're just not usually nice to me, and usually I'm really good at pretending I don't care. It's just hard. You see, it's been nearly two weeks since we've held family home evening, and you would think that would be enough time away from him to get over this, especially with Thanksgiving break, but it just wasn't working.

I mean, take a look at this new girl that Marcus is flirting with. Miriam's my FHE sister, so I have to like her, but what is it about her that makes her more special than anyone else—namely, me? Alright, she has really long hair that's blonder than mine and her complexion is flawless. She's calm under flirting pressure, which means that she's used to it, and she's completely unattainable. I guess the answer was obvious, wasn't it?

The only good thing about her was that Marcus had competition for her hand. His roommate collapsed on the couch on the other side of Miriam and smiled at her. Logan was the ward hottie with chiseled cheekbones and an athletic build, and this would have been an intimidating moment for almost any girl, but not for Miriam.

"Hey there," he said.

Miriam returned his smile, her eyelids half closed in a half-amused, half-prove-yourself-to-me look. Why couldn't I perfect that? Logan would be eating out of her hand in no time at all, and he would be a good catch . . . if she could do it without him knowing it.

"You're actually kicking a hook on the ceiling?" she asked. Her voice revealed her scorn and she pulled her dark blue jacket closer to her, acting like she was still too cold to take it off. It was the perfect damsel-in-distress act, making her appear more delicate than the rest of us. It might even earn her some guy's jacket; but there was no way she could actually be cold. The heater blasted from the vent on the ceiling, and we had the misfortune to be under it. The great heating struggles were the biggest point of contention with my roommates . . . thank goodness Miriam wasn't a roommate.

"It is common knowledge that a hook that hangs from the ceiling must be kicked," Logan told Miriam in his haughtiest voice. "You should try it. It makes you feel better about yourself."

"I don't think so."

"Why not? Samantha did it."

Miriam turned to me and I just shrugged, playing with the pockets on the knee of my flair khakis. I couldn't pretend to be above kicking the hook—I'd invented it. Another strike against me. Miriam rolled her eyes and brought her attention back to Marcus.

I began to fan my face. The heater wasn't letting up. How could Miriam keep her cool under this? I pushed back the ugly flowered curtains and forced the living room window open. Cold air splashed against my face and I breathed a sigh of relief, watching the snowflakes float gently down from the dark sky. I watched the shadow of mountains in the distance and wondered what sort of view we were treating the people to outside. I'm sure it was amusing.

Logan poked me in the side. "Hey, Samantha, why don't you sit down?" he said. "There's room for you on the couch."

"It's a little tight," I said. That was an understatement. The couch was packed. We didn't have many chairs in our apartment, and there was no way I was squeezing next to Marcus.

"There's always room for you," Logan said. He patted his knees and I laughed at him, appreciating the sentiment. At least Logan was good for a self-esteem boost, though he couldn't be taken seriously. He flirted with everyone.

Marcus quickly stood up, not one to be outdone in looking chivalrous. "Take my seat."

"Uh, don't worry about it," I said, not wanting to get between him and his new conquest. Talk about uncomfortable. Besides, my roommate was trying to get everyone's attention, which meant the seat fight was over.

"Hey, listen to me!" Brooke shouted through the din. "Give me your attention . . . *now.*"

Brooke was the FHE "mom" with the air of a drill sergeant—she had to be with Marcus as her coleader. Despite her tough air, she was the only girl in the room who actually dressed classy with a button-up shirt and black dress pants. She flipped her long, red hair, almost hitting me in the face. Her green eyes were serious as she tried to bring us to control, a nearly impossible task.

"It's time for refreshments," she said, hoping everyone would take the hint and leave. I could read it in her expression, but it was an impossible dream. No one would leave until they were good and ready.

The only one who even listened to her was Scott. He was leaning against the wall, a serious look on his face. His brown eyes missed nothing. What could one expect from such an artist? Tall, dark, handsome . . . a musician. Scott looked like he had just walked out of a club in Seattle. He had on light brown cords worn low on his hips like an alternative rocker, and a striped button-up shirt that was supposed to look ugly. He was everything that was cool. Nothing left his mouth unless it was poignant. Now, he was looking at me and I glanced away. I couldn't let him know that I was interested.

You see, no matter how laid back they look, Mormon guys are different from any guys I've ever met. They're scared of everything because everything means commitment. If a girl happens to show interest, it means she wants to marry him and it freaks him out. He won't ask a girl on a date unless he's ready to marry her, which freaks him out again. So then, when we get tired of waiting to be asked on dates, we ask the guy out instead, and guess who freaks out? Yep, every guy here would deny it, but it's true. Mormon guys are overly sensitive. We girls have tried to fight this fear, but it just won't die, and so we're forced to play mind games by acting completely harmless with our interests hidden away until even *we* forget about them.

So besides a few staring games, Scott and I weren't destined to go far because he never made a move. I tried to push all thoughts of him from my mind, listening to Brooke sigh loudly beside me. Calling her as FHE mom was pure inspiration. She disliked anything that came between her and her homework, so this was the only way to get her to FHE. But now she had a plan. She would thrust the refreshments on us and then hide out in the back rooms like she did every week.

"Listen to me!" Brooke shouted to the uncaring crowd.

But even Scott had lost interest. He leaned next to the turtle cage, inspecting the dirty water. The rotund turtle scratched angrily against the side of its plastic cage, trying to escape, an example of true perseverance. "Whose turtle?" he asked.

I snapped to attention. This was the moment that I had been waiting for, a chance to capture the musician in a somewhat meaningful conversation. I had to see what deep thoughts lay buried in such a brilliant mind. The trick was making turtle talk deep. Of course I could always turn its endless scratching against the cage into an analogy. "The turtle's Brooke's," I said, moving closer to him. "His name's Zooga."

Scott's lips lifted slightly. "*Her* name's Zooga," he said. "She's a girl."

"What?" I inched even closer. It was a perfect excuse. "How can you tell?"

"The shape of her shell."

"His shell," Brooke cut in. He didn't even flinch, and I think that put her off guard. Her green, almond-shaped eyes narrowed. No guy could stand up to Brooke. She was the master of intimidation, which meant this guy had guts. I was impressed. Even more astonishing, he started opening Zooga's cage. "What are you doing?" she cried.

"I'm taking Zooga out, which is more than I can say for her owner."

Brooke gasped. "Put him back right now!"

"You really need to clean her cage," he said, pulling the slippery turtle out of its water.

"I do clean her—his cage, every other day. He's just messy."

Scott cradled Zooga in his strong hands. They were fascinating hands, artist's hands. I wondered how they handled a guitar. Scott glanced at me and melted me with a smile. "What do you feed her?" he asked.

"We feed him food," Brooke answered for me, but fortunately she was momentarily distracted from us. Our FHE group was getting out of hand, building to a chaotic roar. She desperately tried to call us back to order, but there was only one person she could count on. "Emma," she called. "Go get the treats."

Emma turned, miraculously hearing Brooke through the chaos. She had pulled her brown hair back in a ponytail, and it bobbed with her head. "Sure," she said, smiling pleasantly. Emma still had on her blue jumper from work. She had so many jumpers that I couldn't keep track of them all, but what could I expect? She worked at the MTC *and* was the Relief Society president, so it came with the job description. And whether it was because her mission hadn't rubbed off yet or because it was just in her nature, she was sweeter than any of us were capable of being.

"Would you please go help her, Sam?" Brooke asked me. She pulled Zooga from Scott's hands and put the turtle safely back in his/her cage. She looked so frazzled that it would have been sheer cruelty to refuse. I pulled reluctantly away from Scott.

"You'd better wash your hands," I told him. "We don't need another salmonella case on our hands."

"Do those happen often around here?" he asked.

"Only when I cook," I said. Scott laughed, only because he didn't know how true that was. Emma was disappearing into the back, and I quickly excused myself to help her. I shoved my way through the crowd of FHE siblings into the kitchen.

"Oh, Sam, you don't have to help me." Emma was already cutting apples, her ponytail bobbing with her quick, little fingers. "I'm fine here. Why don't you rejoin the party?"

"No way," I said. "I'm tired of taking Kick the Hook pictures. I need to talk to someone sane."

Emma nodded. "And how are you doing?"

I stiffened, knowing exactly what she was talking about, but I pretended innocence anyway. "What? Fine, just fine." I moved across the black-and-white checkered floor. It was like a chess set. I grabbed some apples from the big bowl on the table.

"Oh." Her big blue eyes looked too big for her small face. "How is it between . . . you and Marcus, I meant?"

I shrugged, picking up a butcher knife. I applied it to the first apple. "Well, he wants to be friends still. I'm pretty good at ignoring him."

"Is it hard on you?"

"Whatever!" I managed a smile. "I've hardly talked to him all night. As far as I'm concerned, he doesn't exist. I don't care what he does anymore."

The fluorescent light buzzed crazily over us. "Where is he?" Emma asked in a worried voice. She was probably afraid he would overhear my mean candor.

I snorted. "Sitting on the couch next to Miriam, flirting with her and everything else that moves." I was cutting three times slower than Emma. She really didn't need me, but I needed to talk to her.

Emma nodded understandingly. "Well, I'm sure she's a nice girl."

"No, she's not."

Emma gasped. "Now, is that very nice?"

I laughed. That was Emma's favorite thing to ask me. "No, but it's the truth," I said, but I lowered my voice anyway. "Miriam's one of those girls who string guys along because she likes the attention. She's never interested . . . unless they're not interested back and they're a challenge. The more fans she can find the better, so she can act superior. Marcus has awful taste in women."

"He liked you."

Ouch, Emma. But I knew she didn't mean anything by it. "Well, yeah, but he should at least upgrade."

"Impossible."

"Oh." I smiled. Emma was also good for a self-esteem boost, but I quickly changed the subject. "I like Marcus's roommate, though. He's really cool."

"Logan?" Emma asked.

"Yeah."

Emma finished her last apple, and her knife hesitated over the table. "Didn't he just break up with . . . ?"

My head lifted. I didn't even know Logan had been dating anyone. He had always flirted with me. "When was he dating someone?" I asked.

"Oh, we shouldn't gossip." Emma began sliding the apple wedges into the big bowl with her knife.

I leaned my head back. What did she think we had just been doing? This was Emma's favorite trick. She got me all excited for the latest news and left me in suspense because she couldn't gossip. I watched her take the caramel dip out of the microwave and set it on a platter. I didn't even think to ask if she needed help. I just followed her into the living room, my curiosity driving me crazy.

An excited murmur met Emma's entrance, and she brought the apple slices and caramel-dip platter into the middle of the room. She set it on the floor, where the boys attacked it—except Derek of course. That boy was always so considerate. He had to be. He was the elders quorum president. In fact, everything about him was friendly—his crooked grin, his disheveled red hair, the way he made his way around the room. The only problem with him was that he was far too nice and I could never tell exactly who he was interested in, though he certainly had his pick.

Derek had every girl's heart, including mine. He talked to each one of our FHE sisters, easing some of them from their wary positions against the walls before he got to Emma and me. Then he thrust his hand out, shaking my hand missionary style. Derek could certainly pass for a missionary with his button-up shirt and dark slacks. The only thing missing was a tie.

"How's my favorite girl?" he asked.

As soon as he relinquished my hand, he leaned way too close to me. Now *that* wasn't missionary style. Did he mean something by that, or was he just being friendly? There was no way to tell. I regained my wits with a quick smile. "I'm better now that you're here," I said.

Derek laughed a low rumble in his throat and pulled even closer, his foot almost touching mine. My eyes flicked to his friendly ones. Maybe he was trying to tell me something. You may think that I'm being ridiculous, but you see, a girl will look for any sign from a guy she likes—a token of a man's affections if you will—before she makes a fool of herself. But it's still sticky, because even if a girl finds out that a guy likes her, she will still make a fool of herself if she thinks it's safe to proceed. The fact is, no matter how many positive signs you have, you can never act on them. It will turn the guy off.

Now I know this in theory, but not in method, and so I felt my breath catch in my throat when I noticed Derek's eyes still on mine. I struggled for something witty to say. Nothing came out, and I was actually relieved when he turned from me to glance down at Emma. The top of her head didn't even reach his shoulders. "Emma, did you buy the treats? They look delicious."

She dimpled, enjoying the attention—his mother had taught him well. "Why don't you try them?" she said.

"I'd better before they're gone."

The statement was true and I frowned, almost forgetting to act like a lady. "Excuse me," I said politely, and then I fought my way through the boys. "You're eating everything!" I cried. "Marcus, Logan, save some for us. What's the matter with you?" There was hardly any left. The pigs.

Marcus stopped eating midbite and offered the half-eaten apple slice to me. I drew back appalled, but my roommate Ashley just laughed behind me. She tugged her black shirt down over her low-riding jeans in a preemptive strike before kneeling next to me to accept the proffered fruit.

I just glowered as she smoothed back her long, black hair. Ashley could have any guy she wanted, which is why she wanted none. She could be a movie star, which is why she never cared how she dressed. She was shaped like a model, which is why she had no interest in being a lady. In fact, she never wanted to do anything at all, except play her drums and make boys cry. I was jealous. Everything came far too easily for her.

She dipped the apple slice in the caramel, of course not worried about the extra calories because nothing she ate had any effect on her. "Samantha," she said. "Try it. It's delicious."

My plan had been to take the plate away and give it to the more polite portion of the FHE family, but out of spite, I snatched an apple slice with an angry jerk. "I'd better before Marcus eats it all," I said with a pointed glance at him. I was just about to bite it when he stole it from my hands.

My eyes widened, but he just dipped the apple slice into the caramel and gave it back. "Sugar won't kill you," he said.

"How do you know?" I asked.

Ashley smiled at Marcus, directing all of her charm at him. "But obesity will."

"So will anorexia," he said.

My lip curled in irritation. What was he saying? "I'm not anorexic," I said, biting into the caramel for emphasis. "Just because I didn't get the caramel doesn't mean that I have an eating disorder."

Marcus just smiled benignly at me until I turned angrily away. He then redirected his attention to Ashley, which is probably where it had been all along. "Ashley doesn't care what she eats," he said.

"Have you been watching me?" she asked.

He laughed, and I groaned. The problem with roommates is that they can either be a rival or a best friend. I always make the tactical error of making them my best friends, and then I lose all my guy friends to them. But really, one girl can't take all the guys, right? Wrong. I've learned that the hard way. Ashley might not care about guys, but she still stole them. And don't get me wrong. I didn't actually *like* this particular guy anymore, but it was annoying to watch.

I turned away from the new flirting couple only to have someone try to stuff another apple into my mouth. I pulled away with a gasp. This was outside of enough. I shoved the apple away from me, seeing intense gray eyes and unkempt hair. Griffin! He was crazy about me and it was just my luck. Murphy's Law works every time. You want the guy, and he doesn't want you. You don't want the guy, and he wants you—especially if he's a weirdo. Okay, so I'm not supposed to judge . . . but they say don't judge *unrighteously*—that's a pretty big amendment. I mean, we were given our intellect for a reason, so we can protect ourselves from guys like this.

"I can feed myself, Grif," I told him. "I'm not a baby."

"You looked hungry," he said. And *he* looked a little hurt.

I stared at him. Griffin could actually be cute if he tried, but his real problem was that he was scary sometimes. I could stand the occasional nerd having a crush on me, even the guy who never brushed his teeth, but I couldn't handle the ones who leered, especially with such an unblinking stare. Call me crazy, but I sensed danger a mile away when Griffin was around. It was as if he were plotting ways to confine me to a dreary existence where he would force me to ponder the meaning of a righteous life—but that self-righteous brooding nixed having any fun.

He crossed his pale arms over his cream-colored sweater vest, and I knew it was time to make him disgusted with me—that was the only thing that worked with this kind of guy. It had been idiotic to give him a first date anyway, but it wasn't my fault. The stake presidency had lectured us at stake conference that it was our duty to accept every first date, and Griffin just happened to ask that very week when I was still feeling particularly dutiful. It had been a disaster, especially since it had raised his hopes.

"I don't want to ruin my appetite," I said. "I haven't had dinner yet. I was going to make some Cocoa Pebbles."

"*Make* Cocoa Pebbles?" He wiped at his nose, and I mentally told myself not to shake his hand anytime soon.

"Uh, yeah . . . for dinner." I stood up and towered over him. He was nearly a foot shorter than me it seemed, which should have turned him off in the first place, but since it hadn't, this would be a difficult procedure. It was a good thing I excelled at this. "I eat Cocoa Pebbles for breakfast, lunch, and *dinner*—I get my vitamins that way. It's all part of a nutritious breakfast."

"Food is overrated," he said. "I don't even eat dinner."

I frowned, seeing that he had beaten me in the disgust category, but I was determined to make this work. "Well, I don't cook dinner because I'm a terrible cook. My poor husband will starve to death . . . not to mention my gaunt, malnourished kids . . . ." I hesitated, watching his enamored face, my lips mirrored in his glasses. The normal tricks wouldn't work for this guy, would they? If I told him that kids were just a nuisance and another mouth to feed, he would probably like it, so when all else failed, I revealed my age. "Not that I'll have any kids," I said, "not at the rate I'm going. I'll never get married. I'm twenty-five. Yeah, I know, old."

His expression didn't change. "That's not old," he informed me.

"Yes, it is," I argued. "I have my walker in the back."

He snickered, and I stifled a groan. Why couldn't I resist a joke? I had ruined it for myself, and now I deserved what I was going to get. The truth is, I attracted weirdos because I was one myself. That's why I had such a hard time being mean to the kid. Wouldn't I want someone to be nice to me—break my heart gently? Dash everything. I didn't want to break anyone's heart. Being single is so hard. I just wanted to get married so I had a reason to reject guys, but how did one get married, anyway?

CHAPTER 3

"By George, Samantha, the men of BYU will be groveling at your feet by the time I'm through with you."
—Harrison Bean (Mon., Nov. 29th)

Just then I heard the crazy wreath singing maniacally outside our front door. The wreath had a motion detector, and it went off every time anyone came to visit. It worked as a great alarm system, too. No one could sneak up on us, though now our neighbors hated us since our numbers of visitors were growing. There was always a constant medley of Christmas songs screeching from our apartment.

Grateful for any excuse to leave my stalker, I lunged for the door, tripping over the coats stashed in a crumpled heap in the corner. "I've got it!" I shouted, but when I saw who it was, my hands dropped limply to my sides.

Harrison stood outside on the snow-covered balcony. He was the perfect English gentleman with compressed lips and a purposeful manner to his stride. He walked into the room, and I half expected him to take my hand and kiss it. Of course, it wouldn't have meant anything to him. It just would have demonstrated his knowledge of propriety long since dead, and emphasized his eccentric behavior. Besides the loose green T-shirt, blue jeans, and BYU baseball cap, everything about him was dramatic—jet black hair, and piercing blue eyes that missed nothing.

He tried to get past me, but unfortunately I happened to be standing in his way. I tried to sidestep and so did he, which just made things even more confusing until we almost ran into each other. He halted and looked directly into my eyes. "Care to dance?" he asked in a perfect English accent.

I felt the color rise in my cheeks. I loved his accent. Too bad it didn't reflect his personality. He was just being sarcastic, which was usual for him. "Maybe later," I said. "Why don't you come in first?"

He already was in, and he nonchalantly perused the room and our awe-inspiring Christmas decorations. "Who are you trying to scare?" he asked.

"You," I said.

"It almost worked," he said. "Your apartment is ostentatious, to say the least." I didn't even pretend to know what he was talking about. "What's going on here?" he finally asked. The slight amusement in his voice belied his superior glance.

"We were kicking the hook," I said, trying to keep my voice from sounding guilty. I couldn't let him know that he had put me on the defensive. I pointed to the hook hanging from the ceiling. "You want to take a go at it?"

He looked at me like I had just grown two heads. "I'd rather die," he murmured, then abruptly headed for the kitchen. I rolled my eyes and saw Emma too late. I tried to look happier, but even her sweet smile was a little forced.

"Oh look, that nice English boy is here," she said.

"Don't be fooled," I said. "That's no nice English boy." He was a pain, and who knew what he was doing in our kitchen?

"He's nice to me," she said.

"Yeah, because he likes you—probably because you can't remember his name. Guys are twisted that way." I chased after Harrison, weaving around the people in the living room until I saw Scott too late. He was brooding in the hallway and I smacked right into him, almost pushing him over the Chastity Line. He teetered over the invisible barrier that exists in all BYU apartments between the front room and the hall that leads to the bedrooms. Scott grabbed at me before he could fall completely over the line that no man can pass, but instead we both toppled over it. He fell onto his back and I landed against him.

Scott glanced up at me, his brown eyes full of concern. "Are you alright?"

I couldn't help it, but I started laughing. "We're all over each other," I said. What a great way to get to know a guy, especially one as cute as this one.

"Hey," Brooke yelled out from the back. Scott's eyes filled with what could only be described as fear, and we both scrambled back into the living room. He helped me to my feet just as Brooke sprinted around the corner. "I saw that," she said, stepping into the hall, her red hair flying over her pale face. "Scott, what were you doing in the back?"

"What were *you* doing in the back, Mom? How could you desert us like that?"

"First the turtle, now this!" Brooke's face was flushed with anger.

I snickered, but stopped abruptly when I heard the commotion in the kitchen. Scott could take care of himself, but the kitchen couldn't. I stomped into it, leaving Scott to contend with Brooke. Harrison was already writing on our whiteboard. Where had he found the dry-erase markers anyway? My eyes fell on the overturned flowerpot on the table and its scattered contents. Oh.

"What are you doing?" I asked, annoyed at the crack in my voice.

"My job." He was writing our names on the board next to different times. "The bishop wants to see you and Ashley on Sunday. It's time for the ward draft."

"Oh." My heart fell, but I should've known. The semester was ending. New callings were already being extended to replace the students leaving. That's what it meant to live in a transient ward, namely a college ward at BYU. Except I liked my calling now—activities committee cochair. In fact, I had been preparing for that calling since the day I was born . . . well, since I even knew it existed. It's an excuse to hang out with guys and throw parties. Why would they take that away from me?

"Dash everything," I said. That's what I said when I was only *slightly* irritated.

Harrison glanced up in time to catch my less-than-enthusiastic reaction and he smiled briefly, putting the cap back on the marker. He was the ward executive secretary, but he couldn't just call to make an appointment. No, that would be too normal. The fact was his visits always held some sort of hidden agenda, though we could never really figure out what that was. My theory was that he just liked to mess with our minds. "Dash everything? Have you suddenly turned British, then?" he asked.

"I haven't stooped that low."

"Surprising," he said. "Apparently you have a problem with the time of your bishop's appointment?"

No, no problem. It just meant that I had to wake up earlier to get to church, which meant I couldn't stay up as late the night before, which meant a damper on my social life. No, no problem at all. I shrugged, knowing that I was just being difficult because I didn't want to let go of my calling. "I'll be there," I muttered. I turned to leave the kitchen and almost tripped over Ashley.

She tucked her black hair behind her ear. "Were you talking about me in here?" she asked.

Harrison straightened, almost losing his calm reserve . . . almost. It was common knowledge that Harrison did not like to be touched, which we all respected—not having the inclination to do otherwise—but Ashley was different. Just the fact that the English boy was in any way vulnerable was too much of a temptation for her to bear. She sauntered to his side, a mischievous glint to her eye.

Harrison backed up against the wall. "I'm just setting up appointments with the bishop," he said. His discomfiture amused Ashley and me.

"Oh, really?" she said, lifting her hands in a threatening way, almost touching him.

"Quit it with the magic fingers, Trashley, or I'll do something you'll regret," he stammered.

"Like what?" she asked.

"Uh, never mind, I'll probably regret that too, so forget it."

Emma laughed from the opening in the doorway. "*That* is going on the quote board," she said, and we reluctantly concurred. You see, every apartment has an apartment historian, though we were all the historians here. Every inch of available space in our kitchen was covered with slips of paper, quoting everyone that happened to say anything even remotely clever. It made for very messy cabinet doors.

Harrison's head shot up when he saw Emma, and I smiled. Perhaps he wasn't so different from the other guys after all. Harrison would never admit it, but as I looked at his face, I knew the truth. Call it intuition, or call it that he was exhibiting all signs of possibly liking her. They were not the usual signs, mind you, but for a guy who spared no one's feelings, actually deigning to be nice to a girl meant something. Comparatively speaking, he treated her like gold, saving only his harsh words for us. Too bad she could never remember his name.

"Hello, Emma," he said, "I'm so glad you've come to restore some sanity into my life."

She laughed, probably not understanding that he'd just dissed everyone by complimenting her. I felt stupid for not seeing this new development earlier. The sarcastic, mean ones always liked the quiet, sweet ones.

"Oh great." Brooke followed Emma into the kitchen. "Who let the annoying guy in?"

"And now the sanity is gone again," Harrison retorted.

To my irritation, and most likely to our FHE brothers' once they became aware of it, I realized that Harrison had managed to capture the attention of all the girls in our apartment, leading us away from our own FHE group like the mad pied piper he was.

"How goes the love life?" he suddenly asked me.

My eyes widened. What did Harrison know? He was always trying to get information out of us. I wasn't about to let him have it. "It's okay."

"Hmm." He stroked his chin. "That's only because you don't know what you're doing as of yet. With the proper training, I would chance to say you fine, upstanding ladies could become the hottest commodity in the ward. Not only would you have a date every night, but you would have *multiple* dates every night. Men would stand in line waiting for you to pencil them in for half-hour time slots, just salivating for the privilege of lavishing their money on you. Think of the free dinners at the Skyroom, the operas in Salt Lake."

I scoffed. Where did he get off making fun of our love lives that way?

Brooke snorted. "Just what we need—to fail all our classes for a few stupid dates."

"Your FHE sister Miriam wouldn't know what to do with herself," he finished, ignoring Brooke's comments.

I stilled. He knew what button to push, didn't he? And I wondered how he knew so much. Besides the definite sag to my already-lowering grades, I liked the sound of making Miriam suffer, but as usual, Harrison was being completely ridiculous. "You sound like a miracle worker," I said dryly.

"I am." Harrison paced the room, circling me. All he needed was an eyeglass. I tried not to flinch at what he must see. Okay, let's just say that Audrey Hepburn–sized girls were the bane of my existence and I just waited for the day when the Marilyn Monroe look came back in style. I enjoyed my flares and cords, but I definitely had to be careful picking out the cut of my jeans. And there was no way I could ever stop working out. I pulled my black shirt over the ribbed waistband of my khakis, and Harrison smiled.

"By George, Samantha," he said finally, "the men of BYU will be groveling at your feet by the time I'm through with you." My eyebrows lifted. What did Harrison mean by that? He must have been blind.

Emma clapped her hands after the initial silence. "That's going on the quote wall," she said. "That is a perfectly adorable thing to say, Harrison."

"Dash diddly," I said. That meant I was even more irritated. "Don't encourage him," I added. Harrison had far too many quotes on our wall as it was. My fists landed on my hips and I decided to play dirty. "Emma," I whispered, "ask him to kick the hook."

"Only fools kick the hook," he said, overhearing me. He watched us under heavy lids.

"Emma kicked the hook," I said. "Do you think she's a fool?"

"Only blinded by the evil designs of wicked women."

"Is that true, Emma?" I asked. "Are you too stupid to know whether you want to kick the hook or not?"

She dimpled, refusing to take offense.

"C'mon, Harrison, kick the hook. It's fun," I pushed.

"I refuse to be a sheep."

"What's so bad about sheep? Aren't we all sheep in the flock of God?" I asked, smirking condescendingly at him when he cast me an irritated look. I was exactly what he would describe as a conniving Babylonian temptress.

"You have to see this wall of fame," Emma said, completely unaware of my goads. "C'mon." Emma led the poor fool to the pictures that covered our wall, passing the guys as they began filing from the living room into the kitchen—apparently they had just noticed our absence, though it didn't do them any good.

"Everyone on it has kicked the hook," Emma said. "And you can do it too."

"Fools," he muttered.

"You will join those fools," I promised. "C'mon, it's not that high. You can do it."

He rolled his eyes, but stopped when Emma's hand landed on his arm. "Come look at these other pictures that Samantha put up."

I tried to follow, but was stopped by a low voice that sent chills down my back. "I'm practicing to be a massage therapist," Grif said behind me. I stiffened, though I couldn't help but note the poetic justice in it as I saw Harrison slip away from my grasp, only to be caught myself. "You look tense," he said.

Of course I did. The huntress was becoming the hunted, and I pulled back. "I'm fine," I said, but Grif's eyes didn't leave mine.

"Let me work out the knots in your back. You'll be glad you did."

"No, I don't think so," I said, looking around frantically.

He reached for me, but was stopped by Marcus's laughing voice behind us. "Quit putting the moves on Samantha," he said.

I reddened. *Putting the moves on me?* Not only did I feel incredibly stupid that Marcus had to come to my rescue, but why did he have to use that phrase? It would only give Griffin ideas. I wasn't sure who to smack now.

"I'm not putting the moves on her," Griffin said. "I'm giving her a massage." He reached for me again, but Marcus's hand landed on my shoulders and he steered me away from Griffin's reach. I wasn't sure who he was protecting, since he knew I was quite capable of violence myself.

Marcus carefully kept the telling expression from his face. "It's getting late, Griffin," he said. "Shouldn't we be leaving now?"

"Well, you're touchy," Griffin told me, still taking offense that I'd refused the massage, despite Marcus's interference that made me appear innocent.

"No, I think you're the one who's touchy," Marcus said, not able to resist the pun. Ashley laughed and I cast her an annoyed glance. There was no need to bring undue attention to Griffin's embarrassment. He would just take it out on me.

Griffin reached for his cell phone at the same moment it went off. It was such an opportune moment that I couldn't help but think it was contrived. He answered it in an important voice. "Oh, I'm busy," he said into the receiver. "I'm not sure if I can do it . . . I'll have to get back to you on that one." He clicked it off and shrugged. "I get calls all the time. I probably shouldn't have gotten the cell. I can't get a moment to myself, but it's the latest model. I had to buy my dad one of these too, they're so advanced. It takes better pictures than your digital. You can even set the clock to . . ."

Brooke looked at our own clock and her jaw dropped. It was almost midnight. Nobody's FHEs lasted until curfew, except ours. If she was a cussing girl, she would've cussed. Instead she clenched her fists. "It's Cinderella time," she announced. "Everybody get lost."

Scott snickered behind her. "Thank you," he said. "Aside from that exciting stumble in the hall, I thought FHE would never end."

"No one asked you to stay," she countered.

"You know, Mom, sometimes I think you don't care." He glanced at me, but didn't even spare a thought for his short, stalker roommate as he deserted Griffin, the wreath singing Scott out the door.

Griffin didn't seem to care about being left, which I suppose guys never did. Instead he knelt next to our DVD collection. It was stacked against the whole side of one wall. Brooke had quite the array of movies.

"If you want to check one out," Brooke said sternly, "you write it on the whiteboard."

"Whose *SpongeBob* is this?" Griffin asked.

"That DVD's mine," I said. "It doesn't leave the house." Marcus rolled his eyes. His arm was still on my shoulders but I knew it meant nothing to him, though it might deter Griffin. I chose the slightly lesser of two evils and didn't shrug him off.

"Really? Whose *Arthur*?" Griffin asked, picking up the DVD.

"That's mine," Emma said. "You can borrow it."

"And keep it forever," I muttered.

Marcus perked up in sudden interest. "Arthur? Isn't that some happy kids' show that promotes world peace, love, and harmony? What could you possibly have against that, Sam?"

I tried not to say anything, especially with Emma standing right there, but I wanted to rip right into him. Poor Emma had been deceived by Arthur's apparent lack of charm. She probably felt sorry for the whiny little brat and therefore chalked the show up as educational. Now SpongeBob, there was a lad who had character.

Ashley just shook her head at Marcus. "We're actually pretty sensitive about the SpongeBob/Arthur issue around here."

"I didn't realize there was an issue," Marcus said. He was trying to keep from laughing.

"Of course you didn't," I said. Marcus never kept up on the hottest debates. To him SpongeBob was insignificant and random, but this issue was a defining point of character. Any guy who liked SpongeBob was fun-loving, clever, and forgiving. But usually if someone liked Arthur, they were depressed, introspective, whiny, and dramatic (minus innocent Emma, of course). Basically, the shows helped separate the wheat from the tares in my dating book.

"I'll take the *Arthur*," Griffin said. He turned to me. Apparently Marcus's arm didn't do the trick of fending him off. "Hey, are you doing anything tomorrow, Sam?"

I purposely misinterpreted the question, trying to ignore the offending *Arthur* DVD in his hand. "Yeah, school," I said. "Well, see ya later." I smiled a bright fake smile, and he had no choice but to follow his other roommate out the door. He tried to run past the wreath to keep it from going off, but it was in vain and the wreath sang jolly Christmas carols after him at the top of its mechanical voice.

Marcus's arm finally left my shoulder and he reached for something more interesting. "Hey, whose walkie-talkies?"

"Mine," Ashley said. "You wanna borrow one?"

I stifled a gasp of horror. That would mean constant interaction with Marcus for who knew how long. She couldn't be serious, but even as she said it they turned them on, talking into them though only ten feet apart.

Derek touched my arm, directing my attention away from them. "Thank you for a very pleasant evening," he said. "The entertainment was as enjoyable as the company."

Marcus glanced up at that, but he wasn't the only one to notice the pretty speech given by the elders quorum president. Harrison smirked, his gaze running from Marcus to me, which surprised me.

Harrison prided himself on reading people, and I knew that he was doing some sort of psychoanalysis on us, but there was no way he could know I had ever been interested in Marcus, could he?

"Oh, really?" I turned to Derek hurriedly. Being the middle child of seven, I thrived on attention, but when I finally got it, it made me nervous. However, the best way to take a compliment was pretending that you liked it. "Say more things like that."

Derek's hand transferred to my elbow, and it took every ounce of self-restraint not to raise my eyebrows. Every girl knows what an elbow squeeze means . . . unless, of course, he's just a friendly guy like Derek. He smiled encouragingly at me. "We'll have to get together sometime and play some equally random game at my place, you and . . ." his gaze swept behind me and he winked at Emma, "all your roommates."

"Sure," I said. He nodded, and with one last elbow squeeze, he too ran past the singing wreath.

Harrison took this as his cue to leave. To my annoyance, he glanced significantly at me and then at Marcus. "Happy hunting," he whispered for my ears alone, and he stepped out the door, boldly striding past the wreath.

I gritted my teeth at the insinuation. Happy hunting indeed. Besides a few shocked glances, Marcus was pretty good at ignoring me. Now he was making eyes at Ashley.

"Get out," Brooke said.

Surprisingly, Marcus took the not-so-subtle hint. He lifted the walkie-talkie to his lips. "I am now making my way out the door," he said through it.

Brooke stormed the kitchen and flushed Logan out of it and away from Miriam. "I'm going. I'm going," Logan said, but his footsteps stilled as he watched Marcus land on his hands and knees at the front door. "What's he doing?" he asked me.

What did it look like? Marcus was trying to get past the wreath without setting it off. Apparently it was the newest challenge, and it didn't take Logan long to join in the fun. Marcus was already army crawling under the wreath when Logan threw on his gray coat and followed him, inching his way past it too. We watched in silence.

"Slowly, slowly," Marcus whispered. "Only through the means of our athletic stamina will we be able to sneak past the vigilant guardian of the C6 chicks—and I'm not talking about Brooke." Logan hunched over, creeping over the threshold, close to his roommate's heels. Their coats swooshed—the only sound that broke the silence.

Despite myself, I listened for the wreath to go off, but so far it was still. Even Brooke waited tensely.

"We're almost through," Marcus whispered. His voice resonated from Ashley's walkie-talkie, and we craned our necks in suspense.

"Almost . . ." he said.

The wreath opened a glowing eye and we jumped, listening to it go off. Its thin mouth moved up and down in eerie rhythm to the music as it belted out another Christmas carol.

Dash diddly dog, it was good.

CHAPTER 4

"Ah, sweet nothings, empty promises, chocolates—you can tell me anything you want . . . as long as you don't mean it."
—Samantha Skyler (Wed., Dec. 1st)

The snow fluttered gently over my head, and I clutched my American Heritage book tightly against my stomach. It was getting colder and I had only my jean jacket to protect me, but there was no way I was wearing my "Stay Puft" Marshmallow jacket. I might not have money, but I had my pride, especially in moments like these. I watched as a guy in baggy jeans barreled in my direction. He was bent double under his backpack, and he steadfastly avoided eye contact as we passed—until I almost tripped over him. Then he nodded—the typical BYU greeting.

I sighed. Four more blocks until I reached my apartment, and my back was killing me. I had stuffed as many books as I could possibly squeeze into my frayed backpack, and I still had to carry the heaviest in my arms. On the bright side, I was going to be buff by the end of this semester. The American Heritage book was quite the workout, though I should've taken the class freshman year and gotten it out of the way.

Yeah, twenty-five years old with another semester to go until I graduated in the spring—with one of the shortest majors at BYU. But let me explain myself. Besides my conflicting plans for life giving me ADHD on my choice of majors, there was no way my parents could fork out enough money to pay for seven kids to go to college. Even if they could, they didn't raise us to be wimps. We were scrappers, or so they told us, which meant that we had to pay for school ourselves. For me that meant taking lots of breaks because there was no way I could work and go to school at the same time . . . not with the way my life went. I was already struggling with the finals coming my way.

I listened to the wreath go off at my apartment and stilled. No wonder our neighbors hated us. That thing had volume. I was only a block away from my apartment, but I slowed my steps, desperately hoping that the eerie Christmas carols marked the coming of roommates and not visitors. I was no longer looking my best.

My hair, which I had taken such pains to straighten, had frizzed into curls under the wet snow, making me look like Little Bo Punk. My army boots with the chunky soles just added to the look. You see, no matter how tough I tried to dress, my fashion always tended toward cutesy military brat. It was terribly embarrassing. The red hearts stitched to the pockets of my flared jeans didn't help either.

I poked my head around the corner and my heart dropped. Marcus stood on the balcony three flights above me. He turned and saw me, and it was too late for me to jump behind a bush. "Hey, Samantha, we were just leaving you a message," he yelled down at me.

"Really?" I shouted. "Then why don't you leave it and leave me alone?" I smiled up at his startled expression. I have lots of practice pretending to be happy. Logan's head pushed over the balcony, and my smile turned more genuine. At least good news traveled with bad. I could take a Marcus dose if his roommate was there to cushion the blow. I was always ready for a good time, even if it was mingled with danger. "What kind of message?" I asked quickly, not wanting to chase Logan away.

"A message of love," Logan said.

Marcus cast him a furious look. Logan dimpled, in no way apologetic. Trust Logan to be scandalous. He was so much fun. I smiled, well aware of Marcus's watchful gaze, and decided to play along.

"Who is it from?" I asked. "You or Marcus?"

"Who do you want it to be from?"

"Definitely not from Marcus." I cast Marcus a mean look and he just leaned against the balcony, ignoring me. I pulled up the three flights of stairs. I dropped my backpack at their feet and both Marcus and Logan jumped back at the loud clunk against the cement. The wreath reacted with another loud carol.

Marcus ignored the goad, his eyes intent on my backpack. "Mercy, how many books do you have in there?" he asked.

"Believe it or not, I actually go to class every once in a while." I pushed past him, standing next to Logan, belatedly noticing that I was stooped from my backpack. I straightened my shoulders, working on my posture. It wouldn't do for Marcus to think that he had broken me.

"Of course," Logan said, leaning against the balcony, but mostly toward me. His eyes were steady on mine. He had a way of making me feel very attractive. I liked that. "There are probably lots of cute guys there," he said. "We can never compete."

"They're not as cute as you." I returned the compliment while fishing in my pocket for my keys. My hand brushed past nothing. Dash everything. I glanced up, seeing Marcus's watchful eyes on me. I had locked myself out . . . unless the keys were somewhere in my mess of a backpack. "But they're still tempting," I managed to say, trying to keep their attention from my lost keys.

"Then I'll never let you go to class again," Logan said.

Marcus cast Logan a quelling look as if that would stop his constant flirting. "How about we take this inside?" Marcus said. "It's freezing."

"I'm not hot enough for you?" I asked, trying to keep from looking trapped. I tried to keep my gaze from the flowerpot. It would never do if they knew where the spare key was hidden.

"No one's hot enough to combat this cold weather, pumpkin," Marcus said. "I know you don't care if we see your messy apartment, and we don't care, so let us in."

Well, that about did it. Even if I hadn't locked myself out, I wouldn't let him in after that. I crossed my arms across my chest. "Sorry guys, I can't do that."

Marcus looked startled for the second time that day, and I quickly hid a smile. He almost made getting locked out worth it. "I mean," I said in a fake-sweet voice, which I knew he would immediately sense as trouble, "what's wrong with the porch? It's such a beautiful day."

The snow drifted over our heads and I enjoyed Marcus's discomfort immensely, even though I was feeling it too. Logan, on the other hand, looked very amused. He gave Marcus a knowing smirk as if he knew this had something to do with my hurt feelings. Marcus just glowered.

"Well," Logan said. "Since this is only a business trip, I suppose we can wrap this up fairly quickly."

"Go ahead." I pulled my gloves off with my teeth and began rummaging through my bag. My keys had to be in there somewhere.

"We need to plan the ward Christmas party," Logan said. "It's already December."

Of course. Logan always thoughtlessly loaded everything on my shoulders. Well, not thoughtlessly actually. He was under the impression that I enjoyed it, which I did. We had the perfect working relationship—both of us pretty much did what we liked, so I could only imagine Logan's surprise when he found out I would no longer be his cochair in a week. It meant that anything he assigned to me would be completely moot by Sunday. I smiled, deciding to play with him.

"What do you want me to do?" I asked, pretending I still had a say.

"Well, we need to figure out what we want to do, for starters," Logan said in his most charming voice. Normally he had a willing slave on his hands.

"I'm sure I could think of something by Sunday." I couldn't help the crocodile smile spreading across my face. "Anything else?"

"We need to have a committee meeting," he said. "The bishop has been getting on my back about it."

"How about on Sunday?" I said, knowing perfectly well that I would be out of the clear for that one. I was actually a little sad about it.

"Yeah, that sounds good." Logan leaned closer to me and I followed his lead. It was really fun to flirt with such a charmer. "Remind me to make this up to you, Sam. I owe you dinner or something."

Logan always threatened to do that and never followed through. "Ah, sweet nothings," I said. "Empty promises, chocolates—you can tell me anything you want . . . as long as you don't mean it."

"Oh, I mean it," Logan said, gamely keeping up the flirtation.

Marcus frowned, casting his roommate an annoyed glance. Man, Marcus must've really thought that I was a pushover. And normally I was, except not in the regular sense of the word. I liked to be in charge of everything.

"Could you make up some fliers for it?" Logan asked.

"Of course," I said, almost feeling disappointed that I couldn't. I made good fliers, but I was enjoying the joke too much to be that sad about it. "I'll make the fliers next week."

"What?" Marcus exploded. "Are you going to make her do everything, Logan?"

Logan looked surprised, and I just smiled, looking like the perfect martyr in sheep's clothing. Logan tried to defend himself. "She likes to make fliers," he said.

"That's what she says," Marcus said.

"Are you calling me a liar?" I asked sweetly.

Marcus floundered at that one, and I smirked, knowing I had effectively caught him between looking like an idiot and a jerk. "Not exactly," he murmured.

Logan glanced down at his watch. "I would love to stay on the cold balcony with you, but I've got to get to class." He grabbed my hand, pulling me away from my backpack. "It's good doing business with you, cutie."

My face turned red and I steadfastly avoided Marcus's eyes, knowing he would be laughing at my reaction. I tried to cover it up.

"Until we meet again," Logan said.

"I'll be counting the hours." I quickly returned the sentiment, wondering if I really would.

Logan pulled away. "It will be sheer torture being away from you." He bounded quickly down the stairs away from me, contradicting his words.

"I hope I'll be able to subsist during the long hours of . . ."

"Knock it off," Marcus said. I glanced at him, and the smile drained from my face at the look I saw on his. He was not amused. Why didn't he ever enjoy a good joke like his roommate did? "Aren't you going inside?" he asked.

"Yeah."

"Well, what are you waiting for?"

"For you to leave."

He laughed dryly, knowing better. "You're locked out, aren't you?"

Sometimes Marcus saw too much. I pulled away from him, leaning against the wreath. It began singing wildly behind me. Its jaws hit my head and I pulled away from that too. "Don't worry," I shouted above the din. "One of my roommates should be coming home pretty soon. I'll just wait for her."

"Ashley?" he asked.

I wasn't prepared for the surge of annoyance that hit me. Don't get me wrong, I was over this guy, but he didn't have to act so interested in my roommates. "Why?" I asked. "Did you have something to tell her?"

"I'm sure I could think of something," he muttered when the wreath finally stopped singing. He began searching through the dead flowers and Christmas lights, getting dangerously close to the spare key. "Don't you leave a spare key under a flowerpot somewhere?" he asked.

"What, are you kidding?" I blocked him, practically pushing him back. He glanced at me in confusion. "Where anyone can steal it?" I asked. "Provo's a dangerous place." If he found the key, he would cause no end of havoc until we hid it again, and then we would most likely forget where the new hiding spot was.

"You're right," Marcus said. He pulled off his black gloves with his teeth. "We were just waiting around to steal your couches until you came home and thwarted our plans."

"Look." I threw on a backpack strap, acting as if I were going to leave. "I was thinking of going next door anyway. I'll be fine . . ." He began pulling out the screen on our kitchen window. "Hey!" I tried to tug him back, but he easily warded off my efforts. "There's a fine if it gets broken," I said, putting my fists on my hips just so he knew I wasn't about to let him win.

"Like your manager would make you pay for anything," he said. "He loves you."

"Well, he wouldn't if he knew half of the things I've done," I said.

Marcus ignored me, prying the screen out of the window and setting it at my feet with a clatter. He began wedging the glass open. It was disconcerting how expertly he did it. I glanced behind us, seeing a group of students walk past us, but they didn't even blink. This kind of break-in was a normal thing in Provo. With a final jerk, Marcus got the window open and pulled himself over the window pane, jumping into my kitchen.

I glanced through the window, meeting his eye. "Welcome to C6," he said. "Would you like a hamburger with that shake?"

I pursed my lips. Just the thought that he had full access to my apartment made me nervous. "Would you just open the door?" I said.

"What will you give me?"

"What do you want?"

"Information."

"Forget it." I tried to pull through the window myself, and he just pushed me back with one hand.

"Hey," I said. "It's cold out here."

"Really? Maybe you should put your gloves back on."

"So I can your box your ears with them? Not a bad idea."

"Oh, come on, you're not still mad at me, are you?"

"Why would I be mad at you? You would have to cross my mind for that. I wouldn't even spare you a thought—"

"Except for moments like these," he finished for me, giving me a maddening smile. "Let's talk."

I stilled. That sounded awful. "About what?"

He shrugged. "I don't know. Let's try small talk first—how are your novels coming along?"

Good. I could handle that. As long as we never said anything of importance, we could still be friends . . . sorta. "I'm coming up with a doozy of a plot actually," I said.

"Really?"

"Yeah." I cast him an evil look. "I've got the perfect villain."

"This isn't based on anyone we know, is it?"

"And get sued? I don't think so."

"Oh come now, your roommates wouldn't sue you. What else are you doing with your life since we last talked? You aren't still planning on becoming an actress, are you?"

I stiffened. He might as well have called me a flibbertigibbet and gotten it over with. "I wouldn't count being in one student film becoming an actress," I said. But yes, if I didn't get married, there was no way I was wasting my life on some boring job, so maybe I would try something like that. Who knew?

Marcus glanced at my electric guitar propped precariously against the wall in the living room. "Whatever happened to your band?" he asked.

I winced. The last talent show we had been in had been a complete disaster. I had taught Emma her part on the bass guitar, but unfortunately she didn't know how to tune it when someone knocked it over. Ashley couldn't hear any of us and her drums were off beat, throwing me off on the guitar. Brooke, of course, was perfect on the cello, but besides that, the whole thing had been a disgrace and we had banned The Cranberries from our apartment. The sad thing was that the song had sounded pretty good before we got on stage and ruined it.

"We haven't been able to practice lately."

"Oh, too bad," he said. "You need it."

Trust Marcus to make me feel incredibly stupid just making small talk, but apparently he had lost interest in the conversation because he began wandering around the room. I was almost grateful. "You don't mind if I make myself at home, do you?" he asked. Without listening for an answer, he went to the cupboard and rummaged through the glasses.

"I've got a good idea," I said in a fake, bright voice, slinging my backpack over my shoulders again. "Why don't you let me into my apartment?"

He pulled out my SpongeBob glass, not listening. "What's this?" he asked. "The famous SpongeBob. This is yours, isn't it? Where's Emma's Arthur cup?" I molded my expression into a casual one, so he wouldn't know he was making me nervous. "This isn't fragile is it?" He lifted the glass as if he was going to dash it against the sink.

"Hey!" I pulled myself over the window in one swift movement, but my fat backpack caught me on the top and I lurched to a stop. "Put that down . . . gently!" I kicked my legs and managed to throw one over the windowsill, knocking a plant over with my army boots. It crashed against the floor, flinging dirt all over the kitchen. *Dash diddly!* "Look what you made me do!" I shouted.

He didn't seem ruffled in the least. "Oh, typical girl, blame the guy."

"Because guys are always the ones at fault." I tried to disengage my leg from the side of the windowsill, realizing I was in an awkward position. No, it was worse than awkward, I was stuck. I tried to shrug off my backpack, but it wasn't working.

He set the SpongeBob glass on the counter. "Let me help you."

I tried to push him away. "No, I can do it." I tugged uselessly at my foot. Why did these things always have to happen to me? I tried to seem as calm as he was, but it was hard when I felt myself teeter over the sill. Instead of moving forward to help me, he stepped back, laughing. .

"Well, this should be amusing to watch," he said, knowing full well I couldn't get through by myself. This would end in tears, but I would definitely make sure they belonged to him. I felt the windowsill digging into my leg and I wriggled around like a worm, my heavy backpack definitely not helping me keep my balance.

The wreath went off behind me and I felt hands on my shoulders, shoving me into the kitchen. "Boo."

I screamed shrilly, having no hands to protect my fall. I fell straight into Marcus's arms. Fortunately for both of us, he had been ready, and he dragged me unceremoniously to my feet just as I heard Ashley erupt into giggles at the window behind me.

"Awkward," she said. "No, don't let me interrupt you."

I gasped and scrambled away from Marcus as fast as I could, turning to glare at Ashley. "Oh, c'mon," she said, recovering quickly at my look. "You would have done the same thing to me, admit it." She disappeared from sight, but I could still hear her talking. "Hey, why did you break in? Isn't the key still under the flowerpot? It is."

I avoided Marcus's eyes, silently wishing Ashley far, far away from our apartment. But wishing was futile and she let herself in, making her way into the kitchen. She was the only girl I knew who could pull off high heels with jeans. Her red heels clicked against the linoleum like the world was her runway, and she threw her sleek black coat on the table, not caring that it was covered with breadcrumbs.

"Why didn't you just grab the spare key?" she asked me.

"She didn't want it to fall into the wrong hands," Marcus said. I met his eyes and tried not to look guilty.

"We really should close the window," I said. "It's freezing in here."

"Really? I thought it was getting pretty hot," Ashley said. She began prowling around the kitchen and opened the fridge, perusing the goods. She reached for the milk. "But maybe it's just the company." She smiled at Marcus and he gave her a genuine smile in return. Ashley was so insincere with her flirtations that anyone could relax around her, especially Marcus lately. I tried to ignore it. "What are you doing back so early?" I asked her.

Ashley took a long swig from her milk carton. "I'm skipping class," she said once she caught her breath. "Looks like you are too, Marcus."

He shrugged. "It's just Marriage Prep. I'll copy Miriam's notes later."

My eyes narrowed. *Miriam?* No wonder our FHE sister was so tight with Marcus lately. Besides her perfect looks and perfect behavior, they had been spending some quality time together in a class devoted to dating and marriage. Well, what did I care?

"Or maybe I'll just get your notes, Samantha," Marcus said. "Aren't you taking the same class on Tuesdays?"

"Don't look at me. My notes are worthless. I'll never be ready for marriage at the rate I'm going."

"I'm not sure anyone would be ready to marry you," Marcus muttered.

I swiveled around, catching him with an angry look. "I'm not doing *that* bad in the class. I totally aced the Marriage Prep midterm, except for one question—it was one of those 'on your honor' questions. They asked if I'd done the assigned reading . . . and of course I didn't. And you have to answer those questions correctly or you're going directly to the hot place. Dash everything. It dropped me two letter grades." I was so annoyed I suddenly realized that I was babbling.

"You're taking Marriage Prep with Miriam?" Ashley asked, pulling out the one topic of importance from our practically meaningless conversation. She was wiping off crumbs from her red velour sweater.

"I'm not taking Marriage Prep *with her,* with her," Marcus said as if defending himself from the Inquisition. "We just happen to be in the same class."

"Too bad," Ashley said. She slammed the fridge door shut and stretched lazily. "We could have spread some really good rumors . . . Of course, we still can."

"Go ahead. Miriam's hot."

That took Ashley off guard. She tilted her head as Marcus started for the hall, and she almost didn't have enough presence of mind to stop him. "Are you going home?" she asked him.

"No, I'm heading for school. I've got to study."

"Me too," she said. "I have to take a test. I just forgot my ID card, just a sec." Ashley disappeared into the back, her long, black hair trailing behind her.

I looked everywhere but at Marcus, still very much aware of what he was doing. He had better not make any fast moves, especially around my SpongeBob glass. He paced the kitchen and stopped at our newest quotes on the wall. "What's this?" He began reading the bottom slip of paper and my head shot up, vaguely recognizing the quote.

"'He said he still wanted to be friends,'" he read.

My eyes widened. No, my roommates hadn't quoted me on my breakup with Marcus, had they?

"'Friends,'" he continued to read. "'I don't even spend time with my real friends, why would I spend time with some guy I can't stand anymore? Thank goodness he was lying.'"

Marcus glanced at me and I felt my whole face go red. I leaned heavily against the wall, wishing I were somewhere else. Not only did I look like a jerk, but now Marcus knew that I had thought twice about him . . . and our supposed breakup, even though we really didn't have anything to break up in the first place.

He studied my face and I was sure that it revealed everything. "Remind me to never say anything incriminating around your roommates," he muttered.

Dash everything! This was the worst thing that had ever happened to me, although I didn't know why it was so completely horrible, except . . . well, Marcus was already so sensitive. I didn't want him to know I couldn't stand him. Except he didn't look heartbroken really, he looked like he had caught a rat in a trap.

"Oh, look—your name's on this," he said, "and it was dated last week. Who could you have had a DTR like this with, I wonder?"

I shrugged, knowing full well he was playing with me. How many guys could I possibly have had a "define the relationship talk" with in a week? He might have thought that I was a player, but I wasn't that good.

"Found it." Ashley jumped back into the room. She threw on her slick, black coat, wrapping her scarf multiple times around her long neck, as graceful as Grace Kelley but with none of the class.

Marcus's hand landed on her elbow, and she didn't even blink twice. She was used to such attention. "Let's go," he said. Then he nodded at me. "See ya, friend." I tried not to shrink back.

"Oh, wait, Marcus," Ashley said, stopping in the hallway. "Didn't you want to get those Marriage Prep notes from Sam?"

"No, I'll get Miriam's notes instead. She has more time."

"Oh, okay."

Marcus opened the front door for Ashley, and I felt the cold air blow back at me. It wasn't just coming from outside. The wreath went off, making the two of us jump, but not Marcus. He didn't even glance at it.

"I'm gonna kill that thing someday," he muttered under his breath. At that moment I believed him.

CHAPTER 5

"He's come to admire you from afar."
—Brooke Hansen (Wed., Dec. 1st)

The door slammed shut behind them and I turned on my heel, stalking to my guitar and shrugging off my jean jacket. I felt awful, but I didn't know why. I was like a boxer with no punching bag. I needed to get my aggression out, and I needed to get it out *now*. I threw the strap over my shoulder. I didn't mean to hurt everyone around me. I just did, but it was *his* fault anyway. Technically Marcus was the one who dumped me! I was allowed to fight back, right? So why did I feel so guilty?

I turned my amp up loud. I didn't want to hear my thoughts—not now and I hoped not ever—but they kept coming. *Be good, be nice, be sweet, be perfect.* But how come I found myself relating to women like Evita and Alanis Morrissette? Why was I so angry, anyway? I mean, I had always thought that I would live happily ever after, but it got to the point where I had no idea what *happily ever after* even meant. It was just that nothing was turning out the way that I had planned. It was like banging against a door that would never open—maybe because it was just a padded cell. Sometimes I felt like I was stuck in an insane asylum.

Brooke came through the front door, and my fingers stilled over the strings. She nodded stiffly at me, her red hair falling like a sheet over one eye as she marched into the back, straightening her striped jacket over her gray power suit. I heard her bedroom door shut and I sat on the ugly couch, listening to the chords fade into oblivion.

I could feel it. I was going back into hibernation mode again, wasn't I? But I couldn't help it. I had to survive . . . I had to prepare . . . I had to live . . . I had to find something to live for. It really wasn't my fault that I was only good at completely ridiculous things. I was going to be a writer, an actress, a rock star . . . the only thing missing from the list was an all-star athlete. I'm always on this quest to make something of myself, not to disappoint that little girl who used to dream about the things that she would do someday because no one believed that she could. When I was a kid, we didn't have enough money to buy shoes, so I had to wear my older sister's hand-me-downs. They flopped so badly that most of the time I couldn't keep up and my siblings had to leave me behind, which left me sitting on the front porch. But I always knew that someday I would buy shoes—lots of them—and I would go places. I got made fun of in elementary school because I didn't have matching socks; well, someday I knew they'd follow my trend. Guys didn't date me for long because they hated my personality. I was too flighty, too obnoxious, too crazy—but soon I'd be so completely out of every guy's reach that they would finally know what they were missing. They say riches are a curse, but so what? Curse me with riches . . . Wait, what was I saying? At least curse me with enough to get by. How did that work, anyway?

Brooke came back into the living room wearing her yellow-ducky pajama bottoms. She was too practical to confine herself to the classic look all day. In fact, she usually spent half of the day in her pajamas while she did her homework. She sat down next to me, setting her smart books down on the carpet. "You're getting better at the guitar," Brooke said, capturing her long red hair with a pen. She spiked it on the top of her head, watching me closely.

I tossed the strap off my shoulder and threw my guitar on my couch. "Well, I've lived longer than you whippersnappers. I've had time to practice."

"No, you just don't do your homework." She looked very stern, not much like a whippersnapper, even though she was three years younger than me. "Battle of the Bands is coming up," she said in a matter-of-fact voice. "Maybe we can put something together."

"Yeah, right. Remember what happened last time? I can't even hear that Cranberries song anymore without wincing."

She laughed, and to my complete mortification started singing, "Zombie, zombie, zombie," in her most mocking voice.

"Stop it!" I shouted. "We've banned that song from this apartment and you know it!"

"C'mon, we can't possibly do as bad as we did last time," she said, pulling open her calculus book. "Well, at least I can't. Oh wait, never mind, I didn't do bad last time. Yeah, you're right, we shouldn't attempt it."

"Are you trying to use reverse psychology on me or what?" I said, feeling somewhat flustered. "Because you're not doing a very good job of talking me into playing—" We were interrupted by the wreath going off outside. The color drained from my face. "Who is it?" I asked.

Brooke stood up bravely, willing to find out for me, which said a lot. She must have sensed that I was having a bad day because she hated visitors, probably more than I did right then, and yet she still peeped through the peephole for me. Her expression grew dark. "Oh, great," she said.

"Who is it?" I demanded.

"Scott."

I straightened eagerly. Scott? Coming here? Musicians were always miserable, that's why they always made me feel so good. "What's the occasion?"

"He's come to admire you from afar," Brooke said.

I smiled. "From afar? I certainly hope not. Let him in."

Brooke shook her head, but she opened the door anyway. "Remember, this was your decision, not mine," she warned darkly.

Scott walked in, his movements liquid smooth. He wore dark jeans and a black shirt layered over a white shirt. His brown hair was unruly in true Byron fashion. You would think someone so well put together would show more cool around Brooke, but after last FHE, he took one glance at the man-eating, man-hating nazi-chick from our ward and made a wide berth around her, heading straight for our turtle. "Hey, Zooga," he said. "Mom didn't clean your cage yet. She must hate you."

Brooke sat down heavily on the couch, throwing her books in her lap. "FHE coleader. Get it straight, *son*," she muttered. "And I just cleaned *his* cage this morning."

Now that he was a safer distance away, he lifted an eyebrow at her ducky pajamas. "You look comfortable," he managed politely.

Brooke didn't seem to care that he was scared of her. She just rolled her eyes and I laughed. Scott turned to me, breaking into a rare smile. He was usually brooding, so any smile from him was flattering. He ruined the moment by sitting safely on another couch, though he still gave me his full attention.

"I heard you playing and had to come see you for myself." He glanced at my guitar, and I hoped that the walls had smothered the sound somewhat.

"Well, I'm not really the talent of the band." I glanced significantly at Brooke. She didn't look abashed. She didn't glance up from her books, either. "Brooke plays the cello and she's really good."

"Really?" Scott asked. "Brooke, why don't you play something for us?"

"No," she said without preamble.

I tried to cover up the awkwardness of the situation. "Why don't you play something for us, Scott? I hear you rock."

"What?" he said. "I can't follow a performance like yours."

It was no time for false modesty. He was the musical genius, not me. "Why?" I asked. "Was I really that bad?"

"Don't be annoying." Brooke flipped another page in her book. We glanced at her. "It's obvious you both just want to show off, so get it over with."

Scott bit his lip to keep from laughing. Neither of us could ignore a bitter challenge like that. He picked up my guitar and proceeded to tune it as inconspicuously as possible. I tried to stop from smiling. He was such a professional. "What do you want me to play?" he asked.

"Are you kidding?" I asked. "You can just play anything on demand?" I was far from that kind of talent. This guy was pure genius.

"Well, I can try to play it," he said. "I can't promise anything."

Brooke rolled her eyes. "And so the play-offs begin," she muttered.

I stood up in my excitement. "Play something from the Pixies— 'Where Is My Mind'?"

"You're a Pixies fan? You're so cool," he said. I preened under the compliment while Scott gave Brooke a mischievous smile. "You be Kim and do the backup vocals."

"Forget it." She cracked her knuckles, her eyes running intently over the pages of her book. She picked up another book, and I wondered if she was reading two at the same time.

He began strumming my guitar, turning back to me. "We need a bass here."

"Oh, too bad Emma isn't here," I said. "She's getting a lot better on the bass."

"Yeah, she can actually tune it," Brooke said, now the official heckler from the peanut gallery. She was starting to enjoy her role.

"Stop," I said. They both stopped and turned to me. "No, that's the beginning part of the song. 'Stop'."

"Okay." Scott pointed to me. "You've got the part. Vocals." I sat down on the orange wingback chair, crossing my legs underneath me as he began to play. I bobbed my head to the music, adding the appropriate backup vocals when needed. Brooke watched us like we were completely insane, which we were, but we didn't care. We were having too much fun.

"Where is my mind?" Scott sang. The rich tone of his voice caught my attention. Not only could the lad play the guitar, but he could sing. I was right. He was the ultimate romantic. I mean, if musicians' thoughts were as deep as their lyrics, they could offer hours of entertainment. Could you imagine getting into the mind of such a man? As a general rule, men were supposed to think in grunts, but to actually find one who thought deeper than me? Just associating with him would expand my horizons.

Scott broke into a guitar solo, and my eyes widened as he ran his able fingers over the frets. It was almost as if the guitar were a part of him, not some alien instrument that needed to be tamed like I made it out to be. He squeezed out a very groovy chord and I almost gasped, hardly believing that this sound was coming from my guitar. It tried to jump out of his hands, he was playing so hard, and he lifted the guitar up and behind his head, not missing a beat—the showoff.

I glanced at Brooke, knowing she would *not* be impressed, but she was despite herself. She even forgot to pretend to read. Well, really, who could read while this was going on?

The guitar solo faded into a steadier rhythm and he nodded at me, and with a little difficulty I resumed my vocals. It was so completely fun and loud that we didn't even hear the wreath go off. Emma shoved her way through the doorway, carrying loads of groceries. She held the door open with a tiny sneaker.

Scott stopped playing, and I listened to the sound vibrate into silence. "You need some help?" he asked her, suddenly acting the perfect gentleman. I was taken completely off guard. The musician had stopped his playing to help a lady in distress. He was now almost perfect in my eyes.

"Oh no. I'm fine." She smiled brightly, her ponytail bobbing. There was a lot of energy pent up in that tiny girl. "You sounded great. What were you playing?"

"Pixies," Brooke said in an annoyed voice.

"Well, how nice." Emma would say that even if we had been playing a polka. She was always so polite. She set her bags down on the ground and pulled off her snow-white mittens. She then tried to straighten the wrinkles from her pink-and-white striped jumper. The phone rang and I jumped from the stiff orange chair and scooped it up.

"Samantha's boyfriend!" Brooke and Emma shouted out simultaneously. No matter their normal reserve in other situations, the tradition would never die. Everyone who called on the phone was my boyfriend.

I put the receiver to my ear. "Hello," I said.

"Sorry to disappoint you." I recognized Harrison's maddening English accent.

"No, you'll do," I managed in my most flirtatious voice . . . and that's pretty flirtatious. He was silent on the other end, and I smiled, realizing I had just freaked him out. Good.

"Uh, do you have a point?" I asked. "Or did you just call to breathe heavily on the line?"

"It appears hunting season has started," he articulated.

My forehead wrinkled. "What? I don't get it."

"Be careful or you'll let your prey escape again."

I looked out the front room window, seeing him in his apartment across the way, a long elegant shadow beside his curtains. "Get a life, Harrison," I said.

"Once I get all you girls married off, I'll feel easier about it," he said. I glanced at Scott as Harrison droned on. The guitar sat on his knee, and he listlessly plucked at the strings with the capable hands of an artist. He was like a deer—one whiff of this conversation and he would run off. "Please don't take on such a heroic role," I told Harrison sarcastically.

"I'm just magnifying my calling. As the bishop's right-hand man, I'm his eyes and ears."

"Quit looking for promotions from the bishop. I'm sure we'll manage fine without you."

"Really?" Harrison asked. "Then who will be the lucky soul confined eternally to you?" I was silent. "Whose name will be etched on your gilt-edged invitations—the bumbling flirt, the scared rabbit . . . or perhaps the eager specimen angling your way? Or maybe," he paused dramatically, "you'll opt for something more familiar, an old flame perhaps—the one who got away."

I hung up the phone.

"Who was that?" Emma asked politely.

I gave an unladylike snort. "Only the most annoying, cold-hearted, idiotic guy . . ."

Emma's brow wrinkled. "I'm not sure . . ."

"With an English accent?" I finished meaningfully.

Emma's eyes brightened. "Oh, Harrison!"

Scott grimaced. "Whoa, brutal, Emma."

"Oh, you've finally remembered his name, Emma," I said. "And I think you've described him exactly."

Her face grew red and Brooke guffawed behind her. "Oh, but Harrison isn't any of those other things!" Emma cried. "I didn't mean that at all."

"Good save, but you're not a very good liar," Scott said as he handed over my guitar and gave me a conspiring grin amidst Emma's protestations of innocence. "We make a good team," he told me.

Oh yeah we did, but I tried not to let it get to my head. "We'll have to play again sometime," I said. "Maybe Brooke can play a cello solo while we're at it."

"Yeah, I'll play it behind my head." Brooke rewound her hair with the pencil and stacked the long red locks over her head, remembering herself enough to glare down at her books. It wouldn't do to give him any attention.

"Man, you're sassy, Mom."

She just growled in response and he let himself out, cool until the end. He gave me one last backward glance and winked. I was completely taken aback. That was very courageous for a guy of his ilk, but then again, he probably didn't think of me as a threat. Too bad.

CHAPTER 6

"Heaven called. They said they were missing an angel. Here he comes now."

—Emma Rose (Wed., Dec. 1st)

I picked up Emma's bags. "Let me help you with these."

She detained me with a smile. "Oh, those are just some more Christmas decorations. Don't worry about those. I'm just getting ready to unpack them."

"What?" I looked around the living room. It already looked like Santa's fanatical little helpers done their worst here. Tinsel hung from our tiny Charlie Brown tree in the corner. Strings of white Christmas lights looped around the ceiling. Santa Claus sat on the piano next to a manger. "Um . . . didn't we already decorate?" I asked.

"Yes, but now that Thanksgiving is over, we can finally put some finishing touches on this place." She surveyed the room, her tiny hands on her hips. "I was thinking another string of Christmas lights for the balcony outside, and maybe we should weave some garland around the railing. We could put some snowflakes on these windows, too."

Brooke had been sucking on a pencil, but she quickly plucked it out of her mouth. "You've got to be kidding," she said.

"Why would I be kidding?" Emma looked shocked, and suddenly I felt guilty. Emma had worked so hard to make this place unlivable, and it couldn't get worse, really. It already looked like a grandma's house gone wrong.

I glanced at Brooke, but she was watching her books intently, the pencil back in her mouth. It meant she couldn't mouth off. "Brooke's just cranky," I said.

Brooke rolled her eyes to prove my point.

"She wishes she had more time to decorate," I said, purposely misreading her reluctance. Only one thing made me feel good about being so nice—it was driving Brooke crazy. "You don't mind if I help instead, Emma?" I asked. "I need something to get my mind off my test tonight."

"Are you sure?" Emma asked.

"Yeah, I really want to." I heaved Emma's bags into my arms and pushed the door open, stepping out into the snow . . . like a martyr marching to the guillotine. The wreath went off and I jumped.

Brooke just twirled a red strand of hair around her finger, her lip curled in amusement. "See you on the other side," she mumbled with her mouth full of pencil.

With a set face, I pulled the wreath from the door and set it inside. I didn't want the wreath to alert our neighbors to our nefarious deeds on the balcony. "Don't make any fast moves, Brooke," I warned. She didn't even look terrified.

Emma closed the door behind us and pulled a few strands of Christmas lights from the bags. She wove them around the railing. I stared up at the blue and white sky, but her next words brought me quickly back.

"Scott looks like a nice guy," she said. Her brown eyes were on me, way too sincere to make her question a calculating one.

"Uh," I said, glancing over at Harrison's window, making sure he wasn't watching. He probably had the place bugged. That was one young man who took his calling of keeping track of the ward way too seriously.

"Yeah, Scott's pretty nice," I said. "And he visits all the time. But he'll never make a move—even if he was interested. Though you can never tell with a guy like that." I sighed. "It will be a blue, blue Christmas this year . . . for all of us."

Emma laughed. "What are you talking about? You've got plenty of admirers."

I shrugged. "None who will do anything about it."

"Oh, I know someone who will do something about it."

I brightened at the thought. What had Emma found out? "Really? Who?"

"Griffin."

My smile faded. *My stalker?* Why were really nice people so stupid when it came to setting their friends up? It's like they had no sense of judgment at all. "Griffin?" I intoned with astonishment. "How could you even see us together? He borrowed your *Arthur* DVD, for crying out loud."

Emma ripped off a piece of tape, her movements mouselike. She hurriedly slapped the piece over a string of lights. Her little nose was red, and it began to twitch as she fought the cold. "What?" she said. "He's nice."

"You think everyone is nice."

"No, I don't."

"You think *I'm* nice."

"You are," she said.

"You really are a saint, aren't you?" I glanced at Emma and she gave me a genuine smile. She always said the right thing, but the problem was that I never believed her.

"You're like one of those construction workers who helped change our flat on I-15," she informed me in a cheerful voice.

"What?" My hands dropped to my sides. Too bad she hadn't stuck with the first compliment. I remembered our blowout with distaste. It had been ten o'clock that night, and the highway was closing for construction when we pulled over. I don't know how long Emma and I had been standing on the highway just outside of Salt Lake City, desperately calling everyone we knew on my cell. But nobody would stop to help us . . . until *they* came, the construction workers with their ratty beards and dirty trucks, spitting and cussing, especially when they found out how long we had been standing out there in the cold.

I stared at Emma. "You just compared me to a construction worker."

"Yep, one of the highest compliments I can think of," she said. "You're one of the spitting, swearing construction workers of life who help change tires on the highway while all the clean-cut, supposedly righteous folk pass by without expression."

You know, there really was something about Emma. Anyone who met her would call her a Molly Mormon, and she was in a way. But for some reason I really looked up to her. We all did. Maybe because she put us all to shame. I turned quickly away from her, trying to hide my laughter.

"Speaking of your suitors . . ." She ripped off another piece of tape and secured the other side of the lights to the railing. "Heaven called. They said they were missing an angel." She laughed at her own joke. "Here he comes now."

I turned, seeing friendly, elders quorum president Derek below our balcony. He wore a dark marshmallow coat over a sophisticated suit coat that contrasted strangely with his unruly red hair.

Now she was beginning to sound suspiciously like Harrison. "He's not my suitor," I said quickly.

"Oh, I think he wants to be."

Good, sweet Emma. I wished it were true. Derek was just so nice. Even now he was engaged in friendly conversation with . . . I squinted and groaned . . . Harrison, of all people. I remembered Harrison's veiled hints earlier. Of course, Harrison would refer to Derek as the fine specimen angling our way. Everybody loved him, including Harrison, who was almost incapable of human emotion.

"Derek!" I yelled down at him.

Derek waved happily, his freckled face breaking into a smile, but then he remembered Harrison and dutifully turned to him. Not even a girl could deter him from saving such a soul. I knew it was only a matter of time before Harrison would take care of the situation for us. I watched the scene play out with jaded eyes, and Harrison didn't disappoint me. He suddenly *had* to go, and Derek made overly polite, almost regretful farewells before Harrison actually nudged him away. Derek wasn't about to be defeated, though. He extended his hand to the devil, giving him a friendly handshake before purposely turning to march our direction.

Derek still hadn't lost his missionary stride, and he grinned up at us. "Hello, girls," Derek shouted. "How are you doing today?" His voice was full of absolute concern.

"Here comes the nicest heartbreaker I know," I told Emma, trying to ignore Harrison, who saluted us behind Derek's back. There was no way to miss the insinuation. Harrison thought he was so smart. I watched him with narrow eyes as he returned to his apartment, but Derek quickly distracted me as he made his way up the stairs.

"We're doing fine," Emma called down to Derek from the balcony, like Romeo and Juliet, except neither of them was very dramatic, and they cared for each other in a completely platonic way. Emma turned to me. "Give him a chance," she said in an undertone. "This one is a nice boy."

"True," I said. "But this brings us to our first dilemma. Even if he liked me, he wouldn't do anything about it. It wouldn't be nice to have favorites."

"Oh, he has his favorites, Sam," Emma said. "Derek," she said in a louder voice as soon as he got closer. "You've come just in time."

"I'm at your service, Emma."

"Good." Emma moved quickly, her ponytail bobbing. She barely reached Derek's shoulders. "Can you hold the end of these Christmas lights on the roof?" He obediently followed her will, his bigger hands looking like a bear's next to hers.

"Sam?" Emma turned to me, and I wondered what meaningless chore she would make up for me. "Can you hold up the other end of this? Kinda string it around the railing." She gently placed the lights into my cold hands, then suddenly stilled. I tried not to smile. The girl was not a good actress.

"Oh dear," she said. "I forgot my . . ." I waited tensely to see what she had forgotten. As a general rule, Emma didn't lie, so she couldn't say that she didn't have tape because she did. "My, my, well, it's in the back anyway. I have to find it," she finished. So, she *was* in cahoots with Harrison. I knew there was something between them . . .

She ran inside, closing the door securely behind her. I'm sure she would procure something to assuage her conscience. I just had no idea what to do now. I didn't have enough nice comments to fill up an entire conversation with Derek. My lip curled at our awkward position. She could at least have left her two lovebirds in a more comfortable situation, but fortunately Derek was grinning, even though I was sure his arms were tingling. "I'm not sure how I feel about this," he said.

I bit my lip, trying to figure out what he meant. Well, yeah, it was obvious that we were being set up, but *did he like it?* was the question. I quickly tried to cover up the awkwardness. "Yeah," I said. "I'm morally against putting up all these decorations too. It just doesn't seem right somehow."

"Yeah," he whispered in an undertone, "it's almost sacrilegious."

His eyes twinkled and I realized that he actually thought I was funny. It was like he followed every commandment, even the "don't judge too harshly" ones usually reserved for me. That was a rare combination and it surprised me. I could actually live with such a personality. In fact, we could have a lot of fun growing old together.

Wait. My nose wrinkled at the direction of my thoughts. How come they always jumped straight to marriage? Now he was staring at me, and I desperately tried to look oblivious to it.

"You've got something on your nose," he said.

That caught me off guard. "What?"

"It's dust." I tried not to flinch as he studied my face. "You must have rubbed it against something . . ."

I cleared my throat, suddenly remembering Marcus's break in. It must have happened when I got stuck in the window. Knowing Marcus, he probably thought it was funny. I was going to kill him. "Well, get it off," I said.

"I'd like to," he said, his eyes suddenly very dark, "but I'm stuck."

"Break the rules for once," I said. "Defy Emma. Make a move without being asked."

He leaned my direction just as the front door burst open. "I'm back." Emma pulled the tape from her pocket and began taping madly before we could ask any questions. She kept casting furtive glances my direction, as if something had actually happened between Derek and me. Well, if she wanted something to happen, she should have left him a few more minutes to propose.

"There," she said, putting the last piece of tape on the Christmas lights. "You're free."

We gratefully pulled away, and now Derek was able to act. Action said more than words, anyway. He squeezed my elbow. "Gotta jet," he said. "I've got a class."

Dash diddly. Mixed signals. My professional guess would be that Derek really wasn't interested or he would have met the challenge of touching my face. But then he hesitated and leaned over to me, brushing my nose free of dirt. He quickly pulled away from the finished product, briskly nodding to cover up any embarrassment.

"There," he said, "nice and clean." Not the most romantic line, but I smiled anyway, more confused than ever. He was either really nice with a professional air or really nice and very conscientious of not getting into my personal space. There was no saying whether he was interested in me or not. I could never tell with these friendly guys.

Emma grinned behind us. "You should've left it," she said. "It was actually kinda cute."

Derek look flustered. "Well, yeah it was cute . . ."

I turned to Emma. "You saw it all along? I trust you to help me keep my nose clean."

"What? Emma isn't a complete miracle worker."

I recognized that low voice. *Marcus!* I clenched my teeth. Two visits in one day? It was his record. Drat that wreath. The one time I take it inside, Marcus slinks by without me noticing.

I turned, recognizing the red Cardinals cap. Marcus leaned against the balcony, watching me with a sardonic gaze. It looked like he was up to something. "Sorry to interrupt," he said. "I forgot my gloves." He reached around me, trying to get them from the flowerpot holding the yellowed stumps of dead flowers. It was where we hid the key, and I tried to block him from it, but my face collided with his chin.

I fell back, grimacing in pain, and his hands landed on my arms. "What's the matter with you?" he asked. "Do you always have to go in for the kill?"

I got a close-up view of his face, close enough to see the faint spatter of freckles on his upper cheeks, and I jerked away from him. "I was just getting your gloves for you," I lied. I stumbled to his gloves while trying to direct his attention elsewhere. "And I suppose you didn't notice that I had dirt all over my face?" I asked.

"Oh, I noticed," he said dryly. He took the gloves from me and began pulling them over his calloused hands. "A friend definitely would've said something."

I seethed. He was bringing *that* up again? Well, he was just proving my theory correct. No matter how rude it sounded, I was right. Being friends was just a line and he knew it.

"Unless your friend thought it was cute," Emma quickly inserted.

Marcus smiled indulgently at her. "Now that's a thought, isn't it?" I crossed my arms over my stomach, not deigning to reply. And he pulled his cap down. "See ya later, Emma," he said. He left and I turned to Derek, once again trying to push Marcus from my thoughts. It was difficult when he was so obnoxious.

CHAPTER 7

"Good luck on your test."
—Samantha Skyler (Sun., Dec. 5th)

I sat across from the bishop, trying to look as innocent as possible. I wondered if he could read my mind. If so, I was a goner, but no suspicion registered on his weathered face. "So, Samantha," he said, leaning back. "How's your social life?"

Was that a trick question? "Oh, well, I'm . . ." I tried to make up something that made me sound successful. "I'm throwing a lot of parties and hanging out with guys."

"Are you dating?"

"No, not really." I wound a short, blond curl around my finger. "But we're hanging out."

The bishop drew in bushy eyebrows, not pleased with this answer, and he made a steeple with his fingers, leaning toward me. "Are you accepting dates?" he asked.

"Uh, yeah," I fidgeted with the pleats on my dark plaid skirt, "but mostly guys just want to hang out." He nodded soberly and I forced a cheerful smile. "But there are so many great guys in the ward that I love . . . hanging out with them," I finished lamely.

Apparently the subject was depressing the bishop as much as it depressed me because he abruptly changed the subject, probably so he wouldn't pull out what remained of his white hair. "I've called you in here today, Samantha, to extend the calling of second counselor in the Relief Society presidency. Will you accept this calling?"

I straightened, not believing my ears. *The presidency—me?* I'm more the Primary teacher type who can make kids sit in their chairs, not the actual teaching type. And grown-ups can tell whether you know what you're talking about or not—especially the RMs. And then a horrible thought hit me. Relief Society! There weren't any possibilities to meet guys with this calling—just girls. Couldn't I work with Relief Society after I got married? And even worse—"Don't you have to be loving for that?" I asked the bishop.

He laughed at what he thought was a joke, but he didn't know that I was about as sensitive as a bag of hammers. Sure, I'll cry at a sad movie, but only if I'm by myself. I mean, once I reenacted all the death scenes in *Les Mis* as a joke because it was Emma's favorite musical. So why in the heck would she even suggest me as her second counselor? It *must* be pure inspiration because there were no other reasons I could think of besides that.

"Sure . . . why not?" I smiled a smile that belied the gut wrench in my stomach.

"As second counselor in the Relief Society, you will be in charge of Home, Family, and Personal Enrichment as well as various other assignments the president may give you."

Ah, yes, that meant crafts. I was crafty. I could handle that. It was called delegation.

"How well do you know the sisters in the Relief Society?" he asked.

My smile grew even more forced. "I know my roommates."

"What do you think about getting to know the *other* girls?"

"I can do that," I said.

What else could I say? The bishop had caught me red-handed. This calling is what you would call an ironic calling. You know, the kind you get when you need to repent.

I got to my shaky feet, reached for the bishop's hand, and shook it firmly at the end of our interview. The firmer the handshake, the more confidence the recipient had in you, and I needed his confidence now. I had no idea what I was getting into.

The bishop sat back down and smiled at me. "Can you call Ashley in?" he asked.

I nodded and left his office, staring at the sign next to the door: *A teacher molds the minds of the future and thus changes the world.* I stifled a snort. Like most bishopric offices at BYU, the place actually doubled as a teacher's office on weekdays. This one actually had quite the professional setup, though. I passed Harrison, who sat at a desk in the middle of the lobby, and he nodded at me. He wore a pinstriped suit, looking like Jimmy Hoffa incarnate, and I quickly turned from him. He knew exactly what I had been up against, the little conspirator.

Ashley sat on a chair near his desk, twirling her black hair between delicate fingers, ignoring Harrison quite successfully. "Next," I said.

She stood up, the tiny pink buds embroidered on her cream-colored skirt swirling around her ankles. I stole her seat since I had promised to wait for her. "Good luck on your test," I said.

Ashley just smiled in return, and I watched her close the door to the bishop's office. It clicked shut with an air of finality, and Harrison tapped a jolly rhythm on his desk. I rearranged my skirt over my knees, trying to ignore him, but I wasn't as skilled as some people.

"Did you pass?" he asked.

"No."

He wasn't deterred, and his tapping continued. "Well, that's okay. How's your dating life?"

I looked up at him. His blue eyes were especially vibrant with pent-up laughter. "Don't even start with me," I said.

"You know, I can help you with your numbers."

I glanced up at him. "How? Are you asking me out?"

"No."

"Then quit talking about it."

Sarcastic people always enjoy sarcasm flung back in their faces, and he laughed appreciatively. "Come to me when you want some *real* dating advice."

My eyebrows drew in, but before I could ask what he meant, Ashley blew out of the bishop's office. To my surprise, she was smiling brightly, and she made a fist of victory. "Yeah!"

"Let me guess," I said. "You just got your dream calling?"

"Just you wait until sacrament meeting."

I shrugged. "I'm sure I'll be surprised." I had just lost my activities committee cochair calling, and judging by how pleased she was, it didn't take much deductive reasoning to figure out what her calling was . . . unless she was the new ward hymnbook passer-outer, because that was the best calling by far, and then I'd really be envious. Without a backward glance at Harrison, we stepped out of the lobby and almost ran into Brooke and Emma in the hall. Emma laughed, but Brooke didn't even change her army pace, so we followed her up the stairs and into the meeting room.

"Good morning." Scott extended his hand, and I prepared myself to once again fail at the most complex handshake I'd ever seen. Scott was the ward greeter, another calling that I would give my CTR ring for.

"Wait," I said, trying to do a snap over his hand. His fingers slid through mine in a quick motion that only a hand used to cradling a guitar could perfect. He thumped his fist over mine and I laughed, finally holding my hand still in his until he had abused it enough to let it go.

"Welcome to church. Is that a new skirt?" he asked me. I shook my head and gave him a mock curtsey with the full, pleated skirt—I looked like a Highlander in it, but apparently that wasn't all because his next words were, "You look hot."

With difficulty I kept myself from being completely smitten. He didn't mean to be so charming . . . he never did. But everything about him was smooth. Scott lounged against the door in the regular Sunday attire, a snowy-white shirt and blue-sheen tie. He watched me under calm, heavy brows, looking relaxed in his dark blue suit coat. So why would a guy like that be intimidated by me? I mean, he wasn't knocking down doors to ask me out . . . unless he really wasn't interested in me. It didn't bear thinking about.

Scott turned to Ashley and she just shook her head, sidestepping him, her flowing skirt flipping saucily at her heels. But Brooke was ready. Secret handshakes were second nature to her, and I watched enviously as she zigzagged her way through it. "Nice," Scott said. "Look how cool our mom is."

Brooke watched him with her no-nonsense air. Her long, red hair was caught up in a sensible knot at the nape of her neck and she wore a dark blue power suit, complete with a straight skirt, giving her an armylike appearance. "Yep," Scott said, "very cool."

"So I'm cool, Samantha's hot. Who's next?" Brooke asked, raising an eyebrow. She wasn't even fazed.

"I don't know." Scott glanced at Emma and she giggled. She wore one of her better jumpers for Sunday, a pink number with white flowers on it, but the whole ensemble was drowned under her green fat-coat, as we liked to call it. We were waiting for the next outrageous compliment, and he didn't disappoint us. "Emma, you look like a budding flower in spring."

Ashley immediately swung back on her heel to join in the fun. "And me?" she asked.

"A fiery Spanish señorita," he said. By now we were all gaping. The man could spout poetry on demand, and we all smiled a little uncertainly. With one mean swipe, he had slain all reservations we had against him. Even Brooke looked a little impressed. More sisters were coming up the stairs, and reluctantly we left him to them. I chanced one last backward glance, and he smiled at me. No wonder the girls loved him. So why wasn't he asking anyone out?

I ran into Brooke as we filed into the meeting room to find a desk—yep, no pews. But as far as I was concerned, we had the best church building ever. Our meetings were held at the BYU Testing Center, where the walls were covered with *You can do it* signs and other inane inspirational thoughts. And although I would never look at church the same again—or at a test for that matter—it was a spacious room with plenty of seating. Gray and cream-colored desks lined the rows, but before we could pick a desk, we caught sight of Derek. His gray suit blended in with the scenery behind him.

He waved us over in his friendly way. "What are you doing here so early?" he asked us. It was normal for Emma and Brooke to be on time, but certainly not for Ashley and me.

"We just got callings," Ashley said. We each picked out a desk, surrounding him with our numbers. We pulled out our scriptures and hymnbooks.

"How about you?" Emma asked.

Derek was the kind of guy who could draw any shy gal out of her shell, and he turned from me, giving Emma his full attention. I left her to him, watching the ward pile into the meeting room as they took the seats in the back; everyone wanted religion, but they didn't want to get too close.

Just for fun I counted the guys and then the girls. I gasped as I worked out the ratio. "Wow, those are pretty good odds," I said, "if you're a guy." Nobody was listening to me and I turned to Ashley. "There are three girls to every guy in our ward."

"Are you trying to depress me?" she asked. But I could tell she really didn't care, resting her chin in her palm and looking out of her dense curtain of hair. What did it matter if there were one or a hundred girls? She could steal any man she wanted.

"No wonder they had polygamy," I muttered.

"What was that?" Marcus came up behind me.

I shook my head. "Nothing."

Logan sat on the other side of me, grinning. "What are you staring at?" he asked.

"You." I glanced at him, seeing his plaid shirt. The guy had a rebellious streak, but the shirt still looked good on him. I wondered what he would look like in a white shirt. With his olive skin and hazel eyes, the contrast would be amazing. I glanced up just in time to see Griffin stare at me from across the room, and there was an open seat next to me. "Marcus," I said, "come here for a sec."

"What?"

"Sit down. Tell me about your life."

He looked very suspicious, but he took the seat anyway, straightening his red tie. "Why are you so interested in my life all of a sudden?"

I averted my head, watching Griffin glare at me from the corner of his eye, and I felt like an absolute cad. "Huh?"

Marcus followed my gaze and snorted, picking up his hymnbook. "I should've guessed."

I watched the girls carefully arrange themselves next to the guys they liked. That was the problem with coming early, you had to wait for the guys to get up the courage to come to you, but at least I was sitting near Derek and Logan . . . Marcus was an unfortunate necessity. I searched the congregation for Scott just as our bishop stood up, following the usual order of opening the meeting with a hymn and a prayer.

I gave up the search during the business part of the meeting when I heard the bishop announce my name: "Samantha Skyler as second counselor in the Relief Society." After an elbow nudge from Marcus, I stood up, enduring the dropping jaws. Except for a little glaring redhead in the front, everyone seemed okay with it.

I squinted at her, but I didn't even recognize her, so why in the heck did she have a grudge against me? I couldn't have wronged her yet. Of course, maybe that was the problem. With some people you had to do something wrong for them to like you.

"Ashley Fox as activities committee cochair."

Of course, but how was she going to work with Logan? She stood up, smiling brightly as the bishop continued calling out the names until almost half the room was standing up.

"Marcus Gray as Gospel Doctrine teacher."

I glanced at him and he steadfastly ignored my gaze. *Ready or not, here comes the false doctrine.* But at least none of us were stereotypes. In fact, we were evidence that the Church was true. We hadn't messed it up yet, and despite everyone's tragic faults, we were sustained.

The rep from the stake presidency stood up to give us our monthly lecture on dating. "Guys, you must ask. It's your priesthood duty. Girls, you must accept. It's your Relief Society duty." See, now everyone knew, but did anyone care? I looked around, seeing nodding heads, but they were sleeping ones.

We stood up to go to Sunday School, and Logan shook Ashley's hand. "So, you're my new cochair? How do you feel about that?" Exactly my question.

Emma hugged me before I could listen for Ashley's answer. "Thanks for accepting," Emma said. "You'll be a wonderful second counselor."

She really was sweet.

"Marcus, congratulations." The voice made my skin crawl. It was Miriam's. Remember my blond FHE sister? Yeah. Her voice was low and husky, and I turned just in time to see her put her hand in Marcus's, and not just to pump it missionary style either. No, Miriam let her fingers linger on his before she pulled away. She was good.

She smiled up at him, her lips parting to reveal perfect teeth. "I'll never miss your lessons," she cooed. "You'll be wonderful."

Marcus watched her with amused blue eyes. *The idiot.* His thick lashes managed to hide most of his expression. "Well, you haven't heard me teach yet," he said. *Ah, false humility.*

Ashley just glanced at me and rolled her eyes. I laughed and tried to brush past them, but then I realized that Miriam was blocking me from getting by . . . on purpose! What? Did she think I was going to try to steal Marcus away? I might not like her, but there was no way I was getting in the way of ridding myself of him forever.

"I'm positively stuffed from last night," Miriam told Marcus loudly. I knew it was solely for my benefit—call it woman's intuition, or suspicion, or something like that.

Marcus laughed. "But you didn't eat anything."

She played with the ends of her long, blond hair. "It doesn't take much to stuff me," she said. "I eat like a bird."

"Actually, birds eat nonstop," I said. "Excuse me. Can I get by?"

Miriam's catlike eyes narrowed. "It's an expression, dear."

I froze. Every girl knew what *dear* meant, it was a direct challenge to fight. I listened to her drone on, ready to pull out her hair. "I did love the play, Marcus. I've never been to an Italian opera before," she said.

Play? Marcus never even spent a dime on me, not that I recalled. "Thanks, narrator," Ashley said. She shoved her way through, more pushy than I could ever be. Emma followed her and nodded politely to Marcus. I just avoided his gaze. If this was the kind of girl Marcus liked, then I was glad to be free of him.

"Yeah," Marcus said. "Thanks for inviting me, Miriam," he added, a bit louder.

I quickly turned. So that was it. Marcus was proving to be a challenge. That's why Miriam was hanging all over him. I tried not to laugh at the thought. And he thought I was bad? I wondered how Marcus, the great relationship Houdini, would avoid her.

She touched his elbow and let her hand linger there. "I trust you'll return the favor?"

He shrugged, smiling. "Of course."

Uh-oh, she would hold him to that.

CHAPTER 8

"All in favor, say, aye."

—Marcus Gray (Sun., Dec. 5th)

We stared up the stairs, waiting for the other ward's elders quorum to be released from their classroom. The wait was always worth it. The doors opened, and the girls from our ward turned as one to gape at the hottest guys ever. They were separated from our ward by cruel fate and ward boundaries, only across the street from our apartments really, situated forever out of our grasp. They marched down the stairs.

"The first item of business for the activities committee," Ashley said, "will be to combine our ward with this one and have a dance. Maybe we'll make it a combined Christmas party. Who knows?"

Brilliant. Ashley hadn't even been set apart yet, but already she was receiving inspiration. I pushed Emma and Brooke toward the door, knowing that Ashley didn't need any prompting, and we passed the men in the narrow staircase on our way into the classroom. A few locked eyes with us and nodded, and I desperately wondered how to get more than a "Hello," from them—like an "I can't live without you" or an "I love you." I'd even settle for a "Can I have your phone number?"

I was at the end of the staircase and out of luck when we reached the classroom. Lucky girls—whoever's ward those guys belonged to. By the sounds of things, the guys seemed eager to reacquaint themselves with the girls downstairs. My roommates and I were the first ones in the classroom. Emma collapsed into a desk. Brooke sat down primly, opening her scriptures, and Ashley threw hers on a desk behind her, leaving us to go talk to *our own* guys in *our own* ward. I turned to the chalkboard.

Good luck on your test.

I got up and erased "on your test" and wrote "in Sunday School."

"'Good luck in Sunday School,'" Emma read slowly. I suddenly noticed the volume of girls gathering in the front row and my heart sank. *Oh no.* Marcus was teaching up here, wasn't he? Ah, the tides of fate. Resigning myself to it, I sat behind Emma, waiting to see who would deign to sit by us. Scott appeared in the doorway, looking very debonair. I tossed my curls, preparing myself and . . . He passed me without saying a word. *Excuse me, but do I have a disease?* Scott nodded at Brooke on his way to the back row and she scowled. I made a sound of irritation. I mean, c'mon, at least I smiled at him. Was he afraid of friendly girls?

I turned to Emma. "You'll still be my friend, right? You can pretend that I'm likeable at least."

She patted my hand, not sure what this was about. "Sure."

I saw Derek walk through the door, but by this time my confidence was shaken. The odds that he would sit by us again weren't very good. After all, the friendly guy had to spread himself around, which meant that we had to make our own odds. "Hey, Derek," I said once he made eye contact. "Sit down. We saved you a seat."

Notice I said *we?* Yeah, perfect, no suspicions that I'm a calculating female, just an affectionate one. At least I hoped it sounded that way. Apparently it did because Derek immediately sat across from me, completely at ease. He winked at Emma, and she ducked her head, dimpling. Logan saw me from across the room and smiled, making his way to my side. It took me completely by surprise. That was the second time today . . . and I didn't even try to arrange it. Now *he* was the one who was looking suspicious. Of course, I didn't mind at all as he sat down beside me.

Marcus walked into the classroom with Miriam like he was walking the red carpet to the Oscars. The girls in the front row looked visibly disappointed, but walking into a classroom with a girl didn't mean he was engaged to her—or did it? I smirked. If he could take that particular girl out, it would mean less competition for the rest of us. Miriam sat in the corner, framed by the window. She crossed her long legs, her elegant gray skirt trailing the ground.

Derek stood up. "I'd like to announce something before we start."

"You're engaged!" Ashley shouted.

"No, now listen." He already had the girls' attention in the class, but being elders quorum president, he was probably trying to get the guys to listen instead, which didn't seem likely since they were busy trying to steal back the girls' attention from him.

Marcus leaned against the podium in the front of the classroom and held up his hand. "Hey, guys, Derek has an announcement. It's about dating." A hushed silence filled the room. Marcus gestured grandly to Derek. "You have the floor."

"Last week, we didn't get all the slots for safewalk—"

"Safewalk!" the guys echoed in a thunderous bass. They shouted it out every time their elders quorum president made the safewalk announcement, and it still managed to fluster him.

"—filled," Derek finished lamely. "So, I'd like to pass the schedule around in Sunday School if I could. I've already taken the 11:45 times . . . except Friday night, of course." There was an audible gasp at this and a twitter from the girls' section near the front. That time, 11:45, was a sacred time; it was the biggest sacrifice, since that's when the library closed—not like anyone would be asleep at that time. "This is really important, brethren. We cannot have the sisters walk home from school at night by themselves."

"Hear, hear!" Marcus took the sheet from Derek and signed his name as boldly as John Hancock signing the Declaration of Independence. The girls in the front craned their necks to see what time they needed to be conveniently walked home. Marcus then gave it to Harrison, who raised arrogant brows and passed it behind him, refusing to sign it. The drama was over and class could begin.

Marcus set his papers in front of him, shuffling through them. "Today's subject is . . . charity."

Everybody sat up nervously. Charity meant love, which meant this would be controversial. "Did anyone review the assigned reading for this lesson?" Marcus asked.

Emma and Derek were the only ones who raised their hands. No one else wanted to spoil the surprise before they got to church.

"Good," he said. "I hope you will have some insight for us, then. Now, who would like to read the first scripture on the board?" The room grew suddenly silent. "Samantha, will you read that scripture?"

My head shot up. How had he known I wasn't paying attention? Even now his eyes sparkled as he watched me flip noisily to Matthew. There was just enough hesitation between his request and my compliance to give away that I had spaced out. As soon as I found it, I cleared my throat. "'And because iniquity shall abound,'" I read, "'the love of many shall wax cold.'" I glanced quickly up at him. What did he mean by that?

Apparently nothing because he began expounding on it. No meaningful glances, no pointed fingers—maybe it was just my conscience. "Now, let's turn our scriptures to John," Marcus went on. "This scripture explains how we can follow the Savior's example. Could I have another volunteer read chapter 12, verse 25?"

This time the girls were ready in the front, and they raised their hands eagerly. "Um . . ." Marcus's hand hesitated until he pointed to the brunette at his side. "You," he said, obviously not knowing her name.

She didn't take offense at this, pulling the scriptures closer to her. "'He that loveth his life shall lose it; and he that hateth his life in this world shall keep it unto life eternal,'" she read.

"Now what does that mean?" he asked.

Emma raised her hand. "It means that if we spend our whole life trying to please ourselves, then we'll end up wasting our lives and the talents that our Heavenly Father has given us, but if we forget about our own problems and help others, then we'll have joy because we'll be doing what our Heavenly Father wants us to do."

"Not only what He *wants* us to do," Derek added, "but what we were *meant* to do."

I squirmed in my seat, feeling guilty. What exactly was I meant to do anyway? It was so unclear, even for a girl who had been taught all her life. I was *meant* to get married. I was *meant* to have children. I was *meant* to be on my way to eternal happiness and bliss, but nothing seemed to be falling into place for me. So how on earth could I help others when I couldn't even help myself? To be perfectly honest, besides teasing my roommates out of their occasional bad moods, I wasn't helping anybody.

"Good comments," Marcus said. "Anyone else?"

"Yes," Derek said. "Blah, blah, blah . . . love." Well, that's all I heard. I watched Marcus's eyes go glossy too.

Scott decided to add to that, and then I heard *blah, blah, blah* again. I think it was basically the same thing, but my attention was caught by Brooke's bobbing and weaving. She was falling asleep, but she was fighting it on general principle. Since she was just across from me, I felt it my duty to press my hand over her head, weighing it down to her desk. Logan laughed.

"And therefore . . . ." Scott continued.

Marcus nodded. "You both have excellent points." I doubted if even he knew what those points were.

Ashley raised her hand. It always surprised me how active she was in these group discussions. "Look at the stripling warriors," she said. "They were young—maybe only twelve years old—and yet they had so much love for their people, for their liberty, and for God that—"

"No . . . fifteen," Griffin said, not taking his eyes from me. "They had to be at least fifteen to fight."

"Well, they were young," Ashley said, trying to continue with her point, "but they were willing to give their lives—"

"Have you talked to a fifteen-year-old lately?" Logan interrupted her. "The stripling warriors were probably nineteen at least, the same age as missionaries."

"How about we take a vote?" Marcus suggested. "All in favor, say, aye."

Everyone read the warning look in his eyes and shut up, and Emma handed me the safewalk schedule. I was supposed to pass it on, but I wrote "hot" next to Derek's name instead, then scanned the rest of the contents. Scott had taken all the ten o'clock slots. He must have been feeling particularly dutiful. What had gotten into him? Of course, they were the best slots. I took note of it and passed it behind me. "Here ya go, Logan."

He didn't see me and I waved it ineffectually at his head until I noticed that his hand was raised. "Who wrote the foreword on this manual?" Logan asked Marcus. I stifled a gasp. This was the closest to heckling the teacher anyone could get, and the safest procedure was to turn the question to the class, but Marcus seemed to be considering it. *Turn the question to the class, turn it.* I tried to coach him through telepathy, but it wasn't working.

"I believe so-and-so wrote it."

Okay, so I didn't listen to the name, but the fact was that he knew it. Incredible!

"Then what about the foreword on the Book of Mormon?"

"Can somebody shoot him?" I muttered.

"McConkie."

A couple of the RMs in the room nodded and my eyes widened, my gaze going from one roommate to the other. There was no way Marcus could have answered that off the cuff. It must have been a setup to make him look smart. I wouldn't put it past the two.

"Thanks," Logan said. I shoved the safewalk paper at him again and he took it, glancing at the available times. "Yeah, right," he muttered. He quickly passed it behind him without signing it. I set my chin on my hand, playing with my pen, watching Marcus suspiciously.

Griffin raised his hand. "Having love for God means giving up all we have for Him. Many of the prophets in the scriptures have given up their worldly possessions to follow Him. As we all know, Lehi was a jeweler—"

"No, we don't."

I looked up from my doodling . . . did Marcus just say that? But he was the teacher. He was supposed to be diplomatic, veer the subject away from offending anyone. "But you're right," Marcus quickly backtracked, seeing the veins stick out on Griffin's neck, "he did give up everything to follow God . . . whatever occupation that might have been."

The ward's engaged couple raised their hand. And I say raised *their* hand because I wasn't sure whose hand went up, they were so tightly intertwined. Apparently Marcus had a hard time differentiating too because he just nodded at them. "Yes?"

The guy answered, "We can also show our love for our Savior by following His example and learning to love like He loves us." His fiancée gave quick nods of appreciation. "Without learning true charity," he said, looking deeply into her eyes, "we can't progress, we can't gain eternal life."

I sighed. *True charity.* That was my downfall, wasn't it? I glanced over at Miriam. She was playing with her hair, then I turned to Griffin, but not for too long because he could sense when I looked at him and then he got ideas. I concentrated on Marcus instead. I really needed to be better. Emma was wrong. I wasn't like a spitting, swearing construction worker. I was one of those uppity drivers who turned away without expression.

The bishop raised his hand. "I agree. My son Joe just recently got engaged, and as we were sitting in the living room with him and his fiancée, we could feel the love radiating between them. They were both just so happy and excited to spend the rest of their lives together and for all eternity, and I must admit that the feeling was contagious. That's what I'll think of now when I think of perfect love. I just hope that all of you will be able to experience that same joy that comes from eternal marriage."

Marcus smiled. "Good story, Bishop, and good little plug in the end. I'm sure we could all benefit from marriage." He nodded at a petite redhead in the front whose hand was up. She didn't look happy; her face and neck were blotched with red. With a start I recognized her. She was the one who had glared at me when I was called to be second counselor.

"Uh, you," he said.

"Well," she lowered her hand, blinking rapidly, "maybe if the guys would ask us on more dates we could experience the *joy of eternal marriage.*" I winced for her. There went all her dates for the next semester.

Logan snorted behind me. "Quit trying to hurry us. Guys should wait at least six months after their mission before even thinking about marriage."

I winced again. Logan must not understand that he was messing with an emotionally charged girl and, just as I thought, she bristled. "Excuse me?" she asked. "Should he also lead girls on and throw the line that he's not ready for marriage at her when she actually decides to take him seriously? Or should he be so indecisive that he can't even make up his mind between four girls? Or how about this? There are a few people I know that won't even say hello to me on campus. Should he do that?"

"Just say no, Logan," I whispered.

"I am tired of guys who are too lazy to ask girls out!" the girl bellowed.

Griffin turned to her, his eyes unblinking. "Do you want to go out?"

Her expression grew even darker and mine turned eager. Was I losing my stalker? But no, she just avoided his gaze, and Griffin turned his stare back on me. *Dash diddly dog. No luck.*

"Is that what this lesson is about? Dates?" Logan growled behind me. "Not everything is about dates." Wow, that was a sore spot . . . and strange coming from him. Brooke woke up with a snort, looking around the tense room. I wondered what she thought was going on. She smoothed her red tendrils back into her French knot, her green doe eyes glassy.

Ashley sat behind her. She met my eyes. "They used to date," she mouthed to me.

Suddenly it all made sense. This little fireball had dated Logan. Was she the one he had just broken up with? Maybe that's why she hated me. We had been sitting together during sacrament meeting and now we still were.

Marcus took control of the discussion again, and for once I was grateful. "No, not everything is about dates," he said. "You see, the trick to charity is actually looking outside of yourself, and we can't do that unless we force ourselves to be happy no matter what situation we're in. I mean, if you're miserable now, you'll just be miserable when you're married."

Whether Marcus knew it or not, his comment was aimed directly at me, and I tried not to squirm.

Derek looked concerned. "I agree with you. The point is that we should follow the Savior's love by having unconditional love for our fellow man . . . no matter what is happening."

My mouth dropped open. No, he didn't. Not the controversial *unconditional love* topic! It wasn't a controversy anywhere except at BYU. If you don't believe me, just shout "unconditional love" on campus and listen to the uproar that follows. Or even better, listen to this:

Logan was the first to break the silence at Derek's words. "Where in the scriptures does it say God has unconditional love?"

Oh, I should've known Logan was an *unconditional love* debater. *Just keep your mouth shut, just keep it shut!* Besides, unconditional love totally worked on Logan's behalf. If this redhead practiced some unconditional love, it would get Logan off the hook for dumping her.

Derek was taken aback, but Scott was more than happy to take over the debate for him. "Well, where in the scriptures does it say to get a year's supply?" he asked.

"It doesn't."

"Exactly, so what was your point? Are you saying that we don't have the right to modern revelation?"

"No, I'm saying that no modern-day prophet has ever uttered the word *unconditional love.*"

"That's two words," Marcus quickly intervened. "And nobody cares either way."

I gaped . . . could a teacher say that? But Scott didn't listen, and I wondered if he was playing devil's advocate for the heck of it, or just because he didn't like Logan. "So are you saying that God doesn't love us, Logan?"

"No, but I'm saying that he has *perfect* love, not *unconditional.*"

They went on like this back in forth, and our heads rotated from Scott to Logan until we were dizzy. I felt like I was watching a tennis match, having no idea who I was rooting for, only hoping that someone would get knocked out with the ball so they would quit playing. "I don't see the difference," Scott said.

"Well, I do. Preaching that God loves you no matter if you're good or bad borders on apostasy."

Whoa, pretty big words for Logan.

"Is that what some teacher at BYU told you?" Scott asked. "Is he *your* prophet?"

I groaned. Those were fighting words.

"Why are we even fighting about this?" Marcus shouted. "This is stupid."

The bitter girl raised her hand. "Nothing about this changes the fact that guys aren't asking us out on dates. What are you all—chickens or something?"

Griffin nodded, still staring at me. "Well, it seems to me that there are two kinds of people," he said. "Those who like Arthur and those who like SpongeBob."

"Don't even go there," Marcus growled. I was beginning to suspect that he liked Arthur. I preferred SpongeBob hands down, and he knew it. Lucky for him, and for all of us, the bell rang.

CHAPTER 9

"Perfect love casteth out all fear."

—The bishop quoting the Bible out of context (Sun., Dec. 5th)

The boys left for Priesthood so they could argue about unconditional love and SpongeBob for as long as they liked, and I headed for the chalkboard. "Good luck in Sunday School," it still said.

The reminder hadn't given Marcus any luck, but I erased "in Sunday School" and wrote "Bishop" anyway.

Good luck, Bishop. It was time for the once-a-semester chastity talk, and I glanced at the bishop. He had an uneasy smile on his face. "You nervous, Bishop?"

"Nope. Perfect love casteth out all fear." He fidgeted in his chair, and even with all that white hair, he looked like a scared little boy.

"Excuse me."

I swiveled on my heel at the irritated voice, and now it was my turn to look scared. It was the angry redhead. She watched me with watery blue eyes, looking at me like I was the clumsiest girl in Relief Society. "Go ahead," I said, quickly getting out of her way.

Unfortunately she didn't take her opportunity to brush past me. "Isn't Emma your roommate?" she asked, crossing her arms across the large flowers on her dress.

"Yeah," I said.

"So, that's why you're her second counselor?" she asked in a snotty voice. She didn't wait for my answer. "I always thought Emma was so sweet."

"She is," I answered in Emma's defense. It was almost as if this redhead was talking about her in the past tense. Was she going to kill her for having inspiration?

"Didn't you go out with Logan's roommate?" she asked.

"Sorta," I said. There was no way I was going into details with her.

"Well, it didn't last long," she said. I gave her an uncomfortable silence, but she didn't seem to notice. "How old are you, anyway?" she asked.

Whoa, babe. I didn't even know her name. "Older than you," I said. "Any other questions?"

She shook her head and swept past me, but I should've known better than to relax. "You have a run in your nylons," she retorted as a parting shot. I hid a gasp, having no idea what to say to that.

Emma saved me the trouble. She made her way to my side, and I glanced down at her, wanting to grab onto her like a lifeline. "Okay," Emma told me, "you'll be conducting today. You do the announcements first. Here's the list. I'll write our schedule on the board." She glanced at "Good luck, Bishop" with a grimace and erased it, writing down the opening hymn in its stead. I tried to call the room of giggling sisters to order, but it was hard considering the drama that had just occurred.

"Okay," I said, remembering my Primary classes with a scowl. "No rolling around in the aisle." I paced the front of the room. My theory is that if I'm more active than the audience, then they'll be confused enough to listen. If it worked for the Primary in my home ward, it definitely could work for the Relief Society here. I heard giggles and whispers. Hmm, I guess I was wrong. I changed tactics. "Sisters, do you know what today is? Chastity-talk day. Yay!" I pretended to be excited.

The room got silent and I bit down a smirk and executed the rest of the business. It wasn't too tough, and before the bishop even knew it, he was standing up.

"Now, I've heard girls complain that they're tired of hearing the chastity talks, and there's a cure for that." The bishop gulped before he continued. "Get married."

There was an audible gasp in the room, and a few chuckles, mostly coming from me. "Alright, I know that isn't as easy as it sounds," he said, softening the blow. "Only thirty-five percent of females marry before graduation. That means sixty-five percent of females leave BYU without getting married."

In other words, we'd better start planning our careers now. I raised my hand, ready to give the bishop a hard time. "Hey, where do we apply for the refund?"

"What?"

"'Ring by spring or your money back,' right? Well, I want it back." The girls behind me murmured in agreement.

"Yeah." The redhead was at it again. "The boys won't ask us out."

The bishop cast me an annoyed look before continuing. "Now, don't get frustrated. They're just as concerned about dating as you are, and it's a hard role that they have to play. They are intimidated by all the amazing sisters in the ward. And why wouldn't they be? All they need to do is close their eyes and point to find the perfect woman. You are all that special. And that's another thing. Don't compare yourself to other sisters in the ward. Look at Alicia Stormbuck."

I followed everyone's turned heads to find Alicia Stormbuck, half of the engaged couple. She looked like she didn't know what to do with her recently emptied hand. "She is engaged," the bishop said, "and Sarah Binhampen and Cathy Muckbecon." I smirked. They probably just wanted to get married so they could get rid of their last names. "Do you see how different each of them is from the other?" he said. "They aren't more special than any of you, but they are all very good sisters. The point is, sisters, you must be encouraging to the boys."

"What if we don't want to?" Brooke said under her breath.

I couldn't believe she'd just said that. Even the bishop heard, but fortunately he just laughed. "Give the boys a chance. Don't get me wrong. You shouldn't get married just to get married, sisters. Such an important decision isn't something you should rush into. Statistics now show that one out of seven marriages will end in divorce—even temple marriage, sisters. Why do you suppose that is?"

"Selfishness," Emma said. "We're worried more about our own desires than our partner's."

"Exactly. Marriage is a partnership—a man and a woman raising children, working toward eternal life. Our lives, not the certificate, should be evidence of our temple marriage. In fact, my wife's values were the first thing that attracted me to her. I knew that she was a hard worker and that her heart was in the right place."

Ashley's head lifted at this. "I thought that you said she was the most beautiful girl you had ever met."

The bishop's lips curled upward. "Well, everything about her intimidated me, and her values were a part of that. In fact, I fell in love with everything about her. And that's the next thing I would like to discuss with you—your values. When you *do* find the man of your choice, remember that intimacy is about getting to know the whole being, not just getting to know the physical aspect of another person. Bridle your passions so that you may be filled with love."

I leaned back. This talk didn't really apply to me. I didn't even get dates, so how could I have a chance to mess up? "Girls," the bishop said, "you must wear modest clothing. Guys won't respect you if you don't respect yourselves. Cover the parts of your body that you should be covering." My eyes quickly drew to my Highlander skirt and I tugged it over my knees as inconspicuously as possible, which was hard since I was sitting in the front. "Now, are there any questions about what I'm talking about?"

We were silent.

"Good." He pretended to wipe his forehead. "I didn't really want to get into details." He picked up the chalk and turned to the board, writing "Spectrum of Love."

"Now, I'm sure you're all familiar with this," he said. We were, except the girls who weren't in the ward when the bishop gave us the talk before. He drew a straight line across the board and turned to us. "Now, remember this spectrum isn't really a flat line. Somewhere in the middle it turns into a ski slope, an almost vertical slant. Okay, now what are the different steps of showing physical affection? First we have *arm's length*, then *just friends*." He wrote those down on the beginning of the line. "Next, we have *snuggly-buggly*, then *handsy-wandsy*, then *hugsy-wugsy*, then *kissy-wissy*, *necky-pecky* and *naughty-waughty*."

"There needs to be *elbow-squeezing*," I said. "Call it *elbow-welbow* or something, and put it after *just friends*."

"I think *hand-holding* should go before *snuggly-buggly*," another girl suggested.

Ashley's hand shot up. "Then *hugs* should go after *hand-holding*."

The poor bishop tried to rearrange everything in accordance to the proper order of courtship until he finally lost all patience with us.

"You get the idea. Now, who wants to be our volunteer?"

You mean victim? I tried to hide a smirk when the angry redhead raised her hand and the bishop called on her. "Okay, Veronica," he said. I took a mental note of her name and which exit to run to after this game was over. "How far would you take your physical demonstrations when dating?" he asked.

"What do you mean?"

"How far is too far? Would you allow the guy to hold your hand? Kiss you? When would be the appropriate time? You have to decide your limits now before the situation comes up. I'm going to draw the line across the spectrum, and you tell me when to stop. Are you ready?"

"Yes." Veronica stared at the board intently, steadying herself.

"Then let's go." The bishop drew a quick line across the spectrum past *just friends* to *naughty-waughty* before she could even open her mouth.

"Stop!" she screamed. "Not so fast."

"Yeah," he said. "You get it."

CHAPTER 10

"If you can't say something nice, write it in a honeypot note."
—Ashley Fox (Sun., Dec. 5th)

"Who wrote that I was a great guy and any girl would be lucky to go out with me?"

I watched Scott at the microphone. He was trying not to laugh. The sleeves of his white shirt were rolled up to his elbows, and he lounged against the podium in true poetic fashion. "You failed to leave your name," he said. "So next time you decide to write me a honeypot note, will you please sign your name on it? Thanks." Scott pulled away from the podium and made his way to his seat.

Griffin stood behind him at the podium, his eyes wide behind his glasses. He was the ward-prayer director and it seemed that even ward announcements were getting too off-the-wall for him, but what could one expect for a Sunday night in the cultural hall above the Manavu Chapel?

"Uh . . ." he took over the microphone, straightening it, then bending it. "Do we have any more announcements, brothers and sisters?" Griffin cleared his throat. "Please keep them short."

Emma stood up, almost as tall as me, except I was sitting down. She made her way to the podium with a determined flounce. Her ponytail bobbed up and down, and her pink jumper was slightly crushed. "Okay," she said, pulling the microphone to her lips. I just hoped that she didn't break it in half. "Some of you don't know how these honeypot notes work. You write on the little papers we provide for you, using the gel pens in the jar, and then you put the note into the envelopes for the corresponding apartment." She hesitated, trying to get her courage up. "Now, remember that you are supposed to write nice things on these notes, like "I enjoyed your talk today" or "thanks for smiling at me." You know? Not . . . other things." Emma was bright red and she quickly retreated, allowing Griffin to take over the microphone.

She collapsed on the chair next to me. "Good job," I said. "I'm sure everyone gets the idea now." But of course they didn't.

"Anyone else?" Griffin asked. He swung his green tie like a pinwheel over his face, trying to fan himself. It was getting hot. The heater had been turned on full blast to combat the cold night outside, and all of us had peeled off our coats under the sweltering heat.

Derek raised his hand, making his way to the podium. His gray suit wasn't even wrinkled, though he had been in it all day. How had he managed that? Harrison was at his heels. He had changed from his impeccable pinstripe suit into a black sweater and jeans. Now he looked like a disdainful James Bond, and if he opened his mouth, he would appear even more so. Derek nodded at us, but of course Harrison didn't even spare us a glance, his bored gaze elsewhere.

"I just wanted to remind you," Derek said, his voice echoing through the chaotic room, "that there are still available slots for safewalk."

"Safewalk!" the guys shouted out around us. It acted as background music to his announcement and Derek jumped. You would think he'd be used to the elders quorum's ways by now, but he still wasn't.

"I'll be passing the finished copy to the girls so that they will know what times safewalk will be available . . ."

"*And* what guys will be safewalking them home," Brooke whispered to me. By the tone of her voice, she was clearly above such things. I wasn't, but I didn't let on. Derek's gaze met mine and he pulled slowly from the microphone, smiling at me before he returned to his seat.

Harrison took his place at the microphone. "Institute will be . . ."

"Harrison is hot!" Ashley shouted. Harrison was clearly used to her eccentric behavior and suffered the catcalls with a dignified air.

"Are you quite finished?" he asked in his snooty English accent.

Ashley didn't even have the grace to blush. "No." She tugged the cream-colored confection of skirts back over her ankles, giving him an innocent look, quite in contrast to her nature.

He rolled his eyes. "You are all formally invited to attend institute in this building on Tuesday at seven o'clock, where you will have the chance to meet the eternal companion of your dreams, and, if you've the inclination, share an intimate conversation over a light repast afterward."

A lot of blank stares followed his announcement, and I wondered if he knew none of us spoke his language. Logan leaned over my seat, trying to get Ashley's attention, and I felt the warmth emanating through the thin material of his plaid shirt. It was really wrinkled, but his cologne smelled great. "Let's announce the ward activity," he said.

Ashley pursed her lips and shook her head. I didn't blame her. After all her catcalls, she could expect the worst. "Go ahead," she said.

Logan snorted, and to my chagrin, left us, taking his manly scent with him. "One more," he said, practically pushing Griffin out of his way. "There's an intramural basketball game and we need your support. Come cheer us on."

I leaned over Emma, trying to get to Ashley's ear. "That's our ward activity?" I asked. "What happened to the combined Christmas party with the hot-guy ward?" She shrugged a delicate shoulder. "Logan had a game . . . and he thought he could combine the intramural sports with the activities, just killing two birds with one stone. It's genius."

"That's lazy," I accused.

"Nope, smart."

"Oh, and one other thing," Logan said, watching me mischievously. "C6 is serving brownies and ice cream after ward prayer."

Brooke stood up. She had changed from the drill-sergeant outfit into something more practical for a Sunday night: khaki pants and red T-shirt, and now her face matched it. "No, we're not." But her voice was drowned out by the excited murmur filling the room.

Logan laughed. "So, if you're interested in homemade cooking, bring your appetites to the C6 chicks and be ready to eat a tasty treat." He gave a slight, mocking nod at our dismayed faces and sat back down with a smirk.

Ashley twisted in her seat, meeting Logan's nonchalant hazel eyes. "That was stupid," she told him.

"Yeah? Well, next time come up with me, then maybe you can stop me."

She just snorted. None of us would be home tonight anyway. It was a roommate tradition to deliver honeypot notes all night, speed delivering them to the girls, lingering with the boys until we were kicked out at curfew. Even Brooke would be coming with us, especially now. She didn't want to be the only one home at our apartment to greet the torrent of confused visitors.

Seeing there were no more announcements, Griffin dismissed us and we filed into the foyer to write honeypot notes . . . or to attend what was more aptly entitled the "flirt fest." Griffin followed me and I grabbed a handful of paper, stuffing myself in a corner. I rearranged my pleated skirt over my knees. Griffin slid down the wall, settling next to me. I tried to concentrate on my notes, which was hard with his eyes on me. "What are you doing?" he asked. "Writing a novel?"

"Not today," I said, carefully keeping my voice neutral. I have a tendency to play dumb. I don't know why I do it, but I always think it's funny until it's too late. Griffin probably thought I was oblivious to his intentions.

He chuckled, staring at me appreciatively. "You think you're such a great writer. Why don't you tell me a story?"

"Uh . . . no. Here." I gave him a slip of paper. "Write a note to somebody. Make their day."

Griffin stared at the paper. "I don't have a pen."

"Well, you'd better get one before they're all taken." I turned back to my notes, burying my nose in them. After a moment, he got to his feet. By the time he could find a gel pen that worked, he would've forgotten all about me, and even better, Logan took his place.

He scooted down the wall next to me and turned to me with a smile. "Hi, I'm Logan Smith and I'll be your official stalker for today."

"The position's already filled," I said.

"Really? That's disappointing. I thought that I was the only man in your life."

I took out my chapstick, applying it to my dry lips. "I wish."

"Hey, you want to share some of that with me?" I stopped midapplication and stared at him as he puckered up. "Your lips are amazing, do you know that? They were made for kissing. How many guys have you kissed anyway?"

I almost choked. I mean, I like to pretend I'm scandalous, but I'm not. "With or without the chapstick?" I asked.

"What are you talking about?" Griffin cast a shadow over us.

I smiled an oblivious smile up at him. "Oh, nothing."

"Well, I'm just going over here. If you need me, just call."

"Oh, okay." It was obvious that Griffin was trying to save me from this "bad influence," which sealed the deal. I liked this Logan guy . . . well, sometimes . . . when he wasn't mouthing off in Sunday School.

"Well, well," Logan said, "look who just walked in." Marcus had come in late and Logan whistled, seeing he was with the blond again. Miriam had changed from one Sunday dress into another with a pale blue overskirt. She pulled her fur-trimmed coat closer to her, looking very chic.

"Hey, what's going on?" Ashley kneeled next to us, trying to get in on the conversation. She glanced back to see what had caught our attention and tossed her dark hair. "Those two seem to be spending quite a bit of time together," she said with obvious distaste.

"Seem?" I said. "They are." Why couldn't I have held Marcus's attention like that? I leaned back and thought. You know, you should know better than to believe your mom. No matter how much she says that you're the most beautiful, most talented, most personable girl that ever walked the earth, she's wrong. There's always someone out there a smidgeon better than you are. And you can never compete with someone just a smidgeon better . . . Well, at least I couldn't. Ashley shook her head, playing with her black hair as Marcus and Miriam approached us.

"How was ward prayer?" Marcus asked us.

I could've said something flirtatious, but it just wasn't the same with Miriam at his side; in fact it seemed a little sick and wrong. "Uh . . . good."

He was disappointed with my answer and turned to Ashley. "Anything scandalous happen?"

She stood up with long, graceful legs, ignoring Miriam easily. "Of course. I was there, wasn't I? Where were you?"

Marcus smiled appreciatively and Miriam's eyes narrowed. "Why? Did you miss him?" Miriam asked.

"Of course."

"Well, don't make it so obvious."

Ashley swung around. "What do you mean?" she asked sweetly— too sweetly. Something was up.

"What do you mean?" Miriam mocked her voice and Ashley's eyes widened. "Don't you get tired of playing a part?" Even though Miriam's voice held a joking note, she had shocked us all. She didn't seem very secure in her relationship with Marcus at all . . . or very nice for that matter, but then again, I had known that all along.

Ashley seemed ready for it. "I wouldn't know," she said. "Do you?"

By then I was exchanging nervous glances with Marcus. Miriam's smile was icy cold. Ashley matched it easily. "You shouldn't act so desperate," Miriam said. "Someday the guys will believe you're sincere."

I cringed.

"Are you talking from experience?" Ashley asked, looking as fake sweet as Miriam.

"Ashley," I said, standing up. "Come here for a second."

"In a minute."

"Hey, Miriam," Marcus said. "There's the bishop. I think he's trying to get our attention."

"No, he's not."

What we needed now was Emma's kindness to splash over this fiery blaze, and I waved her wildly over. Brooke followed her with quick, jerky movements. "What's going on?" Emma asked. Her eyes sparkled . . . in definite contrast to Ashley's flashing ones. Brooke crossed her arms over her stomach, reading Ashley's look, and she became militant. You mess with one roommate, you mess with us all, and Brooke turned to Miriam defiantly. It looked like the beginnings of the rumble on *West Side Story*, and I got ready for a dance-off.

"Ah," Marcus said quickly. "Look, we've managed to capture the attention of all the C6 chicks. Such a charming group of ladies."

"Yes," Logan said, "if we could put all of your finer qualities together, you could make one man such a charming wife."

Marcus coughed then tried to look serious. "But since that's impossible, we'll just have to bring polygamy back, so I can marry you all."

Miriam gasped and stomped off. She grabbed the first cute guy she could find and began talking animatedly to him. Not a good move on Marcus's part, especially since he was trying to get our goat instead.

"Polygamy?" I asked him.

"Oh, yes, it would solve so many problems." Marcus was doing a good job of ignoring Miriam's outrageous behavior and he leaned against the wall, his blue eyes dancing.

By now Brooke was seething at the choice of topic, but I easily ignored her. "I agree," I said. "I mean, the best guys wouldn't be taken anymore. And if I ever got tired of my husband hanging around me all the time like a disease, I could just pawn him off on another wife. Then I could get things done . . ." I trailed off, seeing Scott behind Marcus, and I almost bit my tongue off.

Apparently he had caught the tail end of the conversation because he was running his hand through his already disheveled hair. "It's not actual doctrine that polygamy will be reinstated," he said.

"Thank you," Brooke said, which surprised me. I never thought she'd ever be in accordance with Scott.

"Polygamy would never be an ideal situation," Scott said, "especially for me. I just want one wife. That way I can spoil her. I guess I'm just a romantic that way."

The girls gasped at this and the guys just rolled their eyes.

"Yeah, you're right, a whole horde of women nagging at you doesn't match my idea of romance either," Marcus muttered. Most likely he'd had his fill of them today.

"Oh, blah, blah, blah," I said.

"Yeah, just like that," Marcus said, cutting me off. "Can you imagine about a dozen Samanthas following you around making that noise? I don't even want one."

I glared, having no idea why that was such a painful assessment.

Logan put his arm around my stiff shoulders. "Don't worry, I'll take her."

"Good luck." Marcus abruptly left us, going to Miriam's side. Unfortunately, she allowed him to talk to her.

"Logan!" a girl called behind us. His arm left my shoulder. "I heard that there were desserts at your place instead of at C6?"

"What?"

The females surrounded him and I turned to Scott, seeing my opening. "Any luck with your honeypot-note scandal?" I asked.

He shook his head, leaning against the railing on the stairs. He gave a conspiring wink to my roommates. "I've been watching the drop-off spot, but the girls are good. So far I've only caught one actually putting a note in our apartment's envelope."

"Was it for Griffin?" I asked.

"No, but it was from Veronica, and the love note couldn't have been from her."

"Why not?" I asked.

"She's a chemistry major."

"So?"

"Her come-on lines would've completely given her away—'Come over here and complete my octet' or 'Let's share electrons and make a double bond.' I just don't see it." Brooke broke out into laughter and I chuckled, pretending to be smart. What was he talking about? "But I've actually narrowed it down to two girls," he said.

"Really?" I asked before he could bring up chemistry again. "Who?"

"Oh . . . wait, more girls are dropping off honeypot notes. I'll be back." He inched secretively toward the drop-off, and Ashley and I broke into laughter.

"What's so funny?" Emma asked.

"You wouldn't happen to have anything to do with this?" Ashley asked me, taking Scott's spot against the railing. "If you can't say something nice, write it in a honeypot note," she teased. "I know that's what you do."

"What? Me?" I turned back to my honeypot notes. It was too funny to resist, and before I knew it, I was writing "It was me" on a blank slip of paper. Now the trick was getting it to the drop-off.

The girls who had been on their way to the drop-off had stopped to talk to Scott, and he had no choice but to pretend that he'd cut them off because he was actually interested in them. Even now he was filling their minds with sweet nothings as I passed him, pretending I was trying to wrap things up, the incriminating honeypot note firmly in hand. Marcus didn't even glance up at me as I passed.

"Okay!" I shouted to the room in general, acting as innocent as possible . . . which was pretty hard for me. "Everybody hurry up with your notes!"

Logan tried to trip me and I stepped effortlessly over his leg. I poked my head into one of the church offices. It was filled with honeypot-note writers. "You almost done?"

Derek glanced up worriedly from a desk, his red hair slicked back from his forehead. "No."

"Why not?"

"Hey," Veronica argued, pulling from her uncomfortable position in the corner. "You're not in charge of honeypots, Emma is."

"Yeah, so? She won't ever make you stop, and then it will take us forever to deliver these things . . . and then you'll never get your notes . . . and your special someones won't get them either," I added as further incentive before dragging myself away from the door.

Scott was still by the drop-off and I brushed past Marcus again, yelling at the people on the stairs to wrap it up. Marcus acted like he didn't even hear me, his eyes on Miriam. Her rosebud lips moved up and down in a constant rhythm, and he was completely entranced.

I went to another room, seeing Harrison and Ashley. They were arguing and I paused to listen. "Oh yeah?" she said. "Well, how about this?" She wrote something on a honeypot note and gave it to him with an angry whip of the hand.

He read it out loud. "'You're a simple man with a dumb accent.'" It sounded even more scathing when read with the said accent, and I smiled.

"Well, how about this?" he said, writing furiously. He gave her the note and her eyes widened at it.

"'You're a pernicious, insipid, insidious strumpet,'" she read. "'You wouldn't get a date unless they reenacted the law of consecration because it would be the sacrifice of all things.'"

She gasped and I cleared my throat. "I'm sorry," I said. "I didn't realize this room was taken." They stiffened guiltily. "Let me leave you alone."

I closed the door on them and laughed when they came charging out. I passed Marcus with no reaction from him and I swung around and passed him again—just to test him, mind you—but again no reaction . . . interesting. Was Miriam really that enthralling? Before I could do anything about it, my elbow was stolen from me. I looked down, seeing Derek's hand on it.

"I'm so sorry that we took so long with the honeypot notes." His concerned eyes were on me.

"Oh." I unconsciously tuned my voice about two times sweeter. "Well, don't worry about it. I'm just giving everybody a hard time . . . to be funny." I wondered if he understood that; it was so foreign to his nature.

His mouth broke into a generous smile. "Well, you were right. We *do* want our special someones to get our notes."

"Oh," I said, "did you write to me, then? You're too kind."

He laughed at that. "No, *you're* too kind."

No, not really.

But I smiled in response and he released my elbow.

"I'll go so you'll have time to deliver your notes to us tonight. See ya." With a murmured farewell from me, he left, the door swinging behind him.

Marcus caught it in midswing and left without saying a word, making it painfully clear what I meant to him . . . I was nonexistent, which I already knew, except . . . *Okay, stop thinking about him,* I commanded. *Why do I even care?* Next . . . I turned to Logan. His hazel eyes locked with mine, but he was still surrounded by girls. I saw Griffin. *You know, if he had a little more sun . . . Wait, can someone save me from myself?* I was lacking some sort of self-restraint. Was I going to flirt with anything that moved? What was I thinking? *Oh yeah, Scott . . .* He was properly diverted now, and this had been the moment I was waiting for. I passed the honeypot note drop-off and slipped the evil little note into his apartment's envelope.

Mission accomplished, except I glanced up just in time to see Harrison's all-knowing eyes on me. His lip curled mockingly. His arms were crossed across his sleek black sweater.

"Yes?" I asked.

He simply shrugged. "And so the game begins."

CHAPTER 11

"You got the stuff?"

—Marcus Gray (Sun., Dec. 5th)

Fliers and leftover paint from pranks gone wrong covered the door in a splatter of graffiti. The apartment building could have belonged to the poorest section in downtown L.A., but it was just a guys' apartment in Provo.

Marcus opened his door, looking at my flimsy jean jacket. "That isn't a winter coat," he told me.

"Yeah?" At least it matched the rest of my outfit. I glanced down at my pleated skirt and slippery, patent leather shoes. My black tights were the only things keeping me warm. So what? He had caught me being too fashion conscious, that's all. I shoved my way into his apartment and the rest of my roommates followed me in.

He shut the door quickly, only wearing a short-sleeved, white T-shirt and long, black basketball shorts. He had cute scrawny legs and I tried not to think about that. A large window stretched across half the room and, since it was dark outside, I used it as a mirror to fix my strings of blond hair into curls. I hated having ADHD hair. I mean, no one would know that I had spent hours trying to straighten it into the perfect punk look. The snow had destroyed it pretty fast.

"See, now that's a winter coat," Marcus said, taking in Emma's attire. I swung around. She was wearing her green marshmallow coat and a thick, striped stocking cap. Brooke was dressed similarly in a sensible brown jacket and a black stocking cap shoved over her long, red hair. They began pulling off their heavy gloves.

Ashley stepped into his living room looking like a Russian spy. "Don't even start with me," she told Marcus. She began peeling off her long, sleek jacket then proceeded to unwind her long scarf from her delicate neck.

"Why don't you make yourselves at home," Marcus said dryly.

"Thanks." I wandered around his living room. The apartment was just as bad inside as it was outside; basketballs and sneakers were thrown into a pile in the corner, DVDs were piled on the twenty-five-inch TV, couches were stacked against the bare walls . . . My attention was caught by a cross-stitch hanging on the wall. "This is new, isn't it?"

"Uh, yeah."

I kneeled on one of the deflated tweed couches and squinted at it. "'It's better to fail than to never have tried at all,'" I read.

Emma smiled. "Well, that's nice."

"Where did you get it?" Brooke asked. "DI?"

Marcus bit down a smile with difficulty. "My mom sent it."

"And I put it up," Logan shouted out from the back. He cleared the corner, wearing his striped pajamas. We whistled. He looked great . . . in a strange way.

"Who are you trying to impersonate?" Ashley asked. "Sherlock Holmes? Where's your smoking jacket?"

"You're jealous, aren't you?" He catwalked around the room, and I laughed when he even managed to make that look good.

Marcus sat on the bony arm of his couch. "So, you got the stuff?" he asked.

"Stuff? Oh yeah, of course." Emma dug into the honeypot envelopes, finding their notes. It was a fat pile of nonsense and the guys began dividing them out.

"Where are your other roommates?" I asked.

"Engaged," Marcus said, "nonexistent . . . same difference." He split the pile of honeypot notes like a deck of cards, giving half of them to Logan.

"Oh, this is priceless," Logan said. "Listen to this: 'Why don't you come over to my place and visit some time, I've been dreaming of holding the priesthood.'"

"Who wrote that?" Brooke asked.

"Some sweet Relief Society sister," Marcus said.

"Probably the same one who wrote this one," Logan laughed, holding the note up so we could see. "'Nice plaid shirt today, can I talk you out of it?'"

"Anonymous," Marcus said. "They're always anonymous. Where's the fun in that? There's potential here for a really brutal honeypot note war . . . if we just knew who these were from. Dash diddly dog." He unconsciously used my phrase, picking up a note from Griffin.

My curiosity got the best of me. "What's it say?" I asked.

"Uh . . . something about how he was right in class and everyone else was wrong."

"Well, that's true," I said. "There really *are* just two kinds of people, you know. But the question is what kind of man are you, Marcus? An Arthur lover or a SpongeBob fan?" Apparently no one knew how important the question was because they ignored me.

"What's this?" Logan asked. He slid out a fat envelope from the bottom of the pile, pulling out picture after picture. One was of the back of his head, another one taken of his foot, another was of him opening the door, looking out blankly. He read the accompanying note. "You're just not worth it anymore." His forehead wrinkled. "What's that supposed to mean?"

"Oh, dear," Emma said.

Creepy. I couldn't help it, but it was pure genius. I snickered. "Your stalker gave up on you? What did you do? You big meanie."

Logan stood up. "This is going in the honeypot bucket of fame." He threw it in the trash can.

"That's your bucket of fame?" Ashley asked. "Aren't you afraid someone might throw it out?"

"That's just a chance we're willing to take."

"It isn't one I'm willing to take." She stomped into the kitchen, rescuing the pictures from the trash can. "This is too brilliant to throw out. I'm hanging them on your wall next to the cross-stitch. Where's your tape?"

"What?"

"Hey, is this from you?" Marcus asked me. He held up a black spot.

I tossed my blond curls. "No, why would I give you a black spot?"

"I don't know." He leaned closer to me, but I refused to step back. "Why would you?"

"I . . . I . . ." I looked everywhere but at him. "I wouldn't even make the effort," I said.

"Oh, because it takes so much effort to make a black spot? C'mon, I know you did it now. You look guilty."

I squirmed. I looked guilty because I was trying not to. "I didn't do it." He looked dubious and I stood up quickly. "Hey, c'mon girls, it's time to get the rest of these honeypot notes delivered."

Logan followed Ashley out of the kitchen. "Where are you off to now?" he asked me.

"Next door . . . Derek's apartment."

"Good luck," Marcus muttered.

"What's that supposed to mean?"

"That's your favorite apartment now, right?" Marcus managed to keep an innocent expression. Apparently he had perfected it more than I had—he probably had lots of practice in deceit.

"We don't have favorites," Emma reassured him politely.

"Hey." Logan stopped me before I could walk out the door. "You wanna play Ultimate Frisbee with us on Saturday? It's a reading day, and we need to do something relaxing before finals."

I smiled at him, seeing Marcus's annoyed look behind him. "Sure."

"Could you make the fliers for it?" Logan asked. "I've got it all planned out. We could have a picture of a Frisbee and then some sort of dramatic depiction of a guy running." He gestured wildly, the sleeves on his pajamas flying over his hands. "Or maybe even a—"

"I'll take care of it," I said, cutting him off. This kind of thing was right up my alley. I knew exactly what I was doing. "The flier will be amazing."

"You need to pass them out by Wednesday so there'll be a big turnout."

"Consider it done."

"Oh, Samantha," he called from the door. He swung the door playfully back and forth. "Do you think you could do the basketball fliers too while you're at it?"

I rolled my eyes at Ashley. I still wasn't happy that he made the game into our ward Christmas party. "Only if you do something really nice for me," I said.

"Of course . . . I'm always nice!"

"Yeah, right." The door closed behind us, choking off my words as we went to Derek's apartment.

"Stupid boys," Ashley said.

"Hey, that wasn't very nice," Emma said.

Brooke barely had her gloves on by the time we reached Derek's door. "She's just returning the favor," she muttered.

"Yeah," I said. "Marcus actually accused me of giving him the black spot."

Brooke cracked a smile that didn't quite fit her elegant face. "You would never do that."

"I know."

"Me too," Ashley said. "That's why *I* gave it to him." My eyes got wide and she laughed. "Well, he broke up with you. What could he expect?" She knocked on Derek's door as my mouth formed an O. Now that was loyalty, and though I appreciated the sentiment, I wasn't sure if I wanted it.

"We weren't really going out," I argued weakly.

"Whatever . . . practically."

Derek opened the door, dimpling when he saw us. Seriously, I have never seen such darling dimples on a guy's freckled face. He was so cute. "Uh . . ." I lost my train of thought.

"Honeypot notes," Emma announced bravely. She pulled out another stack of honeypot notes. His pile was unusually high.

I managed to find my voice. "Derek, I think you won again. You got the most honeypot notes in the whole ward."

He just laughed. "I'm sure most of these are for my roommates."

They weren't.

"Do you want to come in?" He opened the door wider, stepping back with bare feet. Night was the only time we would see him in shorts and a T-shirt, but he looked so adorable without the tie, which made me wish that he dressed down more often.

Brooke shook her head. "We're not going to get these all delivered in time if we do." Her warning was directed at me and I reluctantly concurred.

"Would you like something to eat? Something to drink?"

I was almost halfway into his sparkling clean apartment when Brooke grabbed my arm. "Maybe next time."

He winked at her scowling face. Nothing could ruffle his friendliness. "Okay, I'll consider that a rain check."

"Enjoy the notes!" I yelled over my shoulder. He nodded and closed his door, once again separating us from his remarkable presence.

How did he get so many honeypot notes, anyway? Half of the ward must be in love with him . . . Wait, the girls outnumbered the guys in this ward, so it was very likely that *more* than half the ward had a crush on him. An amazing thought. "They were all boring, though," Ashley said, breaking through my thoughts.

Emma was shocked. "What? You read some of his notes?"

"No . . . I read *all* of his notes." We swiveled on her and she shrugged. "They're just a bunch of 'thank yous' and 'blah, blah, blahs.' Boring. You'd think he was a saint."

"He *is* a saint . . . a Latter-day Saint," I finished lamely. My roommates just shook their heads at me.

We made our way up the windy staircase, the wood creaking under our shoes. It barely held the four of us. "Get Griffin's and Scott's notes ready," Brooke told Emma, "then we can get this done faster."

"Who cares if we get this done faster?" Ashley said. She reached the top floor and tap-danced across the balcony, making a loud staccato through the silent night.

Emma felt around the empty envelope. "Oh dear, I can't get them ready . . . Their apartment already has them."

"What?" I glanced at Ashley's distraught face. "How could you allow Scott to take them? Now we have no reason to visit."

"Well, you can ask how he liked his honeypot notes." Emma suggested tentatively.

It just wasn't the same and she knew it. I wanted to see Scott's reaction when he got *the* note, but I didn't have to wait long. He poked his head out of his door, his scruffy, brown hair more disheveled than I had ever seen it. Before Brooke could object, he dragged me into his apartment, my roommates in tow. It seemed we had been too loud on the stairs.

"Alright." His hand was still on my wrist, and he was close enough for me to get a whiff of his cologne. He smelled great. "I'm checking every girl's handwriting in our ward. I'm going to figure out who wrote this." He maneuvered around his guitars and amps and handed me a piece of paper attached to a clipboard. "It was me" was written halfway down the page next to a variety of girly signatures.

"Let me guess," I said, trying not to laugh. "You want me to write "it was me" on this?" He nodded, and I glanced up at Griffin, who had just shuffled into the living room. He had wrapped his bathrobe over his pajama bottoms, still watching me intently. He would never put the crush to rest, would he?

I sighed and balanced the clipboard on my knee. "It was me," I wrote, changing my handwriting into blocky letters. No one would recognize it. "What if she disguised her handwriting?" I asked mischievously.

"Believe me," Scott said, tugging on the collar of his white T-shirt, "I would know."

Well, we would see, wouldn't we? I handed the clipboard back to him and he studied my handwriting, comparing it to the infamous honeypot note. I watched him in breathless suspense. "Was it me?" I asked finally.

He ignored the sarcasm, shaking his head. "Nope. Emma, Ashley, Brooke, get over here." They groaned, but he made them sign it too, though he had to browbeat Brooke into doing it. Then he stared at the list with a critical eye.

I leaned against the wall, my hair brushing against the Argentine flag behind me. "Any winners?" I asked.

"Don't you worry. I have a pretty good idea who she is."

"Who?"

He met my eyes briefly then shook his head. "Nope, not telling."

Brooke looked at her watch. She was the most dedicated taskmaster I had ever seen. "We only have fifteen minutes, guys," she said. "We've got to keep moving."

"Well, by all means," Scott said. With one last glance at me, he headed for the back in true absentminded genius fashion, leaving Griffin with us in the living room. We shifted awkwardly.

Emma was the first to break the silence. "Well, see ya later." She was also the first out the door, followed by Brooke. Fortunately Ashley stayed by my side. We made a quick, albeit casual, dash to the balcony outside.

Griffin walked us to the door then leaned against the doorframe. "I know what you did," he informed me.

I turned. Squealers were the bane of a mischief-maker's existence. "What?"

"It was you . . . and I can prove it."

My smile didn't even dim. "Tell," I said, "and I'll make sure you never get a date in this ward again." I guess there was no sense in beating around the bush.

"There's no need for that. I'll keep silent . . . *for a price.*"

I matched his stare with one of my own. Maybe he was just trying to be cute, but it just wasn't working.

Ashley was just as shocked as I was. "Don't do it," she said. "Nothing is worth that." Forgetting her former animosity toward a certain English boy, she knocked hurriedly on his door. "We'll see you later, Griffin . . . much later," she said under her breath.

CHAPTER 12

"I'll take a stiff English boy over a stalker any day."
—Ashley Fox (Sun., Dec. 5th)

Harrison answered the door, but not soon enough. His eyes roved lazily over us, still managing to look haughty in a black T-shirt and blue BYU shorts that showed off his hairy legs. "Ah look, it's the passionate service committee," he drawled.

We barreled into his apartment and Brooke and Emma gave surprised grunts, not aware that we were making our escape from Griffin. "It's the *com*passionate service committee," Emma corrected him, "not the passionate."

"Same difference," he said. He closed the door behind us, and I gave a sigh of relief now that we were free of Griffin. Harrison's apartment was tidy, but not too stifling. The uniform ugly couches were actually on the floor, instead of propped up on cinderblocks, and a few pictures, though not too many, decorated the walls. I felt myself relaxing in what could only be described as the home of a true English gentleman.

Ashley collapsed onto the nearest chair, free, at least for the moment. "We couldn't have bolted out of there a moment too soon," she whispered to me.

"Yeah, but now look where we are," I said.

She tossed her hair. "I'll take a stiff English boy over a stalker any day."

Harrison didn't even bat an eyelash. "Flattering sentiment, Ashley. What can I do for you fine ladies today?"

"We have your honeypot notes," Emma said, trying to change the subject.

"But of course," he said. "Excellent plan. You get to acquaint yourself with all the men in the ward. You happen to make *accidental* contact as the notes exchange hands . . ."

Emma was denying it as she handed him his notes. "That's completely untrue . . . Where are your roommates?"

"The dumb oxen? They passed out an hour ago. Why? Were you hoping they'd be here to greet you?"

Emma gasped and tried to reassure Harrison that he was just as agreeable a host as they were while Ashley turned to me. "Were you the one who wrote that note to Scott?" she whispered.

"I only wrote the second one. I couldn't resist messing with him."

"Well, if it comes down to it, just let Griffin tell him. I wouldn't even try to bribe *that thing.*"

"That seems a bit dramatic," Harrison said. I glanced up at him. He was sifting through his collection of honeypot notes. "Correct me if I'm wrong, Emma, but aren't there supposed to be some honey in these notes?"

"Oh dear, what do they say?" she asked. I noted the heightened color on her cheeks.

"I'm sure you already know. Didn't you read these before I got to them?"

"Why, of course not." Emma was shocked.

"Why should we bother?" Brooke said dryly. She purposely didn't look at Ashley.

He shrugged. "To discover the latest tantalizing on dits, why else?"

We were silent, just a little confused . . . If I didn't know better, I'd think he was a fan of romance novels. At least he talked like one with his highfalutin language. "Come now, don't be missish with me." He collapsed into a ratty love seat. "Tell me everything."

Ashley was the first to come clean. She balanced on the edge of the love seat, leaning toward him. "Let's just say we know all the gossip."

"Really?" he asked "Did you happen to know where I was last night?" He handed her a honeypot note.

"'Leave small, unmarked bills in a place soon to be specified if you wish for strict confidentiality,'" she read. "What?"

"Exactly my thoughts."

"Well, that's strange," I said as I plopped next to Harrison. He stiffened and I remembered too late that the boy had a huge bubble; he was probably one of the biggest advocates for personal space that I knew. "Yours are actually much more interesting than mine," I said, stealing another note from him. "'I couldn't help but notice your nice cufflinks in church today,'" I read. "'I'll take them from your body after we're finished with you.' Interesting," I mused. "These writers know you well, don't they?"

"This one is even better." He handed me another one, letting me inspect it.

"'I know where you hid the bodies. I'll keep silent for a price.'" There were dollar signs all over the paper. *Wow.* These were amazing. I picked up another one, feeling strangely like Nancy Drew.

"Oh, that's not mine," he said.

He was right. It was addressed to all the inhabitants of P3, and expressly *not* to him. "What do you do to these women?" I asked. His honeypot notes were practically death threats.

He propped his long legs on a chair. "I drive women crazy with my indifference, that's what."

We looked at each other. "Really? Who would've thought?" It came from several sources.

"Oh, here's a nice one," Emma said. She was desperate to find something good. "'Thank you for . . .'"

"Let me see that." He stole the note from her and ripped it up. The scraps floated to the ground. My eyebrows rose. "Insignificant trifles," he said.

Brooke's expression grew colder. "Remind me never to write you anything nice," she said.

"I doubt that you would." At her furious look, he shrugged. "It's a waste of time. What do yours say?" he asked me. "Are they love notes?"

"I . . . no, they're mean."

"Well, they're not as nice as they should be," Emma whispered.

"Really, I thought that girls actually got nice ones. You are the Relief Society, aren't you? Let me see." He snapped for them, and I found myself mindlessly reaching into my pockets for my stash.

I supposed I could let him see a select few. "This one's from my official stalker." I handed it to him.

"'You make a great honeypot-nazi,'" Harrison read.

"Here's another one. Apparently this guy thought it necessary to reassure me that he'd do polygamy with me anytime." I handed him that one too. "And this one's for our turtle. He gets more notes than we do." Some were the cheesiest notes in the history of mankind, but that was the point. If the notes were cheesy enough, they were ensured a spot on our quote boards. "Oh, that's funny." I dug deeper into my empty pockets, pretending astonishment. "I didn't get any notes from you?"

He rubbed the bristle on his chin. "I don't write notes."

"It's beneath him," Ashley said. Her eyes locked with his and they both glared at each other.

"If you must know, yes, it is. Besides that, doing absolutely nothing suits my purposes."

"What's that supposed to mean?" Brooke asked.

"Women flock to a challenge. For example," he read another honeypot note to us, "'If you need a green card, Harrison Bean, here's my number.'" He shrugged. "It appears that I don't have to do a thing."

"Doesn't that bother you?" Emma asked.

"Of course not, girls, it's part of the game. Speaking of the game," he turned his probing blue eyes on me, "how are your advances proceeding with Brother Marcus J. Gray?"

My mouth flew open. This boy was too observant. "You are way off the mark," I said.

"I see. Have your affections wandered to his roommate then?"

"What are you talking about?"

"Secure an invitation to Ultimate Frisbee, and it's in the bag. You'll have him wrapped neatly around your little finger in no time at all. Maybe a ring, too."

"They've already invited us to Ultimate Frisbee," Ashley said.

"They had to," Emma said. "Samantha's making fliers for it. She's also making fliers for their basketball game."

I shot her an angry look, but she was really too innocent to know that she was making me look like an idiot.

"Really?" he asked, one eyebrow already up.

"Look, it wasn't really a big deal. I type faster than I talk. I'm already writing a dozen English papers on the side. I might as well whip up some fliers while I'm at it."

"You're an English major?"

"Yes," I articulated slowly, "I study English."

"So, you're studying me?" he asked.

I couldn't help but laugh at that one—if anyone was trying too hard, it was him. "How many times have you used that line?" I asked.

"Honestly? Never. I just wanted to see how it affected you."

"My heart just went pitter-patter," I said dryly. "I was just about to beg you to propose. Happy?"

He leaned back. "Not yet."

Brooke glanced down at her watch, seeing it was curfew. "Finally," she said in relief. "Let's get out of here before we turn into pumpkins." We all stood up reluctantly. Brooke already had the door propped open with one white sneaker, and Emma and Ashley filed through it, passing Harrison on their way out.

"You'll never catch a man the way you're going," he whispered to me as a parting shot. "You're too obvious. You might as well set up a sign at a booth and write 'Desperate, come and get me.'"

My brows shot up in surprise, but I had already stepped outside. The door closed behind us, making a reverberating sound.

Desperate? The word rang in my ears. Was I desperate? Maybe a little. I mean, look at me. I was flirting with these guys like crazy, actually giving them the chance I'd never have given them a few years ago, but did that make me desperate?

According to Harrison, it did.

CHAPTER 13

"I think I've hit my quarter-life crisis."
—Samantha Skyler (Tues., Dec. 7th)

"Are they coming?" I asked.

Ashley shrugged, playing with the ends of her black peasant shirt. "They said they were."

I tapped the kitchen table in a steady rhythm, trying to pretend that I didn't care. My mass of curls bounced along with the rhythm. I had decided not to flat-iron it today. It looked punky enough.

Brooke splashed around in the sink, getting more soap onto her khaki flairs than on the dishes, and Emma set her scriptures on the table and began thumbing through them, crossing one tiny sneaker over the other. "Is your lesson done yet, Samantha?" she asked.

"What for? I'm not giving it for two more weeks."

"A week and a half . . . right in the middle of finals."

"Yeah, and I'll probably get it done the day before. Don't worry, it will be great."

Ashley straightened, hearing the guys come up the stairs. "They're here."

Brooke dried her hands on a towel, and I noticed her face was turning as red as her hair. No matter how much she pretended not to care, she did. "Are you sure?" she asked. "That doesn't sound like a group of guys."

The wreath went off, singing Christmas songs in maniacal glory, followed by the unnecessary ringing of the doorbell. Emma pulled away from her scriptures to answer it, the hem of her jean jumper rustling at her ankles.

We listened to the male voices in the living room, and we followed her at a more sedate pace, then froze. There were only two of them . . . there were four of us. Don't get me wrong—they were perfectly nice-looking boys, dressed up in khakis and matching striped polo shirts. They were Harrison's roommates to be more specific, both of them football players—a starter and a halfback, but they promised us a real group date, not just hanging out this time.

"Hey," I said, smiling to put them at ease, but my hands clenched over the hips of my loose-fitting jeans. "Where are the rest of you?"

"Oh, yeah." They looked blankly at each other. "Well, we can get two more guys," they offered quickly.

"Okay," Emma said. She sat down on the couch. "But we can't be too late. The movie starts at nine."

"We'll be back in a second," the halfback said. They quickly escaped and we looked at each other, listening to the ticking clock.

"I thought they were going to set us up on blind dates," Ashley said. She paced the room, her brown cords swishing along with her long legs.

"They are," Brooke said. "Polygamy style, one girl on each arm to lead them blindly around. I'm sure they've done it before."

The walkie-talkie beeped on the end table and I flinched, but Ashley made a running leap for it, diving on the couch and scooping it up in one motion. She had been talking nonstop to Marcus for I don't know how long on that cursed thing.

"Hey, you got your ears on?" she asked, tucking her shirt back into her cords. A long beep was her answer, and she beeped back, then he returned it, then she did. It went back and forth, back and forth forever until I was ready to chuck it out the window.

"Turn it off," I hissed.

"Wait," she said. "He's going to talk pretty soon."

I clenched my teeth. I wasn't normally this testy, but it was Marcus, and he was driving me crazy.

Emma sighed. "Did anyone get the mail today?" She should have known better. We shifted, looking around guiltily. It was delivered eight hours ago, and no one ever got it but Emma. "Okay," she said. "I'll get it." She hopped out the door with no trace of anger on her face. Amazing. She was nothing like us. The wreath sang gratefully at her.

"Why are girls so hard to read?" Marcus asked over the walkie-talkie.

I swung on my heel. "What did he just say?"

"One second they're all over you and the next they won't even return your calls."

Ashley smiled, bringing the walkie-talkie to her lips. "Did Miriam break up with you?"

"Well, we weren't really going out."

"If you kissed her, you were going out," Ashley reminded him, swinging her legs.

He was kissing her? "Already?" I blurted. How come Ashley knew that? And how come she didn't tell me?

"Cool it," Ashley told me. "I'm teasing him."

His answer was smothered by the singing wreath, and this time I got the door, still shaken. Before I could pull on my jean jacket, I stepped back as a group of girls crowded into the living room, almost running into Ashley's drums. Our two football-player studs stood in the middle of them. "We're back," they chorused.

"Yeah?" I asked. "Where are the rest of the guys?"

"Oh, well, we couldn't find any more guys, so we found some more girls."

Ashley dropped her walkie-talkie. It landed dully on the bald spot on our orange carpet.

"Is that okay?"

"But . . . but . . ." I tried to clear my head by shaking it. Now there would be two girls on each arm. "Well, I just remembered that I can't go," I quickly fibbed. "Why don't you go without me?"

"Uh, me too," Brooke said. Ashley still hadn't closed her gaping mouth. She just stared blankly.

"Here," I said, handing them our tickets. "Go without us." They were only Tuesday night fifty-cent tickets, so it wasn't that big of a sacrifice, but still we watched them leave in a sea of confusion.

The door slammed and Ashley punched the cushion on the couch. "This would never happen to me anywhere else," she said. "Only here . . . in the *city of men!*"

"Apparently this *isn't* the city of men," I said. "We've got to find someplace else where they're more desperate, maybe . . ."

Emma flung the door open again, the wreath singing her in. "Hey, they're leaving without us. They just passed me on the stairs."

"Complete with their harem," Brooke muttered. "Did I get any mail?"

"No, but Samantha got a *Rolling Stone* again," Emma said.

I winced. "Again? I thought they were going to cancel me." Emma handed me the magazine, complete with the cancellation notice. "Oh no, they're going to cancel me again. How many notices does this make, anyway?"

"I don't know," Ashley muttered into the couch. "Maybe this should teach you not to sign up for freebie magazine deals anymore. Maybe this will teach all of us." Her words were lost in the cushions.

"Why would I be even tempted to renew my subscription when they keep sending it to me?" I asked.

Brooke leaned against the wall, burying her face in her hands. "You would think they'd make good on their threats to cut you off forever."

"I wish."

"Maybe *you* should cut them off."

"I don't have the energy."

Ashley reached halfheartedly for the walkie-talkie. She pressed down on the button with what remained of *her* energy. "What are you having for dinner?" she asked Marcus. Was it too much to hope that it was a rhetorical question?

I turned, shaking my head quickly. "Don't you dare invite him for dinner."

There was an elongated silence before he answered, "Cranberry sauce . . . maybe over some ramen noodles."

Once again, he had shocked me. "You've got to be kidding."

"What are you having?" he asked her.

"No," I pleaded. "Don't do it."

"Steak," Ashley said.

"Yeah, right," his answer crackled.

"Why don't you come over here and find out?"

"That's tempting."

I couldn't take it. I headed for the back rooms, but Emma stopped me with a worried look. "You got something else, too," she said. My heart fluttered when she handed me an envelope with our address printed on the front with my own handwriting. It was the answer to my query letter. It always meant a rejection for one of my books. But maybe this time . . . I sliced open the envelope.

"Uh-oh." Ashley pulled away from the walkie-talkie. Brooke pulled her head out of her hands to watch.

"'Thank you for sending us your book,'" I read, "'though we are sorry to say that it does not meet our needs at this time.'" Another rejection. I leaned my head back. If adversity revealed our true characters, it only proved that mine was a poor one. "I can't take any more of this," I said. But then again, I had to. What else could I do? I felt trapped.

Ashley turned back to the walkie-talkie. "Are you coming over or not, Marcus?"

"I don't know if I should. Is steak really on the menu?"

"If you want it."

Oh, shut up. I stalked into my bedroom and pulled out my guitar. Everything was hitting me all at once, every insecurity, every disappointment, every failure staring me straight in the face . . . until I couldn't stand it anymore. The more you put on the line, the harder you fall. I knew that already, so why was I always putting everything on the line?

I threw the strap over my shoulder and with difficulty pushed the tight sleeves of my blue hoody to my elbows, then turned my amp up loud. What was wrong with me? I wanted to be happy, but I had no idea how to go about it. There were so many miserable people out there. I had always promised myself that I'd never be one of them. I just didn't know how I would avoid it without the inevitable self-destruction. I was pushing everyone and everything out of my way just so I could prove myself. I thought of church. It definitely didn't put me in the lose-my-life-to-find-it mode, but what else was I supposed to do if I wanted to succeed at something?

Never give up. It was drilled into me. Yeah, you can't change your circumstances, but you can change your attitude. Can you change how you *feel?* Trying to be happy felt forced, like I was a chameleon pretending to be something I wasn't. And I didn't want to be something I wasn't. I wanted to be strong. I wanted to fight whatever obstacles came my way. There was no way I was going gently into that good night . . .

I just hoped that my energies weren't channeled in the wrong direction. It wasn't as if I didn't have righteous desires, but they just weren't working out for me right then, so I'd decided to work on other things. Nothing evil of course, just less spiritual. I just wanted to be successful, socially adept . . . significant somehow—starting that moment. But it just wasn't happening. Dash diddly dog. I wasn't perfect. Of course, no one was, but it wasn't like I was comparing myself to Emma or Brooke or Ashley. No, my problem was that I was comparing myself to what I wanted to be.

You see, what I was is *not* what I'd hoped for. I was hopelessly flawed. And it's strange what parts of my personality popped up the older I got. I was far behind where I wanted to be, and it became more obvious with everything I failed in. At least I was honest about it. That was one thing I prided myself in.

Emma waved in front of my face, shouting. My fingers stilled over the strings, and I turned. I hadn't even noticed that she had come into the room. "Can I close this door?" she asked.

"Uh, yeah."

The door slammed behind her exit. I sat on my bed, thinking. I *was* sabotaging myself, wasn't I? But I wasn't sure how or why. I thought of how I'd handled Marcus and how I felt about others around me. Who would have thought that the pursuit of happiness meant hurting yourself and everyone around you? I know how I appeared to everyone: superficial, idiotic, inconsiderate, a flibbertigibbet.

If I didn't prove that I was something and quick, I would really end up being what everyone thought I was. So even if I was looking in all the wrong places, I would never give up. I had to keep going, even if it hurt. Because there was no way I could fail. I wasn't crazy. I wasn't worthless . . . and I had to prove it somehow.

Brooke shoved through the door. "Hey." She knocked belatedly, even though we shared the same room. She sat next to me on the bed, flinging her heavy brown shoes off. "What's the matter?" she asked. She knew me well, didn't she?

"I think I've hit my quarter-life crisis," I said. "I'm trying to better myself."

"Good." She stared at her toes, wriggling them. "Does that mean you're up for that redemption concert?" she asked.

I laughed, but she watched me with all seriousness. I cleared my throat. "Well, if we can actually get our band together to practice . . ."

"That should be pretty difficult," Brooke intoned ironically. "We only live in the same apartment."

"And we have absolutely nothing to do with ourselves right now," I muttered, especially since we had dumped our polygamist boys.

"Well, we could do our homework," Brooke reminded me. Her eyes twinkled. It was clear she knew what buttons to push.

Homework—at night? I winced, then I winced some more when I heard the wreath singing outside. "Is that Marcus?" I asked.

"No, he opted for cranberry sauce. Strange guy."

"Lazy guy. He didn't want to make the trip across the street." And I was grateful. I listened to the male voice in the living room, trying to guess who it was, then leaned my head back when I realized what I was doing. Just like Harrison said, I was desperate . . . *Desperate for this crazy dating game to end.*

"You brought us cookies?" Ashley asked. Cookies? That sounded like the right kind of male to me. I jumped off the bed and Brooke followed. Please say that they had chocolate in them—and no methylene blue.

CHAPTER 14

"It isn't about fun, it's about marriage."
—Harrison Bean (Tues., Dec. 7th)

"No, I didn't bring you cookies." It was Harrison's voice and it was filled with disgust. "What do I look like—a girl? Someone doorbell-ditched you . . . except I came at the opportune moment and would've caught the miscreants if I felt like running after them. I think the wreath scared them, too, though I couldn't be sure. They could've been having seizures."

I started blocking out his babble, staring at the cookies in his hand instead—that was all that was important. "It's a dangerous world out there," he told us. "I had to duck some carolers to get here. They tried to suck me in with their insidious levity, but I resisted soundly." He glanced up at Brooke and me. "What? Are you hungry?" he asked.

Wasn't that obvious? He relinquished the cookies and oh, they *did* have chocolate in them. *Bless the doorbell-ditchers.* I grabbed two, and Brooke followed my example as we quickly made them our dinner. Ashley came behind us, snatching a few. Emma just waited politely in the kitchen. Harrison joined her, towering over her. He made a strange sight in our kitchen. He was elegantly dressed in a dark blue T-shirt and dark jeans . . . wait, not elegant exactly, but he always managed to trick the senses.

"Oh look, a death threat." He leaned over the sink. "'Do the dishes or die,'" he read the sign. "Let me guess—Brooke put that up? Aren't there laws against this kind of intimidation in the U.S. of A.?"

Brooke ignored him, sitting down on a rickety chair in the kitchen. I sat on the round table, pushing aside cereal boxes and the bowl of leftover apples. Ashley pulled next to me, tapping her foot against the dingy table leg as Harrison quickly skimmed through the quotes taped all over our walls. Then he got to the honeypot notes, and he lingered. "Oh, this is tender," he said. "'Santa has something special for you this year,' signed anonymous."

"Yeah, thanks Harrison," I said.

"Why would I write something like that?" His gaze moved to another honeypot note. "Oh, I guess this one's true at least."

Emma smiled. "What is that?"

"'You sisters really are sweet spirits.' What kind of drivel is that?"

Emma frowned, but I ignored him. "I'm still hungry," I said. "Ashley, where's that steak that you were talking about?"

Ashley laughed, putting her arm around me. "I just wanted to see what would bring Marcus over here."

"It isn't food." Harrison was slowly perusing the kitchen. The cupboards were full of nothing and he opened them to make sure; there was just junk from Christmases past, jars of peanut butter, a milk jug filled with sugar. He got to one of our refrigerators and stopped in his tracks. *So that's what he was looking for* . . . But he didn't open the fridge. Instead he stared at the wedding announcements that decorated the whole front of it. "Well, well," he said, "your refrigerator is covered in yet more signs of your failure . . . or do you keep these announcements up here as your inspiration?"

I felt those words bubble up in my throat, you know, the ones that I've been trained my whole life not to say. I slid off the table instead, casting a languid glance at the pictures. "Oh, these are just warning signs so we don't end up the same way. Take a good look at those guys. Losers, all of them. We're just grateful these girls took them off the market." Even Harrison looked shocked, and I smiled wickedly, tossing my blond curls.

In the sudden silence, we listened to the carolers making their rounds outside. They were coming closer.

"Whoa," Ashley intoned nervously, "don't say things like that . . . or you'll end up with some ugly guy and spend years trying to convince people that you really do love him."

"Oh, all guys look pretty much the same five years after marriage anyway," I said. "So what's the difference?"

Brooke rolled her eyes, but Emma looked concerned. "Now, Samantha, that wasn't very nice."

"Why? I'm just telling you to marry for personality. If he's bald, cross-eyed, or shorter than you, you always have the resurrection."

Emma gasped. "Now, that isn't very respectful."

"Yep. So the fact is,"—I was on a roll and I strutted around the checkered kitchen floor, careful not to step on the black squares (there was really no need to step on a crack and break my momma's back) —"I'm not nice and I'm not respectful . . . and that's why I'll die an old maid and be perfectly content with it."

"So then act like it," Harrison said. He pulled a seat away from the table. Most of its back was missing. What was left of it jutted jaggedly from the ruins. He grimaced at it, but despite his usual disdain, he still sat next to Brooke. She didn't look happy about that, but he didn't care. Instead he played with the markers in our flowerpot, acting innocent . . . almost like he hadn't just said that.

I swung around, facing him. "What do you mean?"

It was a stupid question that was sure to burn me, and of course, Harrison took it as his opportunity. "I've seen the way you flirt with every guy that moves. You're desperate to bring a souvenir home for Christmas."

I stilled. Was that how I was acting? Or was he just trying to get to me?

"The fact is, if you even had the slightest inkling how to play the game," he said, "you'd have any guy you wanted."

"That's a laugh." I had been trying harder than I had ever tried before, but the funny thing was that besides Griffin, I wasn't getting anywhere with anybody. It's not the disadvantage of my age. That never stopped my admirers before. It's not my face—I mean I have two eyes, a nose, and a mouth, though not necessarily arranged in any artistic fashion. And even though I don't think I'm the best-looking girl alive, guys think I'm pretty and I take advantage of that. Okay, so I admit that my personality is lacking some refinement, but no one cared about that before, either. So could Harrison be right? Was my complete inexperience with the game the real root of my problems?

"Even if a guy were interested in me," I said quickly, "he wouldn't do anything about it."

Harrison dug his chin into his palm. "And what do you do if *you're* interested?" he asked.

"Nothing."

"Why?"

"Because I don't want to be annoying." I leaned against the refrigerator, feeling my face go red.

"Hmm, so between the two of you, *nothing* will happen."

I was silent.

"So tell me," he went on. "Who is the *lucky* man you've set your sights on now?"

"I'm not telling you anything, Harrison."

"Alright, then let me guess. You're working on melting the heart of the staunchest, most noncommittal bachelor in our ward while dabbling with the affections of the quorum leader."

I stilled as he began outlining all the men in the ward that I had ever been interested in. ". . . followed by a full-fledged love affair with the activities director, topped off with a torrid romance with the ward greeter," and he went on and on. "So, who's it going to be, Samantha? Who will you take home to Daddy for Christmas break?"

I laughed away my unease. "I think you're giving me more power than I have, Harrison." I wondered why my roommates weren't coming to my aid, then noticed they were watching in complete fascination. And how could they not? This was no guy. He was too observant, freakishly so.

"I'm giving you more power than you're willing to use, you mean," he said. "You have all the equipment."

"Dash diddly. What are you saying?"

"You can't tell me that you don't want to get married, and I wouldn't believe you if you tried."

"If I tell you that I want to get married, I'll end up on a mission. If I tell you that I don't want to . . . I'll find myself leg shackled before I know it. The fact is, whatever I want, I'll get the opposite. That's why I make it a point not to spill my guts . . . or pray for patience while I'm at it either."

Harrison shrugged. "God isn't a leprechaun. He doesn't try to find tricks in your phrasing . . . and He doesn't give you the opposite of what you want just to mess you up." He leaned against the table, resting his chin in his hand. "No, the only reason that you're not getting married is because you're desperate."

"What?" I shrieked. I couldn't help but give a good reaction, and it always proved my undoing, but he was using that *desperate* word again. Harrison smirked at my scowling face. "Maybe you're right," I said. "I shouldn't date. I should just give up and become a Mormon nun."

"But then you won't get your eight-carat diamond ring."

I stared at him. Who cared about the diamond ring? I wanted a husband, kids—seven to be exact, though the number was dwindling the older I got. I was wasting good childbearing years . . . and there was no way I was going to admit any of that to him.

"You're right," I said. "The bigger the ring the better . . . and once he gets that on my finger, it will be 'thank you and good-bye.'"

"I don't care about that," Emma said soberly. "As long as I marry a man who treats me with respect."

"Respect?" Harrison said scathingly. "Whoever wrote about the eight-cow wife should be shot."

Brooke met his eyes challengingly. "*I'm* worth eight cows."

"I'm worth eight mad cows." Ashley leaned toward him.

Harrison snickered appreciatively. "You're right."

She scowled.

"Okay." I waved in front of them to get their attention. "Let me get this straight—no girl cares about the diamond, no girl I know anyway, so your point is absolutely moot."

"You'd be surprised . . ."

"Whatever. Listen to a girl. A girl wants a man who loves her, and if there's anything I've learned, you can't force anyone to love you. I don't like stalkers either, so I try to apply the golden rule and not stalk."

"Who says?" he said.

I was growing indignant. That was more than enough. "I don't stalk anybody!"

"No, I mean why can't you force a man to love you? It's called the commitment pattern."

"I believe that's the manipulation pattern," Brooke said.

"And you care?"

"No," I said, "except it doesn't work."

"But what if it *did* work?" He leaned back in his chair, languidly pulling the top off one of our black markers. "I believe that I've got a proposal to present before the council of spinsters."

At that moment the carolers outside screeched a high note, which was completely appropriate for this moment. "Why are you here at BYU, anyway?" Harrison asked. "And don't tell me it's to find yourself by honing your talents and finding a career. You are on a mission, girls . . . a mission to get married."

We exchanged glances. He was off his rocker. The carolers were coming closer and Harrison quickly stood up. The windows were fogging up and he rubbed at them. It was snowing gently as he peered into the darkness outside. Suddenly he jerked and closed the curtains hurriedly.

"I think they know we have a guy in our apartment," Ashley whispered.

Brooke fixed Harrison with a dramatic look. "They're coming for you."

Emma bit her lip worriedly.

"Yeah right," I said. "That would be too good to be true."

Harrison wasn't taking any chances. He began writing on our whiteboard with all the seriousness of a man giving his last piece of advice with his dying breath. *It isn't about fun, it's about marriage,* I read. "This is your mission statement," he said. "And consider this your first district meeting."

Emma perked up excitedly; being an RM, she recognized this. The rest of us just watched the board blankly.

"Now I want an honest report of your stats this semester." He drew a quick chart and wrote "contacts" in the first box. "Samantha," he barked. "You're our first victim. What contacts have you made so far this semester?"

"What kind of contacts?" I asked. "Elbow squeezing? Hand holding? What?"

"No, this is your finding pool," he explained patiently. "How many guys have you found as potential dating material?"

I froze, listening to the carolers outside. Our wreath went off, followed by the girls' screams and giggles until they too began to sing along with its eerie melody. I turned to Harrison. "They're here," I said in a haunting voice.

"Don't answer the door," he said.

Emma ignored him, going to the door, and he groaned, pointing at her as if that would stop her. "Emma, Emma, didn't you hear me? Pretend like we're not home. Don't you dare let them distract you from the work."

She opened the door, letting in the cheerful blare of carols from outside. She smiled prettily. "You sound wonderful."

"What is she talking about?" Harrison mouthed. "They're the carolers from—" He took one look at Brooke's stern face and modified his words somewhat, "—heck."

The carolers piled into the living room, singing another jolly song for good measure. Harrison rolled his eyes to the music until they stopped. "Are you quite finished yet?" he asked.

"Harrison!" Feisty little Veronica pulled from the crowd of girls. "I didn't know you were here."

"Yeah, right," Ashley muttered. Brooke cast her a warning look.

"I've got a grand idea," Veronica said, definitely not looking at Harrison the way she had looked at me in church. "Why don't you come caroling with us? We need a bass."

"Actually, I'd rather die."

They giggled in response. "Come on. C6, you should join us too."

"Uh, no, I'm tired," I began. We made our various excuses and Harrison nodded in approval. I tried to ignore that.

"Well," Veronica said, "if you change your minds, just follow the music and we'll be there." They waved and we waved back; this went back and forth until they left. The wreath opened its glowing eyes and we quickly shut the door on it.

Harrison led us back into the kitchen. "I admire their determination," he admitted. "I want to see that same determination in all of you."

"Oh brother," Brooke said, but she looked fascinated. Harrison was really very entertaining.

"Take this seriously," he said. "Ashley!"

"Huh?" She glanced back from the window, a dreamy smile on her face. She held the walkie-talkie.

"We'll get to your stats in time," he said. "Now, put your attention on me. Samantha, report your contacts for this semester."

I laughed. It was an unwritten rule to never break the code of silence and reveal the men you liked to another man, but maybe I was what he said . . . *desperate*, sorta, so I decided to play along. "You want *all* of their names?"

"Uh," the marker hesitated over the board, "a number for now."

"I don't know a number."

He sighed. "Well, let's fix that. Where's your ward selectory?"

"Directory," Emma corrected him.

"Same difference."

Ashley stood up and clogged to the counter, where she picked up the ward directory and flung it at Harrison. He caught the red and pink, heart-covered book one-handed. "First of all," he said, "is there a guy in the ward that you *don't* like?"

"Sure," I said.

"Who?"

"I never bothered to learn their names."

"You're hopeless. So every guy whose name you know, you like?"

"No."

"That's not what the guys think," Brooke said. "You say hello to them and they think you're in love with them."

He shook his head, flipping through the pages of eligible young men and women from the ward. "We can completely skip over the girls' section," he said. "Why haven't you torn these pages out, anyway? They're useless to you."

"It would make our intentions too obvious," Ashley drawled, evilly fluttering her fingers together. She really was getting into this, wasn't she?

"Don't play with me," Harrison muttered. She sat next to him, practically leaning against him to peer at the directory, and we joined her, forming a semicircle around him like he was our mommy reading us a book. The ward directory never seemed so interesting. Harrison finally found the guys' section and Emma peeked over his shoulder, still too short to see the pictures.

"Let me see," she said. He lowered the directory for her benefit, and there they were—the guys in all their glory, complete with pictures and captions loaded with highly personal information. It read like a singles ad: age, major, hobbies, likes and dislikes, and was complete with a quote. It was all there, a compact dating directory.

"Well, it seems someone has already taken some initiative," Harrison said, noting the stars and slashes next to the guys' pictures. "Would you like to let me in on this little secret code?"

Ashley giggled. "It doesn't mean anything."

"Let me see." Harrison flipped the pages to his picture and saw a star over his face. He gave a short bark of laughter. "What's that mean?"

"Nothing, now go on." Ashley smirked proudly, looking more mischievous than anything else. It wasn't every day someone gave Harrison a taste of his own medicine.

He stroked his chin. "It appears you need to take a few tips from your roommate, Samantha. She's already started her contacts. But don't worry, I'll crack this code. Now, before we start, what are you looking for?"

"Friendly, intelligent, good conversationalist . . ."

He watched me incredulously. "No looks?"

"Of course looks," Ashley said, taking over, "and an accent." He stiffened when she met his blue eyes. "That's about the only good thing about you, actually, Harrison."

"Really?" he replied in his stiff accent. He pulled away from her. "Just think of what I'm going through. You all have accents to me. Now," he turned to me, "start pointing out your men, sister."

I sighed, mentally preparing myself. I would have to start this out differently for once. This could be my last chance to finally go for the right guy . . . the perfect, nicest guy I could find, one who wouldn't turn on me. Of course, there weren't that many to pick from out of our ward, but I was going to try anyway.

"You realize that I'm putting you in my strictest confidence?" I told Harrison. He nodded. "And you realize what will happen if you cross me?"

"Let's start on page one," he said, his face serious. He flattened the page so we could see it properly.

"Boring," Ashley chirped.

He cracked a smile. "Really?" He turned another page.

"Boring."

"Ashley, it's my turn."

"Well, those apartments are boring," she said.

"Not for me."

Harrison quickly flipped back to the so-called boring-but-not-for-me page. "Ah, yes, I suspected as much."

"Derek Johnson," Emma said with a sigh.

Harrison squinted at his picture. "Perfect marriage material: elders quorum president, good . . . nice."

Ashley snorted. "He's *too* nice."

"That's why I like him," I said.

"Whatever. You'd kill him."

"No, I wouldn't. He's perfect." It was obvious by Ashley's unmoved look that she didn't believe me. "Look," I said. "I'm tired of choosing the wrong guy, alright?"

"I'm not," she said.

"Are you sure?" Brooke asked. "He'll be rich."

Emma gasped. "That doesn't matter."

Ashley echoed her gasp. "You're so right. He's going into chemical engineering." She tugged his picture closer; it wasn't his best—too close up and his nose looked huge. She wrinkled her perfect nose. *Good, no competition there,* I thought.

"There's only one problem," Harrison said. "He's still in missionary mode."

"No, he's not," I said. "He always touches my arm."

"The elbow?" Harrison asked. I nodded. "Sounds promising," he said. "Okay, tally him on your list of contacts."

He flipped to the next page and I stopped him. "There's Scott," I said. Now, *he* had a good picture, but how could he not? He was the hottest guy I knew, and so romantic when he set his mind to it. I couldn't believe that he wasn't dating anyone. "I like him too," I said, almost wincing at the sound of it. It sounded so stupid verbalizing it.

"Ah, the poet," Harrison said. "Always looking for his one true love to dote on."

Brooke rolled her eyes. "Looking so high that he can never find her."

"He's looking for a sweet girl," I said. "I'm not really sure if I'm his type."

Harrison turned to me, studying my face. "There's a possibility."

"Not really. He won't ask me out."

"That doesn't mean anything. You could have intimidated him out of his simple mind."

"Or he's just not interested," I said.

"Not possible."

I looked at Harrison with new eyes, suddenly realizing how useful he could really be. "Could you find out?" I asked.

"Possibly . . . of course guys don't talk, but there are other ways of knowing."

"How—through grunts?" I asked.

"Men can read men."

"I don't know," Ashley said, still studying Scott's stats. "Could you really live with that last name?"

"Turnipp?"

"Well, telemarketers won't have any problems pronouncing it," Brooke pointed out.

Ashley sucked on the ends of her black hair in deep thought. "At least think of your kids, Samantha."

"Oh, c'mon, give him a chance." Emma stood up, stretching her legs. She shook out her hands then touched her toes. "You've got a lot in common. You're both musicians."

"True," Harrison concurred. "We'll add him to your list of contacts. Next?"

"How about Griffin?" Emma said. "He likes you."

"What?" I had never been so insulted. Why was she bringing him up again, especially after the violent reaction I had given her last time? How could she possibly think that Griffin and I would be a good match? "I'd rather live with twelve dozen cats and die a spinster," I said.

Brooke choked on a laugh. "I think that's a no," she said.

Emma straightened. "I like cats."

"Okay, then *you* marry him."

"No." The finality in her voice was the closest that Emma ever came to being mean.

The walkie-talkie started beeping incessantly behind us and Harrison smirked at me. "What about Marcus?"

"Never," I said, too quickly.

"Good," Ashley said, "because I want him." Harrison's eyebrows went up, as did mine. I glared at her. "What?" she asked.

"It's your funeral," I said.

"Well, you don't want him."

By all rights I shouldn't. "Yeah, but you would just be wasting your time with him. He won't commit."

"I'll get him to commit."

She was probably just as noncommittal as he was, so they would probably get along just smashingly. "Okay," I said. "Fine. Then I want his roommate Logan." All of a sudden, I felt like a petty school-girl fighting over Ken dolls.

"You like Logan?"

"Well . . . yeah." But only because he was the only guy that showed any *real* interest in me. That and he was Marcus's roommate and it would make Marcus mad if we got together.

"Oh, working the roommates, are you?" Harrison said. "Very difficult."

"No, I'm only working one roommate," I said. "I'm done with Marcus."

"Are you?"

"Yes."

"Well, if anyone can do it, you can."

I rolled my eyes. "I told you, I'm only working one."

"Sure."

I glared at him. "Even if I tried, I wouldn't have a chance with *that* one."

"You mean he doesn't have a chance with you."

"What?" I hadn't even considered that before.

"Don't go for Logan," Brooke said, completely missing Harrison's insinuation about Marcus. "He always goes for the pretty girls who date all the time."

"You're pretty," I said.

"That's not my point."

"Oh wait, Mayday," Harrison said. It was obvious that he was thoroughly enjoying himself. "Logan's a biology-composite-teaching major. He won't be able to support you, let alone himself."

"He will too," I said. "Teachers make more outside of Utah . . . or he could go on to be a professor at BYU."

"Ah, stupid, blind love. Okay, so you've decided on three Mr. Possibilities: Mr. Friendly, Mr. 'Fraid, Mr. Flirty . . . and let's add a fourth, shall we? Mr. Freaked Out."

"The fourth?" Ashley asked. "Who's the fourth?"

I sighed. *Marcus.* "Whatever, Harrison. You can count him, but I won't. He's history."

Harrison added four on my list of contacts, then put one on Ashley's list. "Any more for you?" he asked her.

"One's good enough for me. I don't want to divide my efforts."

"Excellent strategy," he said.

"I would've considered you," she continued inanely, "but it never would've worked. I think it's your name. That's the first count against you. Then it got worse from there."

"Thank heaven for small miracles," he muttered, turning to Emma. "It's your turn. Choose your dating pool."

She shrank back. "I like everybody."

We sighed. Emma was so nice it would be hard to get anywhere with her. "Yeah?" Ashley asked. "But do you like *like* all the guys like that? You know what I mean?"

"No." Her forehead wrinkled and she turned to me for guidance. "Who do you think I should go for?"

"Nope, it doesn't work that way," I said. "You've got to find a guy for yourself or else you're just forcing it."

"I don't know who I like."

"Yes, you do," Ashley said, "you're just not telling us."

Emma watched us helplessly, and I took over, turning to our mentor. "Count out all the bitter guys and the ones with tempers, Harrison . . . and forget the I'm-different-and-more-special-than-anybody-else mentality guys, too. Now who's left over for Emma?"

"Nobody."

"Well, you took all of them," Brooke accused. She shoved away from us, pacing the room, only stopping to lean against the announcements on the fridge.

"Okay, then who do you like, Brooke?" I asked.

"I'm not telling you."

"Please," Ashley begged.

"No . . . I don't like anyone."

"Let's rephrase the question then." Harrison brought his fingers to his lips. "Is there a guy you can tolerate?"

She was silent.

"A man you're attracted to?"

"Just think of it as an experiment," I said, pulling to her side. "You can prove how . . . stupid boys are."

"Yeah." Ashley quickly caught on to my line of reasoning. "If this works or if it doesn't work, you can prove how stupid boys are either way. It's easy."

Brooke leaned her head back, her long, red hair swishing against her back. "You're the ones who are stupid. I'm not a romantic, okay. I'm more rational, and I don't think this little game of yours is going to work."

"Just give us your numbers," Harrison said.

"I don't have any."

"Because you aren't giving them out. Let's work on your finding methods." He wrote down "numbers" for Brooke and put a big fat zero underneath it. "Have you received any 'referrals'?" He wrote that on the board, too, and waited tensely for her answer.

"I hate blind dates—you should've seen the one we almost had today." Another zero went up, which was pretty galling for a girl who always got hundred percents on calculus tests. She tried to pretend it didn't matter.

"You're just going to have to revert to the less-effective method of street contacting. Well?" His marker hesitated over the board. "Opening your mouth isn't necessarily less effective, just desperate. Let's write down FTC, 'flirt to convert.' Samantha and Ashley will just have to show you how it's done and then make you a believer in the process, but it's basically BRTing then waiting for an opportune moment. Any of those?"

Brooke was just silent.

"Oh, BRTing means 'building relationships of trust,'" Emma told her eagerly. Brooke remained silent.

"Okay," Harrison said. Another zero. "Tell me your mincing hours."

"What?"

"How long does it take you to put that face on?"

"Zero. I wake up with it."

He mimicked a buzzer sound and I felt like I was on *Jeopardy!*. "Wrong answer."

Emma pulled to the sink, getting a glass of water. "And what about *your* finding pool?" she asked Harrison in a kind voice between sips.

"Don't worry about my stats."

A mischievous smile spread across Ashley's face. "Oh, I think we should. Why should we make you our fearless leader if you can't even do this yourself?"

"Yeah." I strutted over to his side. "I don't see you getting married, hot stuff."

"I'm not trying to find any more contacts," was his cruel rebuff. "I'm trying to get rid of the ones that I already have."

I pulled away from him. "So you have commitment problems, then?"

"No, but it doesn't matter if practically all the girls in the ward like you if not one of them suits your fancy."

"And you couldn't possibly like any of them back?" I asked.

"Perhaps a few."

We waited to hear, but he was silent. "Well?" I tapped my fingers over the kitchen table.

"Like I'm stupid enough to tell you."

I straightened. "But we told you."

"Exactly."

"I didn't tell you," Brooke said. And she looked very smug about it. "Neither did Emma."

"That's because she didn't know who she liked," Harrison said. He watched Emma push a tendril of chestnut-colored hair behind her ear, and I resisted the urge to point out exactly who Harrison liked, but there was no way I was going to now. That boy held some dangerous information.

CHAPTER 15

"Let's set the date, shall we?"

—Harrison Bean (Tues., Dec. 7th)

Harrison pulled away from the refrigerator, stuffing the Tupperware container of nondescript leftovers under one arm so he could balance the burnt bratwursts and expired milk in his hands. Unfortunately he had picked my shelves to steal from, except now I really didn't care. He had that much of a grip over his audience. Harrison set the stolen goods down heavily on the table, and after a brief intermission of perusing the items and shoving them away in disgust, he continued.

"Now that you've found your contacts," he said, "the trick is moving them from your finding pool into the dating pool and making them your investigators."

"And how do we do that?" Ashley was all business, and I realized that I had never seen her pay attention to *anyone* so closely. She ran her fingers through her black hair, deep in thought.

"The first thing to remember is that you know nothing—nothing about men . . . and nothing about yourself, for that matter."

Ashley nodded. "Yes, master."

"I agree," I said. "Guys are more complicated than they think they are."

"No," Harrison said. "That's another point to remember. Guys aren't complicated. In fact, they're very simple to understand."

"So, you mean that they're shallow?" I asked.

"No . . . simple and deep."

"Like one of those kiddie pools that rats drown in," Ashley said. A deep dimple showed at the corner of her mouth.

I snorted at that philosophy. "No, they're more like toilets that suck you in. Guys just think they're uncomplicated because they're so complicated that they can't even understand themselves. Girls, on the other hand, are straightforward. A guy would have to be blind not to know that we're interested."

"Not blind," Harrison said, "purposely oblivious."

"What?"

"Which brings me to my next point, a girl needs to make the guy *believe* that he wants her. That will be the only way to meet your marital goals for this semester, sisters."

"That figures," Brooke said. Her freckles seemed more pronounced than usual, which was what always happened when she got angry. "The girl always has to do all the work—it starts with the dishes, then changing the diapers and making the dinners, then going out in the workforce, and now dating . . . someday we won't even need men at all. And then there goes the mess and there will be nothing for us to do."

I stood up, shaking my head. This was something I knew about. "A girl can't do *everything* in a dating relationship because then she wouldn't be a challenge. But the problem there is that if she is a challenge, the guys will give up on her anyway, so we're in a no-win situation."

"No." Harrison was trying to be patient with us, but it wasn't working and he began to pace the floor. "Let's address your first problem . . . the hook. You've got that, but he can wriggle out of it easily. It's what *keeps* the male hooked that's the important element for you to learn."

"Oh, I see," Ashley said. "You have to make him believe that he likes being strung up like a dead fish."

"Merciful heavens." Horrified, Emma was rooted to the spot, having no choice but to listen to more.

"Now you've got the point," Harrison said. "There are four main qualities that a guy will look for." We straightened eagerly. "And there's no reason to beat around the bush. The first, my dear sisters, is—sadly—looks."

Brooke groaned. "Of course."

"You've got a lot of work ahead of you," he said. I tried not to be insulted by his observation. "This will be your motto: 'I will always look my best.'"

Whoops. I tried not to think of all the times I had been caught in public without my face on.

"To quote an Apostle," he continued, "'even an old door could use a fresh layer of paint.'" I snorted. I wasn't sure if that was the exact quote, but it worked.

We glanced at Brooke out of the corners of our eyes. "Quit looking at me," she said. "I don't feel like wearing makeup, okay?"

"Then men won't feel like dating you," Harrison drawled. "You have to trick him into thinking you're a girl. That means you walk like a girl, talk like a girl, think like a girl. Got it?" Brooke made a face and he shook his finger at her. "By next district meeting," he said, "you will be the epitome of femininity. Gone are the days of being referred to as sweet spirits. You got that?" He straightened, looking just like a drill sergeant, and marched over to the honeypot note taped to our wall. He ripped it off. "Are you sweet spirits?" he shouted, waving the offending note in front of our face.

"No!" Ashley and I chorused. Brooke rolled her eyes.

"Good, that's the right attitude." Emma took a bite of a cookie, and Harrison turned on her. "Put the cookie down and back away. If the men want to go to SeaWorld, they'll go to San Diego or Orlando or San Antonio, not to C6."

She kept chewing.

"So you expect us to starve?" I asked.

"Until you seal the deal with your man, yes. A girl can't be out of shape. She has to be fast enough to catch her man. And sisters, exercise is not just lifting a credit card. It's going to the gym, which can actually give you more finding opportunities. But don't wear BYU issue clothing, that's bad, bad," he said to Brooke. She just glared back at him. "Remember, it isn't *chaste,* it's *chased.*" He spelled it out on the board. "Let's talk about spandex—less effective . . . no one can get away with it unless they're Barbie, and even then . . ."

Ashley raised her hand worriedly. "What if a certain girl has a hard time getting up the hill to campus?"

"Well . . . as long as she *looks* in shape, it's okay." Brooke opened her mouth angrily and he lifted his finger against her mouth, soundly shushing her. "Speaking of figure, Emma, how many sizes too big is that jumper?"

She dimpled and swallowed the cookie before answering. "Five . . . I lost weight on my mission."

"Less effective. Get something less baggy. You got it, you flaunt it."

Emma gasped.

"I got it and I don't flaunt it," Ashley said with a challenging glare.

Harrison sighed, running a hand through his already disheveled black hair. "Just make sure that your clothes aren't from an exclusive Amish catalog." He lifted an eyebrow at Emma. "It isn't, is it?" Emma shook her head. "Good. Any sister who wears a floral jumper to the next district meeting will get negative stats, do you understand? You will wear appropriate proselyting clothes. No more power suits, no more ugly skater shirts, no more army boots. Is that clear?" I tried to hide the dismay from my face, especially since he was looking straight at me. "I want your mincing hours higher next week," he said.

There was nothing like fulfilling a prophecy from Isaiah. I winced, getting a sudden image of us wearing cauls, mantles, wimples, crisping pins and all other sorts of doodads, which was pretty amazing since I had no idea what those really were. But I could imagine making a tinkling with my feet and mincing while I walked. "So you *do* want people to refer to us as Sister Trollop, then?" I asked.

"Definitely not," Harrison hissed. His pupils weren't getting it, and he looked so harried that I almost felt sorry for him. "You want to say toodle-loo to all your contacts, Samantha? Huh? Huh? We want to avoid that at all costs. This is BYU for heaven's sake!"

"I was joking," I said, trying not to break into a smile.

"Well, don't ever scare me like that again. From now on, you will be known as Sister Friendly . . . and that's the next quality on the list. Never talk bad about guys to other guys. They understandably get nervous when they leave the room or turn their back on you, and why shouldn't they? You're going to rip them apart. Don't be so snotty." He was looking directly at Ashley. "And never show your anger."

"What?" she said, laughing. "I'm a cheerful person."

"Try bipolar," Brooke said. Ashley scowled at her.

"Don't talk about how much money Daddy makes," Harrison said, "and don't be all girlfriendly in private but not in public . . . and don't squeal at a movie and say the main guy is hot in front of your contacts."

"So guys are insecure?" Ashley asked.

"In a way . . . except I would label that behavior as more annoying than anything else. It's like watching him drool over a voluptuous babe on *Babewatch*. Get the picture?"

"Yeah. So be friendly." I made a fake check in the air.

His eyes didn't leave mine. "But not too friendly."

"What's that supposed to mean?"

"I mean too clingy."

I knew where he was going with this. "Clingy girls get married too," I pointed out.

"Indeed? Look *what* they're married to." He made a sweeping motion at the announcements stuck to the fridge. "If the girl acts too desperate for a guy, he begins to wonder what's wrong with her. She can't be too forward. Wait, no, it depends on the girl . . ." He smiled a secretive smile, then continued, "But she definitely can't be a pushover."

I tried to play dumb. "What are you talking about?"

He wouldn't let me get away with it. "Let me give you some advice. When a guy asks you to make fliers, pretend you won't and then do it at the last second as an act of mercy."

"But I wanted to make the fliers."

"I see. Why don't you just shorten your name to two letters—E and Z?"

I gasped. "I hate y . . ." But I hesitated. He was right. Whenever I was in a possible relationship, I found myself getting too excited and doing the *Chris Farley*: I killed the sale every time. Had he witnessed this? ". . . oo . . . thank you," I finished.

"Do you ever wonder why the only guys who actively seek you out are your stalkers?" Harrison asked.

Oh, I knew this one. "Because they only like you if you don't like them," I said, "and once you like them back, they won't. It's twisted. I think I'm the same way." Wow—was that why I referred to stalkers as stalkers—because I didn't like someone who liked me? I was starting to put this together. Did *everyone* have a self-esteem problem, then? I had been fighting these tendencies in myself forever. I just didn't realize everyone else was too.

"Men can sense when you want them around and when you don't."

"Not all of them," I said.

Harrison shrugged. "It basically comes down to this—guys like a challenge."

So, it was all about following *the rules,* was it? It was so not me, but if you followed them, you'd get the guy—one who had no idea who you were or what he was getting into. I sighed, feeling myself grow depressed. Why would I want a guy who didn't want me? Perhaps this was going to take a complete personality overhaul. "What if I'm so inaccessible I put myself in hibernation for a year?"

"You won't if you know the tricks," he said. "And the trick is pretending not to be interested, and then turning it around at just the right time."

"But how do you turn it around?" Even little Emma was intrigued.

"You give the guy the look," Ashley said, getting so excited that she used Harrison as her dummy. "Touch him briefly on the arm, tickle him, then pull away. Leave him wanting more. You're a challenge—but not too much of one."

"The look?" he asked scathingly. "A man can't read your mind. The look is completely useless. Proximity is more effective. Stare at his lips, make comments about them, lean . . . take matters into your own hands—pun intended—and seize the opportune moment."

"No, *he* seizes the opportune moment," Ashley said. "As a girl, you can't overdo it."

Harrison watched her with sardonic eyes. "So why don't you follow your own advice?"

She shrugged. "It's convenient to chase guys off. It saves me the trouble of breaking up with them."

He turned to me. "Is that what you do?"

"Uh, well, kinda . . ." How did he know I sabotaged myself? "I just tell the guy how old I am right away, or I act too crass and obnoxious, or even too girly, for that matter . . . I actually act too much like myself and it usually does the trick."

"But you end up being too honest with a guy whether you like him or not," Brooke pointed out. "You're honest 'cause you don't care or you're honest inadvertently 'cause you're nervous. It doesn't make a difference."

I took a deep breath. "Well, yeah . . . but it takes a little longer for him to get disgusted with me if he doesn't see the real me at fir . . ."

Brooke nodded. "So, it's a complete accident that anyone gets together . . . unless you find someone who actually likes you for you."

"No." Harrison intervened before he lost his following altogether. "You want a man with intelligence."

We gasped. "Excuse me?" Ashley said, rising to her feet. "Any intelligent man would give his Palm Pilot for a girl like me, thank you very little."

Harrison wisely ignored her. "That means he'll be looking for a girl with some intelligence too . . . or at least one who acts like she has it. Men look for *qualities*, not personalities." He ignored Ashley's harsh glare.

"A girl who acts intelligent when she's not?" Brooke mulled that over. "That would be very difficult for a stupid girl to pull off, wouldn't you think?"

"Girls do it all the time," Harrison said.

"What about the ones who are intelligent and act stupid?" Brooke asked.

Harrison pointed brutally at me. "Don't do that."

I tried to defend myself. "But it's funny."

"Well, I suppose a girl can be so beautiful that her stupidity can be overlooked, but then she's only good for a month or so." His words did the trick and I vowed to act more intelligent, though I knew my sense of humor would probably get in the way again. I was a lost cause to the genius line.

Emma's hands landed on her hips. "What a thing to say."

Brooke snorted. "You've got it totally wrong, Harrison. It's a turnoff if the girl's smarter than you."

"Not possible," he said.

I laughed at that one.

"But since you're not going for me . . ." He rested his chin on his hand, looking at Brooke. "In your case, you're going to have to dumb it down a little. What's that book you have there?"

She lifted her hand from the textbook lying on the table. "Math 97."

"Hide it," he snapped. "They'll think you have a mind."

Ashley picked it up. "It's mine. And in case you didn't realize, I'm like a creative-advertising major, so I don't have to learn such boring subjects anyway. I'll make my millions doing what I love to do while you mathematicians slave away at a desk all day."

"Congratulations," he said. "You won a prize for the most words used to convey the least amount of meaning."

"Excuse me, Mr. Eloquent . . . like anything you've said has made any sense so far, you're like . . . ridiculous."

"That's another thing to work on—your vernacular. If there was a finite use allowed for the word *like* in the universe, you would have expired it long ago."

"Yeah? Well, you're solely responsible for using up all the oxygen produced by the Amazon rain forest . . . today . . . just this last half hour even."

He shook his finger at her. "Nuh-uh, men like sassy women, not *witches*." He ignored her enraged face. "Now, let's proceed to our numbers." He turned to our whiteboard. "Visits?"

"What do you count as visits?" Brooke asked. She was starting to participate, albeit begrudgingly.

"The guy comes without your making an appointment with him, and for no particular reason except to visit."

"Well, guys come over here all the time," Emma said. "There's no way to know."

"How about in the last week?"

"No way," I said. "We can't come up with that number. It's infinite. Ask our neighbors. They seem to be keeping track of how many times the wreath goes off."

"Okay, fine," he said. He wrote zero. "What are your stats for phone calls?" Again we shrugged. "Alright, I'm not talking about calls with a purpose. I'm talking about calls for the sole purpose of BRTing."

"Ashley got a few," Emma said. "She's good at building relationships of trust."

"Yeah, but not with the investigator I'm working on now," she said, "unless you count walkie-talkie conversations."

"No, they're very noncommittal. How about ACT: animate, close in, and touch?" We shook our heads. "Hugs?"

"No."

"Holding hands?"

"Like we're going to be holding hands when we haven't even ACTed yet," Ashley said.

"Hey." I raised my hand. "I got an elbow squeeze."

"Ah, good, that's a golden contact." He put down one tally on the board. "How about CKs?" he asked. At our blank look, he elaborated. "*Courtesy Kisses.* You can't tell me that you've left a date without the investigator giving you a CK?" We drew back. I for one was glad that the CK wasn't normal for my end-of-the-date ritual. It was already awkward enough. "Hmm," he said, "well, kissing has a lot to do with your breath, you know, so keep it fresh. Now how about your PDAs?"

"We just said we didn't CK—that means no public displays of affection," I pointed out.

"NCMO?"

We gasped in shock. "Erase that," Brooke said, "or we're not playing your little game anymore."

"What? Oh, fine, forget make-out sessions, committal or no. Regular kissing then, and I'm guessing no." He didn't even glance back to see our shaking heads. "How about gifts? Did he spend *any* money on you at all? None?"

"Oh," Ashley said. "My contact left a plate of old mashed potatoes from Thanksgiving on our doorstep . . . uh, a week ago. It was pretty funny. He left a note . . ."

"That counts as negative gifts." He wrote a negative one under Ashley's "gifts" box. "Love letters?"

"Marcus wrote that Samantha was a snothead with the mini-letters on the refrigerator," Brooke said, now thoroughly enjoying herself.

"Wow, it seems these relationships will go far." We tried to ignore his sarcasm. "Flowers? No?" We were shaking our heads so much we were getting dizzy. "Engagements?" he asked. "You're pathetic. These stats are worse than a freshman's grade in American Heritage. Do you live vicariously through TV or something? I hate to break it to you, but guys do not like antisocials. Spend more time out of your books." We laughed, which he didn't appreciate. "Let's learn about a little principle called *resurrection,* 'CAUSE YOU'RE ALL DEAD!"

"But, but, but . . ." Emma was distraught and we couldn't blame her. We were looking like total losers on the board. "We can't get good stats unless we get a date first."

"What about your infinite number of visitors?"

"We just hang out all the time."

"Then as your district leader, I will issue the challenge of turning the constant barrage of visitors into real first dates . . . not just safety dates." I guiltily thought of all the hanging out I had been doing lately with guys who were "just friends." It always gave us something to do on the weekends and there was absolutely no pressure involved, but they were also dead-end dates and would take me nowhere.

"Easier said than done," Ashley said. "We have to somehow manipulate the guy to challenge *us* to a first date first. We can't just ask him out."

"That is why you must learn how to prep the investigator." He began writing new stats on the board. "You need to make dinner appointments, cookie visits—you've already converted your apartment into a visitors' center, which is a relief. It will suit your purposes because you must keep in daily contact with your man. We all know the relationship doesn't end on the first date unless *you* end it. You know nothing about each other at this point, except mutual attraction, and there's no way for either of you to make any sort of decision about your future through just a couple hours of mutual activity where you're probably too stressed out to make any sort of a good impression anyway. That's why you need to advance your investigators through the dating pool, past the second date, the third, the fourth, the fifth, and sixth. That's the only way to reach your engagement goals."

We were completely stricken dumb at this. It made sense on the board, but would it work?

"Determination, malevolence, audacity, and throw what you have left of your scruples away. Yes, you will be rejected, but not every time. And, as we know, you need only one engagement."

Ashley's hand went up.

"Any more might raise ethical issues and a few eyebrows," he said.

Ashley's hand went down.

"Always keep your goals in mind," he continued. "Make each discussion quality, issue a challenge on every date, and follow up on those commitments."

"What kind of commitments?" Brooke asked.

"Small ones at first, like taking out the trash, giving you rides, walking you home, fixing your car . . . make the commitments bigger and bigger until he's ready to make the biggest commitment of all."

"What if we aren't sure he's ready for engagement?" Emma asked. "Should we discuss the relationship?"

Harrison slapped his forehead, acting like his favorite pupil had just stabbed him in the back. "Okay, all of you, put your right hand up and repeat after me. Right now!" We obeyed in a confused daze. "CTR, don't DTR," he said.

"CTR, don't DTR," we repeated in confusion.

"Good. Always *choose the right,* never DTR. It only clues him in on your intentions. It doesn't stand for *Defining the Relationship,* alright? It stands for *Destroying the Relationship.* Keep him as confused about the relationship as you are . . . even a little insecure—not enough to scare him away, mind you. Oh, and watch out especially for DWRs—Define *What* Relationship? Those are completely embarrassing and needless. You got me? There must be a relationship first before you can have any discussions. Now, let's set our goals for this semester."

"You don't expect us to do anything now." Ashley said. "We have less than a month left."

"Then let's get to work, sister. We're planning our time effectively. Don't waste your time dating losers when you should be out there building relationships of trust with real Mr. Possibilities. So far, we only have elbow squeezing from Derek, but we must take it to the next level. He should be advancing through these dating pools at a more rapid pace." He turned from the board, glancing at me. "How many dates have you gone on with him?" he asked.

"Uh . . . not any."

Harrison froze.

"He's my home teacher," I said by way of apology.

"Then you've been double dating at least once a month for the last four months. Next time he asks for special needs, you abuse the system. Ask him to put more passion in your life. It won't hurt him. It will just give him an opportunity for more blessings." He saw only blank expressions. "Shall we role-play?" he asked.

We pulled back as one. "No." It was the most unified answer from our apartment in a long time.

"Let's see who's on the safewalk list." Harrison walked to the list that Derek had given us. We had taped it next to the telephone. "Convenient," he said. "Safewalk is the perfect proselyting opportunity, when armed with effective teaching techniques, that is."

"But I'm never up on campus when it's dark," Ashley said. "It depresses me."

"Get over it. Are there any dances coming up?"

"No," we chorused, though what a dance had to do with furthering ourselves in the game, we had no idea. Guys never danced. It was just us in a lame circle, hopping around like sick birds. But could you imagine what would happen if guys actually danced? The possibilities were endless.

Harrison looked to be deep in thought. "You have already secured one proselyting opportunity, the Ultimate Frisbee game. Perhaps when you throw the Frisbee, you'll throw a few kisses too."

My eyes brightened. That would be a perfect line for the fliers.

"Now, let's set the date, shall we? According to my calculations, we can set your engagement goals for Christmas break."

Brooke guffawed. "That's less than a month away."

"Then get out there and flirt, sisters. Make your district leader proud." Emma looked so shocked that I thought she would faint. At least the rest of us knew Harrison was joking.

"Oh, and we're supposed to get engaged in a couple weeks with finals coming up?" Brooke muttered. "You *are* a miracle worker."

Ashley jumped off the table. "What makes you think I want to get married already?" she asked, stretching lazily. "I'm not ready to be a grandmother yet."

Emma couldn't take it anymore. "Harrison," she said. "I can't believe that you would suggest such a thing." I had never seen her react like that before, but her face was flushed and she acted as if Harrison had just murdered someone. "That is the unhealthiest, most unwise suggestion I have ever heard come from your lips. Marriage is a sacred institution. You can't take such a decision so lightly. I thought better of you."

I didn't take his suggestion lightly, but there was definitely a method to his madness. I had just one nagging doubt on my mind. "I couldn't move any man through the dating pool this whole semester," I said. "What makes you think I can do it in less than a month?"

"Have a little faith, sister. All you need to do is resolve concerns. When your contact isn't ready to make a commitment, find out why. If he was just flirting for fun, step up the game and be more fun than anyone else. If your interest far exceeds his own, make yourself more interesting. And if he perchance gets a girlfriend . . ." He hesitated, gauging Emma's reaction closely. "That's when you start poaching other people's areas."

"You can't do that," Emma said. She was definitely getting frazzled, and I hid a smirk. Harrison had just ensured a place in her memory. There would be no chance of forgetting his name now, but I wasn't so sure his strategy was a good one, since now it would go down in infamy.

"Oh, yes you can poach," Ashley said, smiling suddenly. She had her sights set on Marcus . . . if just for a little while. He would be quite the feather in her cap, and she could easily tug the cap on and off when convenient, especially since Miriam wanted him. And though Marcus wouldn't be so easily taken in, she was free to try.

"Shall we sing a *him* before we close? H-I-M?" Harrison spelled it out on the board and we groaned. "Just a suggestion," he said. I stared at his face, his calm expression, his debonair grin. Even though this would prove to be a most hilarious adventure, how could I trust him?

"Why are you doing this?" I asked.

"Isn't it obvious?" he said. And I guess it was, but after his crazy antics, I wasn't sure if Emma would want him.

CHAPTER 16

"If you can't join them, beat them."
—Samantha Skyler (Wed., Dec. 8th)

The library was a great finding opportunity. Guys were everywhere here . . . the only problem was that they were all as busy as I
was . . . well, as I was supposed to be. I had a ten-page essay to write
for my American Heritage final, but instead I found myself here. I
stepped through a row of books, trying to match the call number on
my card. I leaned over, almost tipping myself upside down to read the
ensuing numbers. It was making me dizzy. Just before I gave up and
was ready to reveal my incompetence to a librarian, I found it at last:
Artwork for the Less Artistically Minded.

I threw my backpack down on a desk and sat down, pulling off
my gloves so I could flip through the pages. The first one was a
picture of a ship with tall masts and billowing sails reaching for a
perfect blue sky. I studied the decks, imagining myself on one of
them . . . I'd most likely be swabbing it.

I turned the page, seeing a girl with a pale face, a dirty scarf
wrapped around her head, and pearls in her ears. Pearls in her ears? I
pulled the book closer to my face. Where did a peasant get a hold of
those? Interesting. I was supposed to be writing papers, but this was
so much better. You see, nobody knows, but I'm a research junky. I
love paintings, though I can't really draw; I love information and
words and facts, though I have to write them down because I'll never
remember them; and this has nothing to do with my personality. I'm
supposed to be reckless and wild and care for nothing . . . and stupid.
I grimaced. I hated how everyone assumed that I was stupid just

because I was a little carefree, and forgetful, and maybe even a little crazy, too, but no one took into account that I was something more. No one seemed to even care, so why did I try so hard to break free from that mold? Probably because I never could.

EFY speakers, they're the bane of my existence. They told us we could do anything we wanted to do, but it took me a decade to realize how wrong they were. Talk about traumatic experiences. I rested my head in my chin and pulled out my rejection letter from my backpack, glancing at it, trying to revise my strategy somehow. But how many of these was I destined to get? I'm not normally a bitter person or a jealous one. In fact, I'm usually really happy, but not lately, not when everything was going wrong. It was times like these when I wished God's time coincided with mine. I was nearing graduation with an English major, but what was I supposed to do with that? Especially since I wasn't publishing. I thought that writing would be my saving grace, but it just wasn't. I was so idealistic sometimes . . . *Wait, what am I talking about?* I am *all* the time.

I ran my fingers through the blond tendrils of my hair, pulling out some split ends while I thought of my options. They were slim, but most of them involved sitting behind a desk for the rest of my life or teaching a roomful of bratty kids. And though the bratty kids might be amusing for a while, that was no way to make money. I wanted to get my parents out of debt, pay everyone back for everything they did for me—and speaking of debt, get myself out of it while I was at it. I had spent hours and hours writing just to make a better life for myself, but instead I felt like a rat on a treadmill, constantly running after that carrot (yeah, don't worry about it; I mix up every analogy). But the fact was I'd done so much running trying to prove everyone wrong that I was tired, and mostly of myself.

Why couldn't life just be simple? I remembered when I was young and the sewage overflowed in our backyard. My dad and my brothers had to dig a huge hole in the ground so they could fix it. It took them forever to fill it back up, so it became my new obstacle course. I would jump over it again and again and dream that I was flying, but now I just didn't appreciate the simple pleasures anymore.

Of course, I didn't have a sewage pit to jump over either, well, not any literal ones anyway. Everything challenging just ended up being frustrating . . . except I couldn't get that "district meeting" out of my head. Now that was one challenge that could actually end up being fun. Dash everything . . . just like a pit, I suppose. I could also fall into it and drown in the sewage.

But what if it worked and I actually snared a man? Of course, I wasn't sure how much I wanted to date someone right now. You see, I'd done everything on my own, so it was kind of hard imagining myself with someone else. But then again, it would be nice to find someone I liked. Perhaps it could turn into love—but to actually be loved back? Even with *my* imagination, it was hard to picture. And what if I actually got married? Me? And to a nice guy, even? Now that would take a miracle.

Did I believe in those? Angels administering, sure, but did I believe in a little miracle for me? It seemed so easy for others to be in good, healthy relationships, but for me nothing was easy. Yeah, I knew that nothing was impossible for God, but sometimes it seemed impossible for me. I guess my lack of faith in myself hampered my faith in God because I always felt like I had to prove myself worthy of not being alone. Of course, there were times when I would rather be alone . . . especially times like this.

I saw Griffin across the room and made a mental note to change the floor I studied on. *Too late.* We made eye contact and I slammed my book shut. It wouldn't do for him to be asking questions, but he did anyway. "Aren't you skipping English 415R?" he asked, leaning over my shoulder. Uh-oh, he knew my schedule.

He dumped his books next to mine, pulling up his green cords to sit next to me. I shot to my feet. "You're so right," I said. "I've got to get to class."

"You only have five minutes left."

I gathered up my books. "You're right again. Well, I'm . . ." My footsteps didn't slow and he matched my stride.

"Where are you going?" he asked.

"To go meet a guy . . . I like." It was too harsh, even for me. And I felt like I was completely overreacting, but the truth is that guys always scare me a little bit—especially ones like Griffin. Griffin was the epitome of my nightmares, actually—being stuck with someone I couldn't stand . . . forever. I had to escape.

"I'll walk with you," he said.

"Okay, but I'm meeting . . . some guy at the LRC to type up some fliers."

"No problem. I need to go there too."

"Oh, I just hope that guy's still there," I said lamely. "I kinda lost track of time. If not, I'll probably still type the fliers when I get there." He just stared blankly at me, and I quickly turned away from him, seeing that no one I knew was miraculously waiting for me at the entrance. "Oh, he's not here." I laughed nervously. "I'm always standing guys up. I'm so mean. Who knows who I'll turn on next? Oh well . . . uh, thanks, Griffin, for walking me to the computer lab."

"Hey," he said. "I've got my eyes on you."

That got my attention and I hesitated. "What?"

"You're a honeypot note stalker. How bad do you want to keep that a secret?"

I grimaced. "I don't know. Well, see ya later."

He stood at the LRC entrance and watched me select a computer. I was just glad that there wasn't a line or Griffin would've insisted on waiting with me. He probably would've heckled me further about Scott's honeypot note while he was at it. Ah, how the world spins; the persecutor so easily becomes the persecuted. When would I ever learn?

I sat down and purposely turned my attention away from Griffin, quickly typing in my password to log in. The longer I kept my eyes on him, the longer it would take him to go away; a watched pot never boils, you know. I might as well work on the fliers instead and then do my English papers, maybe another query letter for one of my books, too. I inserted my disk and pulled out the file and glanced at the query letter. It was short, concise, to the point—and, I thought, attention grabbing. Apparently the publishers didn't think so though . . . I was beginning to wonder if Griffin was still staring through the entrance when I felt a hand squeeze my shoulder. Instinctively, I hit him back and heard a grunt. That wasn't Griffin! I turned, seeing Marcus.

"Hey." He smiled slightly. "I thought that we were supposed to be friends. Friends don't hit."

He said it so sincerely that I stared at him in confusion, seeing him rub the sleeve of his black shirt. Why wasn't he getting it? He knew what I thought of the "Let's still be friends," line. I didn't care if it made me seem shallow or immature. It was true—no one could still be friends after dating, especially the two of us. "I'm sorry," I said. "I thought you were someone else."

"Who?"

I shrugged, suddenly remembering that my query letter was on my screen for anyone to see. I quickly minimized it. It wouldn't do for him to know that I still had ambitions.

"What are you writing?" he asked.

"I'm writing a discourse on the differences between SpongeBob and Arthur and the people who love them . . ."

"Oh." He didn't seem to care. "What are you doing tonight?" I couldn't believe my ears. Was he asking me out after he had decided to call whatever we had off?

"My roommates and I are bored, and we wanted to do something," he said.

Nope. He was only calling on me when he was bored, and this sounded like another hanging-out party. Well, I wasn't going to do it again—Judas Iscariotting myself by allowing him back into my life. And that's when I decided if you can't join them, beat them. I'd play Harrison's little game and show Marcus just how fine I was without him.

"Oh," I said, "well, *we're* not bored. We have cleaning checks tomorrow morning, so we're going to be cleaning tonight. It's awful. We have to wipe out the gray gunk from the windows, and you know that stuff's really dead skin. We have to vacuum under the seat cushions, too, and I've found the most disgusting things imaginable down there—old, rotting food and other slimy things. Hey, come to think of it . . ." This would be a perfect way to make him reject me instead of the other way around, and then psychologically he wouldn't want to ask me out again and play with my emotions. "Would you want to help us out?" I asked.

"No."

"Well, if you change your mind, tell me." *Not likely.*

He nodded and found a computer next to mine and checked his e-mail, his chair squeaking under his weight. He read it, chuckling to himself. It was probably from Miriam, and I sighed. In the last half hour I had flung two guys out to dry . . . And I didn't even feel bad. Was my conscience seared? I sincerely hoped not. One thing was for certain, my district leader would have my hide if he knew I was throwing out perfectly good man flesh, but what he didn't know wouldn't hurt him, right? It was time to concentrate on nicer, tamer prospects.

CHAPTER 17

"You really need to work on more effective door approaches."
—Ashley Fox (Fri., Dec. 10th)

Snow fluttered over my head and I shivered in the cool morning air. My jean jacket was too flimsy for this kind of weather, but everything I owned that was warm was too flamboyant to wear out in public. I clamped my gloves and the Ultimate Frisbee and basketball fliers under my armpit. They were complete with Harrison's quote: "A chance to throw a Frisbee and a few kisses, too." It was brilliant.

"I've almost got it." Ashley wrestled with the tape that we had stolen from Emma's dresser. We were sure it was foreign tape from her mission in Guatemala because it wouldn't break off properly. Ashley finally ripped off a piece and attached it to a flier. Her long scarf had worked itself free from her neck and she pulled the scarlet thing from the snow, brushing it off. "Okay, it's all yours," she said.

I almost had the thing on Derek's door before he opened it, and I barely stopped myself from taping it onto his forehead. I handed it to him instead.

"Hey, what's this?" he asked. It was obvious that he was heading for school. He had on his blue coat and a backpack packed with smart-guy books. His red hair was combed missionary style.

"Oh, well, it's for the Ultimate Frisbee game tomorrow," I said.

"And this one's for the basketball game next Tuesday," Ashley said, stealing it from me to hand to him.

He turned the basketball flier over in his hand. "These are neat. How long did it take you to make these?"

I shifted, stomping the snow off my chunky black shoes. "Not long."

"Wow, so is this is our ward activity—basketball?" He glanced at me. "Are you on the activities committee still?"

My eyes widened. "No, but Logan asked me to make these . . . ur, Ashley did really and . . ."

"Why?"

"Because . . . uh . . ." Before I knew it I found myself blabbing everything to him. "Well, if I admit I wanted to make the fliers, I won't look very cool, so I can't do that."

"No, you can't." He laughed and patted my back. *More golden contact,* Harrison would be proud. Ashley just smiled next to me, taping bits of tape to her pinstriped pants to use for the next doors. "You're cool, no matter what you do," he said, "so don't worry about it."

"Really?"

"Yeah." He walked us to Marcus's door and took my elbow. "Catch you later," he said with a wink. I watched him leave, and I put my hand on my hip. Derek had a way of making me feel pretty good about myself. I liked that. Absentmindedly, I rested my hand on Marcus's doorknob, and it turned before I realized that I was breaking and entering.

I stuck my head through the doorway. "Hello?" It was silent inside. "Hello? Is anyone home?" The apartment was empty . . . and unlocked. I turned to Ashley in shock. "What were they thinking?" I asked.

In Provo, you don't necessarily have to worry about thieves, just girls—evil ones like us—and it was quite uncommon to find someone's apartment unlocked like this. We stepped brazenly into the living room, looking for something exciting to hold hostage . . . something nice, but what? Their walls were empty, except . . . my eyes locked on the inspirational cross-stitch on the wall.

It's better to fail than to never have tried at all.

And before I knew it, I had detached it from its safe perch. "It's beautiful," Ashley said, kneeling on the shabby tweed couch with me. She took the fliers from me while I inspected it.

"I know."

We heard a door slam in one of the back rooms and we stilled. Someone was there! Serious tactical error . . . unless they hadn't heard us. So far there were no running footsteps down the hall. Even so, our clothes were dark enough to camouflage us in the shadows of the dim living room. If we could get the cross-stitch out while someone was actually there, it would make this coup even more triumphant. I brought my finger to my lips, and Ashley's smile broadened. We slid silently off the couch and tiptoed across the orange shag carpet. The front door was already open, letting in the frigid cold air, and we closed it behind us before we burst into giggles.

"C'mon," I said. She followed me up the stairs to Harrison's apartment, and we listened to the guitar music blaring from Scott's. *My little musician.* Ashley handed me two fliers complete with mutilated tape, and I kissed them and slammed them on Scott's door as we passed.

"Hey." His door opened and I threw the cross-stitch behind my back, faking a bright smile. How in the heck did Scott hear that? Or did he see us coming through his window? I really hoped he didn't see me kissing his fliers. That would be beyond embarrassing; I'd look like a stalker.

"Hey," I said. "How's it going?"

"Good."

Well, he looked good. His brown eyes were unusually dark and brooding this morning. He wore loose-fitting jeans and a brown long-john shirt over a white T, the sleeves shoved to his elbows as usual.

I was very conscious of the cross-stitch and desperately tried to distract him from my suspicious behavior. "Did you find the girl?" I asked. He looked blank, forcing me to translate what I was saying. "You know," I said, "the honeypot-note girl. *It's me?*"

I flinched at my words. It sounded like I was confessing.

"No," he said, "but I'm still looking."

"Well, good luck," Ashley said, waving the fliers in front of him. "We just have to deliver the rest of these."

"Yeah," I said, "be sure to come tomorrow and play, huh?"

Scott turned and ripped the fliers off his door. "Sure." He retreated back into his apartment, and we listened to his guitar resume its dirty sound. He was brilliant, and I wondered briefly if he would ever lower himself to play with our band. It could be more golden time spent with him.

Ashley glanced at me and sighed. "You really need to work on more effective door approaches."

"I know, I know," I said.

We knocked on Harrison's door. Thankfully, *he* opened it and not his deadhead football-player roommates. His T-shirt and BYU shorts were wrinkled. It was obvious that he just woke up, the slugabed. "Give me your computer," I said, marching boldly to his desk. Ashley followed. I flipped the cross-stitch over and slid it out of its frame.

"What are you doing?" Harrison asked in his throaty accent. He took a bite out of a half-eaten bagel. It was slathered in strawberry cream cheese and looked absolutely delicious, but there was no time for that.

Ashley crossed her arms over her scrawny stomach, leaning toward him. "Isn't it obvious what we're doing? We've got Marcus's cross-stitch."

I sat down, pulling the keyboard closer to me and made a new document. *It's better to never try than to fail so pathetically . . . like you have, you loser.* I typed it in quickly, changing the font and coloring to match the stolen cross-stitch across my lap. I wiped my hands across the side of my dark jeans in anticipation. "Do you have paper in your printer?"

"Yeah."

I printed it out and stood up, putting the new *inspirational* thought into the cross-stitch frame. Now the trick would be getting it back on the wall with whoever that was still in their apartment. But I had full confidence in my abilities. If we could get the cross-stitch out, we could get the fake one back in, even if we had to pull a moonlight and fake a visit.

Harrison rubbed at his tired eyes. "This is ludicrous," he said. "*Stealing* isn't part of your stats."

Ashley laughed behind me. "We're not stealing, we're BRTing."

"No, that's building relationships of trust. This is the opposite."

"It's all part of our strategy," she said.

"No, it's not." I shook my head vigorously. "Marcus left the door open, so of course we're going to do something. What does he expect?"

"It's Logan's apartment, too," Ashley pointed out.

"And it's Marcus's cross-stitch," I said. "I hope he feels this in his gut."

"Interesting." Harrison settled himself on the arm of his couch. "You're making quite a bit of effort for him. He's going to think you like him." His voice sounded a little too dry for my taste.

"That's a chance I'm willing to take," I said, not meeting his piercing gaze.

CHAPTER 18

"Saturday is a special day . . . it's a day to play Ultimate Frisbee."
—Brooke Hansen (Sat., Dec. 11th)

The snow pelted the window like feathers from a pillow fight, but it didn't matter if it was snowing. It didn't matter if we caught our death of cold. It didn't matter if we slipped on the snow and died. It was Saturday and we would play Ultimate Frisbee.

"Hold still," Ashley told Brooke. I pulled away from the window, witnessing Brooke's complete makeover. Her red hair looked especially vibrant against her pale face, and she knelt in front of Ashley like she was awaiting her execution. Ashley dabbed cover-up onto her cheeks.

"No," I said. "Keep the freckles, they're cute. Any guy would go crazy for them."

"They haven't yet," Brooke muttered.

"That's because you didn't have eyelashes before," Ashley said, using the cover-up to disguise the dark circles under Brooke's eyes. Didn't that girl ever sleep?

"Girls!" Emma shouted from the next room. "Was that a very nice thing to say?"

"Nope," I said, "just honest. Face it. Every girl looks scary without makeup on."

"True." Ashley tugged her black shirt back over the waistband of her sweats. It was the first time that I had seen her do anything with her long, black hair. It was caught up in a French twist—compliments of Emma. "What do you think I do?" she said.

Brooke made a face. "Oh, so you're just going to deceive the guys and be something you're not?"

I shrugged. "What they don't know won't hurt them."

Emma walked into the living room. The usual ponytail was gone and her chestnut hair swung over her shoulders, giving her a soft, elegant look. She wore my straight-legged jogging pants, which were a little too long, but they showed Emma had a figure. I swallowed the pangs of jealousy. "Hey, no poaching in my area, huh?"

"Of course not." She stopped short, seeing the new Brooke. She looked like a beauty queen in sweats. "Sweet merciful heavens, Brooke. Wow."

"I feel ridiculous."

"Who cares?" Ashley said. "You look good."

"I should be studying." Brooke sat down heavily on our ugly couch. "Today's a reading day."

"Yeah," Ashley said. "That's why we can goof off and procrastinate our repentance."

Brooke began nervously twisting her red hair between her fingers. "Saturday is a special day," she sang sarcastically. "It's a day to play Ultimate Frisbee."

Speaking of which, I turned to the clock. The hands had been moving incredibly slowly, but at least now we would be fashionably late . . . just as planned. "To the Loner," I said.

I opened the front door, feeling the cold blast of air rush over my bare skin, and I ran my fingers over the goose bumps that immediately popped up over my arms. Harrison had told us not to wear sweatshirts, and glancing back at the others, I realized that I was the only one stupid enough to obey. And worse, my blond curls were going to string once they got wet, and then they'd go fro in the car. Dash diddly.

"Go, go, go!" I shouted, trying to cover my hair. Our jogging shoes punched through the powdery snow as we raced for the Loner. It was something we'd have to get used to, since we'd be running in this stuff for the next two hours. Ashley pulled open the rusty door in the front of the Loner and dove inside. Of course I never kept the Loner locked. No one would want that piece of trash unless they wanted to use it for a demolition derby. The car cost me more to decorate than to buy—two hundred bucks was all I paid for it. The sellers should've paid me to take it off their hands.

Ashley landed on the leopard-print covered seats, pulling out the snow scraper and a dirty plastic cup in one practiced motion. She handed them off to Brooke and Emma. They went at the windows, scraping off the snow like a well-trained team of race-car mechanics.

I slipped around the side, the ties on my loose-fitting black sweats swinging as I jumped into the driver's side. Now was the moment of truth. I inserted the key into the ignition and prayed for a miracle as I turned it. The engine made a dying noise. No problem, it was just warming up. I started it again and it putt-putted. We listened closely for the noise to pick up into a dull roar, and it didn't disappoint us. It exploded into a healthy growl, and we shouted out for joy. Don't pretend you've never heard that sound before. It's the usual shout of joy you hear when a car starts in a college town, and we echoed it as generations of students have done before us.

Brooke pulled into the car, kicking the trash away from her feet. "This is horrible," she said. She threw the dirty cup on the front seat.

"I know," I said, not particularly caring. I accepted the snow scraper over my shoulder from Emma, throwing it at Ashley's feet.

"Don't you ever clean this thing?"

"Hey, why don't you start lecturing Ashley?" I said. "She's the one that never takes her trash in."

Ashley shrugged, pulling on her seat belt. "Anyone for some tunes?"

She flipped on the old-school radio and we listened to the fuzz from the radio station, but we were well trained. Ashley simply placed her finger over the metal circle on the radio, making herself into a human antenna, and the fuzz cleared into full-blown music. Brooke was silent, anticipating the game. Emma just smiled a little to herself, playing with the fog on the windows.

I knocked the fur dice from my vision and we were on our way, driving through the grid streets of Provo.

CHAPTER 19

"Love's a game—trash-talking required."
—Harrison Bean (Sat., Nov. 11th)

"Where's Ashley?" Harrison asked. His black hair was slicked against his forehead, and he pulled at his black sweatshirt. It was covered in mud and I envied the extra layer.

"She's over there." I pointed to the sidelines where Ashley hopped from one foot to the other. "She doesn't like games."

"Yes, she does."

"Not these ones."

"Then she's missing the point . . . incidental contact." Harrison pointed brutally at her. "Ashley, get over here. Action's only for those that play."

"Keep your voice down," I said, seeing Scott move out from the Ultimate Frisbee players.

He was only wearing a dirty white T-shirt and long basketball shorts. The musician must be chock full of warm blood to subsist in this weather with so little covering. He ran across the field, pulling next to me, elbowing me playfully in the side. "How did you get Brooke to come?"

Brooke scowled, breaking the perfect line of her brow. "They didn't tell me you'd be here—that's how."

Emma fixed a determined smile on her face, listening to Brooke murmur her indiscernible complaints. I shifted, feeling my sneakers slip over the snow, and stifled a groan. The odds of getting hurt were almost nonexistent the first time I had played, but since this was my fifth game, I was due for an injury. It just made me wish that I had better insurance.

"I'm freezing, Harrison," I muttered into my hands, blowing at them and rubbing them together intermittently.

His bored gaze met mine, but before he could answer, Marcus sprinted over to our little group, slapping his blond hair from his face. "Hey, why didn't you wear something warmer?" he asked me.

"I don't know," I said, casting Harrison a dirty look. "I thought I'd get hot playing."

"Here, I'm burning up." Marcus peeled off his sweaty BYU sweatshirt and threw it at me. "Take this until you get warm."

"Thanks," I murmured. It was filthy and smelly, but I was desperate.

I pulled it over my head just in time to see Harrison mouthing something to me. "See, it worked," he said. I turned steadfastly from him, trying to ignore him under Marcus's watchful gaze.

"Where's Miriam?" I asked, looking for an elegant blond. Somehow it seemed silly for her to be roughhousing with all these boys. It would be an interesting sight, but it was denied me. I didn't see her anywhere.

"She's studying for finals," he said. That's what I should have been doing, except I really didn't feel guilty. Marcus suddenly smirked. "I got your message last night, by the way."

"Huh?" I pretended innocence.

Judging from the twist of his lips, he knew better. "I'm just wondering how you got into our apartment."

"Hey, Marcus," Ashley interrupted us, and I quickly backed away from them. She had made a subtle beeline to his side, and even now she had him by the arm. "Are we on your team?"

"Uh, let me see. Logan, get over here," he shouted at him from across the field.

Logan broke reluctantly from the rest of the guys, ordering them to put a hold on the game. "What do we have here?" he said, wiping the sweat from his chiseled cheek. Maybe it was me, but he didn't seem very happy to see us.

"Four new girls," Marcus said. "We've got to divide them up."

"Are you any good?" Logan asked me. I shook my head.

"Yeah, she's good," Marcus said in a voice that brooked no argument.

"Are you just saying that so she won't be on your team?" Logan glared. He looked way too serious, and I shrugged. I was an Ultimate Frisbee loser, but it could be worse. My roommates had never played before and were still under the misconception that it was easy to throw a Frisbee.

"Nope," Marcus said, "but you waited too long, she's on my team. Pick your next player."

Derek came up behind Logan, smiling at us. His kind eyes rested on the runt of our litter, and his next words didn't surprise me. "We'll take Emma on our team."

Logan's eyes widened. "Hey, we didn't decide that together."

"Big deal," Scott said, also joining us. "We'll take Brooke too." He met her eyes. "Let's see what you've got, Mom."

"Good, we get Ashley," Marcus said, winking at her. She stretched like a lazy cat and smiled, not really caring whose team she played on. She would just stay near Marcus's side. "Harrison, show her the ropes," he said.

Harrison smirked, his knowing eyes on her. "I already did that."

"Fine," Logan said. "That means two girls for each side. They can guard each other."

Well, that was no fun. Harrison sidled next to me. "Your contacts are all on the other team . . . besides one."

"I know, too bad."

"No, this is a perfect opportunity. You can guard them. Don't let them out of your clutches."

"You know, Harrison, sometimes you worry me."

"Don't give him another thought," Marcus said, coming up behind us. He had the Frisbee in his hand. "I'm keeping my eye on you . . . and I like what I see." He laughed at my grimace as we made a line with our other team members on the field. Ashley poised, waiting for the throw. "Ultimate!" Marcus shouted. He chucked the Frisbee through the air in one practiced motion, and the other team rushed forward to catch it on the other side of the field.

Logan caught it with a snap and Brooke rushed past him. "Throw it to me," she shouted. For a girl who complained the whole way here, she was surprisingly competitive. Logan looked everywhere but at her. At last he turned to Scott, seeing he was finally open. He threw it and Scott caught it easily. Brooke sprinted toward the goal line and swiveled on her heel. "Over here," she shouted again.

"No, Scott," Logan ordered. "Throw it over here." In a flash, I was on him, trying to block him from Scott's view, but Logan still egged him, trying to make him throw it past me. He obviously had no faith in my defense skills, probably for good reason too.

Scott ignored Logan and threw the Frisbee directly at Brooke and she ran for it, flipping her glorious mane of hair behind her as she caught it midair. She landed on the ground with the Frisbee still in hand. Despite myself, I was impressed.

Logan took advantage of my momentary break of concentration and sprinted past me. I chased after him as he ran for the goal line. "Get him," Harrison called after me. He was busy covering Scott.

"Easier said than done," I said. The guy was too fast for me . . . in more ways than one. I glanced over at Marcus. He was guarding Derek, or at least trying to, and Ashley . . . she was looking at her nails.

"Over here, over here!" Logan shouted. I jumped to his side and he made a sound of irritation when I tried to guard him. Brooke didn't even glance his direction, throwing the Frisbee to Derek instead. It stayed in his hand a mere millisecond before he threw it across the field to Emma. She had been standing across the goal line for some time now.

"What are you doing?" Logan shouted. "She'll never get that." But he was wrong. It seemed Emma was a natural. Harrison deserted Scott, trying to divert the sudden catastrophe just as the mischievous little imp reached out with tiny hands and snatched the Frisbee out of nowhere. It was a beautiful play. And the other team shouted out triumphantly.

I was completely out of breath, and I turned to Logan with a smile. "It's hard keeping up with you."

"Then stay out of my way," he said. I frowned, hearing the angry note behind his words.

"Actually," I said, "I'm only getting started."

He glared at me and made his way to the other side of the field, leaving me to close my dropped jaw. Dash everything. What was wrong with him? He was normally so cheerful, but it seemed the game had a monstrous effect on him. Was Logan a poor sport?

"Okay," Marcus said, interrupting my dark thoughts about his roommate. "When they throw the Frisbee, I want whoever catches it to throw to me, and then all of you run for the goal line and wait. I'll throw a hammer."

Ah, Marcus's famous hammer throws. One minute the Frisbee was on one side of the field, the next it was on the other, which was great if you were on his team, but if not . . . it was like he was running circles around you. I could see only one problem with his strategy, and I raised my hand. "Uh, I can't catch those."

"Then act as a distraction," he said. "If you all run for the goal, they won't know who to cover."

"Okay." I could handle being a distraction. I did it all the time, so why not in a game?

"Ashley," Marcus said. "Look a little alive next play, huh?"

She rolled her eyes. "Whatever."

We straightened, waiting for the other team to throw the Frisbee. "Ultimate." Derek threw it and the Frisbee cut through the air.

I ran down the field, amazed at how out of breath I got just running up and down in a field of snow. I didn't even have to play to get a workout. I broke through the other team's line, passing Logan, then Scott, then Brooke, then Derek, and finally Emma. No one was bothering to stop me from sprinting to the goal line and I didn't blame them. No one was going to throw it to me either. I just enjoyed the invigorating jog until I reached the goal and swiveled, seeing none of my teammates standing next to me. Well, that was strange. They had all been stopped farther down the field. Marcus had the Frisbee in hand and he pointed at me.

"What?" I shrieked. "No, not to me. I'm just the distraction!" But he didn't listen, and I groaned as he chucked it across the field. This was the horrible thing about the game, looking like a complete idiot. I scrambled around the goal line, trying to judge exactly where the Frisbee would fall, not like it would do me any good. I squinted upward. Dash diddly. The Frisbee was white, wasn't it? It blended with the snow perfectly. It sailed straight for me and I made a pitiful noise as I reached for it, only to have it smack my hand and rebound into the air. Brooke was behind me, and she made a dive for it the same time I did.

Her hands wrapped around the Frisbee just as I got a hold of it, and we fell to the ground in a heap. I tugged it from her grip. Wait, was I supposed to do that? Derek ran up to us. "Who got it first?"

Uh . . . I kind of stole it from her . . . after we both had it, except I wasn't sure whose hand was on it first. "I don't know," I said. "We both caught it, but . . ."

"Samantha didn't have it." Logan grabbed the Frisbee from me. "Brooke caught it first. It's ours."

Derek turned to me, the perfect mediator. "Is that true?"

"I don't know."

"See? It's ours," Logan said. He looked around, but he didn't see any guys besides Derek, who was busy offering me his hand, so Logan threw the Frisbee to Brooke as a last resort. She caught it, and they left me behind while they brought it down the field until Emma made a score. Logan whooped loudly, skipping madly over the goal line. My eyes narrowed.

Marcus ran across the field to my side. "That's alright," he said. Harrison just snorted, but Marcus ignored him determinedly. "Now, next time, uh, Ashley . . . if they happen to steal the Frisbee from us, you need to take Brooke." Ashley blew the long tendrils of hair that had escaped from her French twist out of her face. "Samantha," Marcus said, "you stay on Logan."

How had he known that I wanted my revenge? "No problem," I said.

"I've got Emma," he said. "Harrison, take Scott."

"Can we switch?" Harrison asked.

"Sure."

We barely had enough time to break our huddle before they threw the Frisbee at us. I took a deep breath and ran down the field, once again passing effortlessly through the line. I just hoped that this time I was *really* the distraction, but as I reached the goal line, I twisted in time to see Marcus throw another hammer at me . . . again! I groaned. What was this insane belief he had in me?

I steadied myself, but this time Logan was onto us. He rushed straight for me just as the Frisbee sliced toward my knees, and I had to make a split decision to catch the Frisbee or live. I noticed the snotty look on Logan's face and made my decision. There was no way he was going to get away with being a complete jerk. My knees landed in the snow just as the Frisbee slammed into my stomach. Logan plowed into me at the same time, and I stuck my elbow out to at least give him something in the gut to remember me by. He returned the favor by cracking my back for me and we skidded backwards, landing face-first in the snow. I rolled away and before I knew it, I was on my feet, holding the Frisbee high. "Ha, Logan! In your face. Ha!"

"Good catch, Samantha." Harrison was already by my side and he gave me a high five, knocking the snow off me. "You know," he said, his voice suddenly getting lower, "if one cougar scores, we all score." I shrugged. "That was some clever incidental contact, by the way," he said.

"That wasn't incidental contact . . . he steamrolled me—the jerk!" I glanced down at my nails. They were *all* broken from the Frisbee. Man, Marcus had an arm on him. And speaking of arms, mine were turning black and blue. Ugh. I'd have to wear long sleeves for a week or someone would mistake me for a battered woman. How embarrassing.

Logan was already heading toward his teammates. He passed Ashley. "Hey, hot stuff," he said. She ignored him and I was glad.

"Oops," Harrison said. "You'd better act fast. You're losing him."

"Correction," I said. "I lost him."

Harrison smiled slowly. "Remember, love's a game—trash-talking required. Besides," he parroted my words back to me, "he flirts with everybody."

I clenched my teeth. "Then he lost *me*," I said. I was tired of selling myself short for a mess of pottage, and that's exactly what this boy was—a mess.

"Well, you're difficult," he said, but he was laughing. "Okay, so Flirt lost out, but what about Friendly? I see he took advantage of the situation earlier."

Derek *had* been very kind to help me up. "He's . . ." I trailed off, seeing Scott pass us on his way to the other side of the field.

Scott had one eyebrow raised. "I love playing on opposite teams from you," he said, "especially when I'm guarding you. It means I get to keep you close."

I blushed bright scarlet and couldn't think of anything to say, so I gave a choked laugh. "'Fraid is getting bolder," Harrison murmured once he was barely out of earshot—*barely*—Harrison liked to push it.

Marcus was smiling when we reached him on the other side. "That was amazing cherry picking," he said. I nodded, still clutching tightly to the Frisbee in my hand. "Why don't you go ahead and start us out?"

I grimaced, remembering just how smooth my throws were. "Okay." I glanced at the other team, seeing they were barely assembled. Good. They weren't paying attention. "Ultimate!" I shouted and threw it to the side . . . way off to the side. Oops. We charged down the field, and I headed for Logan just as he snatched it from the ground. He was getting ready to throw it to Scott when I hopped up and blocked his throw. Miraculous. It scraped past my fingertips and landed dully in the snow.

Logan looked at me like I'd just given him a cheap shot, and I smiled when Ashley picked it up. His face cleared. "Oh, she'll be easy to cover," he said, smiling slightly.

Ashley's eyes narrowed. "What?" Well, she wouldn't be now. I dodged past Brooke and ran for our goal, since I was now the designated cherry picker. Harrison raced next to me to the goal, dividing the other team so they didn't know who to go for. We watched as Marcus and Ashley passed it down the field.

"So, what about Friendly?" Harrison asked once we were standing on the end zone. My gaze went to Derek, seeing he was acting the perfect gentleman, which was probably why it was so easy for Ashley to get past him.

"The same," I said flippantly. "Friendly, but I probably shouldn't take it personally. I don't think he's interested."

"That's because he doesn't know *you're* interested," Harrison said. "It's all about strategy, you know." We were silent for a moment, watching the teams race for us. "Cookies will seal the deal."

I snorted. "Not *my* cookies."

"Then get someone else to make them, sweetheart."

"Okay, district leader. Then what's the secret to 'Fraid's heart?" I watched Scott guard Marcus ahead of us. They were getting closer.

"Safewalk," he said as if unveiling the master plan. It appeared he had been deliberating on this for some time. "He's a slave to duty. Shall we say more aptly, a slave to women. Romeo cannot allow a BYU coed to walk home unattended."

Scott jumped in front of me and I jumped back, giving a yelp of surprise. Please say he didn't just hear that. I couldn't wonder for very long though, especially when I saw the Frisbee fly right at me . . . I didn't even have time to reach for it before it smacked me in the mouth. I flew back, making a snow angel in the snow.

"Samantha, are you okay?"

Whose hand was that? I didn't reach for it because I really didn't want to be standing up right now. Marcus knelt beside me in the snow. "You okay?" he asked.

"Marcus, is that you?"

He laughed, though a bit nervously, and helped me sit up.

"I knew it," I said. "I was due for an injury. You can't just keep playing without expecting something like this to happen. Am I going to live?"

"Oh, c'mon." His fingers were light on my lips. "It's just a split lip." He brought his hand back and it was covered in blood. He winced and I recoiled at the sight of it. "What? It's yours," he said. "Look, at you, your first war wound." He tried to wipe his fingers off on me and I shrieked.

"You're sick," I said. "I'm wounded! You can't mess with a wounded person."

"You're right. What was I thinking? You're wearing my sweatshirt. I don't want to get blood all over it."

"Would you hurry up?" Logan said behind us. "Samantha, give us the Frisbee. It's our turn."

I scowled up at him. Logan was socially retarded, wasn't he? "I think it's time to change your dating pool," Ashley said, leaning over us.

"Dating pool?" Marcus asked, "What's that supposed to mean?" Ashley quickly pulled back when she realized her faux pas, leaving me to clean up her mess.

Emma knelt beside us. She had no qualms about revealing everything. "Oh, it's just something that Harrison is doing with us. We had a big district meeting a few days ago . . . like the mission."

"Hey, let's get some ice on that lip," Derek said above us. "Maybe we can use this snow."

"Emma." I gave her a warning look. "Don't you dare say anything else."

"Do you want me to give you a ride home?" Scott asked, inter-rupting my threats.

I flinched, wondering just how much my finding pool had heard about our evil plans. "No, I brought the Loner."

"Well, I'll drive it home for you," Derek said. "I have to get some homework done anyway." He offered me his hand and Scott offered me his other and between the two of them, I was efficiently dragged to my feet. Before I knew it, Derek was leading me to my car, leaving Marcus behind in the snow.

"I like the wheels," Derek said, bringing my attention back to him.

"Yeah," I said. "My little brother spray-painted the hubcaps gold." I opened the door and a Coke bottle came rolling out the side, landing dully in the snow. I met his shocked eyes. "Uh, I don't drink that," I said, quickly stuffing it back in with the rest of the trash. "It takes the rust off the battery. It gets . . . rusty all the time . . . and then the radio won't work."

I chanced a glance behind me, seeing Marcus smirk, though at the same time, he looked completely dumbfounded, probably because I had suddenly become such a hot commodity. Well, too bad for him. I just wished that my roommates hadn't blabbed about the district meeting.

He would cause trouble if he knew too much.

CHAPTER 20

"Doing a little 'boy' scouting?"
—Marcus Gray (Sat., Dec. 11th)

"What happened here?" I stepped around the cinderblocks in our living room, balancing the laundry basket on my hip and my notebooks under my arm. It was time to get some late night studying and laundry done before Sunday came. Cinder blocks were stacked high on both sides of the front door. I stopped short, seeing them blocking the front door too. "Hey."

"Yeah," Brooke said. "We got cinder-blocked inside." She hauled another cinderblock away from the door. Her red hair swished against her back as she walked.

Ashley came running from the back, wearing her white pajama bottoms and black shirt. "Why didn't the wreath go off?" she asked.

Emma pulled Mr. Wreath from the door, inspecting it. The back of her hair stuck straight up. It looked like she had just woken up, though it was only eleven. "They turned him off," she said finally.

I glared at it. Lousy guard dog—or whatever it was—thingy. I just couldn't believe that I had missed the commotion the cinderblocks would have brought to our doorstep, but I guess that's what happens when you listen to your music too loud. Brooke and Emma had pulled out most of the cinderblocks in front of the door; now they were only stacked two high. I stepped over them with my laundry basket, walking out into the snowy outdoors.

"Uh, what are you doing?" Ashley asked. "You haven't put in your mincing hours, have you? Remember, always look your best."

Brooke snorted at that. My hair was caught up in a claw and I wore what I always did when I had nothing else clean, my baggy jogging pants, freaky black T-shirt, and clunky army boots for the snow. It wasn't a good combination, but my fat lip from Ultimate Frisbee pulsated with pain, and I really didn't care about anything else.

"You'll get negative stats for that," Brooke said.

Emma shrugged. "Oh, no one will see her in the laundry room. It's eleven o'clock at night."

"Well, if Harrison sees you, he'll read you a lecture," Ashley warned me.

I kept marching to the laundry room. What were the odds that someone would see me anyway? I dragged my dirty clothes down three flights of windy stairs and opened the door to the expansive laundry room, breathing in the fine scent of laundry detergent. I cringed when I saw Marcus sitting on a dryer, wearing his red Cardinals cap. Why was he doing his laundry on a late Saturday night? By the looks of things, he hadn't reached the last scrap of his clean clothes. He looked halfway decent in a green T-shirt and relaxed jeans . . . I, on the other hand, didn't.

He glanced up from his organic chemistry book, and it was too late for me to beat a hasty retreat. Oh, dear. Well, I guess Marcus didn't count as a guy anyway, which was good since he always saw me to my disadvantage. I squared my shoulders, passing him as I headed to the washers. "Hey, Marcus."

"Hey." His forehead wrinkled. "What does your shirt say?"

My hand flew up to the "Boy Scout" label imprinted on the front of my black T-shirt. I had completely forgotten about that. "Nothing."

"Was that your brother's shirt?"

"No."

"Were you in Scouts?"

I noticed a deep dimple at the corner of his mouth. He was laughing at me. "Doing a little 'boy' scouting?" he asked.

"Go away," I said, flinging open a washing machine. I dumped my clothes into it and searched my coat pocket for some change. My pink planner came flying out instead . . . and I mean *flying out*, fluttering to the ground at Marcus's feet. I choked back a gasp. I was cursed, wasn't I? Before I could stop him, he had jumped off the washer and was picking it up.

"What's this?" he asked, turning it over.

"Uh, nothing interesting." I snatched it away from him. We thought these were so hilarious when Harrison first presented them to us a few days ago, but now it had my stats in it. "Harrison's just having fun with us . . ."

"Ah, Harrison the philosopher. Does this have something to do with the famous district meeting at C6?"

I stiffened. My roommates were a bunch of turncoats, but I still couldn't believe he had figured it out. Then again, he was very intelligent. That's what I had liked about him, but now he was on the opposing side . . . and I had to keep it that way. "Something like that," I said.

"Really? What do you do at these district meetings—complain about men? Tell me, what is it that you don't like about guys?"

I rolled my eyes. "Oh, we never complain about guys. It's not their fault that they're so oblivious." I dumped my detergent in the washer.

"I'm not oblivious," he said. "I read the signs girls give."

"Yeah, like what?"

"Like if she touches her nose, followed by her ear, then she's madly in love with me."

"Brilliant."

He shrugged. "Well, we cracked the code in *our* district meeting at the beginning of the semester." He crossed his arms across his chest, looking mischievous. "Our meeting didn't amount to much of anything either."

I stiffened at the insinuation. "Yeah, what were your goals?"

"Well, they were actually a little lofty. We had a goal to go on a group date, but it never worked out. We'll have to start lower now."

"Oh, good." I matched his sarcasm with some of my own. "We've started low too. It's a new program—engaged in under a month." I slammed the washing machine shut and set it on . . . What did I put in there—colors or whites? I couldn't look now that Marcus's eyes were on me. My hand left the dial and I searched my pockets for quarters instead.

"Engaged in under a month?" Marcus leaned across my washer. "You can't be serious? Do you know how many divorces we already have in the Church? That is the most idiotic thing I've ever heard you come up with."

Dash diddly. Marcus really needed to get a sense of humor. Of course we weren't serious about the engaged-in-under-a-month plan, but I decided to play with him anyway. His sudden protectiveness surprised me. "So marriage is idiotic now, is it?" I asked.

He shook his head. "If you make it that way," he said. "And you actually trust Harrison of all people to help you pull off this scheme?"

"Why not?" I asked, a smile playing on my lips. "He's taken Marriage Prep three times."

Marcus was trying to act nonchalant now, but he had given too much away. I wished he'd let down his guard more often, I loved it. "You know what they say?" he said finally. "Those who can't reach it, teach it."

My fists landed on my hips. "Oh, he can reach it."

"Oh really, is he married?" he asked.

"Are you?" I asked.

"No."

"Then you have nothing to say about it." My quarters had completely disappeared, and it just figured since I was growing desperate to get out of there.

"Yeah, but I know a lot of married people . . . and I recognize the signs." Marcus set the dial of my washer on colors and inserted some quarters into the coin slot.

"Thank you," I said, trying hard to keep my mad voice up. "Now, what are you talking about?"

"He's not having these district meetings so he can get you and your roommates hitched."

"Why do you say that?"

"Because no guy cares about the dating average of females unless he's interested in one them . . . and I think he's interested in you."

I smiled. I knew better. "Don't judge. The only reason he's doing this is because it amuses him." I suddenly snickered. (Did I just say that? I was spending way too much time with Harrison.)

"Really?" he asked. "Are you *just friends* then? Oh no, probably not or you wouldn't want to spend time with him." He was laughing.

This was not funny! He moved closer. "So, who's on your Christmas wish list this year?" I didn't answer, but that didn't impede him at all. "Is my roommate one of your investigators?"

"Nope, he just X-ed himself." I smirked, but it hurt my fat lip and I grimaced, gingerly touching it. I glanced up to see him staring at me.

"I can't figure you out," he said suddenly.

I shrugged, pretending I didn't care. "That's because you can't fit anyone into a cookie cutter. Don't feel bad. I can't figure you out, either." I picked up my laundry basket and set it on my hip. I had to get out of there. Things were getting dangerous. He was starting to open up to me. That had never happened before.

Marcus tugged on his Cardinals cap and I bit my lip, recognizing his nervous habit. I had gotten to him. That hadn't happened in a while. "Don't do something you'll regret," he said finally.

"Of course not." I pushed on the door, feeling the cold winter wind rush into the laundry room. I shivered.

"Wait." Marcus stopped me from going out. "The fat lip is the perfect touch. You'll definitely catch more guys with it."

My breath quickened and I quickly nodded. That was my cue to leave.

CHAPTER 21

"You just showed me how to lose a guy in an hour."
—Samantha Skyler (Mon., Dec. 13th)

"Derek, there are daughters of Zion at the door."

I laughed outright. No one had ever called me that, not outside of church, anyway. Derek's roommate just gave me a confused look and my laughter abruptly cut off. He was serious, wasn't he?

"Derek?" he called again.

Derek came out from the kitchen, and his eyes brightened when he caught sight of Emma and me. It wasn't even Sunday, but he was still dressed up in a collared polo tucked into blue trousers. It made me wonder if he ever left anything untucked, and though I wished he did, I forgave him the fashion faux pas when he smiled at me. He dried his roughened hands on a pristine white towel. He turned down the classical music on his stereo. "Hey, girls, I was just doing the dishes. Won't you sit down?"

"Thanks," I said.

"How are you enjoying your reading day? Are you getting a lot of studying done?"

Emma nodded and I tried not to look too guilty as she sat down on the soft, brown couch, rearranging her jean skirt while I held out my offering of cookies. This was a monumental moment. This came from a girl who never cooked, who was forced to wash dishes while the football players cooked the éclairs in high school cooking class. I burned everything. Of course, I had taken it all in good stride and became the best little dishwasher there ever was, and before these roommates came along I ate Cocoa Puffs for breakfast, lunch, and dinner. If Derek had any idea what I went through to bring these cookies to him . . . well, it might scare him away. "We thought we'd make you some cookies," I said. "Something to get your mind off finals."

"Oh, chocolate chip," he said. "My favorite." He sniffed them. "They smell so good. Would you like some?" I shook my head, taking a seat next to Emma. He took a cookie from the plate and placed the rest near a pile of cookie plates on the end table. Wait. I did a double take. There was a whole pile of them—chocolate, sugar, pumpkin, ginger. Everyone and their dog had delivered cookies to Mr. Friendly. How did he keep from getting fat?

He bit into one of our cookies. "Very good," he said. I doubted that, but to his credit, his nose only wrinkled slightly. He lowered himself on the couch across from us and crossed his legs. I felt like I was having an interview. "So what can I do for you fine ladies today?" he asked.

"We were just delivering cookies and thought we'd come by to say hello," Emma said pleasantly. I was glad that *she* had said it. It would've sounded false coming from me.

The doorbell rang and I shuddered. Judging by the accumulation of cookies on the table, it was probably more girls. Derek answered it and he stepped back in genuine pleasure. "Marcus Gray—what brings you here?"

I groaned, having an idea. Marcus walked into the living room, grinning smugly at me. He made quite the contrast to Derek, wearing his favorite faded orange shirt and loose-fitting blue jeans. "I just saw your lovely visitors heading your direction," he said, "and thought I'd pay a call. Oh, look, cookies." He didn't sound surprised.

"Would you like some?"

"Who made them?" He grabbed two.

"I did," I muttered.

"Oh." He quickly put them back. "I probably shouldn't."

I glared. Marcus sat on the rocking chair in the impending silence that settled over us, a smirk on his face. He was probably laughing that I had actually donned an ironed shirt for the occasion. He picked up a CD cover from the end table. "Oh, Enya . . . is that what we're listening to?"

"No, this is Mozart," Derek said without a trace of snobbery.

Marcus nodded. "Hey, have you heard any of the songs that Samantha's written? She's a musician."

Derek turned to me. "Really? What a thing to keep from your home teacher. What instrument do you play?"

I shifted guiltily. "The guitar."

"Ashley plays the drums that we're always tripping over at FHE," Marcus said.

"And what do you play, Emma?" Derek asked her.

"Uh, Samantha is teaching me to play the bass guitar, and Brooke plays the cello . . ."

"Really?" Derek was intrigued. "What kind of music do you play together?"

"Uh," I hesitated. Would he agree with it? "I like all kinds of music."

"Celine Dion?"

I nodded stupidly. "She's alright . . . Yeah . . ."

"Yeah, what?" Marcus laughed. "She doesn't like Celine Dion. She likes alternative. I would say there's a definite Alanis Morrissette twist to her music."

"Oh," Derek said.

"Without the swearing," I said, giving Marcus a pointed look, but he just grinned.

"Oh, you don't swear, do you?" Marcus rocked back and forth on the rocking chair like a deranged monkey. He was clearly enjoying himself.

"No, she doesn't," Emma said in my defense. I was glad that she stood up for me because my word was beginning to mean nothing right now.

Derek brought his fingers up to his chin as if in deep thought. "Who's Alanis Morrissette?"

"Oh, just some bitter rock chick who makes bitter-rock-chick music about men . . . kind of like Samantha."

"I'm not bitter," I said. "I like guys very much, thank you."

"Yeah," Marcus was inspecting his nails, "but everything we do is stupid. Hey," he said before I could contradict him. "Do you remember that basketball game we went to?"

"I remember that we lost."

"Yeah, basketball . . . another stupid guy thing, remember? Dribbling the ball . . . doesn't that seem pretty mindless?" He mocked my words.

My fists clenched. "If I didn't want to be there, I wouldn't have gone."

Marcus tilted his head. "How did you get in anyway?"

"Uh . . ." I hesitated, looking from Emma's innocent face to Derek's. "I used Ashley's all-sport pass."

"Isn't that dishonest?" Marcus asked.

My eyes widened. "Uh, yeah." Marcus was ruining my dating pool . . . on purpose! It was so easy to point out what was wrong with me. It wasn't that I wasn't *trying* to be good, but it was a daily struggle. "But Ashley got the ticket for herself," I said. "She just couldn't go."

"Why not?" Derek asked. He was completely entranced with the story, right where Marcus wanted him.

"I don't know. She was watching a movie," I said. *Please don't ask what movie it was. Please don't ask.*

"That's right," Marcus said. *"The Matrix."* I stiffened, knowing exactly where he was going to go with this. "Can I borrow it?" he asked before I could even defend myself. He had no problem smearing his own reputation, as long as he took mine down with it. "That's your movie, isn't it?"

"Yeah," I said sweetly, "but we got it at Clean Flicks, so you're not going to get the swearing. Sorry." I cast him an angry look and it bounced off his supposedly oblivious one.

"But they don't really take out the violent scenes, right?"

"Yes, they do." My voice was getting high pitched. "There was a whole scene that went black, and we had no idea what was going on!"

"Well, aren't you noble . . ."

The phone rang and Derek's roommate answered it in the kitchen. "Derek," he called. "It's another daughter of Zion. She wants to talk to an elder of Israel."

"Excuse me for a minute while I get this."

Derek left to get the phone and I turned to Marcus, leaning over the cushions of the couch to get closer to him without Derek hearing me in the kitchen. "Hey, Iago," I whispered. "Knock it off."

"What are you talking about?"

"Oh, let me think. I listen to heavy rock, I hate guys, I'm dishonest, and I watch R-rated movies."

"You do?" he asked.

I snorted. "What are you going to do now, tell him I burn CDs? You big tattletale." Derek hung up the phone and walked into the living room. "You'd better stop it," I said under my breath.

"What are you going to do—kick me out?"

"No, I'll kick your can, spazoid!"

"What?" Derek asked.

Oh, dash diddly dog, he caught me faux swearing. I smiled at Derek as he sat across from sweet little Emma, good little Emma, who would never be caught saying anything like that.

"She's just joking," Marcus said. "She's so mischievous sometimes. You should see some of the pranks she's pulled on my apartment." I glared at him and he smiled sweetly at me.

"Oh." Derek's face clouded over. "You really should be careful with pranks. People's feelings get hurt." He glanced at Emma. "Do you do that?" he asked.

Emma held her hands primly in her lap, the perfect lady. "Oh, I just hear about them, but they sound quite exciting."

I stood up. "Oh, wow, look at the time. I have some studying to do. Thanks for having us over, Derek." He quickly stood up to see us out, grabbing my hand for a hearty handshake . . . no elbow squeeze. I'd get Marcus for this.

"You're right," Marcus said. "I'd better get going too." He stood up and followed us out the door. "Hey, Samantha, I wanted to borrow some CDs from you."

I slammed the door behind us before his next words could reach Derek, then I stormed through the parking lot. Poor Emma tried to keep up with me. Marcus easily matched my stride. "That wasn't funny!" I snapped. "You just showed me how to lose a guy in an hour. What was that all about?"

He snorted. "Look, you can't keep yourself hidden from him forever."

"What's that supposed to mean? You think that I'm some sort of swearing, spitting slob? A construction worker maybe?" Even as I said it, I felt guilty. I remembered Emma's words about noble construction workers and wanted to take it back.

"No, but you're not yourself around him either. How long were you planning on keeping the act up?"

I screeched to a halt, glaring at him. "For as long as it takes."

"Why?"

"The less he knows about me the better."

I shocked Marcus with that one and I stifled a smirk. I couldn't have gotten a better reaction. "Why?" he asked. "You don't think he'll like you?"

It was the general consensus at the district meeting that my personality was lacking. I looked back at Derek's apartment for open windows. Thank heavens it was winter. "Of course he wouldn't."

"Then why do you want him?"

"He might have *grown* to like me." I articulated slowly for his benefit. Marcus didn't seem happy with that answer, and even though it was partly a joke, I was half serious. I waited for Emma to catch up with me. "Just leave me alone," I said, "and I'll leave you alone."

CHAPTER 22

"You can't just hang up a love plant. It's dangerous."
—Samantha Skyler (Mon., Dec. 13th)

"Hey, district leader!" Emma shouted at Harrison as soon as we opened our door. He was sitting next to Ashley on our overstuffed green couch, and he turned to Emma with a shocked expression on his face. He shot to his feet, his brown Docs digging into what chunks were left of our orange carpet.

"Don't ever use that name in public . . . the door's open. If anyone finds out about this, the jig is up."

Ashley's gaze went to the door and she ran to shut it behind us. "Actually," she said, "Marcus already knows."

"*What?*" At least Harrison was just as disturbed about it as I was. It made me feel justified. "You girls couldn't keep quiet about this?" He studied Emma and Ashley's shamed faces. "What was I thinking? Of course you couldn't."

"Well," I said, peeling off my jean jacket, "it makes things a little more difficult, but I can get around him. We just need to change our strategy." I was determined that Marcus wouldn't win now. I wasn't sure how, but I would make him pay for what he did.

"Exactly what I've been thinking," Ashley said. She fidgeted with the V-neck on her scarlet shirt. The color accentuated her pale skin and brought out the red in her lips, making her look as innocent as Snow White—until she pointed above the door with a mischievous expression. "We should hang some mistletoe."

"Mistletoe?" My mouth dropped open at this outrageous suggestion. "That doesn't work in the LDS culture."

"Oh," Ashley said with a determined look on her face, "I'll make it work."

"It'll just work on the wrong people," I said, trying to make her see reason.

"Speaking of that, Samantha, you missed a visitor." Ashley pulled a long-stemmed rose from the table and danced it to me. "He left a note, too."

"What?"

A card dangled from the stem and she flipped it open. "'It's me,'" she read. Her eyes widened at the significance.

I snatched the rose, note and all, and stuffed in it the trash. *It's me?* What a blackmailer. Griffin would keep silent *for a price?* Well, perhaps I would let him see how costly that price would be.

"We'll just make sure there's no mistletoe when Griffin's around," Ashley said. "No problem."

I gulped. Well, at least something good happened from going to Derek's. I wondered how long Griffin had waited for me before he gave up. "No," I said. "You can't just hang up a love plant. It's dangerous."

"In the wrong hands," Harrison said, standing up. He crossed muscular arms across his dark blue sweater, looking very wicked. His gaze roved over the crammed room, quickly past the Christmas lights, even more quickly past our pathetic *Charlie Brown* tree. He grimaced.

"With all these garish decorations, no one would blink at another ostentatious adornment," he muttered. "It's time to step the stats up, sisters. We only have a week before Christmas break, and so far you can only mark off a cookie drop-off. We're wasting valuable time." Harrison glanced briefly at Emma. She was innocently hanging up her green marshmallow coat. "You should have all been engaged by now," he said. It was completely for her benefit.

Emma's back stiffened, but she chose to ignore the goad, brushing invisible pieces of lint from her coat instead. Harrison never used to tease her like this. He was really desperate for her attention, wasn't he?

"Ashley," Harrison ordered. "Check the safewalk schedule."

She ran to his bidding, having too much fun to care that I was glowering. This stat thing was humiliating. "Well, look who's doing safewalk," she said. "Scotty the hotty."

"No." I collapsed on the dingy couch. "One failed attempt is enough for today."

"Failed?" Emma asked. "Delivering cookies was a success."

"No," I said, shaking my head. "He hates me now. I might as well admit it." Emma's face fell at my proclamation, but it didn't make me feel any better. "Look," I said. "I just need to give my heart a rest, okay?"

"There will be no rest for the wicked," Harrison muttered. Emma nodded, setting her face in determination. She began picking up the newspapers on the floor, folding them under her armpit. "And then there's you," Harrison said, turning on her suddenly. "Your only hope for wedded bliss is to marry a man who wants a maid. I want you to start flaunting your feminine wiles, not your domestic skills. The men are already aware of the obvious."

I think it was Harrison's misguided effort to give Emma a break, but she was undeterred, tugging a newspaper away from his foot. "Are you hungry?" she asked him.

"I think I just lost my appetite."

"That's because he already finished off my dinner," Ashley informed Emma. The walkie-talkie beeped next to her and she gasped. "Oh it's Marcus. He's so cute."

If it was possible, my expression grew even darker. "That must not be the Marcus I know then."

"Hey." I listened to Marcus's gritty voice through the walkie-talkie. "Is Samantha there? I wanted to borrow some CDs from her."

"She's here. Come on over."

"No!" I shouted.

Ashley turned from the walkie-talkie. "Look, I have to make my stats too."

"I can't stay for long," Marcus said through the receiver. "I've got a date in an hour."

"You see," Ashley told me, "I have to work fast. Things are getting desperate."

I shot to my feet. "I'm gone." I grabbed my jean jacket only to have Harrison shake his head at me.

"Are you dotty? Don't take your coat to safewalk."

"Oh no, I'm not falling for that again." I threw my jean jacket over my flimsy pink shirt, not that it would do me any good in this sixteen-degree weather.

"Hey, you've got a mission," Harrison said, but it was obvious that I wasn't going to listen to him. "Well, at least don't bring the gloves," he said, "or you can't use the 'my hands are freezing' line. You need to get him to invite you to the basketball game on Tuesday."

I pulled on my black, glittery gloves. "Why can't *I* just invite *him*?"

"Have you forgotten everything? He's Mr. 'Fraid. He loves women, he loves romance, that's why he's terrified of it . . . commitment, affection, rejection, everything that he wants, but doesn't. You have to create the mood of a completely carefree, noncommittal date, then strike like a snake."

"That's too difficult," I said.

"Not really. Get him to take you the scenic route home."

"Wear this." Ashley brought her pink perfume out from the back and sprayed it onto me. She then proceeded to dab it on her slim neck. "It always works for me," she said.

"Really?" Harrison asked. "Is that what you wear? Very effective. If I wasn't such a hard man, it would've completely done me in."

She grinned mischievously, and that practically sealed the deal for me. If the perfume almost did *him* in, it would certainly affect a mere mortal. I grabbed it from Ashley and put on another spray for good measure. I opened the door and Harrison stopped me before I could completely slip away into the darkness.

"Have him take you down the stairs. That way it will look more believable when you trip and fall into his arms. Then he can get a good whiff of the seductive perfumes you applied so painfully."

"Yeah? What if I twist my ankle?"

"Perfect. Then he can carry you home, and you can begin your safewalk into eternity."

CHAPTER 23

"What are you, then—a shotgun or a sniper?"
—Marcus Gray (Mon., Dec. 13th)

There's something ironic about walking through the darkness just
so you can get safewalked home, but I didn't put too much thought
into it as I shoved through the glass-paned doors of the Harold B. Lee
Library. I stopped short, seeing Brooke waiting on the wooden
benches with calculus textbooks in hand. It actually wasn't a surprise
to see our apartment's study queen. She had pulled her red hair back
into a bun with a pencil, her reading glasses still perched on her nose.
Harrison would've gone ballistic if he saw her, but I dismissed her as
any kind of competition.

"Let me guess," Brooke said, glancing up at me, "the mission?"

"Of course. It's Scott's shift." I sat next to her on the bench, realizing that I had forgotten to take my backpack with me. "Hey, can I
borrow one of your books?" I asked. She shrugged and tried to give
me a calculus book, but I shook my head. "No, he'd never believe that
one," I said.

"How about *History of Utah?*" she said dryly.

"Sure." I took the white book and opened it to look at the
pictures.

She smirked. "Well, that should keep you occupied. There are
some nice panoramic views of Utah . . ."

"Yeah," I said, looking up at Scott. He emerged from the back of
the library, his book bag slung over one shoulder, a whistle on his lips.
He wore a white T-shirt and jeans with faded stripes, the hems ragged

from being constantly treaded on—my white knight and alternative musician all wrapped into one, set to take me home . . .

"Brooke, Samantha," he said. "I'm a lucky man."

Brooke just rolled her eyes, stuffing a black stocking cap over all that glorious red hair. She then proceeded to hide her figure under a baggy brown jacket. Since I only had my jean jacket, I actually kind of envied her . . . until Scott tried to give me that crazy handshake again. I just held tightly to his hand to put a stop to the ridiculous greeting until he broke away with a laugh, except . . . this time he lingered.

"Samantha, what are you wearing?" He sniffed and I tried to hide my smirk . . . until he sneezed, and sneezed again. He pulled away from me. "I think I'm allergic to you," he said with a wink, but his eyes were watering.

"Oh," I said, amazed at my own ability to keep calm, "it must be my lotion. Remind me never to wear it when I'm around you."

"It smells great." Scott sneezed again and I leaned my head back. I'd kill Harrison for this one. "Are we ready to go?" he asked. It was obvious that he was eager to get out into the fresh air, and I nodded vigorously, hoping that the perfume would fade once we got outside.

He opened the door for us and we filed past him, and I tried to keep my distance from allergy boy, which defeated the whole purpose of the mission. It would be inhumane to take a scenic route when the poor guy was in pain.

The snow fell over us as he pulled on his black stocking cap and black gloves. It was just another sad reminder of my pathetic lack of covering, and I tried to ignore it. We made our way past the Kimball Tower, the pendulum building, the fish tank, and the JSB until we reached the top of the hill, the city lights of Provo glittering below.

It was the perfect moment to make a move, except I had no idea what to do. *Hey, this way looks dark, let's take it together?* No way—not with Brooke here. I'd feel like an idiot. *My lips are parched, baby— maybe you could refresh them?* Impossible. Maybe animated conversation would be the best option. The city lights sparkled in the valley below us.

"This view reminds me of Paris," I said.

He turned to me like I had just proposed. "You've been to Paris!"

"Nooo . . . but I've seen a lot of pictures." I knew it was time to turn the attention away from me before I showed too much ignorance. "How about you—have you been there?"

"I have. It was amazing . . . I'm planning to take my wife there on my honeymoon someday."

Now he had Brooke's attention too. "Isn't that expensive?" she said.

"Yeah, but it's worth it. We'll honeymoon in Paris then tour Spain." We traveled down the campus hill, and I listened intently as he outlined the most romantic spots of Europe that he would take me to. "We'll travel by gondola in Venice, and I'll kick the gondolier out so I can sing a love song dedicated especially to her on those still waters."

"That's so romantic," I said.

"That's ridiculous," Brooke said.

I shivered against the cold, wishing I had more than my stupid jean jacket. The snowfall was getting heavier, and it stuck to my lashes and hair. My ears were freezing. Harrison really was sadistic, I decided.

I turned to Brooke. "Body warmth," I said through chattering teeth. As a general rule, Brooke had a bubble, but she always bent for me. Both of us had low cold tolerance. She squeezed closer to me, and Scott followed suit on the other side. My eyes widened in surprise.

"That can't possibly be your winter jacket," he told me.

I tried to defend myself. "It's not usually this cold." Though it usually was. I knew I had no leg of reason to stand on.

He squeezed my arm. "Why don't you take my coat?" he said. "I'm really hot." That was for sure, but I couldn't in good conscience take his coat.

"No, I'm fine." I broke into a smile, unable to resist the flirtation. Harrison would be proud. "Just stay close to me," I said.

"No problem."

We hurried past the trees powdered deep with snow, racing the four blocks home. I hesitated at the windy stairs that led to our apartment, getting ready to murmur our tearful farewells, except Scott followed Brooke up them. They were still on the stupid honeymoon debate.

"Traveling isn't a waste of time or money," Scott said. "It's a good experience, and it makes you realize that you're not so isolated in this world." I smiled, seeing he had every intention of coming up to our apartment. That was a good sign. He opened the door for us and I frowned, seeing Marcus already sitting on our overstuffed couch.

He glanced up from my CDs and I marched to his side, even while Brooke made her escape into the back rooms. "What are you doing here?" I hissed.

"Nice collection of CDs," Marcus said, watching Scott from the corner of his eye. I knew what he was thinking. My personal Benedict Arnold would try to ruin things again. "Ashley was just showing them to me."

She smiled a brilliant smile, tossing her dark hair, and I turned to her. "Ashley, you had better *watch* him." I wracked my brain for a way to get rid of either Scott or Marcus, or I'd lose my finding pool all in one mean swipe. At least Harrison was there to balance things out . . . of course, he might not be the best mediator either.

"Where did Brooke go?" Scott asked. He pulled off his black stocking cap, leaving his hair a disheveled mess, and I smiled. Man, this guy was cute. "Brooke?" He walked to the Chastity Line and called past it. "Where did you go?"

"What?" she shouted back. "I'm studying."

"Hey, some really hot guys just walked in."

"What do I care?" She came out, only wearing her pajama grubs, having miraculously shed her cute school clothes. I winced for her, but Brooke was looking straight at Scott. "Where are those cute guys?"

"Ouch," he muttered.

"Don't mind her." I sat down on the green paisley couch. "That sounds like an awesome vacation, Scott."

Scott smiled broadly at me. "You approve then?" He sat across from me, not quite chancing to sit *next* to me; once a 'fraid guy, always a 'fraid guy, I guess.

Brooke sat next to him, a stern look on her freckled face. "I don't. The reception's expensive enough."

Marcus's eyes flicked from me to Scott to Brooke and back to me again. He dimpled and I didn't appreciate the insinuation. Apparently Harrison did.

I quickly changed the subject. "Are you going to the basketball game tomorrow?" I asked Scott.

"I don't know," he said. "I've got a paper to write."

"But you're the coach," Brooke said indignantly.

"Well, it's not like I do *that* much. I just stand there and look pretty. I'm just a figurehead really."

"Oh . . . well," I said. "We were thinking of going."

Scott leaned against the hard cushions of our couch. "Well, maybe I'll have my paper done by then."

"If you do . . ." I hesitated, seeing Harrison's hard look. My words fumbled before I extended the invitation. Scott was supposed to do it, not me. But how in the heck could I finagle that out of him? "But . . . we weren't sure if we were going to go . . ."

"Why not?" Scott asked. "Didn't you make the fliers for it?"

"Yeah, but we have no one to go with." I couldn't believe that I had just said that. It sounded so lame.

"Aren't your roommates going?"

I was beginning to believe that he couldn't be this oblivious, which meant only one thing . . . he wasn't interested. "Maybe they . . . can't all make it," I said.

"Who's 'they'?"

"Brooke, maybe . . . or Emma. Maybe Ashley." They just glared at me. "But even if we all go," I said, "it would be cool to go with some fun guys."

Marcus ignored that, picking up the ward directory. Suddenly, he became really interested and I gasped, realizing the dangerous information it held. Harrison had written all over it. "What's this?" he asked. "A hit list?"

I stood up and tried to snatch it from him, but he held onto it firmly until we were engaged in a full-fledged tug-of-war. Ashley came between us, and with a calm look, jerked it from us both. "Don't leave such dangerous information lying around," she said, flipping it onto the table next to Scott.

"Huh?" Scott glanced up from Brooke, having begun again his reverie of honeymoon vacations. I sat next to him, pretending interest. Marcus sat next to me and I gave him a mean look, but apparently he was just as oblivious as everyone else in this room because it didn't affect him at all. I turned back to Scott, nodding as he began to outline the philosophies of travel and life in general and anything deep he could muster from his mind.

I nodded some more and Marcus leaned over me, his orange shirt brushing against my arm. "Blah, blah, blah," he whispered in my ear. "Admit it. You're not paying attention to anything he's saying." I froze. Marcus knew me too well. He must be dealt with. "Why don't you just grab him and kiss him?" he said in an undertone.

I gasped and quickly glanced at Scott. Thankfully he had moved. He was kneeling next to Zooga's turtle cage, despite Brooke's loud protests, and was picking her—or him—up.

He was far enough away not to overhear, but I didn't want to push it. "Stop it," I hissed.

"What? You haven't heard of the courtesy kiss?" Marcus asked, not matching my whisper anymore. He was being way too loud, and I knew that he was doing it on purpose. He was worse than my brothers, and I was about ready to kill him.

"Harrison mentioned it," I said, purposely not mentioning what *it* was. I hoped that would shut him up.

"Well," Marcus said in an overly bright voice. "The courtesy kiss is definitely a good way of knowing if he's interested in you."

I glared. He would love me to sabotage myself like that, wouldn't he? "Don't get desperate for me," I muttered.

"Courtesy kiss?" Scott asked. I groaned. How could he not have overheard? He was sitting right there! He rested the turtle on his knee. "I learned about that in my marriage prep class," he said.

I blushed, not wanting to know how much Scott had overheard. I quickly replayed our conversation in my mind to make sure it wasn't too incriminating. At least no names had been mentioned. "Uh, the courtesy kiss is ridiculous," I said hurriedly. "No one does that."

"No, *you* don't," Marcus said. "Samantha's really picky. She doesn't touch anyone."

I froze. What did he mean by that? "Just because I haven't," I said, "doesn't mean I won't."

"So, you're just waiting for the opportune moment then? When would that be?" He glanced meaningfully at Scott. "Somehow I doubt you're a slow mover."

I flinched and tried to cover it up. "Oh, don't even start, Marcus. If anyone gave you a courtesy kiss, you'd run away so fast—"

"Well, at least the girl would find out pretty fast whether I liked her or not."

"So you'd make the girl do all the work?"

"The guy can't do everything. How much do you think we can take?"

"We work harder than you do."

"Really?" Marcus leaned back on the couch, and I had to follow his lead just to keep an eye on him. "What are you, then—a shotgun or a sniper? Well?"

What was he talking about? I gritted my teeth, but I had to ask. "What's a shotgun?"

"If you're a shotgun, you know what you want. You go for it point blank. There are drawbacks to being a shotgun, though. If you miss—and that happens often—you scare off big prey. Of course, there's less of a chance your target will get away if you hold to your guns."

"What's a sniper then?" Scott asked, completely enthralled by Marcus's theory.

"A sniper sneaks up on the victim and pretends they're just friends." I tried not to fidget next to Marcus as he began describing my strategy to what he thought was my victim. "Then the sniper hides under the brush, and once the prey finally becomes secure that there is no danger, BOOM!" Scott jumped. "They've got you," Marcus said in a low, dramatic voice. He turned to me and smiled. "So, which one are you, Samantha?"

Scott watched me closely for an answer. "Neither," I said.

"So you *do* make guys do all the work." Marcus looked very pleased with himself. Too bad he wasn't going into law. He would've made a good lawyer, because no matter what I said, I'd look bad. "So tell me . . . how many guys have you rejected just this last semester?"

Just Griffin really . . . after that one duty date. But admitting it would be death in Scott's eyes. He was already scared enough of rejection as it was. "Dash . . ." I said.

"Diddly," Marcus said for me.

"Dog," I finished belatedly. He knew me way too well and my mouth fell open at his maddening smile. "Like I would ever tell you that," I said softly.

Harrison quickly saved me. I never thought I'd be grateful to him, but he had a job to do. I just wished he had done it sooner. "Samantha doesn't kiss and tell," he said, meeting Marcus's eyes with a challenging look.

"No, she just doesn't kiss," Marcus said. He couldn't resist a joke, which made him dangerous . . . just as dangerous as me.

"You sound a little bitter about it," Harrison said. "Maybe we can change your luck. There's a basketball game tomorrow, Marcus. Why don't you ask her to go?"

Both Ashley and I gave him outraged looks. He was ruining it for the both of us, and just as I was considering firing the English lad as our DL, the phone rang and we let out a collective sigh of relief.

Ashley jumped up, answering it. "Travel abroad, which broad would you like to study?" She handed it to me and before I could answer it, she shouted, "Samantha's boyfriend!"

I tried to ignore that, especially since it turned out to be Griffin on the line . . . besides that, Scott and Marcus were suddenly watching me closely. "Hello? Griffin?" Marcus winked at me and I turned quickly away from him before I did something stupid, like tackle him.

"Hey, Samantha, would you like to go to dinner with me tomorrow?" Griffin asked.

"Oh, well, I can't tomorrow. I'm going to the basketball game. It's the last one of the semester . . ." I cut off, looking at Scott. The guy was going to think that Marcus was right. I was a rejecting, heart-breaking machine.

"Then let's go together," Griffin suggested.

"Uh, yeah, yeah," I said, "we're getting a *big* group together. Maybe we'll see you there."

"It's a date."

I flinched. "Uh, I don't know if it's a . . ." I stared at his room-mate. Scott watched me as if expecting me to shaft his roommate in one mean sweep. "Sure, it's a date," I said, trying to keep my voice cheerful.

Even Marcus winced.

"Good," Griffin said. "I didn't want to tell my roommate about a certain honeypot note . . ."

What? Now Griffin would think that I was going to give in to his little blackmailing scheme, but before I could retort, he hung up the phone, giving me no choice but to do the same. A sudden silence had permeated the living room, and I sat down, not even noticing that I had taken the seat next to Marcus in my daze. Perhaps Griffin had meant it in a more symbolic sense, not a literal *date* date, right? Just a calendar date, yeah, sure. I was in for it. *That little blackmailing squealer!*

Scott stretched, watching me under heavy brows. "Well, it looks like you've found your hot date for tomorrow . . ." He got to his feet, putting Zooga back in the cage. He gathered his backpack, and I watched him, not knowing how to make him stay. Dash everything!

"Are you going to come to the game anyway?" Brooke asked for me.

He hesitated at the door, his brow furrowed while he considered it. "Yeah, I might crash the party." He smiled, and with a final wave at me, left us, leaving the wreath singing in his wake.

Marcus turned to me. "That was a desperate move."

"You're not the only guy to tell me that," I muttered.

"You dug your own grave, honey." He glanced at his watch. "Speaking of . . . I'm late. I was supposed to pick Miriam up five minutes ago. We'll see ya later," he said.

"Yeah . . ." I glanced up, seeing he was still there. Then I recognized that mischievous glint in his eyes. He had been up to something.

"You might want to look at your picture in the directory," he said, not even trying to mask his smug expression.

"What?" After an accusing glance at Ashley—I knew the table wasn't a safe place to deposit the ward directory—I picked it up and opened it. He had drawn a big black spot over my picture. I looked up at the empty doorway, the wreath's chanting lyrics the only evidence of Marcus's departure.

"I knew it," I said. "It's war. He gave me a black spot. Can you believe it? He gave me a black spot!" Ashley wasn't impressed that Marcus had just threatened me, but I knew exactly what the black spot meant. He was out to sabotage our mission. And since he was a cheater at the dating game, there was no telling what diabolical schemes he planned for us, namely for me. "Don't you understand? This is war." I stared at the wreath's glowing eyes and its incessantly moving jaw. He had declared war. So be it. I reached for my jean jacket . . . no, that wasn't dark enough. Harrison and my roommates watched me in amazement as I flung it to the side. I'd have to change from my pink shirt to a black one. I threw a black stocking cap over my blond curls and snapped on my black gloves like the cat burglar I was.

"What are you doing?" Brooke asked. She watched the determined set of my jaw nervously.

"He's on a date with another girl."

"Yeah?"

"That means he's not guarding his beloved homestead. Brooke, you can pick the locks at Grain Storage Apartments, right?" She nodded. "You're coming with me. Ashley . . . you'll be the distraction if Logan's there. You can easily get him out of the house if you stroke his already-puffed-up, peacock ego. His other roommates are engaged, so that takes care of them." I pulled the door open, but the cold air didn't affect me. My anger kept me very warm. "If we don't return, Harrison, take care of Emma."

Even Harrison looked worried. "What are you going to do?"

I grabbed the wreath midsong and flipped the button off in the back, cutting off its music amid a gurgling note. "Let's just say Marcus won't know what hit him."

Harrison just shook his head. "There's no fury like a woman's wrath."

No, just mine.

CHAPTER 24

"A little Church ball goes a long way."
—Samantha Skyler (Tues., Dec. 14th)

"Is he here yet?" I asked, peering into the gym.

"No," Ashley said.

"Good." I pulled through the entranceway, and Emma looked at me like I was the meanest creature to walk into the Smith Fieldhouse gym. "What? I told Griffin I'd meet him here. I'm keeping my word. If he doesn't show, he's the one that stood me up . . . and then I'll be perfectly justified to do what I'm going to do." *Please justify me, please justify me.*

Emma glanced at her watch, shifting in her khaki skirt. "You're twenty minutes late."

"We didn't discuss what time we'd meet . . ."

"Holy cow, look at the other team," Ashley said, waving her hands in front of her suddenly flushed face. "They're huge and hot. Wow." She shed her elegant black coat and stuffed it in a heap in the corner, and I laughed at her yellow shirt. Harrison would have a heart attack if he saw her. The shirt had a half-human, half-alligator skeleton on the front. *My Friend Jake* was scrawled over the horrible apparition in chunky kid writing. I searched the room for Harrison and realized that his heart was safe . . . for now. He was nowhere in sight.

My gaze went to the other team, seeing only huge heads and hands. "What monsters," I whispered. Our team was completely dwarfed . . . and it showed on the scoreboard. The opposing team had twenty-three points. We hadn't even scored one.

"Well, we need to cheer them on," Emma said in a little, determined voice—as if her cheering would make a difference. She threw off her green marshmallow coat and rolled her hands into fists, marching into the cheering section. She joined the twenty or thirty fans from our ward. Veronica cheered loudly beside Emma, her little face pinched red with aggression—but she probably needed to get it out of her system, I thought, as I remembered Sunday School. I glanced at the other team's fan section . . . zero . . . another uneven score.

"Yay, go team!" Emma shouted. "Oh, good try. Keep at it. Oh, that was *almost* good."

I rolled my eyes. The other team was playing dirty, but Emma didn't seem to notice. A hulking giant knocked Marcus to the ground, and he fell onto his already-scraped knees. "Get off the ground," Emma encouraged.

Another incredible hulk guarded Derek and knocked him down in the process. He went flying, and we watched him limp to the sidelines. "That's a little dramatic, don't you think?" Emma asked. Her worried gaze turned suspicious when she saw Logan try to make a basket. "That's not a shot. They're launching the ball." Suddenly hit by her less-than-charitable attitude, she began clapping to make up for her indiscretions. "That's okay. Good try anyw . . ." Her words trailed off when she saw a large ape thing lurking toward us.

"What's that?" Ashley asked.

"Our mascot," I said.

Marcus pounded the basketball into the ground as he thudded past us. He twisted past the guy guarding him and went up for a layup. The ball slipped through the basket and the crowd went wild at the satisfying sound as it scraped past the net. "Two points! Two points!" Emma screamed out for joy.

The other team watched us in some confusion, not sure what to do. It was *just* two points, but we cheered so loudly that they looked at us like we were daft. Didn't we know who was really winning? Miriam was the only one who behaved herself. She sat on the sidelines, a most decorative fan. She clapped quietly, and only when it was appropriate, which meant her hands had hardly been used.

"It's anybody's game," Ashley shouted. She marched up and down the sidelines, her yellow shirt a blur as she followed the game, though she was following more than just the game.

I leaned my head back and listened to the crowd. "I can't believe it. You rock! You rule—" Hard candy smacked against our faces, stopping our cheers abruptly, and I whipped my head up, glaring at our mascot. He scooped into his bag and chucked another large handful of hard candy at us. "Knock it off!" I shouted, twisting away from his abuse.

"Who's that in the monkey suit?" Emma asked. "Is that Brooke?"

"Excuse me?" Brooke said, coming up behind her. "Am I six-foot-four and stupid?"

"Sorry."

"Wow, it looks like we're catching up." Brooke had her hand in the pockets of her tan canvas jacket and she paced the floor. She was obviously being sarcastic. "This is pathetic."

"What are you talking about?" Ashley said. "I've never had so much fun."

"What's the name of our little team of scrappers?" Brooke asked. The ape lurched forward, swinging his arms. Emma stepped back, watching the ape try to spell our team's name out with his arms. We turned our attention from the game, trying to guess the name of the team, but we couldn't quite get it.

"J?" I guessed. The ape shook his head. "L? No, I?" Apparently we were just as much losers at charades as our guys were at basketball, and the poor ape was beginning to lose patience with us. The sight of Derek nudged me away from it. He was still limping, a damp circle making a ring on the top of his gray shirt. Despite the sweat, he looked really good, which is why he immediately had my attention.

"What's going on?" he asked.

"We're losing."

He laughed. "No, not that, I've been here the entire game. I mean, what are you doing?"

"We're toying with the stupid monkey."

"Well, I need someone to help us with the scoreboard." He glanced at Emma, who seemed to be standing a little farther from the group, and he took pity on her. "Hey, Emma, you want to be a scorekeeper with me?" She smiled at him just as the ape nudged me in the side.

"Keep this low," the ape said, leaning closer to me . . . until he suddenly pulled back. "How long did it take you to apply that stench?" he asked. "It assaults the olfactory gland." If I hadn't recognized the English accent, I definitely would've recognized the bitter sarcasm.

"Well, what was I supposed to do?" I whispered. "I have to keep Grif at bay, Harrison."

"Shhh, don't let anyone know it's me."

I laughed when I realized the enormity of the situation—the stiff English man dressed as our rowdy mascot. He must have lost a bet. "How in the heck did they get you to dress up like that?"

"Don't laugh . . . or they'll make you the mascot next time."

"Is that what happened to you?"

Harrison ignored that, concentrating on the business at hand. He nodded at Derek. "I think you need to give the ol' elbow squeezer a pinch . . . You're losing him."

I glanced at Emma, seeing her smiling and talking to Derek. I just shook my head. "Don't worry." Harrison wasn't going to lose his dear, sweet Emma. "He's nice to everyone," I finished.

Marcus jogged past and Miriam nodded at him. He smiled until he saw me. I stiffened. It was the strangest feeling, but it felt like my nerves were rubbing raw. I tried not to think of the prank I had pulled on him last night.

Logan dashed past us and I jumped back as a massive basketball player from the other team tackled him and threw him soundly against the mat wrapped around the basketball pole. Apparently the other team thought they were playing football. The impact was so great it sent wind ruffling through my hair and I pulled forward, cheering loudly. A little Church ball went a long way. He wouldn't be recovering from that for a while. Ashley elbowed me in the side. "Hey, Logan's our guy."

"Oh, is he? Oops." My laugh caught in my throat when I saw Griffin enter the court. He stood next to the fireball Veronica. Griffin nodded briefly at her and tried to step around her when she ran straight into him. He gave a grunt of surprise and I straightened.

What was she doing? No one was crazy enough to try to get his attention. No matter our differences, I actually felt sorry for Veronica for having the misfortune to get in Griffin's way. But he quickly remedied that and freed himself, his eyes huge behind thick glasses as he stared blankly around the room. He tugged at his sweater vest, and without thinking too much about it, I pulled behind our mascot, trying to gather my nerves. The stupid ape got the wrong idea.

"You're not putting the moves on me, are you?" Harrison asked.

Even that wasn't enough of a threat to make me pull away. I rested my hands on the knees of my black flairs, trying to hide. "Just hold still and keep quiet." Of course I should've known that would be impossible. Besides, I couldn't hide from Griffin all night; one, it wasn't exactly the most acceptable thing to do, and two, it wasn't very practical. Grif could root me out anywhere.

"That was a foul!" Brooke screamed. The refs weren't listening and she was going crazy. "C'mon, guys," she shouted at our team. "You know better than that. No crosscourt passes!"

"No passport passes?" Ashley asked.

Brooke didn't answer, completely intent on the game. "What are they doing?" she mumbled to herself. "Telegraphic passes all over the place."

At least that's what we heard. Ashley looked confused. "Huh?"

"I've hit on the solution," Harrison said next to me. "You need a dessert night."

"What?"

"Show off your culinary skills, the arts . . . blah, blah, blah." Nothing he said made any more sense as my mind went numb at the very suggestion. Mom always wanted me to be more domestic but I just wasn't. But then, look who was worse—Brooke was reckless, shouting angrily beside me. Of course, she knew everything about basketball—play by play. She could probably catch a guy that way, but who ever heard of catching a guy because you *couldn't* cook?

"Dessert night, complete with the mistletoe, should seal the deal," he finished. "Just start making the invites and you're on your way."

"Line!" Brooke shouted. "What's a matter with you, ref?" She marched up to our supposed coach, the sea of fans parting before her. Scott stood on the sidelines. He had actually come, then? And he had dressed up for the occasion. He wore a dark suit and a red sheen tie. In fact, he looked like a hit man.

"You need a time-out," Brooke told him. "Your men are running all over the place like chickens with their heads cut off. You need them to spread out and be in a place where they can actually catch the ball."

Scott turned to her and rubbed at his chin, staring at her with thoughtful eyes. I waited for the rebuff, but instead he shrugged. "You're right."

He called a time-out and our team came running in, wiping off the sweat that trailed down their faces. Logan's face was red, but I couldn't tell if it was from rage or exertion. Marcus mopped off his face with the collar of his blue shirt and he glanced at me, his blue eyes especially vivid. I quickly turned away.

Brooke suddenly transformed into a coach. She knelt on the dirty gym floor in her clean khakis, her red hair swinging at her back. She ripped a paper out of her calculus notebook and started making a diagram. "This is where you are," she said, making little dots that represented them. "And this is where you need to be. Do you get it? When Logan is over there by the key, he has no one to throw it to. You have to situate yourselves so that you're not so easy for the other team to guard." I watched in amazement as our team actually nodded in reverent obedience, even Logan. It appeared that Brooke actually knew what she was talking about.

Ashley leaned over their huddled shoulders, and everyone stared at the yellow shirt with horrid fascination. "If you like," she said, "I'll distract the ref while you beat up the other team so they can't shoot."

Marcus laughed. "Those guys? No, I think we *need* the ref. He's the only one keeping us safe."

"Yeah, right," Brooke said heatedly. "The ref doesn't call anything. He's worthless. As far as I'm concerned, make as many fouls as possible . . . this is war."

The buzzer sounded and our team broke their huddle, jumping back into the game again. Marcus stayed out and came to stand by me, leaning on his knees to catch a breather. He glanced up at me and then at the ape. "You've taken to conspiring with monkeys now?" he asked.

"Maybe."

With difficulty, he took his eyes away from the lurking ape at my side. "How's the mission coming along?"

"Dandy." Though it really wasn't, thanks to him.

"And how's the date?" he asked.

Oh yeah, I guess I was on a date with Griffin, technically speaking. I shrugged, feeling more than a little guilty, but not enough to go to Griffin's side.

"I heard he's planning on proposing," Marcus said.

I shook my head, aware that Harrison still stood beside me. He was turning into a mannequin on purpose, most likely to get more information from this little exchange. "Not even *he* would be that stupid," I said.

"Why not?" Marcus asked. "You gave him a second date . . . unless you're just toying with him."

I blanched.

"The guys are starting to back off now, ya know. They think you have a boyfriend."

"I'm sorry, but it could never work between us," I said. "I like SpongeBob and I have a sneaky suspicion that he likes Arthur. Such a bridge could never be gapped." Marcus probably thought that I was joking.

"Anything is possible with love. Forget the bridge and steal a boat. Just think how romantic that would be." Marcus was clearly enjoying himself, but he grew silent when he saw Griffin catch sight of me and begin to move toward me. I steeled myself for my fate. We had made a deal . . . sorta, except he was a blackmailing cheat.

"Uh, you wanna be my pretend boyfriend?" I asked Marcus.

"Nope."

"Thanks a lot."

"No, *thank you,*" Marcus said. "I got your present last night by the way."

I purposely widened my eyes in feigned innocence. "What present?" I asked.

"Let's just say that Logan dropped a bowling ball on his toe when he got home from his date, though I could only assume that the maniacally singing wreath was meant for me."

"If it makes you feel special, sure."

"Nope, just insecure. How do you keep finding ways into our apartment, anyway?"

"Wouldn't you like to know?"

"Just remember," Marcus said. "I know how to get into your apartment, so don't push me."

I stilled in sudden fear. Why had I forgotten that? Of course there was always time to hide our spare key. The trick was not forgetting where the new hiding spot was.

Logan snatched the ball midair and swiveled outside the key, throwing the ball into the basket to make a three-pointer. We cheered and the scoreboard blinked and changed to five whole points for the visitors' section. Emma held up a candy bar. It was a Skor bar. Man, were we cheesy.

Brooke nodded, standing next to Scott, showing a unified professionalism. Scott caught my eye and winked just as Griffin shoved through the last of the Seventy-Third Ward fans to reach my side. I broke my gaze with Scott and looked down at Griffin. Why didn't he pick on someone his own size?

"Hey, Grif," Marcus said, turning to him. "Why aren't you playing?"

"My nails won't take it." Every pair of eyes swerved to him, even a pair of plastic monkey eyes. "Some people think I'm metro because I get a manicure once a week, but it's worth it."

"And you're obviously not metro," Marcus said.

"Nope." Griffin stared at me and I tried not to flinch. Marcus suddenly smirked and I knew he could guess what I was thinking, but instead of a smart comment, he pulled forward, ready to substitute someone out. "Congratulations on the coming nuptials," he whispered for my ears alone. "You deserve it."

He ran out into the court, and Harrison made a pleased sound beside me. "You've made Marcus nervous," he whispered.

"Really?" I asked carefully, my eyes on Griffin. For some reason the game had diverted his attention from me. "He seemed pretty smug to me."

"All lies. I recognize an act when I see one. Are you going to invite him over for dessert night?"

"Never . . . well, only to witness my victory maybe." But of course, there was no way I was really going to ask Marcus to come. He had already proven that he was capable of ruining everything. Griffin swiveled from the game to stare at me and I stepped back, feeling a twinge of guilt. "You're late," I said. "The game's almost over."

"I was visiting the florist," he said.

"Oh." I hoped he wasn't buying another rose to threaten me. Eager for any excuse to free myself from further intimidation, I turned quickly away from him just as Logan fouled out. We cheered loudly at the honor and he staggered off the court. If only Brooke had been the boys' coach from the beginning, but now the clock was running out. At least we had almost reached half the other team's score.

It was our ball and Marcus dribbled it down the court, handing it off. He sped to the side and caught it again. The monsters guarded him on all sides. He was at an impossible angle, but he went for the basket, peddling his legs through the air to make an impossible shot just as the buzzer went off. We went wild again and rushed the court like a flood breaking loose from a dam.

"I can't believe it!" Ashley shouted.

"You were wonderful!" Emma said.

Yeah, I guess in a way they were . . . well, they were entertaining at the very least.

CHAPTER 25

"Did you propose?"
—Harrison Bean (Tues., Dec. 14th)

I was distracted from the flood of basketball fans as Harrison shouted into my ear, "It's time to make the invites. Go to it. Thursday night's as good as any. It will be a good break from finals."

I nodded, grabbing the nearest sweaty hand and high-fiving it. "Congratulations," I said.

The guys looked like they had run the gauntlet . . . or maybe even through a car wash, something that called for a continual beating. I stopped short when I caught a glimpse of Marcus on the basketball court. He looked horrible. There were red marks all over his wrists and knees, and what was even more astonishing was that he actually smiled when he saw me. He must have really been out of it.

I tried to sidestep him, but Griffin immediately appeared at my side. He watched Marcus suspiciously, never blinking once. I was actually impressed with the stunt. If anyone could win a staring contest, Griffin could.

I found myself face to face with Marcus. "That was an amazing shot," I told him, though a bit reluctantly. After all, he was the enemy. He lifted his hand to give me a fist high-five and got hit in the back of the head with a basketball. I winced for him.

"Sorry!" someone shouted behind him.

I grabbed his arm to steady him, and got a splatter of sweat all over my shirt for my efforts. My lip curled, but despite my disgust I was concerned. "You okay?" I asked.

"Yeah."

It was then that Miriam appeared out of nowhere to come to his aid. She stepped over a dusty blue mat in her delicate tennies. Marcus allowed her to towel off the sweat that poured down his face.

"Oh, dear," I said. "I'm not sure if that's going to do it. The sweat just keeps coming."

Miriam looked distraught, a wrinkle in her forehead marring her perfect brow. I left her to clean Marcus up, but the funny thing was that I actually felt reluctant about it. I *was* a glutton for punishment. However, it was time to search out my finding pool and do a little inviting. I hesitated under the basketball hoop, where Griffin almost trod me down. I stepped away and he stepped on my black chunky shoes. How on earth was I going to do my invites when Griffin was following me around so closely? I needed Harrison.

I looked around for the ape and stopped short when I saw him flirting with all the girls he could find. No wonder he wanted to be the mascot. It suddenly made sense now. I rushed to his side, tugging him away from Ashley and Veronica. "Hey Romeo," I whispered hurriedly at what I hoped was the vicinity of his ear.

"Did you propose?" he asked in a muffled voice behind the mask.

"Not yet. You've got to get my stalker off my back." I didn't have much time before Griffin caught up with me. "If you want me to succeed at all with these invites, you'll take him."

Harrison turned, seeing Griffin closing in on me, and he nodded, cutting him off, which meant I had to work fast. I searched the crowd for Scott.

Emma tried to get our attention, which was hard considering that she was shorter than everyone else. She hopped up and down in her little white sneakers. "Get over there for a picture." She pointed to the key on the court. Derek seconded her, and since he was a lot taller, it was easier for us to see him. Too bad he had such a gentle voice. A group picture would be an almost impossible feat with this number.

"This is the strangest ward," a monster from the other team grumbled under his breath. I passed him, averting my gaze from the enemy, a difficult feat because he was so hot. But it was a good move or I never would have found Scott. He was on his way out the door when I caught sight of him.

"You're not staying for the picture?" I asked, quickly thinking of a pretense to talk to him.

"Nope, I've got safewalk duty."

"But everyone who studies is here." I pointed to Brooke and she gave us a sour look before joining us, her hands deep in the pockets of her canvas coat.

"Yeah, and I need to get back to it," Brooke said. "Maybe it will help me forget what happened here tonight."

Scott watched her with intense brown eyes. "Well, *maybe* if you came on time, this never would have happened, Mom."

"I thought *you* were the coach," she argued.

"My job is to make the team look good," he said, "nothing else."

"Leave that to me," I said, breaking in with a joke. It wouldn't do to have the boy all tense before the big invite.

"I'm sure you could," he said, and I smiled, realizing that Scott was primed and ready for the kill. I just wished that I could get more time with him to BRT. I even started to plot a great dash to the library for the sole purpose of a safewalk, but it was just too improbable. He would probably see through that little ploy and it would put him on edge. The direct invite would have to do. "We're having a dessert night on Thursday," I said, "if you'd like to come."

"We are?" Brooke asked.

"Yes," I said, "would you like to come too?" She snorted at that. "We need a real Christmas party for this ward, anyway," I said, "not just some stinkin' basketball game . . . and we'll have homemade cooking." I avoided Brooke's eyes . . . if dessert night was any kind of success, it would not be *my* homemade cooking. "And lots of games, so say you'll come, Scott. It wouldn't be complete without you."

"If it's okay with Brooke," he said.

I gave her a hard look. "Yeah," she said slowly. "It's okay with me."

He glanced at his watch. "I'd better go do safewalk." he said. "Brooke, are you going up to the library to study?"

Wow, he *was* a slave to duty. They would probably argue the whole way up. I tried to think of an excuse to join them but couldn't find one plausible enough. It would look too ridiculous for me to go up and study at the library anyway, but with Brooke it wouldn't . . . in fact, it would look weird if she didn't.

"Yeah," she said, gathering her book bag. "I've got two tests tomorrow."

They left and I turned, heading for my second conquest, weaving around the scoreboard table and the last remnant of excited fans. I didn't see Derek, but it appeared that Ashley was working on Marcus, and I wondered how she had managed to oust Miriam from the scene. Miriam was nowhere in sight. Ashley was good. I just hoped that Harrison didn't tell Miriam about dessert night. He seemed pretty busy entertaining Griffin with a strange monkey dance, though, and as it turned out, Derek was the one to find me. I felt his hand on my elbow.

"Hey, Samantha, why weren't you in the picture?" Derek asked.

I turned, directing a brilliant smile at him. It appeared that Marcus's interference hadn't done any permanent damage. "I was just seeing Brooke off. We were making plans for a dessert night."

"A dessert night?"

"You can cook?" Marcus asked behind us. The question was completely tongue-in-cheek, and my smile turned icy. I thought that Ashley was *watching* him, but she had wandered off.

"Just because I haven't cooked anything for you doesn't mean I can't cook." Okay, all of that was a lie, especially since I *had* cooked for him. I quickly glanced at Emma, seeing she was making her way toward us. "Emma, I can cook, right?"

She froze and I realized that she was the worst person to ask to lie, which probably made her the perfect character witness. I bit my lip, waiting, and after a moment she nodded a quick, guilty nod.

"I'm looking forward to seeing it," Marcus said dryly.

My mouth dropped. He wasn't invited . . . But now he was, since I couldn't say anything in front of Derek. I glared at Harrison across the room.

"What?" I saw him mouth through the gaping jaws of the monkey suit. I guess he couldn't distract them all.

"Will your band perform at this dessert night?" Derek asked. I suddenly had images of the last time we had performed. It wasn't the way to impress a man . . . especially this one. "I'll go if you promise to perform," he said. This was a strange request coming from Derek.

"Are you kidding?" I asked.

"No."

I hesitated. The performance would reveal too much about myself. I tapped a rhythm on the gym floor, scuffing it with my black-soled shoes as I desperately thought up ways to get out of this newest dilemma.

"Of course we'll perform," Emma said in a cheerful voice. My eyebrows drew in, especially when Griffin had finally attached himself to my side. What happened to Harrison? I glanced up, seeing him arguing with Ashley, probably about her yellow shirt. He couldn't even handle one simple assignment. What was wrong with him?

Griffin tugged me to the side, looking angry. "I want to talk to you."

I gulped. "What did you want to tell me?"

"I'm hungry. Let's go eat something."

"Oh . . ." I wracked my brain for any excuse and picked the first one that came out. "I've got homework," I said. "I can't do that right now."

His face turned even redder. "You can't take one hour out of your *precious* schedule to spend time with me? It's time for you to pay up. I need some incentive for my silence."

"What?" Was he serious about this blackmail thing? There was no way I was going to play his little game, but of course he didn't mean it . . . or did he?

Emma tugged on my arm, unknowingly bringing me back into the circle of somewhat friendly faces, though Veronica was part of that same group and she didn't look too happy to see me. What was her problem? She wasn't afraid I was taking all the boys, was she? I tried to ignore her.

Look, I don't want your man, I tried to send telepathically. I wasn't a threat, but since I was a living, breathing girl, I guess I was.

"We're getting ice cream," Emma said. "Wanna come?"

"Ooh," I said, looking back at Grif. I was a little taken aback by the rage in his eyes. "I'd love to, but like I was just telling Grif, I have so much homework that I can't do anything else tonight."

"Are you sure we can't talk you into procrastinating?" Derek asked. I shook my head and he turned to Ashley. "Well, Emma and Harrison are in. How about you, Ashley?"

"Yeah—are you going, Marcus?"

What? I suddenly realized my danger. If he left, I'd be completely alone with Griffin, and by the looks of things, an angry Griffin. Marcus was trying to wring out his blue shirt. He glanced up at me, then saw Griffin's red face. If anyone saw my danger, it would be him. Marcus wasn't as friendly as Derek. In fact he had always been downright suspicious of everyone, which made him wise to the ways of the world, something I appreciated about him.

Marcus didn't look like he wanted to step in, but he had pity on me and I was glad of that at least. "Nah, I've got too much homework for that," he said. "Samantha, weren't we going to study for that final we have tomorrow? You'd better not stand me up."

"I wouldn't think of it." I normally wouldn't be happy to be leaving with Marcus, but now I clung to his sweaty side, not even minding that he stunk.

"What class do you have together?" Griffin asked, and I groaned. He knew my schedule. "The same class," Marcus said, deftly avoiding the question, "but at different times. Don't worry, Griffin, I'll walk her home. We were thinking of stopping at the library first anyway." He met my eyes and I didn't contradict him. In fact, I couldn't believe that Marcus was doing this for me.

I owed him big time, and unfortunately he knew it.

CHAPTER 26

"Are you ready to make your great escape?"
—Marcus Gray (Tues., Dec. 14th)

"Hey." A furry hand landed on my arm and I swiveled, staring at our big, fat ape of a mascot. "I want your stats after this." I rolled my eyes and pushed on the heavy door, but Harrison tugged me away from it, his hand on my green-and-white striped sleeve. "Are you dotty?" he asked. "Wait for him to open it—that's the trick."

"What if he doesn't?" I asked, suddenly remembering my jean jacket. I marched to a dusty corner in the gym where I had stashed it.

The ape followed me like my shadow. "Then you let it hit you in the face. I promise he'll open it for you next time."

"Or I'll just get really black and blue," I said, not caring who opened the door. This was strictly a rescue operation, nothing else. I threw on my jean jacket and headed back for the door.

Marcus met Harrison's eyes and the ape stepped back, waiting for Marcus to open the door. Marcus didn't disappoint him. He shoved it open and I hesitated, seeing that Marcus was still in his sweaty clothes. I glanced pointedly at his long, white basketball shorts. "Aren't you changing into something warmer?"

"Nope," he said. His steady eyes were on mine. "Are you ready to make your great escape?"

"Okay." I straightened my shoulders, marching through the door under Harrison's and Griffin's watchful gazes.

We stepped into the snowy outdoors, the soft snowflakes floating over our heads. It was deceptively peaceful. "Thanks, Marcus," I said after a moment.

He shrugged, then looked up at the sidewalk with a startled expression. "Look at that." He led me past mounds of snow in the parking lot and stopped in front of a snowman swimming through a lawn. Shark fins protruded from the ground as though swimming after it. The snowman had a worried expression.

"Sick," I said. "You didn't make that, did you?"

"I wish." He gazed at it, his hands in his pockets, his mood as sober as if we were in a museum. Marcus really was amusing sometimes, though this could've been such a romantic scene with a different guy. We walked past another lawn. It had a snowman with its head chopped off. Another maniacal snowman held the head in his arms on the next lawn. Provo had some very disturbed people in it.

Marcus cleared his throat. "I've been thinking of some mission statements that might be useful for your cause—rules of engagement, so to speak."

Oh, no, couldn't he just drop that for a night? I already felt like I had been through a beating. "Why don't you keep it to yourself?" I said.

His eyes twinkled. "And deprive you of finding your perfect match? I couldn't do that to a fellow conspirator. After all, you can't live by certain rules if you don't know what they are."

"What rules?"

"Exactly," he said. "Your first rule, and I believe the most central to your cause, is the flirt clause; 'We believe that through the proper flirting techniques, all women may marry a rich man who vows obedience to her, thereby securing her an eight-carat diamond ring.'"

I turned with a gasp.

He laughed. "You liked that, didn't you? But I patented it, so if you want to use it, you're going to have to pay me royalties. It will be well worth it, though, to get that big diamond on your pretty little finger."

That was amazing. He had completely dumbfounded me, and I struggled for something appropriately cutting to say, but he beat me to it. "How about another rule of thumb—or shall we say, rule of the ring finger? 'We believe that a woman should be called on the phone or by an even more expensive medium at least three to five days in advance before she will accompany an undesirable man on a date.'"

"Only if he's undesirable . . . otherwise we'll drop practically everything," I muttered.

"Thus bringing us to your next rule: 'We believe in the literal gathering of family and friends at the reception where a man will devote his life to satisfy the woman's every whim and desire. There will be an infinite bounty of presents, and the man will be culpable of anything that goes wrong.'"

"Hey, that's completely disrespectful. Stop that right now."

"You first."

"I'm not . . ." I sputtered.

"Really? Then what about your pink planner—or your mission stats—or what is it that you girls plan at your district meetings, huh?" I was silent. "'We claim the privilege of spending man's money and allow all women the same privilege,'" he said. "'Let them spend how, when, and what they may.' Is that what these district meetings are all about? C'mon, you can tell me."

I couldn't believe what I was hearing. "Is that what you think we want—to squeeze the money out of a man?"

"As if you would tell me the truth, though we do believe that women have revealed much."

"What?" My hands clenched.

He quickly backtracked. "But we won't get into that, though *you* will not reveal any information regarding or pertaining to your interests in men, except to the wrong source, might I add."

"You chauvinistic pig." I scraped a handful of snow from a nearby car and chucked it at his face.

He ducked it easily. "Law-breaker," he said. "Where are the cops when you need them? Help! She's throwing snowballs in Provo." He didn't look scared at all, and I tried to change that by throwing another one at him. It flew over his head and I stomped my foot. "'We don't believe in being subject to laws, common sense, scruples, ethics, and morals,'" he said, "'when it comes to deceiving, using, and toying with the minds of men.'" Marcus ducked from another incoming snowball.

"Ooh!" I couldn't even hit him, which infuriated me even more. "If we do, you deserve it," I shouted.

"Of course we do. 'Men will be punished for their own sins *and* for the women's also.'" He sidestepped to avoid another snowball.

"Hold still," I said, and to my surprise, Marcus obeyed with a mischievous look on his face. I tried to pelt it off of him, but the snowball swerved to the side, not even grazing him.

"You're not even trying," he said. I glowered. My hands were freezing without my gloves, but there was nothing I could do. You see, if you're losing in a snowball fight, you're going to keep fighting to get your revenge, but if you're winning, you're going to keep going because it's too much fun. I was obviously in it for the revenge, but either way I was stuck for the long haul.

I watched Marcus scoop up a pile of snow from the hood of a Geo opposite of me. "'We believe in the gifts of flowers, jewelry, liquid assets, furs, and so forth.'" He flung a snowball at me and I ducked behind a Neon. It exploded over my head.

"Yeah? Who's not trying now?" I shouted, bringing my arm back. I clobbered him with a fat snowball and it dripped over his blond hair in clumps, falling over his blue shirt in a heavy snowfall.

He stilled. "You want me to try?"

"No."

Too late, he was after me, snowball in hand. I gave a scared whoop of laughter and ran for it, only to step on a patch of ice. I skidded across it and landed in a mound of snow on the other end. It muffled my screams until I pulled my dripping head out. Marcus came at me with a handful of snow like he was ready to whitewash me, and I stiffened.

"Go ahead," I said. "Finish it. 'We have endured many bad dates and hope to endure no more bad dates . . .'" He was coming closer and I squinted in horrible anticipation.

"Relax," he said. "I'm not going up as another bad date on your stats. Well, actually . . ." He stared at my snow-sodden hair and reached for me, hauling me out of the snow. "It's probably too late for that. What did you do to yourself, anyway?" He tugged off his glove and used it to brush the snow off my jeans. His hand brushed mine and he let out a surprised gasp and jumped back, pulling me with him. "Your hands are freezing," he said. "Don't you have any gloves?"

"I forgot them," I said, finally remembering to pull my hands away from his. My fingers were feeling suspiciously like blocks of ice, and I began to wring them together.

"What are you doing?" He quickly rescued my hands from my abuse, and I noticed belatedly that they were once again in his possession. Why were his hands so warm? He had gloves, but he was still in his basketball grubs. He should be freezing. It wasn't fair.

"Don't rub your hands," he said. "That damages the tissue. Just run them under warm water when you get home, or blow on them. Here." He blew on my palms and I stilled, completely shocked.

You know, it was times like these that it almost seemed like he cared, and I wondered why the thought always amazed me.

"Thanks for the advice, doc," I said. "I'll remember that."

"You've got pretty hands." He turned my hand over in his, and I caught my breath just as he grimaced at my nail polish. "Why did you paint your nails sparkly pink?"

I shrugged, suddenly annoyed. Was he ever going to return my hand? Sure enough, as soon as he realized that he held it, he returned it gladly. So why did that disappoint me? We walked the rest of the way to my apartment in silence.

"Would you like to come inside?" I asked. "I'll show you the mysterious pink planner, you suspicious ol' mobber, then you'll see what a joke this is. We're not a hate-guys club like you think."

He leaned against the railing on the stairs. He must be freezing in those basketball shorts. "I can't. I'm going to Miriam's in twenty minutes."

I nodded. Of course, and it was probably for the best anyway, but he wasn't leaving. "You're not going to give up on this, are you?" he asked.

"Never." If anything, I'd do all this "mission" stuff now just to spite him.

Marcus smiled. "You're hopeless . . . that's what I like about you."

I had to admit that he had surprised me with that one. He liked me? "Thanks," I said, not sure if he was complimenting me. I waited for the insults to follow, but they didn't.

"I'm serious," he said. "You go for what you want. You have a lot of faith in yourself."

I glanced at him in astonishment. That was strange. He never would have told me that before. "I really don't," I said finally. "I'm actually a scaredy cat."

"Really? Then why do you always go for the gut?"

My lip curled. I couldn't believe I was having this conversation with Marcus of all people, but then I surprised myself even more by answering him. "I always leave myself open," I said.

"And you always get up when you fall. You're a scrapper. I wish I could be more like you that way."

I gulped, not sure how to treat this. He was actually letting his guard down with me, which was crazy since he had so much to lose now . . . Maybe he really was determined to be friends. After a moment of silence, he pulled away from the railing. "I'll see ya later," he said. "Put those hands under warm water, not hot, okay? Lukewarm."

"Yeah." I stared after him as he walked away. Was it wrong to go for impossible odds while ignoring perfectly good, sane opportunities? I pulled back, sternly telling myself no. I could see myself doing the same thing I had done before, going for the guy who could care less about me and ignoring the nice guys.

It wasn't so difficult to nip this in the bud, especially if I reminded myself that Marcus didn't like me and was infatuated with someone else. Besides that, he was a complete jerk and a waste of time. The only thought that gave me any real pleasure was that Miriam would be going on a date with a snowman . . . no, it didn't give me pleasure that he was going on a date, but . . . Well, yeah, sure it did. I didn't care, right? But then again . . . I shook my head. No, I had to tell myself no.

CHAPTER 27

"The way to a man's heart is his stomach . . . unfortunately."
—Harrison Bean (Thurs., Dec. 16th)

"We had to invite the other girls to dessert night so we wouldn't look suspicious," Ashley told Harrison. She had reverted back to her signature black shirt and looked unusually serious today, so unlike the carefree Ashley we normally knew. The only sign that Harrison even noticed was a slight twitch in his jaw. "We're not afraid of the competition," she said.

"I'm not complaining," Harrison said in a stiff voice. He was in black too, mimicking the shadows he so frequently liked to melt into. "More girls for me," he said. But Ashley ignored that, already heading back into the kitchen, joining Emma to referee things there.

The Relief Society sisters had brought their desserts into our apartment, splendid course after course: cinnamon rolls, chocolate chip cookies, Rice Crispy treats, cheesecake. There was no way to compete with these girls, and so I didn't—it was better just to pass their stuff off as mine. Either that or blend inconspicuously with the crowd. I even opted for a boring white T-shirt and faded blue jeans to avoid undue attention, but Harrison had other ideas.

He bit into a brownie, though his teeth couldn't quite get through it. His eyes met my defiant ones. "What are these—brownies or cinderblocks, Samantha?"

I shrugged. "Look at the box. It was the only mix I could find in my cupboard . . . Watch out for weevils." I watched the door. People from our ward shuffled past it, talking, laughing, flirting, but they deftly avoided the mistletoe hanging over it. It seemed they had a second sense for self-preservation . . . just like I did. There was no way I could go through with this.

Derek knocked on the door and let himself in, bringing the cold air in with him. I had to laugh because his dark marshmallow coat almost matched Emma's faded green one. He had stripped it off from his semiformal attire, and I sighed. Didn't the man ever dress down? I mean, just to see him in a baseball cap would be an improvement.

"Samantha," he called over the crowded room. "Are you going to perform something for us, then?" He wove around Ashley's drums and Brooke's cello, trying not to knock over the guitars that leaned against the walls. He pulled next to me, brushing my arm with his own. His white sleeve was still cold from the outdoors.

"Brooke isn't here yet," I said, crossing my arms across the butter-flies in my stomach, but nothing would calm them down. "But we'll play something when she gets here." As if on cue, the door opened and I turned, expecting to see Brooke, but Marcus walked through instead. He was surrounded by girls, though Miriam was missing from their ranks. I was strangely elated about that. Marcus threw his red coat onto the pile in the corner and five more feminine versions were tossed over it.

Logan made his way to his roommate; even more girls were flocking around him, which was strange because it looked like he had just gotten back from working out. He wore red jogging pants and a dirty white T-shirt and he smelled. But no matter, his presence ensured that the girls would be kept busy from my conquests, and that was all that mattered.

I turned back to Derek. "You need to try out the desserts in the kitchen. Emma and Ashley are in there. They'll dish you up."

"What did you make?"

"That will be my dirty little secret," I said. Derek headed for the kitchen and I stopped him. "Uh, don't eat the brownies."

"Thanks for the heads up."

"No problem."

Harrison kept gnawing at the brownie, and I had to give it to him, the man had perseverance. "Everything's running according to plan," he said between bites. "The mistletoe, the food," he hesitated, looking askance at the brownie. "The way to a man's heart is his stomach," he said almost to himself, "unfortunately. At least we have the pleasure of your gracious company." His gaze scanned the group of visitors. "Now the question is who will be the first to fall?"

I didn't really care. I could only concentrate on Marcus. He was dressed up like a maintenance man with an ugly, red rugby T-shirt, complete with a *Speed Jiffy* logo. He kept the simpering girls around him occupied with outlandish pranks. Didn't he know that he was making a complete fool of himself? He pretended to kiss some random girl's hand, and I quickly turned away. "Where's Brooke?" Harrison asked.

"At the library. She should be home in a few minutes. She's taking safewalk."

"Who's doing safewalk?" Marcus asked behind us. I jumped. How had he managed to escape his harem so fast? It only proved my suspicions correct. He *was* a wily one. The only comfort I had was that his girls would sense his disappearance in no time and come screeching for him.

"Scott Turnipp's doing safewalk at ten," I said, purposely keeping my eyes blank.

"Oh really?" Marcus said. "Does that mean she's proselyting in your area?"

I swiveled, looking at Marcus. He was despicable. "Why do you say that?"

The door opened, cutting off our conversation. Scott's hand was on the doorknob and he stepped to the side, letting Brooke in. She looked radiant . . . *Of course* she looked radiant. She wore my sleek black pants and Ashley's blue-and-white striped button-up shirt. Her red hair was caught up in an elegant French twist. We had dressed her up before she left for school, knowing she'd be studying all day before coming back for our kitchen performance at the last possible second. One look at Scott's face and I knew he was smitten. His hand was on her arm and they talked in low voices. Bad sign.

And suddenly it all began to make sense. Scott taunting Brooke to be more social . . . Brooke's negative attention seeking. Why didn't I see it earlier, though? Well, that was easy. I was stupid. Girls constantly cut each other out of the picture. You would think I would know better by now, except . . . well, it didn't matter. Now I just looked like an idiot. It was time to flaunt my acting skills and pretend that I wasn't bothered by it.

"I hope you're happy, Marcus," I said, glancing at his knowing face. "Another man is safe from my clutches."

Marcus shrugged. "Well, as long as you don't care."

"I care." I should've been annoyed, but instead . . . I tried to reevaluate the situation for once. Wasn't I a sucker for happy endings? Sure, it wasn't *my* happy ending, but it didn't mean I didn't want my roommate to have one. Besides I could live vicariously through her. Wait. Living vicariously through Brooke? This would take some getting used to.

"Look, if he doesn't like me," I told Marcus, "there's nothing I can do about it." I think I was trying to convince myself and I sighed. "It doesn't mean that he's a bad person or anything."

"No, it just means that he's stupid."

Marcus had shocked me with that one, and I met his amused gaze. I appreciated the flattery, especially at a time like this. No wonder the girls were crazy about him. I quickly tried to backtrack my thoughts from that. "Don't say things you don't mean," I said.

"I mean it." His blue eyes sparkled as he walked away. "I only wish I was worthy to date a girl as fine as you are."

I stilled. Was there any seriousness in that? Most likely not.

"Ah yes, perfect," Harrison said.

I jumped, completely forgetting that he had been eavesdropping on our conversation.

"Not only does the male raise the girl's self-esteem with the 'I'm not worthy line,'" he said, "but he also clears himself of any commitment."

Harrison was right, and I forced myself to steer my thoughts away from Marcus, but Harrison wouldn't let me. "How could you let such an opportunity slip through your normally sticky fingers, Samantha? What's the matter? Did you just turn gutless, or did you lose your presence of mind?"

"What are you talking about?"

"You were both standing under the mistletoe." He was watching me closely, and my face reddened as I realized I was still standing under it, though now with Harrison. I knew that stuff was dangerous!

I tried to edge inconspicuously away. "The mistletoe is broken," I said once I was a safe distance from it.

"Well, get a repairman and fix it . . . I know just the man."

"I'll find my own man, thank you." I broke away from his suddenly amused look and pushed through the crowded room. "Brooke?" I tried to find her, but suddenly Griffin cut me off. I made sure the mistletoe was nowhere in sight before I gave him my full attention. He was actually dressed like a human being today with baggy khakis and a soft black button-up shirt—not tucked in. He had even spiked his hair. He must have taken some fashion advice from Scott, though he hadn't taken any lessons on his manners. He still looked quite angry.

"No," I said, "this is not the time. Can't you see that I've lost him?" I tried for a tragic voice, but failed miserably. "There's no use teasing me . . . when it's ended like this." That managed to confuse Griffin enough for me to slip past him. "Hey." I jumped in front of Brooke. "Let's get this performance over with." Her hand was in Scott's, and she glanced anxiously up at me. I tried to muster up all my good sportsmanship and smiled.

Scott was leaning back on the couch cushions, one leg crossed over the other. He was completely oblivious to any tensions between us, which made me realize that the man had no idea that I had liked him. Good, at least I had that. He reached for Brooke's hair, smoothing it from her face, and he stared at her like she was some fair maiden who had just emerged from a storybook. It was enough to make any girl jealous, even if she hadn't been interested in the guy in the first place.

I steeled myself. "Hey, take off your coat," I said. "Stay awhile."

Scott shrugged out of his rust-colored coat, laughing. "Griffin tells me that he's found my mysterious honeypot note stalker."

"Really?" I kept my voice neutral. Griffin came up behind me as quietly as if he were floating, and I jumped back, my hands landing on my hips. *The squealer!* Now was not the time.

"Perhaps we can discuss this," Griffin said. His nose wrinkled and he looked very smug.

How embarrassing. He wouldn't, would he? There was no way I wanted my roommate's new boy toy to think I had a crush on him.

"I wrote him the first honeypot note," Brooke said, her face was becoming just as red as her hair, "before someone else wrote the infamous, 'it was me' note."

"Really?" Scott watched her even more tenderly. "So, it was you?"

I couldn't help it, but I laughed. Well, now Griffin didn't have anything over on me, the little punk. I glanced at him and shrugged. "I don't think that we have anything to discuss, do you Griffin?" I asked. He glowered and I turned to Brooke. "We've got a performance to do," I said. "You can apologize to me after I get Ashley and Emma."

"Why?" Scott asked.

For stealing my man. I didn't vocalize it, but just walked into the kitchen. Emma was cutting the cakes and pies, looking like Betty Crocker herself, complete with frilly white apron. It covered her blue-striped pants and powder-blue shirt, but it didn't matter. She was still getting frosting all over her clothes. Ashley was filling glasses of punch with a somber air. Apparently she didn't care that she was getting all dirty either. What was wrong with them?

"Brooke's here," I said. There was no need to say anything else. They'd seen the good/bad news for themselves.

My guitar was leaning precariously against the wall and I picked it up. "Make sure your bass is tuned, Emma," I said. "We don't want a repeat of last time." As I said it, my ears caught the end of an intriguing conversation: "Why don't you just grab her and kiss her? We hung the plant of love for a reason."

What? I hesitated. That was Harrison, but what mischief was he up to now? He was talking to Marcus. "Hey, DL, we're BFF, okay?" Marcus said. "Nothing else."

I had the feeling that I was eavesdropping on something important, but the only problem was that I couldn't understand a thing. It wasn't funny.

"We're not in the MTC, RM, so skip the LDS BRT and get to the CK." That was Harrison again . . . I could only recognize a few of the acronyms. I glanced around, seeing Marcus's eyes widen.

"This YM needs to at least DTR before it goes NCMO," Marcus said. "This particular YW from the RS is looking for an MRS degree. This isn't just some PDA from the DI, if you know what I mean."

No!

Harrison laughed at that. "FYI, this ain't EFY either, buddy. We're at BYU."

"Exactly, I'd rather CTR EC, if you know what I mean."

"That's all I'm asking," Harrison said, taking a relaxed position against the window.

My brow wrinkled and I pulled the strap of my guitar over my shoulder. Weirdos . . . except it was kinda cute, too. Wait, no, no, it wasn't. I still had a contact in the dating pool . . . there was no reason to get desperate, which was why I was about to humiliate myself again. Where was Derek, anyway? I found him in the crowd and he smiled at me. I returned it with a nod. Everything about him was right. He was good and kind and sweet . . . unlike some people.

"Harrison," Ashley said, pulling behind him. "This song is dedicated to you."

He just shrugged. No goad, no nothing, and her eyes narrowed. He usually teased her mercilessly, but tonight he seemed uncommonly stiff. And for a girl who craved attention, good or bad, he knew what buttons to push by completely ignoring her. It made me wonder if she had been fighting with him—and about something worse than the yellow shirt she wore to the basketball game on Tuesday—but he just watched Emma, to Ashley's chagrin.

Ashley tossed her dark hair and sat down behind the drums, so distraught she didn't even bother to tug her black shirt over the waist of her khaki flairs. Emma stood next to me, her bass neatly tuned. She smiled brightly at me. Brooke pulled her cello from the corner, a becoming blush on her cheek when she met Scott's eyes. I nodded to my roommates, and Ashley pounded on the drums with unusual vigor. I started my rhythm guitar and Emma followed suit with the bass in a rowdy rendition of "These Boots Are Made for Walking"—the ultimate guy-bashing song, bashing everything that Derek wasn't . . . and Marcus too.

This was idiotic. Well, no, the song was going great, but my feelings, those needed to be crushed. I belted out the last girl-power line, Ashley rolled the drums, and Emma and Brooke finished their last strums. Our ward cheered like we had just scored in a basketball game, which could mean absolutely anything. We could be the best thing they had ever heard, or the worst. I took off my guitar strap.

At least that was done. We had gotten through our redemption concert and could now hold our heads high—until we messed up again. I headed back to the kitchen for a stiff glass of water. Derek stopped me, pumping my hand vigorously. "That was great. I'm so glad I asked for a performance. You really outdid yourself."

I nodded, seeing Marcus behind him. His lips were curled, and I couldn't help but notice that he held a plate of my brownies in a threatening way. "Interesting decor," Marcus said before I could pass him. He mentioned nothing about the performance and I stilled. Was he talking about the silver garland and blinking Christmas lights all over the room? Those had always been there. "Where can you get something like that?" he asked. "DI?"

"What?"

I glanced at the wall across from the Chastity Line and suddenly laughed. Ashley had hung his cross-stitch across the hall where Marcus would be able to see it but not reach it. It was pure torture for any guy bent on having the last laugh, especially one who was torn between being a gentleman and a man.

"You want to see your wreath again?" he asked me calmly . . . too calmly. My gaze was drawn back to the brownie plate. He held up a brownie between two fingers, almost as if in warning.

"Not particularly."

"Then we want our cross-stitch, got it?"

"Oh, you're trying to threaten me, are you?" I was enjoying this more than he knew. "That's sick."

"No," he said, indicating the plate of brownies, "feeding these to a horde of desperate partygoers is sick. Swapping the wreath for your cross-stitch is merely getting your just desserts, pardon the pun."

"I recognize that saying," Derek said, coming up behind us with sparkling eyes. He stared at the cross-stitch across the hall. "'It's better to fail than to never have tried at all.' Hey, isn't that yours, Marcus?"

Ashley jumped next to me, still on a high from playing the drums. "It's ours now." She twirled a drumstick in her hand. With a final glare at Harrison, she turned to Marcus. If Harrison wouldn't pay attention to her, she knew someone who would.

"What can a guy do to get it back?" Marcus asked.

"I'm sure we can think of something."

"I'm sure I can too," he muttered, his eyes on mine. He held a brownie up threateningly and I stiffened. He wouldn't—that would be sure to ruin things with Derek. No one could know those were mine.

"Veronica kicked the hook! Veronica kicked the hook!" Emma shouted. I turned, grateful for even this interruption. Veronica stepped back from the swinging hook, her fists on her hips. The wild-haired redhead had struck again, but it was no wonder that she had kicked the hook. We had all heard her speak in Sunday School. The girl had lots of anger inside. Our little brush in Relief Society was proof of that.

Emma ran to my side. "Go get your digital."

"Excuse me," I told Marcus. "I've got some important business to attend to. I'm the official apartment paparazzi." I glanced at Emma, knowing I could get her to work for me. It was almost like cloning myself. "Maybe you can show Derek how to make snowflakes, Emma," I suggested.

"You're making *more* decorations?" Marcus asked. "Are you out of your mind? Where are you going to put all of them?"

I shrugged. "We need some new decorations for our walls."

"Besides cross-stitches?" Marcus asked. Ashley laughed at that and he gave her an appreciative smile.

"Yeah." I left Ashley and Marcus, an uneasy feeling in my stomach. They were really hitting it off. I suppose that was a good thing. I pulled my camera off the stereo and pounced on the new kicker.

"You?" Veronica asked. "It's your hook?" I smiled, not allowing hurt feelings to get in the way of duty. Everyone must end up on our wall. "Well, I don't want my picture taken," she said. "It was humiliating enough to kick the hook in the first place." She made a small, defiant figure in the middle of the room.

"Come now, Veronica," I said. "No one will know that you kicked the hook without the evidence. Besides, I never take a bad picture." It was only a little lie. She refused to pose, so I snapped it anyway, turning back to Marcus and Ashley. They were deep in conversation. Marcus was leaning toward her and I felt a sinking feeling, which would never do. I had to get rid of it.

Scott and Brooke sat in the corner of the room, smiling and talking. They were holding Zooga, affectionately arguing over the turtle's gender, and I tried to ignore them, searching the crowd for Derek. He was doing his duty as elders quorum president, keeping the girls occupied. Emma was in the midst of them, and he did a wonderful job of including her in the conversation. They were sitting on the couch, busily making snowflakes. I should quit worrying about Marcus and go for the nice guy.

"Samantha," he said, turning to me with a smile. "We were just talking about you."

"Really?"

"Emma tells me that you know how to make these things."

I glanced at the paper snowflakes in their hands, the scraps fluttering to their feet. "Not really. Brooke threw away all the snowflakes I made. I'm actually a snowflake loser."

"No," Emma and Derek chorused, but what they didn't know was that my self-esteem wasn't based on making snowflakes . . . it was based on other things that didn't matter, like writing books and playing the guitar and . . . I sat on the other side of Derek, but before I could relax, Griffin sat between us.

"Things are heating up between my roommate and yours," he said. "How about we follow their example?"

I quickly inched away from him, hugging the arm of the couch instead, watching for any fast moves. I felt Marcus's laughing gaze on me, but his pleasure was short-lived.

"Griffin." Veronica was upon us. "You told me to kick the hook and then you disappeared. Where did you go?"

I watched him cringe, and I straightened in sudden amusement as my stalker became the stalked. If he found her annoying, she must be pretty bad, and I was very eager to see where this would go.

"I was just talking to Samantha," he said.

Her eyes narrowed, and suddenly I understood what she was doing. She was trying to make me angry by flirting with what she thought was my guy. *Well, flirt away, honey.* "You said you were going to try my cheesecake," she said.

Griffin's eyes suddenly lit up. "That was *your* cheesecake? I tried it. Merciful heavens, I loved it."

Veronica smiled. "Thank you." And then with a defiant look at me, she left us. I couldn't help but show my disappointment. Griffin was good. I had no idea how easily he could get rid of a girl . . . Well, I mean I had a little bit of an idea, but he had managed Veronica so easily. I should've taken notes.

And that's when sudden inspiration hit me. No defiant words would deter this lover boy, but one thing would. "I made the brownies," I said. Griffin winced and I smiled. "When I get married that's the only thing I'll make for my husband, brownies for breakfast, lunch, and dinner . . ."

"My, oh my," Derek said, interrupting us. "That's a beautiful snowflake, Emma." He unfolded her snowflake. It looked worse than mine. Dash everything, Derek was nice, but it was then that Griffin did something completely surprising. It appeared he had found something more interesting than me because he excused himself, bouncing off our overstuffed couch to his feet. He shot through the crowd of partygoers.

Derek apparently didn't realize the significance of this, of course, but just smiled at me. "Have you been able to enjoy the snow yet?" he asked.

Besides a near whitewash experience, I couldn't say that I had. I shook my head, still staring after Griffin. He sidled next to Veronica, and she didn't look irritated at all by it. Did my brownies do the trick? "I can't say that I have," I said, pulling my attention back to Derek with difficulty.

"I just got some sleds," he said. "Do you and your roommates want to go sledding tomorrow?"

I brightened. Sure, it was a group invite, but I would take what I could get. And who knows? Maybe Harrison's one-month plan would work, and I could actually get a contact into the dating pool. Of course we only had half a week left to get engaged, which was completely improbable, but Harrison could work miracles, especially if I could get a date out of the deal. A date was practically an engagement anyway, right? Especially at BYU.

There was no way I would voice that to Emma or I'd get a lecture rivaling the one she gave to Harrison. I glanced his direction, seeing him sit stiffly on one of our big orange chairs. He glared at the room in general. What was his problem, anyway? Wait a second. It was obvious, and I wondered why I hadn't seen it earlier. He thought he was losing Emma. Well, for crying out loud, there was nothing to worry about. I could tell when Derek was just being nice to someone and when he was really interested, and now he was looking at me . . . with interest, I was pretty sure of it.

"We'd love to go sledding," I said, and despite myself I met Marcus's eye. He quirked an eyebrow at me, but Ashley had him conveniently distracted. There was nothing he could do about this new development.

Derek stood up, carefully crumpling his snowflake mess into a ball. "How's tomorrow morning?"

"That sounds great," I said, trying to ignore Marcus. He was making faces at me. Emma and I walked Derek to the door, and he gathered his marshmallow coat in his arms.

"Good, I'll pick you girls up." Derek hugged me with a resounding pat on my back. He hugged me! I mean, the pat was kind of a bad sign, but he couldn't show everybody here that he was interested, right? He had to play it friendly because that was his middle name. And of course, he couldn't hug me without hugging Emma too, or else it would look too obvious. Derek pulled away from my smaller roommate, smiling. "See ya, girls."

He left, the wreath blatantly missing from such a poignant doorstep scene, but even so, a happy melody echoed through my heart as I slammed the door shut behind him.

Finally, some sort of success in the wreckage of failures, and of course Harrison could relax about Emma. For a man so observant, I was surprised that he didn't see Derek's interest in me for himself, but then love made us all stupid. I could hardly wait to see what Marcus had to say about this new development, but when I turned, I found him talking to Ashley . . . as if he hadn't even been watching.

It made sense. Now that my swain was gone, he could concentrate on someone else; I started to recognize the pattern. Anytime anyone paid any sort of attention to me, he'd pull in for the teasing, but once they were no longer a threat, he acted like I was completely nonexistent. What a jerk, sorta, except once again, he really wasn't committed to me, so I couldn't expect anything less, right?

Logan joined the two, and Marcus pointed to the cross-stitch decorating our wall past the Chastity Line. Any plans they had for sneaking it out were clearly frustrated, and I grinned. At least we had that against them, but Marcus played it cool, holding up the brownie tray and making jokes.

Ashley took the brownies from him with gentle fingers, laughing, and I stilled, seeing her head back into the kitchen to get him something better. The traitor.

Marcus met my eyes with an ironic look, and I swiveled from him. I gasped at the words written across our fogged-up window— *help me.*

"Hey," I said. "Who wrote that?"

"What can I say?" Marcus said, coming up behind me. "Besides the entertainment, the party's a little dry." My eyes narrowed as his gaze went up to the mistletoe. "But not for you. I'm surprised you didn't take advantage of your little love plant earlier."

"I didn't need to."

"Are you sure?"

I watched Marcus closely. What did he mean by that? He wasn't still planning on sabotaging this relationship, was he?

"It's getting hot in here." Marcus opened the window and leaned against the wall . . . too close to me. It took me aback. "How many guys have you kissed under this thing, anyway?" he asked.

"None," I said. "I only kiss someone when I mean it. No love plant is about to change my mind."

Too late I watched Marcus turn to nod at his roommate, and that's when I noticed Logan had the cross-stitch in his hand. No male would chance his way past the Chastity Line, so who was the turncoat girl who gave it to him? It could've been anyone, since Marcus and Logan had a militia of girls working for them. It appeared Marcus had been the distraction to keep me from noticing them. I was furious.

"No!" I shouted. "Ashley, get over here!"

Logan sprinted for the door, but I was ready. Apparently Marcus was too. He grabbed me before I could tackle his roommate, pulling me easily from the window. Emma shrieked beside me and dove for the door, locking it firmly . . . not that that would keep the miscreants in, but it would at least give us time. Logan wove around the group of people and Ashley cut him off, flattening herself against the door next to Emma. She still held my tray of brownies, almost like they were weapons. There was no way he could get past this army of girls . . . except his escape route had already been planned. Too late, I saw the open window and I fought against Marcus's grip, but he held me tightly.

"Ashley!" I shouted, "the window, the window!"

Brooke saw the danger, even from across the room, and she broke free from Scott, running to our aid with all the athletic energy she could muster, but Logan was already scrambling through it with the cross-stitch. It was only then that Marcus let me go. I stared out the window into the cold night, watching Logan's figure disappear into a lonely dot in the distance. I couldn't believe it. Just like that, the cross-stitch was gone.

"That was easier than I thought," Marcus said, rubbing his hands together. "Thanks for playing, girls."

Emma sighed and Brooke trudged back to Scott's comforting side, but Ashley just smiled mischievously.

What? How could she laugh at a time like this? Then I noticed she was under the mistletoe with Marcus and, unlike me, she wasn't one to let opportunity pass her by. She dumped my plate of brownies on the end table and, with a determined glance at Harrison, grabbed Marcus by the collar of his red mechanic's shirt, tugging him to her and pressing her lips against his.

My eyes widened, but so did Marcus's, except he didn't look like he minded all that much, which just enraged me more. Wait. Why did that enrage me? I had no idea, but my heart beat an unnatural rhythm and I wanted nothing better than to tear my roommate's black hair out. Ashley pulled away from him, smiling slightly.

"Wow," Marcus said, turning to me with a devilish glint to his eye. "You should take tips from your roommate. That's a way to catch a man."

I stepped back and rammed into Harrison's broad chest. He had also witnessed his protégé's success, except he didn't look happy either. Maybe he was cursing her strategy, but judging by the look on Marcus's face, it looked like it had worked. Harrison could relax, but he didn't. He met Ashley's pointed gaze until he finally shrugged, glancing down at Emma.

"Emma, if you even dare follow the footsteps of these little tarts, I'll renounce my district."

"What?" Ashley's face turned red with anger, and Harrison jerked the door open and marched outside, leaving us . . . but not me. With another angry glance at the two guilty lovers, I stole my brownies from the end table and followed him out.

"I hope you weren't including me in your list of tarts," I muttered angrily. "She should never have done that."

"Why?"

I glanced up at him in confusion. I thought that he had disagreed with the strategy too, but now his face had taken on a frightfully calm expression. "Well, he's dating Miriam for starters . . ." It sounded lame even to my ears. Everyone knew those two weren't serious.

"Where are you going?" he asked me, finally noticing that I was following him to his apartment complex.

I shrugged. "Marcus took the cross-stitch."

"No, Logan took it."

"Marcus was the mastermind. It was obvious with the way he was distracting me. I hate how he can manipulate me like a . . ."

Harrison sighed, obviously not listening to me. "Girls are so stupid where men are concerned. Why can't females be more like Emma? She is the epitome of genteelism and femininity, and if certain males can't see her worth, they're completely idiotic . . . especially when you compare her to girls like Ashley, who have no inkling of proper conduct essential to . . ."

I ignored him, my hands tightening over the plate of brownies. "What are you doing?" he asked suddenly. He paused below the stairs to his apartment.

"None of your business." I stopped in front of Marcus's apartment, taking a brownie from the plate. I smooshed the hard chunk into a compact ball and then slapped it against the graffiti-splashed door in one big, black spot . . . well, brown. He would probably get the picture.

Harrison shook his head, clicking his tongue. "Maybe you should forget about him," he said.

"I have."

"Then why did you do that?"

"I don't know." I followed Harrison up the stairs to his apartment. "I've got to keep him on his toes."

CHAPTER 28

"If you change your mind, we'll be at Squaw Peak."
—Emma Rose (Fri., Dec. 17th)

Brooke dug the snow away from our doorstep. Tendrils of her red hair had pulled loose from the tight knot at the back of her head and she smoothed it back, trying to kick back the huge snowball from our front door. I could only guess that it had something to do with the black spot that I had left on someone else's door . . . maybe. Of course, it wasn't every day that we got snowed in by a huge snowball, but it was a nice early Christmas present. I just wondered how they got the hulking thing up three flights of stairs. It was almost flattering.

I listened to Emma in the other room. She was talking to Derek on the phone, working out the details for the sledding party. Ashley sat next to me on the couch, resting her chin in her hand. She had reverted to her black shirt and sweats again, her black hair a springy mess around her face. "I think you have competition," she said. "I saw the way Derek looked at Emma last night."

"What?" I turned to her. First of all I was still a little miffed about Marcus, which I shouldn't be, but now she was really trying to get my goat. "What about the way Derek looked at *me?*" I said.

She shrugged and I tried really hard not to get angry, which was hard considering I was already uncomfortable in my layers and layers of long johns and jeans. Would Derek and Emma ever decide where we were going sledding? It was getting hot. I fanned myself. Brooke finally broke through the wall of snow with a shout of excitement, and then she burrowed through the rest of it to get the mail. Clumps of snow clung all over her dingy green sweater.

"Oh," Emma said on the phone in the other room. "That is so sweet, Derek." My head lifted, and Ashley met my eyes with the *I told you so* look.

"You really shouldn't," Emma said, ". . . you're too good."

My eyes widened. I was a complete idiot, wasn't I? No, don't answer that. But how come *I* didn't see it before now? What vanity. It was happening again. I had been so confident that I didn't see anyone as competition, especially sweet little Emma, who had everything in common with sweet little Derek. I leaned my head back, groaning. Marcus had done everything in his power to stop my union with him, but even this was beyond his control. He'd be overjoyed to hear this piece of news, the psycho.

But Emma? The one who had gone with me to drop off the treats? The one who had gone with me to visit? The one who had encouraged me? The one who looked sad when I told her that I was giving up hope? I felt a little hurt, but let the best girl win, right? Except it was hard to swallow that I wasn't the best girl. I had never even imagined that, especially since I hadn't even considered Emma as competition before.

I mean, it stands to reason that you have to bring a roommate with you when you visit a guy. If you go by yourself, it looks suspicious. But now I understood why some girls left their friends at home, especially when embarking on particularly difficult missions. All this time when I had talked about Derek, Emma had been falling more and more in *like* with him when I had thought they had just been friends. If I knew Emma, she hadn't meant to; she was probably struggling right now under the throes of a guilty conscience. Dash diddly dog. Did Derek like her back? What was I going to do about it?

The walkie-talkie beeped, and Ashley just lounged on the couch like a beached whale, looking blankly at it. "It's Marcus," I said. "Aren't you going to answer it?"

She shrugged, looking depressed. "No."

"What? Why?"

"I don't know."

I picked it up and pressed down the button. "Hey, jerk, you happy? I lost my last contact."

"What?" It was Logan.

I felt my face turn bright red. "Where's Marcus?" I asked.

"I'm right here." For some reason his voice filled me with relief.

"I lost him, Marcus. I hope you're happy."

"You mean *he* lost *you.*"

I froze. That was the last response that I had expected. Why couldn't he gloat like he was supposed to? It would've made me feel better.

"Yeah, right." I sighed, leaning against Ashley. She seemed just as despondent as I was, so she made for a perfect pillow. "But I understand why he would pick Emma over me," I told him. "I'm really just a flibbertigibbet."

"Where would he get that idea?"

I recognized sarcasm when I heard it. "You can celebrate now. Go throw a party or something."

"Oh, come on," he said. "I was just watching out for you."

I stared at the walkie-talkie in my hand. Was he for real? "Well, knock it off," I said. "I can take care of myself a lot better than you can. Don't pretend you didn't sabotage this whole thing."

He was silent for a moment. "Did you even like any of them at all?" he finally asked.

It took me a moment to answer. "I could've."

"But you didn't."

"Well, I didn't even know if they liked Arthur or SpongeBob. How can you even build a relationship on that? But I could've found out." I sighed, feeling like my insides were bruised. I couldn't admit that my heart was broken thrice over. "Tell me," I said suddenly, "which one do you like—Arthur or SpongeBob?"

It was a tough question, and it seemed he was deliberating on it until he answered. "You should know that."

But I didn't.

"Miriam broke up with Marcus," Ashley said.

"What?" I sat up.

"He doesn't seem to care, though."

Brooke pulled through the caverns of the human-sized snowball. Her khakis were soaking wet. "The mail came and you got another one."

I knew what it was before she handed me the letter—another rejection for my book. I threw it on the end table without looking at it. Brooke shrugged, going into the next room, probably to go call Scott . . . or maybe to change out of her wet clothes. She was so secure in their relationship that they were beyond words.

Ashley just stared at the letter, but she couldn't move to open it either, and since Marcus had apparently left the walkie-talkie, I pushed PLAY on the stereo. Emma's *Les Mis* CD was in it and we listened solemnly, completely entranced, especially when we listened to the part sung by Eponine. Could I be like that—so selfless as to give up the man I love . . . well, at least *liked* a lot?

I guess I had done it before with Brooke. I could do it again for Emma. But oh, it would be so easy to steal Derek back with the few right moves; he was such a nice guy and he would make the perfect husband, but then I thought of Emma. No, I didn't want to do that to Emma.

"Charity, charity, charity," I muttered aloud, but what did it mean? It meant that I was about to get hurt, but I had to give him up, this whole game. I had to because I loved her and wanted her to be happy, which meant I had to cut myself out . . . but that would be so painful. I met Ashley's blue eyes and she just stared back at me dejectedly, her bare toes playing with the rags of our orange carpet.

The doorbell rang and I knew that it was Derek. Brooke opened it, having more energy than us slugabeds on the couch. Derek smiled at us, putting his cell phone in his neatly pressed trouser pocket. "Why don't you have your coats on?" he asked Ashley and me.

She mumbled something and I watched him, knowing he was not mine as he nodded kindly. He was so good and sweet and perfect. I glanced at Emma, who had hung up the phone and had come up behind him, sweet Emma in her ugly, flowery shirt and baggy jeans, looking as innocent as an angel, who had always wanted me to succeed. She was the one he liked . . . so what was I going to do? They were so happy together and so nice that they deserved each other. There was a reason that I didn't think of my roommates as competition . . . I'd rather have friends than men. Well, that's what I used to say when I was in my bitter-against-men moods, but now my words came back to haunt me. Maybe it was time to put my motto to the test.

I stood up, tugging the sleeves of my long johns over my hands. "Emma, can you help me with something?" I walked into my room and she followed me, a sincere smile on her face. I closed the door. "You've got to help me," I said quickly. "I don't want to go sledding."

"What?"

"I'm just not interested in Derek anymore, and I don't want to lead him on."

She managed to shut her dropped jaw. "Going sledding with him won't be leading him on," she said.

Good point.

"Yeah, but I'm just . . . you know, I think he likes you and I don't want to get in the way." Her little upturned face turned crimson. Could it be possible that she didn't even know he liked her? Or even that she liked him in return? Well, it was obvious to me, and I wouldn't let her deny her feelings.

"Now," I said, "I know Harrison would agree with me." Boy, would he not. This was cutting him out of the love triangle too. "It's more effective to go on single dates than double." I smoothed her chestnut hair, dragging it to a more attractive angle around her face. "Remember to act like you're freezing so that he has to put his arms around you . . . and he's about eight inches taller than you, so um, let's work on effective doorstep approaches, shall we? You're going to have to kick in his knees, or maybe we can leave a telephone book on the doorstep so you can stand on it when you get back. There's no other way to reach his lips. Was he wearing a tie? Of course, he's always wearing a tie. You can tug on that."

She laughed suddenly. "Are you sure you don't want to come?"

"Yeah, I mean, I feel kinda sick anyway." That wasn't too far from the truth. "Too many brownies probably."

"Oh, then I shouldn't leave you."

"If you mess up on your stats, honey, you'll have more than Harrison to contend with," I said, pulling away from her. "Now, get out of here."

I marched into the living room and collapsed on the couch next to Ashley. I didn't want to stay there and smile while I was kicked in the gut, but I probably should get used to it. It would be my lot for a while.

"I can't go," I announced to the room in general. "I just remembered a homework assignment that I forgot about." Wow, how many white lies was I supposed to keep track of? "Besides, I still have to work on my Relief Society lesson."

"What?" Emma asked suddenly. "You still haven't finished that? You're teaching on Sunday!"

"I know . . . that's why I just can't go."

Derek looked disappointed, but only politely so. That was a good sign for Emma. "I can't imagine such pretty girls staying home on a day like this," he said in true Derek fashion. "Are you sure you can't take a few hours out of your schedule?"

"Sorry."

Ashley mumbled something beside me.

"Okay, well, if you change your mind, we'll be at Squaw Peak," Emma said.

We nodded and they left . . . along with my dating pool. My heart could barely take it. They say it's so easy to find someone else, and maybe it was . . . except my heart wasn't involved in it anymore. I just didn't feel like falling into the wrong-guy trap again. There was more to life than marriage, right?

Ashley glanced at me sideways, not able to turn her head. "I wish I was like you."

I snorted. "Like me? Don't say that. I'm an awful person and I admit it freely."

"Nope, you are an amazing person," she said. I stiffened. Next thing I knew she would start comparing me to construction workers. "Guys aren't everything, you know," she said. "You don't need one to be happy. You have to be happy on your own." She sniffed. "It's more attractive, I've heard."

My forehead wrinkled. Why did she think I needed this lecture? It took me a moment to realize that she was giving herself a pep talk. "I did it to myself really," she said. "When you flirt with every guy, the one you actually like won't take you seriously."

I saw a tear slip down her cheek, and I sat up, hitting her with a hard, green paisley cushion. "What's going on?"

She just shook her head. "Just think of it this way. Your sorrow is another man's joy."

"Yeah, Emma and Derek will be real happy if they can manage to get past their friendliness and get some sort of relationship going. I don't know how that's possible. They're so unselfish . . ."

"No, that isn't what I'm talking about. Now you're free for another man to date."

Oh, so this was what it was all about. Marcus? I steeled myself. Let's see, I might as well give up my last contact who wasn't really my contact in the first place. He wasn't mine. He would never be mine. I still had my writing, right? The thought of the unopened letter Brooke delivered filled me with dread, but I steeled myself.

"Don't worry," I said. "I'm not interested in him . . . You can have him." It almost came out as a croak. You know it was easier to think he was a jerk when I believed I'd never see him again, but it would be harder when he started dating my roommate, since he would probably prove that he wasn't a jerk and that I was the one who was lacking in personality. "I mean, if you still want him," I said.

"I always did. How did you know?"

How could I not know? Ashley was beginning to look hopeful and she sat up, still managing to look gorgeous with tears running down her cheeks and her nose all red . . . and wearing all that black. "But he likes *you*," she said.

"You're definitely seeing things, and besides there's no way I'd leave Griffin for him."

She grimaced through her tears. "I'm sorry to be the one to tell you this, but Griffin has a girlfriend."

"What?" I stood up, scarcely believing it. Had Veronica stolen him from me?

I had heard the party they were throwing downstairs, but I didn't realize what it meant. Everyone was rejoicing that Griffin was safely out of the picture . . . even *he* was taken. My heart dropped at the thought. I couldn't even hold onto a stalker.

What? Why was I thinking that? Obviously I was desperate to find reasons to feel sorry for myself. Even Griffin could find someone when I couldn't . . . there, that was a better depressed thought. Dash diddly dog, I was disturbed. "I'm sure he'll dump her for me," I said, breaking into a sad smile. "Or maybe Veronica will dump him." *Once she finds out I never liked him in the first place.*

"Oh, I don't think so," Ashley said. "Veronica was carrying her cheesecake leftovers home and slipped on the ice. Griffin caught her and the cheesecake splatted all over his face, but he didn't mind a bit. I think he saved it for later, and she thinks he's the most romantic gentleman that ever walked the sidewalks of BYU . . . and *he* thinks that she's the greatest cook in our ward. Maybe she'll fatten him up."

I hoped so. What a great love story, except now I was beginning to doubt I would ever get a chance to dump my leftovers all over my Prince Charming—especially since it seemed he didn't really exist.

CHAPTER 29

"Commitment. That word alone makes grown men tremble."
—Harrison Bean (Fri., Dec. 17th)

I dipped the chocolate bar into the chocolate chip ice cream and stuffed it into my mouth. There's a special chemical in chocolate that makes you feel loved. Don't ask me what it is because I'm not that smart. However, I can put two and two together, and I know that chocolate makes me feel better, except . . . I wiped at my eyes. This was so stupid. The home remedy wasn't working for once, and I was supposed to be cramming for an English final after I was done working on my Relief Society lesson, but I couldn't stop crying.

At least the lesson was on charity, which was something I was probably supposed to be learning. Why else would these things keep happening to me? I was desperate for a little bit of success, but I knew nothing incredible was going to happen, no great cause where I could prove myself . . . nothing. I'd preach against R-rated movies and breaking curfew and crossing the chalk and Chastity Line. I'd go on with my life, but would I ever become anything that mattered? It got to the point that I felt so bitter about it that I didn't even like myself anymore.

"What are you doing?" Harrison had walked into our apartment without knocking, which was so much easier since our wreath disappeared. He pushed his black sleeves to his elbows, looking haughty and hotty . . . well, presentable at least, which was more than I could say for myself. I wore my Boy Scout T-shirt and gray sweats again.

He stared at the chocolate chip ice cream in my hand, shaking his head. "Remember when they told you to be an eight-cow wife? You're taking it the wrong way."

"Really?" I couldn't look at him because then he would know I had been crying. "Would you get out of here?" I mumbled into my ice cream. "I have to finish my lesson."

He clicked his tongue at me. "Effective proselyting areas do not include the frozen food section." He pulled the carton of ice cream from my hands and I let him take it without a fight, which showed just how truly despondent I was.

"Ben and Jerry are not suitable prospects for marriage." He glanced at the empty pizza box on the table, "Neither is the Red Baron for that matter."

I shrugged and he sighed, beginning to pace the room. For once I didn't care. "If you keep going this way, your only chance for marriage will be the reinstatement of polygamy. You'll count as ten wives . . . make it an even dozen."

"Don't give me lip, I don't feel like it right now."

Harrison stopped his inane pacing. "Why? What's the matter?" he asked in an un-Harrison-like fashion.

It completely did me in . . . any pity would, especially his. "Not only did I lose all my guys," I moaned, "but I lost all of my room-mates." I buried my head in my hands. "They'll be busy with their new boyfriends, and I'll be all alone . . ."

"You'll be fine," he said gruffly. "Keep your chin up. Here." Harrison handed me a pristine white handkerchief. Why in the heck was he carrying a handkerchief? No one did that, except crazy English boys, I guess. He would need it once I told him the bad news.

"We should've foreseen it," I said, trying to break it to him in the only way I knew how. "She's Relief Society president. He's the quorum's. It only makes sense."

He helped me blow my nose and I felt like a little kid. He was probably hurting just as much as I was but was afraid to show it . . . or maybe he just didn't understand the significance of what I was saying. "I'm glad that Derek fought so hard against temptation," I said. "He chose wisely. Emma's personality is by far better than mine. All I really am is looks . . . actually I'm not even that . . . I might as well be honest about it, you know?"

"Oh come now," he said, trying to stop my babbling. "This is just like a mission. You get plenty of rejections. There's no need to take it personally. It just means that you have to start all over again."

I hung my head. "It is a far, far better thing that I do than I have ever done."

He groaned. "Oh brother, what are you doing? You're quoting *A Tale of Two Cities* now? What is this—the death march to the guillotine? You're not going to die, get up." He dragged me to the kitchen, where I took a seat on the table and slumped against the wall. He was taking this a lot better than I was. Well, he was strong. I wasn't. ". . . find again." I heard him say through his prattle of words.

I shook my head. "No way!"

"What?" he said. "You don't want to date? Here, let's take a look at your stats. Last week's were pretty good." He picked up the marker and I watched him listlessly.

"I don't want to play anymore," I said. "There's no reason to force myself into something that makes me unhappy. Let's concentrate on something else."

"What do you mean?"

"My career stats," I said. "If I can't do the marriage thing, I've got to concentrate on something else or I'll go crazy . . . so let's concentrate on my career for now."

"Okay, let's look at it."

He wrote "dreams," "strategy to fulfill dreams," "major," "crummy first jobs," "realistic expectations," "interviews," "internships," "real boring jobs" . . .

I stared at the whiteboard, not even wanting him to fill it out, especially when anything he put on there would make me look completely ridiculous. I wanted to be a writer. How realistic was that? And what experience did I have in anything else? "Oh, never mind," I said. "That isn't going anywhere either. I'm a loser, aren't I?"

"A loser? What are you talking about?" He slapped the knee of his jeans at the joke. "You gave those guys away. If anything you're a martyr."

He almost got a laugh out of me. "No, it just means that I'm stupid." I stared at the blank whiteboard, realizing it represented my life. "I'm going to end up being a teacher, aren't I?"

Harrison gave a bark of laughter. "That's okay . . . as long as you don't work in Utah. Their monetary compensation is insufficient here."

"I know," I moaned. "That means I'll have to move, and then I'll never get married. Oh, life has passed me by, hasn't it?"

"Ah, the drama," he said dryly. "Life will never pass you by. You're living it, aren't you? Where's your faith?"

"Nonexistent if it involves me."

"Why?"

"I don't know."

He took my smaller hand in his and dragged me off the table. "Let's go eat, huh? We'll be losers together."

I met his blue eyes, suddenly looking at him in an entirely new light. If he talked like that anymore, I'd fall for him, especially in my desperate straits . . . and he was completely unsuitable for me. He was just as much of a jerk as I was, and I was attracted to that. I'd better stay away from him. "Okay," I told him.

I was crazy, wasn't I? Crazy for liking the wrong guy every single time. What was wrong with me? *Don't do it!* But I was!

Ashley walked into the kitchen, and even my nose wrinkled when I saw her. She looked horrible. Her black ponytail was askew. Her BYU sweatshirt was tucked into her jogging pants. What was she thinking? I couldn't say anything, though, because Marcus was with her. He looked haggard too, though he couldn't quite compare to Ashley. His green shirt was inside out. His jeans were wrinkled like he had just dug them out of a dirty laundry hamper.

If they could stick to each other's sides looking like that, it was obvious that the Thursday night kiss wasn't just a fling, was it? And something else was up. They had a secretive air about them, almost like they were plotting something, but I couldn't figure out what. Ashley took one look at my hand in Harrison's and she backed up, her cupid bow lips curling . . . not upwards.

"Marcus, Ashley, what fortuitous timing," Harrison slurred.

"What's going on here?" Marcus asked.

Harrison just shrugged. "We're just consoling ourselves in the arms of another. It seems to be a common practice around here."

Marcus smiled, but it didn't reach his eyes. Oh no, he was going to get protective again, wasn't he? His next words didn't surprise me. "Well, it doesn't matter how available someone is if they're not the right one," he said.

So, he thought I was desperate, huh? It figured.

"The wrong ones always end up being the right ones with me," I said, trying to defend my actions. What was Marcus's problem anyway? Ashley just stood silently beside him. You'd think she'd look happy. "We're going out to eat," I said.

Marcus glanced around the trash heaped around the kitchen and the empty pizza boxes in the living room. It looked like we had just had a party. "You're taking a much-needed study break I see." It was obvious by the look on his face that he knew none of us had been studying.

I crossed my arms over my stomach, my eyes narrowing. It was really none of his business what I did. "Do you want us to pick up something?" I inquired politely, my voice said otherwise.

Marcus shook his head. "Are you driving, Samantha?"

"No," Harrison said quickly.

"Oh, good."

"What's that supposed to mean, Marcus?" I asked. Both Harrison and Marcus avoided my eyes.

"Nothing," Marcus said hurriedly, "it just means that you'll survive the trip, that's all."

I turned to Harrison. He looked too smug for my taste. "I'm driving," I informed him.

Harrison looked at me askance, and Marcus's lips twisted into a broad smile. "Have fun," he said much too cheerfully. I should've seen something was up, but I was too irritated to get a straight thought into my brain.

"You too," I said, glancing at Ashley. "Where are you two going, anyway?"

"*I'm* going to the Smith Fieldhouse. Can't you tell by the way I'm dressed?"

Not really. Ashley always looked better than this when she left to work out; it was her philosophy. "What about Marcus?" I asked.

"What about him?"

My gaze quickly swerved to Marcus to see his reaction, but he didn't seem too concerned. No, he seemed to be more concerned with me . . . because he wanted to mess things up. "What are you waiting for?" he said. "Get out of here." Harrison walked me to the door, and I glanced back at Marcus.

"Go for him," he mouthed back at me.

I stilled. Was he using reverse psychology on me—or was he just giving me away? I had done this on numerous occasions and was intrigued. Was he doing this because he cared or because he didn't? I just shrugged—did I even care? I was tired of guessing. He probably just wanted to shove two ornery personalities together to see the fireworks. Well, it wouldn't work . . . or maybe it would.

I spun on my heel and Harrison followed me to my car, looking unusually distracted. The Loner looked pathetic under the melting snow and I threw open the door, listening to it screech under its rusty hinges. Harrison opened his own door, kicking the trash back so he could sit down on the leopard-print covered seats. If I had been in the right frame of mind, I would've found it amusing to see such an elegant figure in my dingy car, but I wasn't. He had barely situated himself when I peeled out of the ice and snow, heading for the fattest, greasiest fast-food restaurant in Provo that we could find.

Harrison sighed, pushing the furry green dice from his vision. "Perhaps romance can build on further acquaintance," he muttered. "Just because there are no feelings now, doesn't mean there can't be . . ."

My hands tightened over the wheel and despite my promise to prove Marcus wrong that I wasn't a bad driver, I pushed the gas down harder. What was Harrison talking about? He turned to me. "Friendship first, right?"

"We don't even have that," I said without thinking.

He laughed appreciatively until he glanced at my speedometer. "You're going fifty-three miles per hour."

"Yeah?"

"It's supposed to be thirty-five miles per hour."

"I'm a little dyslexic." I hit a red light and slammed on the brakes.

Harrison's head snapped forward, but he managed to stay in his seat. He righted himself and turned to glare at me. "Where did you say you were from?"

"Not Utah . . . why do you ask?" The light turned green, and I raced a red pinto to the next light then abruptly pushed down the brakes.

Harrison gritted his teeth. "So who just won that race?"

"Me, of course, I'm the fastest. I . . ."—just realized that I was doing everything in my power to turn him off, which is exactly what Marcus had been hoping for. Why?

"Sorry," I said. "I'll try not to get us into an accident."

He sighed, staring straight ahead. "What does it matter? There's nothing to live for anyway." He was talking dismally and the more dismally he talked, the more I couldn't understand him. "Too high-maintenance anyway," he said. "I'm at the prime of my manhood. I'm not ready for commitment . . . neither is she for that matter. Commitment," he growled, and my eyes flicked to him quickly. "That word alone makes grown men tremble. No, it just wouldn't work." He was silent for a moment, thinking his deep thoughts. "But those two don't belong together. She'll kill him . . . she'd kill me too, but at least I would've liked it." He suddenly glanced at me. "I thought you were the solution to my tribulations, but she's just too obstinate."

I met his eyes, suddenly realizing that he was talking about Ashley. That's when I veered the car, taking it back to warp speed. "Where are you going?" he asked, but he didn't seem to care. Even his thick lashes couldn't hide his despondent gaze.

"Not out to eat."

Ashley had been talking about *this* star-crossed lover after Emma left on her date, not about Marcus. I couldn't believe it. Was my female intuition completely out on vacation this month, or what? She was clearly as infatuated with Harrison as he was with her . . . in their strange way. I was blind . . . stupid . . . oblivious, pick one, pick them all!

"Why didn't you tell me?" I asked, but Harrison just stared bleakly ahead. I shook my head. "No, forget it. I should've known. I'm the girl around here." I drove around the block and pulled next to the Smith Fieldhouse, shoving down the brakes for good measure. His head whipped forward. "Go get her, Romeo," I said.

Harrison stared at the Fieldhouse as if waking from a dream.

"Get out of my car," I said. "You and I . . . well, how do I put this gently? We can't stand each other, and we would've broken up after the first week if we had actually gotten together by some curse."

Harrison laughed, but his hand hesitated on the side door handle and suddenly the smooth guy wasn't so smooth-guy anymore. "What do I tell her when I see her?" he asked.

"I don't know, but I can just imagine the fireworks." If anyone had a love-hate relationship, they did, but he wasn't listening to me. Harrison stared through the window as if in a trance.

Ashley was stalking angrily to a tall brick building. She looked horrible, but guess who didn't care? Mr. Everybody-has-to-look-and-act-perfect-district-leader himself. He pulled out of the Loner, and I felt like I was watching a Meg Ryan/Tom Hanks movie as he raced to her side. It was so cheesy, so unlike Harrison, so unbelievable that I loved it. His humiliation was complete.

Ashley crossed her arms over her ugly BYU sweatshirt when she saw him, and he leaned next to her with an apologetic smile, probably saying something flirtatious, most likely scandalous. She stepped back uncertainly, and he showed her a scar on his hand from Ultimate Frisbee. Smooth. Her brow wrinkled and she took his hand to examine it.

Okay, so I can only guess what happened after the "I've got an owie" trick because that's when I drove away.

I sped back to my apartment, thinking drastic thoughts . . . Hollywood thoughts. Alright, alright, don't worry about me, okay? It's not that bad. I'll probably just end up basing this book on all my failures and selling it to make lots and lots of money. Maybe I'll even go to L.A. and do something drastic like waste my life away on parties . . . except I couldn't even do that. I couldn't get an agent because I wasn't published. I couldn't get published without an agent. I felt like I was hitting my head against a brick wall, and to make it worse, nobody was looking.

But at least my parking spot was open. I parked and turned my car off, staring at the ice on my windshield. "I'll probably just have to wait and see if there's a reinstatement of polygamy," I muttered. At least that was my saving grace. I pulled out of the Loner and groaned, realizing what I had just said. *I'll just have to wait and see if there's a reinstatement of polygamy?*

What did I do wrong? I leaned my head against the cold roof of the Loner. It just wasn't my day or even my last two weeks . . . actually my month. I coughed, then stifled a gasp when I realized that I didn't even have my health!

Okay, calm down.

Men . . . I don't like the right ones, right? That's why I had to give them away, which meant I needed to find some happiness elsewhere, go on somehow. And if it meant pretending that I didn't have feelings, so be it. That sounded easy enough . . . except that's when I figured out something about myself, which doesn't happen very often to shallow people like me. I had been pretending to be so many different things with these other guys: sweet girl, talented girl, flirty girl, but the only one who really knew me was Marcus. Maybe that's why his rejection hurt worse than the others . . . because unlike the others, he really had rejected *me*. I laid everything I was out on the table, and he ran the other direction.

But I deserve it. I'm not sure why, but I know I do. I know what kind of person I am, so don't feel sorry for me. I'll find something . . . anything to replace him. The feeling to escape my problems was coming on strong now and riding my emotions, but really, I couldn't escape without money, without preparations, without landing myself into a worse position than I was in now, which meant that I was stuck here in Provo. So what was I going to do? I was driving myself crazy with my thoughts, and that's when I hit on a truism—maybe I should stop concentrating on myself . . .

He that loveth his life shall lose it, and he that hateth his life in this world shall keep it unto life eternal.

The words from Marcus's Sunday School lesson hit me like a battering ram, causing me to lift my head off the cold snow of the Loner. If I was ever going to get over myself, I had to start serving others. Such easy words. So hard . . . but then again, not so hard. Hadn't I already started doing that?

What did I want more than anything in the world but to be happy, and yet I had sacrificed that supposed happiness by helping the ones I loved go for guys I liked. You have to understand, for me it was the ultimate sacrifice. I had no success to fall back on—nothing to cushion the loss like I had planned, no TV interviews, no money, no martyrdom . . . well, a little bit of martyrdom.

So why was I clinging to these hopes as if they defined who I was? Why couldn't I just be happy in the now? There was no point in being so self-absorbed that I made myself miserable, because . . . well, it just didn't make me happy. What made me happy was trusting that

God would help me, even if I wasn't the center of my attention. What made me happy was making others happy. What made me happy was seeing my friends' success, not my own.

Weird. It was the construction worker all over again! My heart lurched. Dash diddly dog. I was a spitting, cursing construction worker changing tires on the highways of life! Emma was right, and I smiled. That was actually kind of cool. And it gave me new purpose. Forget yourself and be a Samaritan.

I could do it. I could get over myself. Even Marcus had called me a scrapper, and so I did it the only way I knew how. I pulled from my car and went up the three flights of stairs to my apartment to work on my lesson on charity . . . and maybe study the ward directory and learn a few names in the Relief Society while I was at it. It wouldn't do for me to call my sisters *hey you* tomorrow, now would it?

CHAPTER 30

"It was almost too perfect, this mistake we were making."
—Samantha Skyler (Fri., Dec. 19th)

I stopped in front of my apartment, shoving my keys into the lock, only to lock myself out. What? The apartment was already unlocked? For crying out loud, everyone was gone on their dates. I realized that Ashley had been distraught, but anyone could have gotten in.

"Excuse me?" I swiveled, seeing a kind-looking young man practically standing over me. His dark hair was cut in a shag, and he wore a red ski jacket. "Do you know my sister? Veronica Killjoy?"

He was hot and I tried to cover the *Boy Scout* logo on my black T-shirt, trying not to look like some punk blond. I was a completely different girl now . . . sorta. "Uh, if she's not home, she's with her new boyfriend, Grif."

"Grif?" He smiled, and I searched his expression, his eagerness to please. You know, besides definite problems with in-laws, there was potential dating material there, but for how long? I guess I should find out, except just before I tried to lure him into my apartment, I managed to get my door unlocked and fell into my living room with a gasp. The couches, the ugly, overstuffed, pea green couches were gone!

"Dash diddly dog," I muttered.

"Excuse me?"

I walked back outside, slamming the door behind me. "Excuse me," I said, practically shoving Veronica's brother out of the way in my haste to get to Marcus. I knew I should've hidden that spare key. What was wrong with him, anyway? The psycho. Wouldn't he ever leave me alone? He won. That should've been enough for him. But already he was trying to ruin my new outlook on life.

I marched down the stairs and dodged a couple of cars, trying to get across the street to wring that soon-to-be-pathetic guy's neck. Only one thought comforted me. Construction workers would never think twice about beating someone up who really annoyed them. I ran into the parking lot, and the sight that met my gaze made me wince. Our fat couches were balanced on top of the red tin roof of his apartment building. How in the heck did Marcus get those up there? How was I going to get up there? And more importantly, how was I going to get them down?

I circled around the side until I saw the ladder. It was too conveniently placed, which meant it was probably a setup. I should've seen it, being a consummate mischief-maker myself, but I was too annoyed with Marcus to care. I wanted my revenge. I grabbed the ladder with both hands and quickly climbed up the side.

The first thing I saw when I cleared the roof was Marcus. He was lying on his back on our couch, his green shirt still inside out, his jeans wrinkled. I tried not to think about how cute he looked as he stared up into the cloudy sky, a particularly blank look across his face, his Cardinals cap turned backwards.

"There you are." I approached him with clenched fists, and to his credit he didn't shrink away from me. "Marcus, did I wrong you in premortality somehow? You won, okay?"

He glanced at me with nonchalant blue eyes. "Won what?"

"Harrison just got too much of a Samantha dose and opted for Ashley. You did it on purpose."

"His loss," he said, shrugging. "I like a Samantha dose."

"No, you don't." I sat heavily down on the couch next to him and stretched my legs out. For some reason I was in the mood to bare my soul. "You've ruined all of those relationships, admit it."

"You did better than I did," he said. "If you had just been yourself, maybe you would've stood a chance."

My brow wrinkled and I grabbed a pillow to hit him with. "Never let them see who you are. That's the first rule."

He grabbed the pillow from me, and I tried to get it back, but he held it from my reach. "I know who you are."

"Exactly," I said, "and I don't see you going for me."

He dragged himself upright from the couch and looked me squarely in the eyes. "What makes you think I'm not?" he asked.

Marcus had dumbfounded me there and I stilled, my hands going back to my side. He had broken up with me. He had just wanted to be friends, and besides that . . . "You stole my couches," I said finally.

"That was a lot of work. I never would have made the effort if I didn't think it would get your attention."

He stuffed the pillow behind him and pulled closer to me. "You know who I am, too."

"Yeah—a complete idiot!" He was obnoxious and rude, and a troublemaker . . . and, and when he put his mind to it really intelligent and sensitive, which was actually the part of him that I had a hard time understanding.

He dimpled. "See, you do know me." He must have seen the sudden spark flare up in my eyes because he hesitated. "Sorry, Samantha, I can't help it with you. You're so fun to tease, but I really *am* sorry for being such a jerk."

"Yeah? Are you sorry for sabotaging me?"

He bit his lip. "No, not really."

I tried not to smile at that. Had he actually been jealous? I thought he was trying to sabotage things out of spite, but maybe he had ulterior motives. I wouldn't mind that.

"But I'm sorry that I made you feel bad," he tried to assure me. "I'm sorry if I hurt your feelings . . . I'm sorry for being born . . . Whatever you want to hear, I'll tell you . . . and I'll mean it." He was starting to laugh, but he was serious. What a sweet-talker.

I turned away from him, my heart beating faster. If I looked at him, he would completely do me in and that would never do. "You won't even tell me if you like SpongeBob or Arthur," I said.

He was silent, and it annoyed me that he wouldn't respond to my question, especially when everything hinged on the answer. I glanced back at him, seeing him staring at me with deep blue eyes, his expression partly hidden under thick lashes. My heartbeat quickened. Dash everything.

"You just like to see me angry," I said. "You want to see the scrapper fight."

"Well, you're quite the prize fighter, you know? I'd put money on you any day, but that's not the only reason I like you."

He *liked me* liked me? But that didn't make sense. If he really cared, he wouldn't have ended things a few weeks ago, right? Unless he couldn't be depended on to make up his mind. "What's the other reason?" I asked, watching him with suspicious eyes.

To my disappointment, Marcus pulled away from me, fidgeting with something at our feet. "I've made lunch. Want some?"

I couldn't believe my ears. This conversation was turning more outrageous by the minute. "You made me lunch?" How did he know that Harrison and I would never get to that restaurant? The answer was obvious, even to me.

"It's a peace offering," he said. "You realize, of course, that once your district leader gets over his freaked-out stage with your driving, he'll come back for you."

Obviously Marcus didn't know what I knew, but I played with him anyway. "Yeah? So?"

"Well, I'm past that stage."

My hands clenched together. Mr. Freaked Out was no longer freaked out? I could hardly believe it. "Yeah?" I said. "And how do I know you won't just get scared again?"

Marcus's eyes widened, and he glanced up at me from the brown paper bag. "Scared—me? Of you? Why would I be scared of you?" It almost came out a stutter.

I leaned back on the couch, quirking an eyebrow at him. "I don't know. Why would you?"

He started tugging on his Cardinals cap, and I knew that I had called it, but there was no way he was going to confess that to me. "I was just confused, that's all," he admitted finally. "You have no idea how hard it is to read you, Samantha. You're like a whirlwind, spinning from one thing to the next . . . one guy to the next." I sensed a little bitterness there, but I let it slide. "I thought maybe you didn't care and I cared too much, and we didn't mesh at all. We're completely different, you know."

"Why—because I'm a little wild?" I asked.

"Oh yeah . . . a lot wild." He leaned back and, to my dismay, didn't hold back at all. "And crazy and mischievous." He laughed.

"Actually it's pretty funny when it's aimed at me." His gaze turned affectionate. "I kinda like it. You're one of the funnest girls I know. And you know what I finally decided?"

I gulped, realizing that I was actually holding my breath. "What?" I asked finally.

"A little dizziness is worth the ride."

At last he found what he was looking for and pulled out some bottled water. It looked like he had just filled the bottle up with tap water. He glanced up at me, catching me off guard with a debonair grin. "You can take me driving anytime, pumpkin."

Liar.

"What did you make?" I asked. He pulled out two smashed peanut butter sandwiches, and my nose wrinkled. "I suppose I'd better get used to this kind of fare," I said. "My roommates can't take care of me anymore. They have their men to worry about now. They'll probably have their rings by spring . . . and I'll have to start looking for new roommates, preferably ones who can cook." I was babbling, but Marcus didn't seem to mind.

"Don't worry about finding new roommates," he said. "I'll take care of it." I turned bright red at the suggestion. Was that a come-on? I hoped it was.

I smiled. "I like that line. I'm using it."

"Where?" He actually looked a little jealous as he passed me the peanut butter sandwich. Our hands brushed, but I didn't mind the incidental contact. In fact, I wouldn't mind putting even more on my stats today.

"I'm putting it in my book," I said, and I would have a great lunch on the roof while I was at it, though I couldn't help the plotlines that ran through my head at that moment and how I was going to make lots of money on the deal in the end. The book would be a romantic comedy adventure, blah, blah, blah. Of course, I was a little too busy right now to work out the exact details; there were more important things to attend to. "So I like SpongeBob," I said, "what about you?"

"Arthur."

"What?"

I jerked away from him and he laughed. "I'm joking. I can't stand Arthur." He pulled me closer, putting a permanent dent in my peanut butter sandwich, and I let him, but only because he didn't like Arthur. We'd work out our SpongeBob differences later. "You'd better give SpongeBob a chance," I said.

Marcus grimaced, sliding my hand into his. He started to inspect my nails. I had painted them a sparkly purple today and he dimpled. "And you have such beautiful fingers, too."

"You're starting to sound like my mom," I said.

He studied my face, his blue eyes melting into my dark ones. "So we *can* be friends?" he said.

I laughed, squeezing his fingers in response. "Definitely not. No, we'll just have to put up with each other." With him, it didn't sound that bad.

"That could be a lot of fun," he said. I smiled. Exactly my thoughts, but I didn't have to say it. He knew it.

We sat on the green couches overlooking the parking lot, the snow fluttering over our heads, eating our flattened peanut butter sandwiches. I couldn't even imagine a more romantic scene. I guess it's like they say, the company is everything, especially since I just happened to be with the wrong guy.

* * *

So that's it. That's my story. No girl-power messages, no poignant thoughts, no award-winning plotlines. Love makes you stupid, except I really liked this ending . . . or this beginning . . . or whatever you wanted to call it. His strong fingers entwined through my sparkly painted ones and suddenly I knew everything about him was right. It was shocking, but he seemed to feel the same way about me.

We were scrappers. Both of us hopelessly flawed and willing to fight for whatever happiness life held for us, willing to lose ourselves in life to find each other. It was almost too perfect, this mistake we were making, but I knew it would definitely make things more interesting in the long run. To be honest, I actually preferred a few bumps in the road. I'll ask him what he prefers later . . . after he watches about six hours of SpongeBob.

About the Author

Ever since elementary school, when Stephanie entertained fellow second graders with the *Donut Mysteries* and wrote the ever-dramatic *Crystal of Darkness,* she has been caught between comedy and drama, as well as science fiction and satire. Stephanie puts the blame for loving this odd assortment of genres on her large family; her family life has always been a cross between *Little Women* and *Little Rascals,* complete with overflowing laundry rooms, whole casts for colorful Nativity scenes, a chamber orchestra with an inordinate amount of violas, and a misfit band of football players. Stephanie ties for middle child in a family of ten going on forty, with new nieces and nephews constantly on the way.

Stephanie served an LDS mission in the Philippines, and though originally from Washington, is a longtime resident of Provo. She has supported her writing habit by falling into swamps at Mosquito Control, getting hit with golf balls while speed mowing, serving fast food with a fake smile, and sitting on the rug enjoying story time with the rest of the first-graders.

Stephanie graduated from BYU in English and communications and keeps herself entertained with kickin' the hook, dessert night, and Phan'm of the Opry pranks. She enjoys performing with her band, We the Peeps, and fills her apartment with the sweet tones of their songs ("Desperate Co-ed," "WWFHE," "Intramural Sports," and the like). In researching for her next novels, she now spends much of her spare time pestering her family, her roommates, and neighbors from her singles' ward.